BRIDE OF THE SWORD

BRIDE OF THE SWORD

HOMER HATTEN

CUTTING EDGE

ISBN-13: 978-1-954840-99-7

Published by
Cutting Edge Books
PO Box 8212
Calabasas, CA 91372
www.cuttingedgebooks.com

BRIDE OF THE SWORD

HOMER HATTEN

CUTTING EDGE

ISBN-13: 978-1-954840-99-7

Published by
Cutting Edge Books
PO Box 8212
Calabasas, CA 91372
www.cuttingedgebooks.com

CHAPTER ONE

Endless mists of tobacco smoke whirled and eddied through the low-roofed room, gray and intangible in the shadows, crimson and gold where they were caught up in the flame of the torches that lined the walls. The long bar along one side faced a crescent of rough tables and long, scarred benches where squat candles dripped and flickered and threw out wavering circles of amber light that alternately advanced and retreated before the onslaught of the night.

They flared briefly when a gust of the torrid night wind swept in from the Gulf, and in the moment of brilliance men's faces were clear and distinct before the brooding shadows descended upon them again. They were strange faces: dark, wind-burned, harsh-lipped, with the flames of recklessness and violence blazing in their eyes. Swarthy buccaneers from all the green sea lanes of the Caribbean, with hoops of gold swinging from their ears and Long John pistols thrust into crumpled sashes of scarlet silk; lean-faced grandees of Spain, somber and inscrutable in the rich blackness of velvet cloaks that revealed Venetian lace at their throats and wrists and scarcely hid the long Toledo blades swinging from their belts; slave traders and smugglers, gamblers and swordsmen, and soldiers of fortune from all the courts of Europe and the half-mythical caravansaries of Asia; Chinese traders and Levantine jewel merchants, sugar planters from the tropic islands of the south and Creoles with a ready challenge on their lips and flamboyant dreams of empire smoldering in their breasts.

La Sirena del Sur welcomed them all, gathering in this horde of wanderers who had forsaken the beaten paths of safety and security to search for fame or fortune—or perhaps for death—in the narrow streets of Havana and the unending leagues of tropic land and sea that lay in the harsh clutch of Spain.

Yes, they were welcome here; welcome to drain their purses of the last silver coin in exchange for the dark rum of the islands or the fiery brandy of France; welcome to have their ears deafened by the unending clatter of bottles and glasses or the sudden explosive melee that erupted in savage violence; welcome to turn curiously in their chairs as the steady throb of a barbaric drum beat down and overpowered the confusion of the room.

The rhythm of the drum quickened, until it surged through the room like the very pulse of this lustrous, lustful land. There was no escape from it. It went on and on in an insistent flow of sound that hammered its way into men's brains and filled them with a strange excitement, like hunting dogs held too long upon a leash.

Suddenly it was silent, and in the instant of emptiness a hidden guitar flung a glittering cascade of notes into the air. The deep resonance of the drum swelled like a dark wave beneath them, and a crystal-throated flute began a wordless tale of ancient skies and watch fires burning far beyond the rim of memory.

The guitar took up the song and, as if it had conjured them up from nothingness, two lines of naked slave girls with flaming torches flowering in their hands filled the empty space before the tables with liquid light that lay like polished jet upon their oiled bodies and flowered in crimson radiance about them.

And then—Manette de Santiago!

A hoarse roar of recognition and welcome swelled through the room. Men leaned forward in their chairs or leaped to their feet to see her better. And at a table just outside the circle of slave girls, a lean, broken-nosed Spaniard thrust his glass aside and unconsciously straightened the froth of lace at his throat.

"So, Ramón, this is the woman?"

His companion nodded, his eyes never leaving the dancer posturing in the pool of light.

"*Si,* Don Nicomedes, it is Manette."

She had come from nowhere, with a swirl of scarlet silk and a half-naked body that was like honey. Her bare breasts were golden apples, fire tipped, and her eyes were like dark stars in a gypsy face.

The slim hips stirred and writhed like a snake's head rising from the earth, and each man who watched her felt his own breath choke him as his mind possessed her and shared the quivering ardor of her flesh. Her finger tips brushed her breasts, and in the instant they grew firm and ardent. The pagan music quickened, rising like a wind that lashed and bent her body into frantic and blindly shivering convulsions of desire and release.

Whirling, she threw the scarlet skirt aside so that her body blazed before them like a living statue of tawny ivory. The torches swirled in a blinding circle of light, and then they were still again, and she was gone.

There was an instant of silence. Then the long room rocked with the roar of men's voices, shouting in Spanish and French and Malayan and English and high-pitched Chinese, calling back this woman of fire and rapture, whose body had trapped them in a dark web they could neither escape nor understand.

Ramón relaxed in his chair and a half sneer twisted his lips as he turned back to Don Nicomedes. "And now, señor? Now that you have seen her, was it not simple truth when I told you that this was the one wench in Havana who could serve you best?"

"Serve us?" The lean Castilian's fingers drummed meditatively upon the table, his mind gnawing at the tangled web of intrigue that was the very warp and woof of colonial Spain. "Serve us? Why, yes, *por Dios!* She'll serve us and serve us well or I'll have that flesh stripped from her body and set her dancing to another tune."

He drained his glass and shoved the chair back from the table as he rose. "I will expect her at the Captain General's quarters within the hour. And my advice to you, my friend, if you would avoid the lash, is to be as prompt and punctual as the coming of the day of God. Don Francisco de Larra is not possessed of infinite patience."

The black cloak swirled about him as he turned away, and Ramón, grinning, stretched out a hand for the half-empty rum bottle he had left upon the table. There was time enough. Time enough to deliver such a woman as Manette to Don Francisco. After that, fate and her own wisdom would decide her destiny. He lifted the bottle and let the dark liquor feed the fire that still possessed him, remembering the proud arc of her breasts and the firelight that had turned her slim thighs to gold ....

The street of Los Mal Casados was dark and narrow, hemmed in by faceless buildings of stone that turned their backs upon the street, rough with the worn cobblestones that rang like dull bells under the horses' hoofs.

At the door of the Casa San Sulpicio, Ramón threw up his arm, gathering the half-dozen hooded riders close around him. His voice was husky and half amused, as if he found some obscene pleasure in the very flagrancy of this foray that paired rapacity with cruelty here in the evil hours before the dawn.

"Miguel, *y mi poco Pepe,* you will go at once to the back of the house. Watch the wall as if you watched for the devil himself, and take and hold whoever may try to escape. As for you others"—his eyes swept the dark circle of faces around him—"you will come with me, remembering that His Excellency requires Manette de

Santiago of us—Manette, and the young virgin sister who came with her from Santo Domingo."

He swung out of the saddle and suddenly the night was bestial with the clamor of his pistol butt upon the wide oak door.

"Open, you dogs!" His voice blared like a bugle, echoing and re-echoing from wall to wall. "Open in the name of His Catholic Majesty the King, before Don Francisco has you whipped through the streets and torn limb from limb in the center of the Prado!"

There was a stir of startled movement inside and a window high above his head swung open, creaking in harsh-voiced but futile protest.

"We are peaceful men here, señor. Surely you seek another door."

"Another door? By God's truth, I'll seek another door, and that one an entrance for you into hell, if you delay me longer! Move now, you worthless whelp, before I have this door torn from its hinges and crucify you upon it!"

"Oh, at once, señor, at once!" The landlord's voice cringed and whimpered like a whipped dog. Ramón laughed as the sound of running feet came to them. "These miserable hounds—"

The door swung ajar, and as it moved Ramón lunged forward to send it crashing back against the wall. White-faced, the potbellied landlord lifted a candle in a trembling hand, and fell back screaming as Ramón's dirk scraped his face. *"Por Dios,* gracious señor—"

"Quiet, you squealing pig! Your noise deafens my ears. Tell me one thing, and then be silent: Where is the apartment of the woman they call Manette de Santiago?"

"Upon the second floor, señor, at the back. If you will permit me to guide you there ..."

But Ramón was gone, leaping up the narrow stairway like a panther that has scented blood and will not be denied. Behind him the heavy boots of his men pounded like sledges against the worn stone steps, their swords drawn and their eyes burning like hot coals.

There was a light in the upper hallway, a thin taper quivering before a shrine. Ramón scooped it up as he swept by, heedless of the fact that this was sheer and awful desecration. There would be time enough to make his peace with God, but as for Larra—no man made peace with Don Francisco if he had once delayed him.

There was a door on the left, and without pausing to call for admittance, Ramón slammed it open and whirled to face the center of the room, the candle high above his head. The breath whistled out through his clenched teeth in a long sigh of relief as he saw the two women cringing against a wall. The night was hot, and they wore only the sheer half chemise of the islands, woven of Chinese silk and fashioned to cover nothing except the breasts and the final upward curve of hips and thighs.

"*Por Dios!* It's seldom enough Larra sends me on a mission that leads to a sight like this. If I had more time and a less cautious regard for my throat, I'd ask no other fee than to spend an hour here before I take you to him!"

He laughed, then threw his head back and roared at the black rage in Manette's eyes. Then he saw the light glitter on the slender poniard in her hand, just as she flung herself at him. With a curse that was like a snarl he lunged aside. His arm flashed out and the rough fingers buried themselves in the flesh of her wrist, twisting savagely until the poniard fell clattering to the floor and she screamed in agony. He pulled her to him, so that her face was crushed against his shoulder, and he could feel her breasts rising and falling against his chest.

"Now, by Saint Christopher!" His voice was harsh with desire. "I'm of a mind to take you whether or no, and let Larra scratch his fleas till we arrive."

"Larra!" She wrenched her head free so that she could stare up into his face. "I have no business with Francisco de Larra. You are mad! You are wild with rum, like some *esclavo* who has traded his daughter for a slaver's bottle! Go now! Go quickly before I call the guard and have you hanged for this night's work."

"Hanged? Yes." He felt the fire go out of him as he recalled the gibbet that grinned and waited above the high sea walls of the town. "But hanged or not, you'll go with me to meet your host, who waits at the *palacio*—you and the maid yonder against the wall."

He half turned and waved the grinning soldiers forward.

"Seize her and bring her to the doorway where the horses wait. Sheathe your knives—and any other weapons you may have in mind. You'll fumble and rumple her enough, God knows, but you can do no more. She is Larra's, she and this bitch who'd have me stabbed and hanged in the first half-dozen seconds of our meeting."

They rode swiftly across the town, clattering like cavalry across the dark emptiness of the vast Plaza de Armas, drawing rein only at the gates of the palace itself. A sentry swung a lantern high, and in the beams of light Ramón saw Don Nicomedes, dressed now in a monk's black robe with a dark cowl half hiding his face. He strode forward until he stood at Ramón's stirrup, his hard snake's eyes raking the half-naked girl who clung to the high pommel of the saddle.

"You run dangerously close to the edge of the hour, *amigo*. Perhaps you thought Don Francisco would be content to have you find pleasure in this wench while he paced the floor and cursed your name?"

Ramón's fingers moved in the swift sign of the cross as he leaned forward in the saddle.

"I swear it is not so! She fought against me and some time was lost, but I have not touched her except to hold her here upon my saddle!"

"So? And yet there is a saying, *la ocasión hace al ladrón.* I hope that opportunity has not made a thief of you, my friend."

He stared up at Ramón until the sultry night seemed to grow cold and hushed and ominous. Slowly he turned away and, in turning, paused to fling a command back over his shoulder. "Deliver them to the guards, and say no word of this to any man if you would live to drink, again tomorrow."

White-faced, Ramón half threw Manette, spitting and clawing like a trapped wildcat, into the eager arms of the waiting guards. He saw the sister, Margarita, suddenly surrounded by bearded men at arms, watched the great gates swing slowly open and then clang shut behind them. He lifted his hand and wiped the cold sweat from his face. It was all well enough to be Don Francisco's trusted *hombre atrevido,* but there were hours such as this when a man's head rested but lightly on his shoulders. He turned and cantered swiftly away toward La Sirena del Sur, where there were other men with passions like his and the swift fire of rum to burn his fears away.

CHAPTER TWO

H AVANA was as diverse, as checkered and contradictory and dissonant, as a symphony so erratically scored that no two instruments followed the same melody or rhythm. It was an old city, even in 1795, for had it not been founded in 1514 by a Spanish adventurer whose very name was almost forgotten? It was a tough, ruggedly enduring city with a power so great that by royal decree it bore the proud title of *Llave del Nuevo Mundo y Antemural de las Indias Occidentales*—Key to the New World and Bulwark of the West Indies. And yet—in its 281 years it had been repeatedly sacked and burned by the buccaneers, blockaded repeatedly by the Dutch, captured and held for a fabulous ransom by the blue-eyed, fair-haired English.

It boasted of vast stores of treasures and there were monasteries and nunneries so rich they could give only a rough estimate of their wealth; yet nine men out of every ten lived in cramped and sickening squalor, unlettered and almost unfed, dying like flies when the yellow fever lashed the city with its pitiless scourge. They worked and prayed and held their peace, these poor and unfortunate ones, removed by the will of God from the orbits of the fabulous grandees who dwelled like kings in great stone houses with wide, steel-grated windows, flat roofs with parapets, and inner courts that were sweet with fruits and fountains and flowering trees.

From dawn to dusk no man of Havana knew the blessed peace of mind that is bred of security and safety. And yet it was a walled city, ringed and guarded by great forts, living beneath the towering shadow of the great Castillo de Príncipe, which crowned the amphitheatre of hills on the southwest, rubbing shoulders with the vast harbor fort of Cabara that stretched a full half mile along the sea wall and housed a garrison of six thousand men.

Nor did men know beauty long, although the Parque de la India was lush and glorious with towering palms and royal piñons loaded with their purple blooms, brilliant with the mango trees and tamarinds and green-crowned banyans. They saw these things, as they saw the macaws and the hummingbirds and the parakeets, but they saw, too, the gutters choked with slime and sewage, the scabrous beggars and the obscene vultures that were the only scavengers of this bright jewel in the crown of Spain.

A turbulent, beautiful, squalid city. A city of strength and power and fear and hopelessness—and in the center of it all, the palace and a half-mad, monstrous man who dreamed of destiny and dealt in death.

His Excellency the Captain General of Havana, Don Francisco Quintana de Larra y Menéndez, was not a big man, either in his physical make-up or in the breadth and tolerance of his outlook on life. But Don Francisco was possessed of one attribute that had served him well: a greedy, grasping, unending hunger for wealth and power. Like a bloated toad he crouched in the sunless depths of his palace, ordering men into his presence when he had need of them, sending them forth on obscure missions that were designed to line his pockets with gold and impress his personal sovereignty ever more firmly upon the lands he ruled in the name of the Spanish crown.

Of late, the crown was a weak and almost nebulous symbol of power as the court of Spain became enmeshed in more and more fantastic and disastrous intrigues upon the Continent. Godoy, the Queen's lover and the personal favorite of the King, had been elevated to the grandeur of First Minister in the winter of 1792, and for the past three years had warred with France in a series of campaigns that was one long catalogue of defeats and failures. The British fleet, under Lord Nelson, had driven the proud armadas of Spain into Cádiz, where the great ships of the line huddled like frightened birds, cut off from the colonies and from the vast colonial wealth that was so grievously needed. For Spain, it was the prelude to complete and terrible disaster, but to Don Francisco, freed from the demands and disciplines of the court at Madrid, it was an undreamed-of opportunity to pile fortune upon fortune and transform himself into a monarch of ruthless and unlimited power.

Tonight, it was his plan to set in motion a chain of circumstances that would destroy a rebel against that power. Cold-eyed, malignant, as charged with spleen as a snake with poison, he waited in the candle-shadowed austerity of his private audience chamber for the woman Manette to be brought before him. He heard a scuffle of feet and a woman's scream in the corridor, and lifted his head as the brass-studded oaken door swung open.

Don Nicomedes came first, pacing slowly in the black monk's cloak and cowl that he affected, contemptuous of the stir and tumult of the women and the men at arms. A half-dozen steps behind him, Manette and Margarita, their scanty chemises ripped and torn till they were no more than rags upon their bodies, twisted and writhed in the grasp of the guards who thrust them forward to face the beady eyes and chalklike lips of their lord and master, Don Francisco.

Don Nicomedes lifted his head as if he were recalling his thoughts from some benign and esoteric meditation. For the first time he seemed to become aware of Larra and of the squalling racket that dogged his heels. His eyes took in the almost naked bodies of the women and then he turned his head to study the squat figure half hidden behind the wide table of mahogany and ebony.

"Your Excellency," and there was far more sardonic cynicism than servility in his voice, "you commanded me to bring these two women of Santo Domingo before you tonight. They are here." His hand sketched a contemptuous gesture. "Is it your wish that I should stay, or would you prefer to talk with them alone?"

"Stay. I may have need of you. Tell me, which is the dancer, the woman they call Manette?"

The soldiers forced her forward, ripping the last shreds of the chemise away so that her slim waist and proud breasts and curving thighs were uncovered to the gaze of the gnarled monstrosity in the tall chair of state. His eyes devoured her. They were cold, measuring her, not for herself but as a tool or weapon that he might turn to his own account.

"And the other?"

His gaze shifted to Margarita, slim and tender in the first flush of adolescence, not yet turned fifteen, yet bearing within herself the bud of beauty that would someday blossom into Manette's own bloom of loveliness.

"The other is of no importance—unless you make her so." Don Nicomedes' voice was rough, impatient of this byplay. "It is Manette who can meet your needs. I saw her dance tonight and the men who watched were like sheep while she led them—and like ravening wolves when she was gone."

"*Verdad?* Then perhaps she can work another miracle and turn a ravening wolf into a sheep for me." He leaned forward across the table so that the candlelight carved deep hollows in his cheeks and set the hard eyes glittering like polished stones. "You are Manette de Santiago. Two years ago you came here with your mother and your sister as refugees from the slave rebellions on the island of Santo Domingo. Tell me, did you not bring gold or jewels with you? How is it that you are dancing like some quadroon in such a place of infamy as La Sirena?"

Manette was like a cat poised to spring, her lips drawn back in a snarl of hatred and her body quivering like a taut bow string. Now she almost spat at him in her fury.

"What I brought and where I dance is no concern of yours! I am a free woman of Spain, a daughter of Don Manuel de Santiago, whose patron was the brother of your Lord, King Philip. When word of this outrage is carried to Madrid, your eyes will be torn out and the vultures will rip the flesh from your bones!"

"So. And yet she could not serve my purpose with her body twisted by fire or scarred from the lash." He sat in silence for a moment and then glanced at Nicomedes. "What is the word of Ramón? Has this hellcat love for her sister, the young and tender Margarita?"

Nicomedes inclined his head. "So I am told. The fool Ramón swears that this virgin sister is the only living creature on heaven or earth that has ever known tenderness from this woman. Is it your pleasure that she should be lashed to make the other talk?"

"Lashed!" Manette's voice was a scream of outrage and fury. "Lashed! Lay one finger upon her and I—"

But Larra lifted his hand in a brusque command and the hard arm of a guard tightened across her throat, turning the threat into a gasp, holding and choking her until her face was flushed with blood and her body hung limp in his grasp.

Don Francisco lifted himself out of the chair and moved, crablike, toward the door that led into the corridor. Seen so, erect, with pipestem legs and a vast paunch quivering before him, he was like a spider moving through a web of evil, a misshapen gnome bearing upon his body his compact with the forces of darkness.

The hall was dark and cavernous, filled with the sound of bats stirring against the ceiling and rats rustling across the stained stone of the floor. At the end it led downward, twisting along a narrow circle of stairs jutting out from the solid rock, winding and turning until at last they stood on a crude balcony that looked down upon a murky room shot with flame and murmurous with the half-intelligible voices of misery and degradation.

Francisco moved his hand in a beckoning gesture. "Bring the woman forward—and her sister—so that they may stand beside me and see what is below." He lifted his voice so that it cracked against the dark walls and the vaulted ceiling high above. "You there, below, line the walls with torches and stir the fires. Rouse the cage of men and bring forth Doña María Castellán, whose husband waits for her upon the wheel."

Dark figures stirred in the murk and torches flamed and drove back the smoky shrouds of blackness. The smoldering fires sprang into life, and in their glow Manette could see a wide room, littered with the harsh racks and wheels and whips and flaming forges of the Inquisition; and at its end a cage of iron bars crammed with a horde of screaming, bearded men who rattled their bars and howled like animals against the mocking blackness of the dungeon that contained them.

Almost directly beneath the balcony where they stood, a naked man lay strapped upon the wheel. Like some tremendous carriage wheel thrown down upon its side, it turned slowly on its axis so that they could see the thongs that bound his wrists and ankles, holding him helpless and spread-eagled on the grim instrument of torture. His beard was stiff with blood and swollen welts upon his naked chest spoke all too plainly of the leather lash that had already torn his flesh. He twisted his head a little to one side as a flurry of tumult boiled up at the end of the room and then, suddenly, he threw himself against his bonds in a par-oxysm of fury.

"*María! Por Dios, María, mi corazón!*"

Manette whirled to follow the direction of his gaze and saw a woman, richly dressed, near fainting in the grasp of two half-naked negroes who dragged her forward. Her hair had fallen about her shoulders and the crimson gown she wore was ripped from throat to waist, so that the white gleam of her flesh reflected the dancing light of the roaring torches. She lifted her head at the sound of the prisoner's shout, and her eyes darted about the room until they found the bound figure of the screaming man upon the wheel. She threw out her arms and would have run to him, but the guards' arms were strong; she was held helpless and sobbing, with only the gaze of her eyes to caress and cherish him.

The prisoner's head snapped back so that he stared up at the half-seen group upon the balcony.

"Don Francisco!" The voice was broken now, importunate. "I beg you to release my Wife! I will confess my treason! I will suffer whatever tortures or agonies you may demand. But spare my María, Don Francisco! Spare her, I beg of you in the name of Christ!"

The sobbing prayer died in the smoky murk and then, finally, the metallic voice of Don Francisco fell like a death knell in the silence.

"It is too late, Castellán. What you confess or deny is of no importance now. I have a use for you—you and the treacherous jade that is your wife. Tonight you shall serve Spain by letting those who are with me now see the ever present fate that is ready for those who dare oppose me."

He turned to the dark-gowned torturer who waited beside the wheel. "Strip the wench and prepare her for the lash—and let her hang so that she may see this stinking carrion who shared her bed."

Rigid with horror, Manette saw the guards strip the woman's clothes away, saw them lash her thumbs together with a wire so fine that it cut into the flesh, saw them swing her into the air, suspended by the wire, so that she swung like a spitted fowl above the floor.

"Señor!" Manette whirled to face Nicomedes. "What devil's dream is this? Must we stand and watch—"

But the dark face was empty of humanity and of emotion, as still and changeless as some evil mask. She turned back to the arena as Larra's voice barked out a harsh command.

"And now let us teach this dog a lesson. Three blows, and let them be struck so that the wench may see."

The hooded figure below them turned a little away, and when he stood again above the wheel they could see the thick bar of dully gleaming steel that glistened darkly in his hands. He swung it high above his head, poised for an instant, and then sent it crashing down in a savage arc that struck the bound man midway between the hip and knee. From the balcony, Manette could see the bloodied flesh torn apart, hear the sharp snap as the long thigh bone crumpled and broke, and hear above it all the unearthly scream of agony from Castellán and the dark murmur that rumbled up from the caged prisoners who watched with bloodshot eyes.

Twice more the bar rose and fell, and each time the body lashed upon the wheel became less a man and more a broken, pulpy mass of flesh. María had screamed once, and then a merciful blackness had overtaken her so that she hung limp and senseless from the taut wire, oblivious of the horror that grew and blossomed in the burning light.

It was a nightmare, and as Manette felt Margarita's quivering body pressing tight against her own, she saw that the younger girl had covered her eyes with her hands and great tears were welling out between her fingers. The inferno of sound and smoke and terror swirled up about them and Manette clung to the railing with stiff, white-knuckled fingers as she fought down the racking nausea that clawed at her throat.

She heard Larra's voice through a whirling mist of dizziness. "What! Does this woman care so little for her lord that she sleeps while he struggles beneath the steel? Wake her, then, that she may taste the ecstasy I have planned for her."

The long lash whistled about the warden's head and then stiffened like a striking snake as it wrapped itself about the soft belly of the naked girl. Her body jerked convulsively in a spasm of searing pain, and her scream slashed the darkness. The whip coiled and struck again, leaving an open gash that spilled blood across her hips and down her thighs.

Manette tore her eyes away to find Larra watching her. "Think of this." His voice was still cold, but there was a throbbing undertone of suppressed excitement in it now. "What has been done to this woman can be done again, tonight, to your sister, Margarita. This, and more."

He turned back to the arena and there was no mistaking the fever of cruel exultation that possessed him now.

"Cut her down and give her to the prisoners!" He swung around to face the howling mob behind the bars. "Take her and use her as you will. A gift—a gift for you from Francisco de Larra!"

The horde roared, fighting and struggling for a place near the barred door that would admit her. A guard threw her limp body across his shoulder, shouted an obscene jest, and strode across the room to the opening door of the cage. He flung her contemptuously inside, and for an instant she was on her feet, screaming and trying to break away from the hands that tore at her and the loose-lipped faces that loomed above her. The roar swelled until it seemed that the very walls must crumple before it; then the dark mass of men surged forward and she disappeared behind the raging wall of their bodies.

"And now," Larra said, "have you repented your defiance, or shall I send the small Margarita to the room below?"

Manette stared at him, suddenly and terribly aware that this twisted dwarf held within himself the dark essence of evil. She closed her eyes to shut out the vision of Margarita screaming beneath the lash, dying before the dawn light at the hands of the brutish inmates of the cage. There was no choice.

"I have repented." She could feel all hope, all pride, all courage falling away from her as she spoke. "I have repented, Don Francisco. Tell me what I am to do."

CHAPTER THREE

S HE WAS to sail for New Orleans at sunset, that windy, light-swept hour when the tides of the Gulf turn back toward the shores of Panama and Campeche and the narrow waters of the Gulf of Darien. Jolting along the quay, with the carriage wheels bumping up and down on the uneven cobblestones and the watchful and subdued Ramón beside her, she reviewed Don Francisco's ultimatum of the night before. They had left the dungeon and gone back to the audience chamber, Larra's little eyes still burning with the strange excitement that had flared up in them when the whip stripped the flesh from María de Castellán's suspended body. Margarita had been white and trembling and Manette's own mind still shocked and reeling from the merciless brutality of the scene Don Francisco had paraded before her.

"Now, señorita," his fingers had drummed on the surface of the table, "I asked you about the money and jewels you may have brought from Santo Domingo, and your connection with La Sirena del Sur. You are prepared to answer?"

She nodded, helpless, knowing that this man held something far worse than the simple power of life and death. "We brought nothing. The slaves were upon us like a hurricane, burning, killing. We fled in the night and took only what little we could seize as we ran. My father—my father stayed behind to hold them back, and we never heard of him again."

Don Francisco nodded, almost as if the story of fire and death and disaster were a welcome tale.

"And your dancing here at La Sirena?"

She lifted her head to stare at him defiantly.

"What else could I do? Less than six months after we arrived in Havana, robbers broke into the small house we had rented. They stole everything we had that was of even trifling value, and left my mother dead upon the floor. I had no friends, no place to turn. I had danced for my own and my friends' amusement in Santo Domingo. It was the only talent I had to offer, and it carried me to La Sirena del Sur."

"Then you have no close friends or patrons in Havana?"

She shook her head dumbly, knowing that she was revealing her weakness and inability to oppose him but unable to offer any defense that would not instantly be destroyed.

"Why, then," he was suddenly at ease, almost genial, "I think you can serve me well. And your first reward, if you succeed, shall be the continued well-being of your little sister, Margarita. If you should fail, of course," his hand made a quick gesture of dismissal, "I would have no choice except to deal with her as I dealt with María de Castellán tonight."

His eyes flicked quickly over Margarita's still trembling body and the strange fires burned again in his eyes, fires like those of an animal watching its prey struggle to escape before it pounces down again.

"I understand, señor." There was no resistance in Manette's voice now. She was like a dead woman, resigned to whatever this hard-eyed man might demand, prepared to sacrifice herself on any altar to protect the slight girl who was her only link with the past. "If you will tell me what you want me to do, I shall try to serve you."

He leaned back in the high-backed chair and his eyes grew thoughtful as if he were considering how best to place the situation before her. His thumb and forefinger stroked his chin as he meditated, and when he spoke he seemed to be weighing each word before he gave it utterance.

"For the past three years we have been almost cut off from the government of Spain. The troubles with France and England have made communication difficult. Difficult and uncertain. Under the circumstances, I have"—he hesitated an instant— "been obligated to accept many responsibilities that would normally be resolved by His Majesty and his ministers. One of these has been the privateers—those captains that some men call pirates—who operate in these waters. They have a base near New Orleans, a Spanish possession and therefore our responsibility."

Manette nodded, leaning forward a little with an awakening of interest in her eyes. The pirate fleets of Barataria and Bonneterre and Cape Minguet were notorious all through the Antilles; freebooters, corsairs, buccaneers who defied every law of God and man and took tribute where they found it, without regard to the flag their victims flew.

"I have heard of them, señor," she said discreetly. "They are, indeed, a heavy responsibility for you to bear."

He glanced at her swiftly, appraising the spirit rather than the form of her comment. This was delicate ground and no one knew better than His Excellency the danger of the admissions he must make to this woman tonight.

"The greatest of them all," he went on slowly, "is one Raoul de Perpignier, who makes his headquarters at the island of Bonneterre, just off the Louisiana coast and some sixty miles below New Orleans. In the past, before the ships of the line were ordered back to Spain, we could control his activities to some extent. But since they have been recalled, matters have taken a different turn. So, unwilling to see the crown suffer here, I made an—an arrangement with Perpignier some two years ago. Briefly, it is a form of tax, a percentage of his loot to be delivered to

Havana. In return, we send no ships against him and allow him to prey upon our enemies, the French and English, and thus, at one and the same time, weaken those who would attack us and enrich the treasury of the Spanish crown. This is clear to you, señorita? You follow these involved matters without difficulty?"

"Oh, yes, Your Excellency. I see the situation clearly—as you would have me do."

Oh, it was clear enough, she reflected silently. Now that Spain was otherwise engaged, Don Francisco had entered into an alliance with Perpignier to ravage the shipping of the Gulf without interference from the small but able Spanish fleet that Larra still had at his disposal. As to the disposition of the gains, it was doubtful if one thin coin of the money Don Francisco received ever found its way into the royal treasury.

He glanced at her suspiciously, but her face was a bland mask of innocence, wide-eyed and intent upon his words.

"It has been an excellent arrangement," he admitted. "Or was until about six months ago. But since that time, señorita, not one peso has been received from Perpignier. Nothing! Nothing of all the rich prizes I know he has taken during the past half year!"

"And so—" Manette's voice was a silken invitation.

"And so I must know why the terms of our agreement have been broken. I must have someone who can win his confidence and find out the source of this strange new insolence of his. That—and word as to his future plans."

"I see, señor. And you have selected me as your ambassador. But have you not tried before? Surely you have not let a full six months pass without making some effort to discover the cause?"

"Tried!" His voice was suddenly stiff with anger. "Do you take me for a fool? Of course I have tried. Two men have sailed from Havana as my secret agents, and both of them have vanished as utterly as if the earth had devoured them. We know that they landed at New Orleans. We have word of them for a few days at the coffeehouses and the slave marts—and then they are gone! This time there is to be no failure. I know that Perpignier is a fool for a beautiful woman, and you are all of that. I am depending upon you to supply me with the information I must have. If you fail," he said, leaning forward across the table, his eyes hot fires burning into hers, "your sister will pay the penalty for your mistakes!"

As the carriage rode on toward the clamoring water front and the barkentine *El Audaz,* which was to take her to New Orleans while Margarita was held as hostage in His Excellency's palace, she sighed, feeling the crushing weight of responsibility she carried; and yet there was a tingling in her pulses at the thought of this new adventure that lay before her.

Some way, somehow, perhaps in the tangled web of intrigue and treachery and blood, she would find a way to win back the freedom and security and pride that had been torn away that awful night in Santo Domingo. Perhaps, before this was done, she would find a key that would release her forever from the grinding poverty she had known during the past year and from such smoke-filled pestholes as the dancing floor of La Sirena.

Impulsively she turned to the silent Ramón, who rode beside her. "Tell me," she said, "what do you know of this affair? Have you been advised as to the reason that I sail tonight?"

He grinned at her, baring yellow fangs in a wide-lipped mouth. "Advised!" he jeered. "Why it was I who first told Don Nicomedes you could act as Larra's agent. It was I who took him to see you dance last night and brought you to His Excellency in the early hours of the morning. I have been advised, and well."

He was boasting, striving to impress upon this lovely woman that he was a man of importance, sharing the confidence of Don

Francisco himself. True enough, the boat would sail within the hour, but even so, many things might be done within that time. If he could convince her it would be to her advantage to bestow her favors upon him ... He licked his lips hungrily, his eyes bold upon the sweet curve of her thighs and the soft mountains of her breasts.

She smiled at him, far too well trained in the hard school of La Sirena to mistake him for anything except the paid desperado that he was. But her face mirrored nothing but his own self-admiration as she leaned toward him so that her shoulder brushed lightly against his.

"Of course. I have seen that His Excellency depends upon you." The words were like honey on her lips, honey sweet enough to lead him along the road she would have him go. "But I know nothing of these things. This pirate, this Perpignier that I am to find and confuse and fascinate—what sort of man is he, and how shall I deal with him?"

Ramón frowned a little. There were other things he would rather discuss in the brief time before them. But, God knew, a woman was a woman and must be humored if she was to be conquered.

"He is an old man," he said contemptuously. "A man well past the half century. He controls his men only because he has been able to attract young and vigorous lieutenants to do his work for him. Raoul de Perpignier is nothing more than a living legend without blood or force. Only a fool would depend upon him for anything."

"And so Larra is a fool?"

Her words caught him in mid-breath, stunning him with the awful insult his heedless attempt to play the oracle had heaped upon His Excellency. He gasped, feeling his lungs suddenly dry and empty and his bones already cracking upon the wheel.

"*Por Dios,* no! I did not say such a thing! It was only that I—that I—"

She was withdrawn from him now, her shoulder far from his, her dark eyes mocking him and a half-smile of triumph on her lips.

"I wonder," she said absently, as if turning over a new idea in her mind, "I wonder what His Excellency would say and do if he heard that his faithful adviser had such a low opinion of him. Would he be pleased, do you think, Señor Ramón?"

"Oh, señorita, gracious señorita!" He was pleading with her now, the light of terror in his eyes and a trembling sickness clutching at his throat. "You would not tell him! You would not repeat a careless joke that meant less than the air that carried it! I beg of you, señorita, in your mercy and wisdom—"

She surveyed him through half-closed eyes, weighing his obvious panic and deciding how best to turn it to her advantage.

"I could forget it," she admitted. "Or I could, at least, bury it so deeply in my mind that it would not arise unless I had some need of it. If I did this for you, señor—" She hesitated and Ramón's eyes turned into those of a pleading dog. "If I did this, could you not find means to extend some measure of protection to my sister, Margarita, and to keep me advised as to the turn of events here that may affect me and the things I do?"

The breath escaped his lungs in a gusty sigh, and he closed his eyes for an instant as a wave of relief swept over him. "It shall be as you say," he swore fervently. "No man shall touch the little Margarita, and as for her comfort, I have friends inside the palace who will see to that."

"And the messages for me," Manette insisted.

"Without question, señorita!" He glanced quickly around and then leaned closer to her. "There is a tavern in New Orleans—on

Conti Street, not far from Royale—that is called the House of the Two Parrots. It is owned by my own blood brother, León Careaga. Ask there for word from me, or leave word with my brother as to where you are, and he will see that my messages are sent forward to you without delay."

They had reached the gangplank that stretched from the barkentine to the quay, and their driver had pulled up the carriage and begun to unload Manette's luggage upon the cobblestones. She turned away from Ramón and silently studied the scene about her for a long, heart-breaking moment that reduced Ramón to his former state of almost gibbering fear.

Timidly he tugged at her sleeve, afraid to have her go without some final word that would give him peace in the long, empty hours of the night.

"You will say nothing, señorita?" he begged. "Nothing of the words that were as nothing?"

She turned back to him and now her eyes were as cold as steel, as pitiless as the hard sheen of an executioner's sword.

"I will say nothing as long as you serve me well. If you are faithful, you may live to die in bed, and if you are not—" She chopped the edge of one hand sharply down into the palm of another so that he saw before him the steel bar of the torturer falling like a sledge upon his flesh.

"You may trust me, señorita, I swear it! By the Mother of God, I swear that you will have no need to speak."

But she had turned away and was stepping out of the carriage, imperiously directing the coachman as to the disposal of her luggage, ignoring Ramón as if he had never been. Lips half parted and eyes haggard and forlorn, he watched her slender figure sway up the narrow gangplank, saw her pass down the deck and enter an open cabin door.

Instinctively he crossed himself and his lips fluttered in a hurried word of prayer. From now until the hour when either he or she was dead, there would be no peace for Ramón. His lust for her had betrayed him, and his life now lay lightly upon the humor of her lips.

CHAPTER FOUR

THE COASTWISE barkentine *El Audaz* was fitted more for the efficient carrying of cargo than for the comfort of its few and usually infrequent passengers. Even so, a half-dozen travelers had chosen to squeeze themselves into its narrow hull for this voyage, and Manette found herself sharing a cabin with a French Creole matron and her two daughters, returning to New Orleans after a visit with their numerous cousins in Havana.

The mother, Madame Julie de Ternant, was scarcely older than Manette herself, and the daughters were so young that their colored nurse was to sleep on the floor between the double row of bunks so she might relieve the young mother of their care. They were unpacking as best they could in the crowded cabin when Manette stopped in the doorway. Madame Ternant looked up with a flash of brilliantly black eyes and a quick flurry of apology.

"Mademoiselle, I am devastated that you find us in such confusion." She was like a small bird, twittering and fluttering in her agitated dismay. "It was our hope to have this bustle and flurry done before you came aboard so that you would not be inconvenienced." Her white hands flickered like pale leaves tossed in the wind. "But with two such monsters, it moves but slowly."

Manette smiled and then directed a grave gaze toward the two children, who had grown suddenly shy and constrained at her appearance.

"Tell me," she said soberly, "are you really monsters?"

The older of the two, perhaps a round half-dozen years of age, shook her head in solemn negation. "No, ma'mselle. I am Cécile, and this is my sister, Désirée. Tante Liche says that we are good girls."

The colored nurse lifted her bent head from her work and snorted in sudden amusement.

"Good girls—when my eye is upon you or when you are in your bed at night."

Manette turned back to their mother, smiling as if they already shared a common ground of understanding. "They are charming, madame. You are to be congratulated upon them."

As she spoke she was appraising the young woman before her, recognizing in her dress and jewels and the black beauty patch upon her cheekbone the hallmarks of the colonial aristocracy that ruled New Orleans with an iron hand and had created there a creditable replica of the gaiety and silken sensuality of the court of Versailles. Such a woman, as a friend, could prove to be of tremendous value to her in this new land that she was about to enter unsponsored and unknown.

"You are too kind, ma'mselle." Madame de Ternant's own eyes were busy, weighing the richness of the dress that Larra had provided, the slimly aristocratic planes of the face that spoke of breeding, and the fluent French that carried the faint but unmistakable accent of the great plantation houses of Santo Domingo. Yes, it would be safe to proceed with this one.

"I am Julie de Ternant of New Orleans. Monsieur is traveling with us, but he is, of course, in one of the forward cabins with the other gentlemen of our party." It was courteously, even graciously done, but Manette recognized it as a bid for information as well as an introduction.

"That is very generous of you, madame, and I am Manette de Santiago, unfortunately"—she sketched a rueful grimace of resignation—"without a monsieur, and even"—her face sobered and she dropped her eyes—"without a mother or a father since the riots of Santo Domingo. I am on my way now to New Orleans, where I expect to join my brother, who is en route there now from the City of Mexico."

She held her breath, wondering if she had overdone the role of the gently innocent orphan, and then felt a sense of relief as she saw Julie de Ternant's eyes soften in sudden pity and understanding.

"My poor dear." There was the sincerity of compassion in the other woman's voice. "So many of those who fled from Santo Domingo have come to us in New Orleans. I almost feel as if I had suffered the horror of it myself. I give thanks that we have been spared that in Louisiana."

She cast a glance of disapproval and distaste about the clutter of the crowded cabin, wrinkling her nose a little as if the very flavor of it were objectionable to her.

"It will be hours before there is any order here." She moved impatiently, like a child willfully restrained by the obtuseness of some adult. "Let us leave this and the children to Tante Liche. She will unpack your bags and we will be able to relax when we return. Would that not be more pleasant, ma'mselle?"

"Tremendously so," Manette agreed. It was marvelous to have won this woman's confidence so quickly. Since she had been involuntarily committed to this adventure, it was only prudence and wisdom to use every means at hand to transform it from a black pathway of defeat to a shining avenue of opportunity. Smiling, she slipped her hand into the curve of Julie de Ternant's arm and they turned toward the deck together, as if they were sisters.

They found Monsieur de Ternant and his friends at ease beneath a striped awning that had been stretched above the afterdeck. He was a lean, stoop-shouldered man with far more than a brush of gray in his hair and with eyes that were eternally suspicious and intent. Meeting him, Manette knew almost in a flash that this had been a marriage of convenience, well arranged to match the still ardent springtime of Julie's beauty with the wealth that it was plainly evident her husband possessed. She turned from him to meet a younger man, Etienne Vincent Chrétien, typically Creole with his blue-black hair and large dark eyes. He was handsome enough. Almost too handsome, in fact, for there was a hint of weakness in the softness of his lips and the rolls of flesh that had begun to gather along his jaws.

He bowed over Manette's hand, and in his quick glance she caught the speculation that this might be a pigeon ripe for the plucking, a woman without visible protectors and yet with an unmistakable light of wisdom in her eyes.

His white teeth flashed in a smile of unhidden admiration. "I had thought the voyage well planned and perfect, with Madame de Ternant to lend her beauty to it, but now we are even more fortunate since the Dieu Seigneur has sent the Señorita de Santiago to us." He lifted his glass and turned to the other men beneath the awning. "Let us drink to this most charming young lady." The others lifted their glasses, murmuring formal words of courtesy, but Manette noticed that Ternant barely touched his glass to his lips and that he watched Chrétien with an oddly speculative look in his eyes.

They disposed themselves in chairs beneath the striped awning and Manette found herself beside Etienne.

He stared at her with a slight frown between his eyes. "I am puzzled," he said, "deeply puzzled, ma'mselle. I know I have seen you before—and recently, at that—but I am unable to recall the circumstances to my mind."

It was like a cold wind suddenly striking through the warm dusk of the tropic evening. She felt her body contract and tighten. This was the hidden danger she had feared, the ever present risk that some man of the party had visited La Sirena and seen her dancing there. If she was ever identified as a dancing girl from a water-front café, there would be no ripening friendship with Julie de Ternant. There would be nothing except ostracism here and some sordid refuge in the dregs of the Vieux Carré when she reached New Orleans.

She forced herself to smile, grateful that the gray shadows of early evening cloaked the deck and no candle or lamp had been lighted beneath the awning. "Why, perhaps you have, monsieur. You may have been a guest at one of the Captain General's entertainments in the palace?" She was stirred by a macabre gust of amusement as she remembered the entertainment she had witnessed there the night before. "Or in some shop or in a carriage on the streets?" She leaned closer to him, well aware that the swooping neckline of her gown had fallen away from her soft breasts, well calculated to drive other thoughts and inquiries out of his mind. "I am sure we have never met before," her eyes were softly languishing as they met his, "for I would certainly have remembered you."

It was well done. Under the flattering implications of her words and the invitation of her breasts and eyes, Etienne Chrétien was no man to waste his time digging in the past for some unimportant and elusive memory. Like a turkey cock he preened himself, unconsciously smoothing the hair of his temples and squaring the shoulders that bulged beneath the thin white linen coat.

"You are right, of course. Certainly such a meeting would not have been forgotten." His lips were parted in an anticipatory smile of warm self-satisfaction and his eyes ranged ceaselessly back and forth between the dark ebony of her eyes and the pale ivory of her breasts. "We must count upon many more meetings while you are in New Orleans. It is a pleasure I cannot deny myself."

"Etienne!"

It was Julie de Ternant's voice, cutting through the warm web of intimacy they had woven, pleasant enough and yet with the faintest possible thread of displeasure hidden beneath it. Manette turned at the sound and caught a quickly hidden flicker in Julie's eyes that could only have been the furious jealousy of a woman obliged to conceal her feelings in the face of a situation that was dangerously close to unfaithfulness.

"Yes, *ma chère* Julie!" Etienne was suddenly all attention and consideration. "I have been telling the Señorita de Santiago of the flowers and the festivals at home."

"Oh?" Julie's voice was carefully detached, skillfully and almost condescendingly amused. "I am sorry to interrupt you, but it grows late. Surely you would not have us all perish here of hunger. Why do you not make inquiries, Etienne, as to when dinner will be served? Ask perhaps, if it could not be here in the open air, like a picnic, so we may escape the heat and stench of those filthy cabins."

Etienne hurried away along the deck and Manette smiled placatingly at Julie, intent upon re-creating the cordiality of their former relationship, all too suddenly and sharply aware that she had been treading upon forbidden ground. She caught a glimpse of Monsieur de Ternant from the corner of her eye and saw that his face was suddenly flushed and fierce as his teeth gnawed angrily upon the corner of his lower lip.

Obviously, some sort of emotional storm was brewing, and she would be wise to avoid even its fringes. She stood up, shaking out the folds of her wide skirt so that it shimmered and moved like silver in the pale half-light.

"If you will excuse me, madame, messieurs, I believe I will go to my cabin for a moment."

Julie smiled up at her, all trace of the previous moment's irritation hidden behind a mask of friendliness and interest.

"But you will rejoin us for dinner, will you not, ma'mselle? It will be our pleasure to have you, if you will honor us."

"Of course." She slipped away into the darkness, thankful to escape for an interval that would allow her time to consider how best to use the situation that had accidentally been exposed.

The party broke up after dinner, the men going to the cabin that served as a dining and lounging salon for cards and brandy, and Julie, pleading fatigue, to the seclusion of the quarters she was to share with Manette and the children. Manette, with a wisdom that warned her to avoid the role of Julie's constant companion, sought a long rattan chair on the lee of the narrow deck, where she could find the peace and relaxation that had been denied her since Ramón stormed into her room on Los Mal Casados some eighteen hours before.

The barkentine had long since cleared the lights of Havana and now it pushed westward in an empty sea, with only the moon and the stars above and its own riding lights to mark its passage. It swung gently in the long swell of the waves, the masts and sails alternately hiding and revealing bright patches of stars as they swayed like grave figures in some formal dance to the rhythm of the recurring rise and fall of the vessel. The cancerous ulcer of frustration and rebellion that had devoured her all through the day began to slip away, to be replaced by a new confidence, even a heady anticipation of some bold stroke of fortune that would make short work of Larra's mission and even lay the foundation for a new life of power and wealth and unchallenged position. She knew the limitations of her arsenal—a lovely body, a pretty face, wits that had been sharpened by adversity, and a ruthless lust for conquest that dismissed and cast aside any impediments of conventional morality or ethics. It was little enough, but properly used, it might be made to serve her purpose.

The sail had swung around so that she was in deep shadow, and as she watched the play of moonlight on the sea, she was suddenly aware of a dark figure standing near the rail. She could see that it was a man, and she strained her eyes in an effort to identify him, but the light was too soft and shifting for her to see his features or the details of his dress. She heard a door close and then the staccato click of high-heeled slippers hurrying across the deck. A woman had come out of the companionway and joined the dim figure at the rail, as indistinct and impossible to identify as the man had been.

He met her with outstretched arms and their forms melted together, clinging for a moment of time. They drew a little apart and Manette could hear the hushed murmur of their voices, the woman's swift and hurried as raindrops pattering on a roof, and the man's as slow and deep as distant thunder rumbling along the horizon.

There was no other sound except the muted music of a guitar and the mournful chant of a group of Carib sailors far on the foredeck—and then, with the harsh force of an explosion, the door of the dining salon crashed open. In the sudden pathway of light that was flung across the deck, Manette saw a man charge through it, a naked blade glistening in his hand and his running feet like drumbeats as he charged down upon the couple at the rail.

They had whirled in quick alarm, and as he approached, the woman broke away and fled down the deck like a startled animal. In her terror she ran directly past Manette, and as she flashed by, Manette saw that it was Julie, her face wild with panic and the breath sobbing in her throat. She disappeared in the shadows and Manette whirled back to see the shining blade of the newcomer poised at the throat of the man who had waited at the rail. In a flash of recognition she knew' that the swordsman was Monsieur de Ternant; there was no mistaking that lean, stoop-shouldered figure. And the other—why, of course, the other was Etienne, trapped in a moonlight rendezvous with Julie by an enraged husband.

Almost without thinking, Manette was on her feet and running toward the two men silhouetted against the sea. There was only the half-formed shadow of an inspiration in her mind as she leaped up, but in the seconds it took her to reach them the entire stratagem of its consequences had emerged as full-blown and complete as though she had pondered it for days.

She flung herself between them, brushing Ternant's wicked blade aside as recklessly as if it had been a wooden lath.

"Monsieur!" Her eyes challenged him and there was the ring of outraged anger in her voice. "What is this crazy jest of charging upon me with naked steel? For a moment I thought we had been boarded by buccaneers until I turned and saw that it was you."

Ternant gaped at her as the sword point drooped slowly toward the deck. "Charging upon you?" There was incredulity and blank amazement in his voice. "You—you were not the woman who was standing here with Chrétien?"

She threw up her hand in a gesture of contemptuous interruption. "Do not bother to play the innocent with me, monsieur. If I choose to chat with Monsieur Chrétien, that is my affair and none of yours. Certainly it is no reason for you to come crashing down like some mad bull in a crowded street. Perhaps, monsieur, less brandy and a greater amount of discretion would help you mend your conduct."

He probed her face with eyes that were like gleaming scalpels, searching for the truth or falsehood that might lie behind her lips. Slowly he turned to Chrétien, and his face hardened as he stared at him.

"Monsieur Chrétien," his voice was cold and brittle as breaking glass upon a stone, "it would appear that I have done you an injustice and I will receive your seconds at any time, if you feel that you require satisfaction." He turned to Manette, and she knew by the bitter twist of his lips that she had earned an enemy who would neither forgive nor forget. "Señorita, I have no choice except to accept your statement and offer my formal apologies. Let us hope that in defending Monsieur Chrétien you have not exposed yourself to any more formidable danger."

He turned away, the naked blade still glittering in his hand. The cabin door closed angrily behind him, and Manette looked up to see Etienne staring at her with a look of mingled gratitude and awe.

"Ma'mselle!" There was almost a stammer in his voice. "I—I do not know what to say, or how to express my gratitude for your generosity."

She smiled at him, knowing the moonlight touched her with a sensual loveliness. "There is no question of gratitude, monsieur. I but repaid a portion of your kindness on the afterdeck this evening. Let us forget it and go on as if this unfortunate incident had never been."

He stepped quickly forward and she felt his hands caressing the smooth flesh of her shoulders. "You are marvelous, Manette! Marvelous!" She lifted her head and let her lips part a little in an image of eagerness as he drew her to him. Softly she yielded herself so that all the slim sweetness of her body was pressed against him. Then, almost reluctantly, she withdrew herself from his arms and turned away with a whispered good night.

She did not look back as she crossed the deck to the cabin where Julie would be waiting. There was no need for that, for as she walked she could almost hear the sound of silver trumpets ringing in the sky. Come fair or foul, good fortune or the ashen face of sheer disaster, she held both Julie and Etienne in a net from which there was no escape, a net she would draw tight when it would serve her purpose best.

CHAPTER FIVE

THE WIND died on the afternoon of the second day. The crest of water at the bow of the barkentine dropped away into nothingness so that finally there was only the slap-slap-slap of the soft waves lapping against the hull. The sun, burning a slow path through a cloudless sky, was reflected from the water in a gleam more dazzling than white fire and the still heat closed down upon the ship until the decks and rails were too hot to touch.

Alone with Julie on the afterdeck, while the men, half naked, tried to relax in the shadow of the flapping foresail, Manette saw the first great waves rolling up from the south. They came slowly, climbing above the smooth-swelling water like strange monsters lifting themselves out of the sea until the jade crest shattered into foam and another began to tower into the sky where the first had been. There was something relentless, almost primeval, about them, as if they swept the waters of the sea before them, thrust onward by some devil's brew of wind and storm.

The first one struck the barkentine from an oblique angle at the stern, lifting the heavy ship like a leaf tossed into the wind, so that for an instant the bow was buried and then flung aloft as the wave rolled onward beneath the keel. Almost thrown from the chair where she had been lounging, Julie scrambled to her feet, her face white with sudden panic.

"*Mon Dieu,* Manette! What is this? There is no storm, no wind, and yet we are almost thrown into the sea!"

"It is *el huracán*—the great wind—I think. Somewhere down there a storm is building up and driving the wind and water before it. I have seen it like this in Santo Domingo—wind and rain that tore the roofs and doors from our houses and threw boats larger than this so far up on the shore that they could never be reclaimed."

She braced herself as the second wave struck, sickeningly aware of their helplessness in the face of this force so vast that it could sweep a beach or an island bare in the space between two breaths. The men were running toward them and she could hear the captain shouting hoarse commands as the sailors worked to reef the sails and lash them down so that only bare masts remained against the sky.

Ternant's face was a mask of grim anxiety when he reached them and his eyes were dark with worry as they raked the rising tumult of wind and water that had already masked the horizon to the south.

"You must go below at once." There was no deference to courtesy in his voice, only the abruptness of a command that could not be disobeyed. "The rain is coming now, with the wind behind it. When it strikes, this deck will be nothing but an avalanche of water."

They could see the dark curtain of rain moving toward them across the waves, shutting out the sea and the sky beyond, flickering like some vast banner above the marching hordes of the rolling tide. There was an eerie, uncanny malevolence about it, for there was no roll of thunder or flash of lightning to bear it company and relate it to the storms they had known before; only the invisible emptiness of the wind driving it on and piling the great swells of foam higher and higher into the sky; only the masses of clouds that fled across the sky like sea birds seeking the shelter of the shore to escape this horror roaring down upon them.

Manette felt a hand upon her arm and turned to see Etienne close beside her. He was dressed only in the loose white trousers he had been wearing as he lounged beneath the sail; and his dark hair had been rumpled and twisted by the wind so that he looked more like a corsair from a pirate's deck than a Creole gentleman of wealth and breeding.

"Ternant is right—although I hate to admit it." He laughed a little and she smiled in answer, remembering the stormy scene on the deck the night before. "Let me take you to your cabin and make sure your doors and portholes are tightly closed."

It was pleasant to have him so solicitous of her, and phrases of agreement were almost on her lips when she caught a glimpse of Ternant's lean figure a half-dozen feet away, and the impossibility of the situation dawned upon her.

"You are thoughtful, monsieur." Her voice was so low that it scarcely carried to his ears. "But you cannot go with me, for it is Julie's cabin also."

"Julie's cabin?" A questioning frown gathered between his eyes and then he threw back his head and laughed as if some rare jest had just been presented to him. "So!" His voice was as conspiratorial as her own. "If Julie thinks that I escort you, there will be fire in that direction ... and if Ternant suspects me of snatching a moment with Julie, he will be at my throat! By God, it seems that I can be neither cavalier nor renegade until we find our feet on land again."

She let her hand rest on his for an instant while her eyes recalled their parting of the night before. "Someday," she said softly, "there will be no Julie close at hand, or any Monsieur de Ternant looking over our shoulders. It will be different then, *ma cher,* I promise you."

She turned away, feeling the wind press the flaring skirt against her hips and thighs and tear at the open neckline of her bodice. "Julie"—she held out her hand in a gesture of invitation— "let us follow your husband's advice and go below before the clothes are stripped from our bodies. There'll be no comfort here between now and morning and I've no mind to be drenched to the skin."

Julie hesitated an instant, shooting a sharp glance at the smiling Etienne, but Monsieur de Ternant's eyes followed hers and she turned away, her mouth a little sullen and her dark eyes smoldering with anger and dissatisfaction. The first drops of rain struck their faces just as they reached the cabin, lashed by a wind so strong they had to throw their bodies against the door to force it shut. The clothing suspended from hangers on the wall swung back and forth like ghosts swaying in the dusk and the torrent of light that had bathed the ship and the sea a quarter hour before had given place to a dull grayness as tangible and ominous as a shroud.

Cécile and Désirée were huddled together in a lower bunk, their eyes wide with excitement and their lips beginning to tremble in a wordless whimper of fear. Liche was trying to soothe them, and as Julie and Manette flung themselves into the cabin she looked up with a muttered ejaculation of relief.

"It looks bad, there on the deck?"

"It is bad." Julie's fingers brushed her cheeks, flipping away the drops of water that had struck her face. "How long do these—these hurricanes—last. Manette? I have heard of them, of course, but I have never had the misfortune to be on the edge of one before."

"No one knows. Sometimes they will blow and rain for days and then turn aside and pass without damage. Then again, they are on you before you know it and there is nothing to do but seek shelter and pray—or console yourself with rum—until it is over. This one, I think, will strike quickly. The rain was so close behind the first waves that the center of the storm cannot be very far away."

The wind screamed across the low roof of the cabin, and after a while it began to drive trickles and then streams of water through the cracks at the sides and the bottom of the door. At first they tried to wipe up the water that sloshed back and forth upon the floor, but as the storm increased they abandoned the effort and climbed up on the bunks, where the water could not reach them. The night came down and it seemed as if the fury of the wind and rain increased. The vessel was a tortured animal, leaping and screaming in agony as it tried to escape its tormentor. Long before midnight they heard the foremast come crashing down, and in the hours that followed the mainmast and the aftermast followed it, striking the deck like great trees falling in a forest and lashing back and forth against the sides until the power of the waves tore them free and sent them careening away in a whirling waste of wind and foam.

All through the night they clung to their bunks, thrown from side to side like puppets on a string until their bodies were sore and their hands were torn and bleeding. Once Manette's head struck the hard corner of the wooden rail and tore a gash across her forehead that oozed blood into her eyes and throbbed and stung from the salt water she used to bathe it. The children sobbed until they were exhausted and Tante Liche, gray-faced, mumbled endless prayers in the gumbo that was the common dialect of the Creole slaves.

By daylight the worst had passed, and when they heard a knock on the door, Manette ran across the cabin to open it. It was Etienne, his face drawn with exhaustion and his eyes salt-rimmed and bloodshot. There was a long red welt across his chest where a piece of flying driftwood had ripped him and his left hand was bound in an awkward bandage stained with blood.

"Etienne, you have been hurt!"

With her emotions whipped to a fever pitch and her nerves as taut as violin strings, she was unable to choke down the involuntary cry that broke from her lips.

"Etienne!" It was Julie crowding close behind her, her cheeks still pale with terror and her hand trembling on the casing of the doorway.

"It is nothing—nothing of importance." Etienne dismissed his injuries almost abstractedly. His gaze swept the cabin and lingered for an instant on the raw gash across Manette's forehead. "I tried to come to you twice in the night, but the water threw me back when I tried to cross the open deck." He looked at Julie, gnawing his lip in indecision. "Monsieur de Ternant—" he paused and then spoke as if his lips were almost too stiff to form the words. "Monsieur has been badly hurt. One of the spars struck him across the temple when it fell. He has been unconscious since before midnight."

"Oh, *mon Dieu!*" Julie's voice was a fading trail of sound, and almost instinctively she looked back over her shoulder at the two children crouching in the bunk, as if she only now remembered that Monsieur de Ternant was their father and the husband she had found it amusing to deceive. "I must go to him." Her slim ankles flashed beneath her lifted skirt as she slipped through the door and ran toward the forward cabin.

Etienne turned back to Manette as he held out his hand to her. "Come out, my dear. It has been a bad night for you."

She lifted her shoulders in a shrug of deprecation. "We survived. I have lived through these storms before." Her eyes swept the deck, taking in the jagged butts of the broken masts, the tangles of ropes and cordage washed against the rail, the broken doors and smashed windows of the cabins, and a long, empty gap where the rail of the ship had been torn away. They were lying broadside to the waves, and the ship rolled sickeningly beneath each onslaught of the swiftly flowing oily-surfaced water. She could see a group of sailors working halfheartedly at a nightmare mass of wreckage at the bow, and in the water-filled well of the open companionway a man's dead body rocked slowly back and forth to the rhythm of the ship.

"We were fortunate to escape with our lives." Her fingers tightened around Etienne's and she lifted his hand until it was firm against her breast. "Will they be able to rig a sail, do you think, or must we wait for the tide to carry us ashore?"

"God only knows." His eyes were bitter as they traced out the details of the ruin that lay about them. "But I've no wish to drift ashore here. Barataria and Cape Minguet are not far ahead, and the island of Bonneterre is less than three miles off our starboard bow. If we should drift ashore there …"

She nodded, remembering all the wild stories of torture and mutilation that had drifted up from these pirate isles. "There'd be little hope and no mercy at all," she agreed soberly. "Even as it stands now, we're better—" Her voice died abruptly as if someone had laid a hand across her lips and she leaned forward, straining her eyes as she tried to pick up the outlines of a dark shadow suddenly glimpsed upon the rim of the gray horizon.

"Look!" She shook Etienne's arm sharply in her agitation. "A ship out there, coming out from the coast! Help, perhaps, or—"

She sobered suddenly and Etienne completed the sentence with a grim note of irony in his voice: "Or perhaps our friends from Bonneterre, coming out to see what sort of cargo the storm has blown onto the points of their swords."

The sailors working in the forepeak had seen it, too, and as it loomed larger on the horizon, they abandoned their task and straggled over to the rail. Lessups and Gronier, who had made up the other two members of the Ternant party, came out of the cabin and shaded their eyes with their hands as they tried to make out the flag or outline of the approaching vessel. Manette and Etienne crossed the deck to join them and stood silent as the dark hull cut a white-fringed path across the waves.

The ship's captain, Martínez, had produced his spyglass, and their eyes flickered back and forth from his taut figure to the sails of the ship that was like an eagle sweeping down upon its prey. An eternity of time was born and died as they waited, and then he lowered his glass. His shoulders drooped and his eyes were like those of a man who had just heard the sentence of death pronounced upon him.

"Pirates." His fingers plucked at the open collar of his shirt. "The flag of Cartagena—and the decks packed with men."

She heard Etienne sigh a little, wearily, as if it were no more than he had steeled himself to hear.

"You will fight them, Captain?"

"Fight them?" He spread his hands in a bitter gesture of despair. "How would I fight them? With my empty hands or a club from this wreckage? Our ship's guns are gone. The powder for our muskets is soaked with sea water. Can I fight them with nothing, señor? Or is it better to deliver the ship peacefully and depend upon their mercy?"

"Mercy!" The word was like gall on Manette's twisted lips. "Mercy! There'll be no mercy here." Her eyes turned to the dark hull slashing through the sea. "Prepare yourselves to meet your God as best you can, señores, for here are men who will surely send us to Him."

She turned away and started across the deck toward the cabin. Halfway there, she heard a hoarse hail from the pirate ship and stopped to listen to the words flung at them across the water.

"Ho, there, you dogs! Stand back from the rail and drop your weapons on the deck. We'll parley with you after we're aboard."

The barkentine's crew surged back toward the shattered cabins like startled sheep, yet Manette saw that even in the flurry and excitement they kept themselves apart from the three passengers who stood tensely erect at the doorway of the dining salon. She frowned in puzzled surprise and then shuddered in sudden understanding as she realized that for common sailors there was always the chance to join the pirate horde, but for passengers there was almost certainly nothing except robbery and fierce torture and an anguished death.

The dark-hulled ship was almost beside them now, and she saw that it carried a vicious long gun amidships and three squat nine-pounders on a side. The decks and rigging were jammed with a howling horde of screaming, half-naked men, and on the raised afterdeck a single figure barked hoarse commands as the schooner swept in. She heard the dull thud as the two hulls met, the scrape of rail against rail, and then involuntarily threw back her head and screamed in terror as the corsair mob came pouring in over the rail, howling like savages in a tumult of confusion and horror that wiped all sense and sanity from her mind. They were a wave, a wave far more savage and terrible than any the hurricane had sent against them. In tattered trousers and heavy sea boots, their heads bound in handkerchiefs of red and purple, they charged across the deck with cutlasses already carving vicious circles in the air and pistols cocked and ready in their hands.

The avalanche of men enveloped the huddled sailors so quickly that almost between two heartbeats the deck was stained with blood and obscenely blemished with the shapeless mounds of dead men's bodies. Some few remained erect, among them Martínez, and as she watched, one squat, red-bearded buccaneer brought a long pistol barrel crashing down upon his head and sent him sprawling on the deck. A smaller group had seized

Etienne and his two companions and forced them back against the cabin wall, their arms wrenched behind them and blood streaming down their faces.

Three men sheered off from the main group and came racing down the deck toward her, howling like animals, with greedy hands outstretched and the fires of madness blazing from their eyes. Now she turned to flee, but they were upon her like hunting hounds pulling down a doe.

"Oh, no, no! *Por Dios—por—*" The broken cry turned into a scream as she felt their hands jerking her to a stop and whirling her about so that she lost her feet and would have fallen to her knees if it had not been for their grasp upon her.

She could not see them clearly. They were only great shapes of nightmare horror towering above her, pulling her back and forth in a stormy tumult of madness and delirium. There was the stink of sweat and tobacco and rum in her nostrils, the half-conscious knowledge of fiery pain as their fingers bit into her flesh, a confused roar of meaningless voices that made a fog of sound and senseless fury about her. Red flame blazed up before her eyes as a hard hand struck her across the face. For an instant there was nothing in all the world except the spasm of convulsive anguish that possessed her. She opened her eyes, feeling a long shudder run down her body as she gasped for breath.

The maniac horror was still about her but she could see it now, see with an almost microscopic intensity the harsh faces and the yellowed teeth and the tattooed arms and bodies that made it tangible and real. She could see, far up the deck, the boiling whirlpool of men's bodies and hear the hoarse clamor of their shouts and laughter as Julie was dragged through a cabin door and flung down on the deck, her dress already half ripped from her body and blood streaming from her lips across the naked flesh of her throat and breasts.

Suddenly, she was no longer afraid. Torture had been piled upon torment and madness upon fear until it was no longer real. It was like a play, a play with an inevitable end, but an end that was too plainly seen to be denied or rewarded with the indignity of protests or of pleas.

Now her mind rejected fear, turning contemptuously away from it so that her body relaxed and she lifted her head proudly to stare up at the brutish faces hanging so close above her own. Her throat was burned and raw from screaming and her face and head still throbbed from the stunning shock of that first blow. Only the first, her mind whispered desperately, only the first of many. But her voice was arrogant, as hot with anger at if she damned some unruly slave from the shadowed veranda of her father's mansion.

"You are dogs!" she raged. "Yes, the worst of dogs, for you have neither loyalty nor courage! What stops you now? Must you call up the others to be sure—"

She felt rough fingers clawing at the bosom of her gown, the sharp jerk of it across her shoulders as the fabric ripped and was torn away. Then hands like claws were digging at her flesh and other hands stripped the last remnants of her garments from her. She offered no resistance, even when they forced her down upon the deck, even when the first slavering-lipped face hung, monstrous and horrible, above her.

No resistance—nothing except the twisted fury of contempt that still clung, strangely, to her bruised and swollen lips.

CHAPTER SIX

MIRACULOUSLY, she was still alive when the black schooner swept in through the east pass to the hidden harbor behind Bonneterre. Alive; and with her, lashed together like slaves, Julie and Etienne and Lessups and Gronier. Even the two children and Tante Liche and Martínez and some half dozen of his men had been spared; spared because Grenaldi, who had commanded the attack, had come raging aboard the barkentine with a fusil cocked and charged and ready in his hands. He had driven the men away like a huntsman lashing a pack of hounds back from their prey.

"Are you fools?" he had stormed. "Idiots? Children who grasp at the first toy they see while the Gulf is still full of other vessels like this that are ready to be had for the taking? Leave the wenches and the rum. We will take them back to Bonneterre and they will be waiting for you when we return, I promise you. Now let me see you gut this vessel of whatever treasure it may have aboard so we may go."

His red eyes flamed with rage and the men fell back, muttering and cursing but unwilling to rise in open defiance against the ready fusil and the crackling lash of his anger. The chests of coins and clothing that the barkentine had carried were transferred and piled high around the mainmast of the schooner. There were kegs of palm oil and long tusks of ivory, and these too found their way to the pirate deck. Monsieur de Ternant's rings had clung too tightly to his fingers. It had been easier to slash the hands away at the wrists and leave him on the blood-soaked bunk that had become his grave. The hands hung now, suspended from the mast, the stumps jagged and black with blood while the jewels on the stiffened fingers gleamed and glittered as they swung back and forth in the glare of the sunlight.

So now they were at Bonneterre, a long, low fragment of white sand and twisted, tortured trees, encircled by the gleaming waters of the Gulf, naked and profoundly desolate beneath the raging fury of the sun. To the north, a score of tropic sea miles lay between the island and the delta of the Mississippi. Without a beginning or an end, the delta was a quaking marsh of unstable earth and sinuous bayous, rank with vegetation, foul with the corruption and the rottenness of a fertility too lush and savage. For sixty miles, between the green Gulf and New Orleans, the delta steamed and stank like some vast primeval beast emerging from a bed of slime.

They went ashore in longboats, to a shining beach ending in a line of stark and beaten oaks that leaned forever toward the north, away from the wind that blew unendingly from the jade and sapphire Gulf. They caught glimpses of rude huts, half hidden beneath the trees, and across the narrow island, built so that it would face the sea, a wide white house standing above a raised basement and roofed with the scarlet tiles of Spain. To the left there was an enormous barracoon, a grim stockade of peeled and whitened logs set endwise in the sand to contain the untamed blacks that were the loot from captured slavers. In the sheltered bay behind them almost a score of vessels still lay at anchor: schooners, barks and barkentines, and trim feluccas with their lateen-rigged red sails like pools of blood against the shifting blue-green pattern of the water.

The line of prisoners moved like a crippled snake, stumbling in the soft sand of the beach, tripped and betrayed by the ankle ropes that bound them together, beaten and shoved and cursed by the barbaric riffraff that drove them on. Their goal loomed up ahead, an ashen-wooded barracoon no better than that provided for the slaves; a little smaller, with a scanty shelter of four upright poles that formed a ten-foot square and supported a rustling roof of dry palmetto leaves. Beyond that there was nothing. Nothing except the empty sky and the scorching sand and the blazing sunlight that burned like a flame above this stark and pitiless prison set down on the rim of a lost island in the strange and savage sea.

The narrow gate of the barracoon slammed shut behind them and the prisoners staggered to a stop. Etienne, midway of the line, dropped to the ground and worked at the rope that bound his ankles. The others, watching, slowly began to follow suit, while Liche, forgetful of herself, tugged and pulled at the rope to free Cécile and Désirée. Manette, whose clothes had all been stripped from her on the deck, was in the grip of a shivering convulsion of horror that shook her like an aspen tree racked by the wind. The torrid heat of the sun beat down upon her, but it could not drive out the creeping cold of nausea that had sickened her as she was ravaged upon the bloodstained deck. A shadow fell across the sand before her and she flinched in terror before she saw that it was Etienne, dropping down beside her to work at the stiff lashing of the knots that held her. She could hear the murmur of his voice, soothing and comforting as if he were trying to reassure a frightened child.

"... over now, and there'll be a chance for ransom once the first excitement's done. Perpignier's not fool enough to let such easy money slip through his fingers just to provide a circus for his men."

Perpignier ... Perpignier ... Through the haze that fogged her mind, she knew dimly that the name should mean something to her, but the memory was twisted and distorted, perhaps a dream, perhaps nothing …. She watched Etienne's fingers struggling with the rope, saw them shift and move as the rope fell away, and suddenly realized that she was free. He was helping her to her feet now, guiding her across the sand to the patch of shade beneath the niggardly palmetto canopy. She stumbled as she walked, glad to have the support of his arm around her, clinging to his hand like a child learning to walk. It was cooler here in the shade, and as she relaxed upon the sand, it seemed as if some of the blind panic that had possessed her had been left behind in the sunlight.

"Try to sleep, Manette." It was Etienne's voice again. "Try to rest a little while and gather up your strength."

She smiled up at him, her eyes already drowsy with the weight of shock and exhaustion she had borne. She touched his hand gently, stroking it as if it were a talisman of hope and courage.

"You are kind, Etienne, very kind …."

Her voice trailed away and the world seemed to roll out of focus for a moment and then vanish into mist and emptiness. She closed her eyes and slept, her body white against the tawny sand, the pouring sunlight golden and intense, hemming in the patch of shadow where she lay.

The day was almost done when she came back to life again; the shadows of the stockade were long and purple across the sand and the heat a little less intense than it had been in the bright glare of the morning. Etienne was sitting beside her and a half-dozen feet away Julie crouched on the sand, her eyes red-rimmed and half glazed, her hair straggling down about her shoulders. She was whimpering softly to herself, and when she saw Manette stir and lift her head she began to cry like a frightened child.

"Oh, Manette, Manette!" She was sobbing openly now, catching her breath in shuddering gasps that tore and racked her body.

"What is to become of us? *Mon Dieu,* we will all be murdered here in this awful place!"

Manette sat up, feeling Etienne's arm supporting her as she tried to blink the dregs of sleep out of her eyes. She was still half drugged by the long hours on the sand and her mind instinctively recoiled from the memory of the night of storm and the later violence that had swept their vessel's deck. But it was true enough. The bleached logs of the stockade rimmed them in. Martínez and his men were sprawled out in the lengthening shadow, and Gronier and Lessups were standing at the gate, staring out at the beach beyond.

Abruptly the sense of her own nakedness impinged upon her and she crossed her arms to hide her breasts in an involuntary gesture of concealment. She looked up to see Etienne smiling at her and she relaxed a little, dropping her arms as she realized the absurdity of such a sudden access of modesty. Julie's voice was still whimpering into her ears and she turned to her with a trace of irritation on her face.

"Compose yourself, Julie." The words were a command. "There is nothing to be gained by sobbing and wailing. You, at least, have a part of a dress to cover you, while I have nothing."

Her throat was parched and dry and her lips were swollen with heat. She glanced questioningly about her and then looked back to Etienne. "Is there any water? I believe I would give my soul to the devil for a drink."

He nodded. "There is a little, Manette. Enough for you to bathe your face and cool your throat." He stood up and unfastened a fired-clay demijohn that was swung from one of the poles. "Hold out your hands and let me pour a little on them. There is no cup and there is little enough of this to waste."

The water cooled the arid burning of her throat and relieved the swollen stiffness of her lips. A little of the irritation she had felt toward Julie drained away and she rolled over on the sand so she could lay her hand on Julie's knee. "I am sorry I was sharp with you," she apologized. "But you must be brave, for yourself and for the two *enfants*. I have seen these buccaneers in Havana and I know that if you show them weakness it only adds to their sport. If they know you are afraid, they will hound you like dogs tearing at a rabbit."

"Oh, I know, I know." Julie's shoulders writhed in despair. "But we are all alone here and you and I are the only women."

"I know, *petite*," Manette comforted her. "But something can be done." She got to her feet, feeling a sudden wave of dizziness assail her. She closed her eyes until it passed and let her breath escape in a long sigh of relief when it was gone. "Etienne," she asked, "do you know where we are?" The memory of the half-heard name of Perpignier was coining back to her, and with it the mission that had been forced upon her by Don Francisco.

"This is Bonneterre," Etienne said. "The outpost of Raoul de Perpignier. I heard enough talk while they were bringing us in to be sure of that. I gathered that he is in New Orleans and is expected back tonight."

"And they will take us to him when he returns, do you think?"

He shrugged his shoulders helplessly. "God only knows. Grenaldi commanded the schooner that captured us and they may hold us for his arrival. I have had no experience in how these things are carried out."

She bit her lip, musing on the coincidence of being held a prisoner in the stronghold that Perpignier commanded. True enough, he had broken off his ties with Don Francisco, but even so, there might still be a tenuous bond of understanding that she could use to her advantage.

"I've no desire to go before either of them in this—lack of costume." She glanced down at her body, aware that already the reflected light from the sand had begun to burn it into a ruddy bronze. There was no help to be had from Julie or Tante Liche. Their own clothing had been so ripped and torn that it scarcely sufficed to cover them. The men were shirtless, wearing only the loose cotton trousers they had been wearing before the storm attacked them. Obviously, if she was to be clothed, it must be with something from outside the stockade. She could see a figure moving back and forth beyond the wide palings of the gate. A guard, of course, and their only possible contact with the world outside. She looked back over her shoulder at Julie and Etienne.

"I think I will talk a little with the guard outside the gate." She moved out into the burning sunlight, heedless of the startled protests that sprang up behind her. The light dazzled her eyes and the sand was like a hot fire beneath her feet, but she walked slowly forward, pushing her hair back on her head and praying silently that the cuts and bruises on her face were not too rudely swollen and disfiguring.

The logs in the wall of the barracoon itself were set so tightly together that it was almost impossible to see out between them. But the gate that provided the only opening in the walls was more like a rude grating, with wide spaces between the criss-crossed strips of wood so that the guards outside could keep a watchful eye upon their prisoners. She stopped beside the gate and studied the man who lounged outside. He was sitting on the sand with his back against a twisted live oak tree. His long musket leaned against the trunk and he seemed to be half asleep as he slouched there with his hands clasped about his knees. He was an old man, bald-headed and skinny and toothless, with a skin like parchment and a twisted foot that sprawled at an ugly angle against the sand. The tendons of his scrawny neck were like sagging wires. Too old, she thought, to fight aboard a privateer.

Too old and crippled, so that now he was relegated to this menial task, cut off forever from the women and the wine and the loot the others shared. She twisted herself against the gate so that her breasts and loins would be presented to his gaze and then called softly, as if she hesitated to disturb his rest.

"*Señor, señor—un momento, por favor.*"

He stirred a little, lifting his head reluctantly and then waking into a more avid interest as his rheumy eyes traced out the curves and color of her body.

She thrust her hand through one of the openings and motioned him toward her. "Spare me a moment of your time, *señor.*"

He spat contemptuously in the sand, although his eyes never left the curve of her breasts and the sweep of her thighs.

"I have no time for you." His voice was a high-pitched squeak, sour with malice and a thwarted, helpless knowledge of his own indignity and insignificance. "Grenaldi will see to you when he returns. He or Perpignier—if the fine gentleman lowers himself enough to spend an evening with us."

"But I have no business with Perpignier, *corazón.*" She seemed to release the term of endearment hesitantly, almost timidly. "My interest is in you—now, and for the future."

She let her body turn a little against the gate, coaxing him with it, watching the glow mount in his eyes.

Her voice was as warm as honey, low, with that half huskiness that all men know as passion. "If you will do something for me, then—when I am free of this barracoon—I will do far more for you."

"For me? What could you do? A prisoner to be lashed or hung up by your thumbs, and then thrown to the men when Grenaldi or Perpignier has had enough of you! You can do nothing for me. Go now, and let me resume my sleep!"

There was no comfort in the words, but she could see the hunger growing in his face, the blind, unmasked desire that even old men feel when the flesh that is thrust before them is young and soft and carries within itself the open promise of remembered pleasures.

She forced herself to smile at him, letting her eyes half close as her thighs moved a little against the gate. "How long has it been since you have known a woman? How long since you have been able to feel one in your arms? How much would you enjoy a woman who could rouse you as you have never been stirred before? Tell me, *querido,* would you not like to have me do these things for you?"

The old man's eyes shifted away and then came back to hers, still unbelieving but unable to repress the desire smoldering in them.

"What man does not enjoy these things?" His voice crackled angrily like dried sticks burning in a fire. "What is it that you want, woman? If you have come begging for release, I can tell you now there is no hope. You're a likely enough wench, but no woman is rich enough to pay for a slow death in the fire."

"Oh, no, *corazón.*" Her voice was a swift blade to cut short the dull flow of his muttering. "No harm can come to you from this. It is only that I am—naked. I need something to cover myself against the sun. A strip of cloth, a worn-out skirt—"

He seemed relieved, as if the request were far less than he had expected. But his voice was still surly and contemptuous. "I have no cloth, no women's gear." He fell into silence and then looked quickly up at her with sly cunning in his eyes. "Perhaps, somewhere, there might be an old shirt that you could wear. You would extend your favors for that, if the time came when you could do so?"

"Oh, yes, yes! For that I would make you the happiest man in the world."

"Well, then—" He got to his feet and whistled shrilly, like a man calling a dog. From nowhere, a half-grown Negro boy came racing across the sand, obviously a messenger stationed there to serve the needs of the guards at the barracoons. The old man's voice shrilled at him in a patois Manette could not understand and the boy sped away, running as if pursued by devils until he vanished behind the line of huts that crouched beneath the beaten oaks. Almost instantly she saw him flying back again, some shapeless material clutched in his hand and fluttering behind him as he ran. The old man took it from him and held it up so she could see.

"So," he cackled, "something to cover you a little—and not too much.' He waved the ragged shirt in the air, a blue cottonade, much worn and bedraggled, a cast-off bit of loot from some lost and long forgotten Spanish galleon.

"Oh, yes," she cried eagerly. "It is perfect, corazón—a gift that you will not regret." She stretched her arms out for it, feeling the rough wood of the bars rasp her skin. "Give it to me, por favor."

The old man shuffled forward across the sand, the shirt tucked carefully under one arm. He came on until his body was pressed against the gate and then the skinny claw of his hand reached through to fasten on her breast. Even in the heat, his fingers were cold and stiff with age, the hand of a skeleton rather than that of a living man. She choked in sudden nausea, swallowing hard to hide the revulsion that sent a shudder through her body. His fingers pulled and twisted at her flesh, cruel with the eagerness of the desire she had created in him. He moistened his lips, the bald-buzzard head quivering upon his shoulders as if he had been suddenly attacked by palsy. The old man's voice was a wordless, obscene cackling in her ears and suddenly she jerked the torn shirt free of his arm and fell back from the gate. His mumbling shrilled up into a sudden howl of rage, his grasping hand still thrust through the opening in the gate.

"Later, *corazón*." She forced herself to smile at him, remembering that he was still their only contact with the world outside, knowing she might have need of him again. "Later, when I am free of this stockade."

She slipped into the shirt, finding it snug and tight about her, barely long enough to touch the tops of her thighs and too narrowly cut to button across her breasts. But there were two buttons at the waist that could be fastened, so that it gave at least a semblance of covering.

She lifted her hand in a gesture of farewell. "*Mil gracias, corazón*. We will meet again." She turned away and walked back toward the ragged shelter of the palmetto canopy. The triumph—if it could be called that—was small enough. A ragged shirt coaxed from an old man whose mind was dulled and appetites brutish from his half senility. Even so, it was something. An omen, perhaps, a step toward the ultimate saving of herself from the danger that surrounded her.

CHAPTER SEVEN

S HE COULD see the men of the island gathering on the southern beach of Bonneterre. Torches moving through the tropic
night, mingling together in a shifting glare of flickering light
in front of the wide white house that faced the sea. Shouts and
curses, snatches of bawdy songs—a reckless, drunken crew pouring in from the huts and the ships to see what sport or spoils the
day had brought and the night would offer.

They had not called up the prisoners yet, so that she and Julie
and Etienne and the others were still able to crowd around the
barred gateway and peer out at the howling mob that swelled and
grew until it was like the black form of some monstrous spider
shifting and moving back and forth upon the beach. The little
knot of sailors standing behind her shifted uneasily, their feet
rustling like dry leaves in the sand. One of them was praying,
his voice a swift mutter of phrases repeated over and over, like
the meaningless sound of a frightened monkey gibbering in the
darkness. She felt Etienne's hand upon her arm and realized with
a sudden shock of amazement that it was unsteady and trembling
a little. So, then, there was a meaning in the lines of weakness she
had seen carved on his face at their first meeting. But he had been
so courageous, so strong, and so stouthearted in the hours since
the great wind struck.

"They'll be coming for us soon." His voice was husky, and
even in the semidarkness she could see that his lips were twitching nervously.

She laid her hand on his, holding it tightly for an instant. It was strange that now she should have to be the one to reassure Etienne. "It will not be too bad, I think. You said yourself that Perpignier would be willing to consider a ransom."

"If he is here! But if he is still in New Orleans and we have only these half-naked devils to deal with—"

"Someone will be here." As she spoke she wondered sardonically what she would do when she was called upon for ransom. Perhaps Julie or Etienne would prove generous, but they had made no offer of assistance and she knew nothing of their finances. It was entirely possible that they had only enough for themselves. She could hardly look to Lessups or Gronier. A chance shipboard introduction was hardly enough to cause those shrewd Creoles to pledge their fortunes or their properties to help her. Fleetingly she wondered if she might turn to Larra, and then dismissed the idea almost as swiftly as it had come. Don Francisco would simply deny any knowledge of her. To do anything else would disclose all the vast web of intrigue he had spun so carefully behind the barred doors of his palace. Well, she still had her wits and a body that men coveted. They might be enough.

She stiffened into attention as she saw a file of men straggling up the sand toward the barracoon. A few of them carried torches, the light moving unevenly across the sand, reflected now and then in the water as they passed some narrow inlet that ran up from the shore. They were shouting and howling, and she knew, even at that distance, that they were aflame with rum and half mad with the twin lusts of cruelty and desire.

Julie screamed as the stockade gate slammed open and the horde of bearded, howling men poured in upon them. Stumbling, wild-eyed, she turned and tried to run, but two of them flung themselves upon her, pulling her down and then dragging her back across the sand.

Even though she had tried to prepare herself, Manette felt her skin turn cold and her flesh shrink. There was an instant when she felt as if she, too, must turn and run and try to hide from this new terror. Then they were all about her, and as she felt their gnarled hands jerk her forward she knew something of the same rage and contempt she had felt on the deck of *El Audaz.* This was the final hour of trial, the test that would determine whether she was to live or die. There was no time for weakness or hysteria now. She threw back her head and moved forward like a queen about to receive the homage of her subjects. One half-drunk ruffian pawed her roughly as she passed and she felt other hands pulling and tugging at her body, twisting and turning her like some inanimate doll thrown to them for their pleasure.

Then they were being herded forward like cattle, the unruly guards all about them and behind them, driving them forward with words and blows toward the blaze of the torches flaming upon the beach. Her body burned and throbbed where they had mishandled her and her throat was so dry that she could scarcely swallow. Her naked feet sank into the soft sand so that each step was a weariness and a torture, but she walked with her back straight and her head erect, knowing instinctively that her only salvation, if indeed there was to be salvation, lay in her own strength and her apparent freedom from fear.

The guards halted them before the wide steps of the long house facing the beach, and she could see now that there was a broad gallery stretching across its length and candlelight streaming out through the open windows. Three men were standing at the top of the steps. One was Grenaldi, who had commanded the schooner that had captured them. The man in the center was squat, thick-legged, fat-paunched. An old man, with heavy, vein-streaked jowls and a head as bald as a round, white-painted rock. He stared out at them stupidly, almost as if he were befuddled with drugs or drink. A gross, shapeless man, so jaded with dissipation that his dull eyes and slack mouth were the measure of the fogged brain that drowsed beneath the naked ugliness of his skull.

But the third man was of a different stripe, tall, lean, wide-shouldered. His eyes were like black fires in the granite hardness of his face. Still young, if she could judge by the arrogant ease of his body and the slimness of his waist and hips. He was dressed like a cavalier in light pantaloons and a sweeping cloak of bottle green that was a background for the snowy whiteness of his ruffled shirt and the gleam of jewels at his throat and wrists. His hair was black and worn so long that it brushed against his shoulders when he moved his head. His right hand lay lightly upon the butt of one of the pistols thrust into his belt, and the other fondled the jeweled hilt of a long sword hanging from his wrist.

His face untouched, unchanging, he watched the guards marshal the prisoners in the circle of torchlight before him. Watching him, Manette came to the swift conclusion that if any terms were to be made, it was this man she must bargain with to save her life. Without speaking, almost without moving, he had managed to convey and define his ascendancy over the two men beside him and the mob of sailors and buccaneers milling on the beach. There was an aura of strength in his very negligence; a feeling of power and ruthlessness so clear and certain that it was beyond any need for demonstration. Casually, almost disinterestedly, he waited until the tumult had died down, until the prisoners stood silent and white-faced before him. He stepped forward a little, so that the light washed out some of the dark shadows that had half masked his face.

"All right." He spoke in French, but it was a French a little twisted and distorted with an accent that was either English or

American. "Which one of you captained this boat that Grenaldi took over? Step out here and let's have a look at you."

Hesitatingly, like a man moving forward to his doom, Martínez stepped forward out of the crowd.

"I was the captain, señor. I am Diego Martínez of Havana, and I have done you and your men no harm."

"Why, no." The voice was half amused. "I don't suppose you have. There aren't a great many men in these waters who are inclined to do us any harm. That's right, isn't it, Perpignier?" He half turned to look back over his shoulder at the gross-bodied older man standing a little behind him. "I never saw a man yet who wasn't a friend of ours—especially after he'd been shut up in a barracoon for a while."

The heavy-faced man nodded slowly, as if he were only half awake. "All friends," he muttered hoarsely. "All friends, MacMurran, when they are close enough to us or the fire is close enough to them."

Manette studied the man in the center with a sharp new interest. So this was Perpignier, this worn-out, fat-bellied parody of a man who was more like a lump of senseless clay than a leader of the buccaneers of Bonneterre. Ramón had told her in Havana that Perpignier was "nothing more than a living legend without blood or force," but she had never dreamed that he was no more than this. Ramón had mentioned able young lieutenants, too, and from the look of it, MacMurran was one of them. He was talking to Martínez again.

"If you have sailed these waters long enough to become a captain, you have sailed them long enough to know our methods. For the prisoners that we take there are three alternatives. You can ransom yourself to freedom, you can join our company—if the men approve—or you can submit yourself to their mercy. Which do you want, Martínez? Can you raise ten thousand dollars for your own ransom and five thousand for each of your men?"

"Ten thousand!" The words died on Martínez' stricken lips. "Señor, I have never in my life had that much money, or even a tenth as much. And my men—Why, señor, you know they are only sailors with nothing on earth except what they earn. They could not raise five thousand dollars among them if they worked from now until the Day of Judgment!"

MacMurran nodded absently, as if it were the answer he had expected. "That's true enough, and yet many of our sailors have had that much and thrown it away in almost a single night. Well, there is always another choice. Do you want to join with us or do you prefer to throw yourself upon the mercy of the brotherhood?"

Martínez' glance darted from side to side as if he were seeking some escape from this trap. It was a sorry choice in either case. If the men turned to piracy, they automatically outlawed themselves insofar as any court in the world would be concerned. If they were caught, they would be hanged; and if they lived, they would probably die in some bloody shambles that they had not chosen. As for the mercy of the brotherhood, that was a grim jest; a joke based upon the universal and unchanging cruelty of this pirate horde.

He twisted his hands nervously before him and Manette could see the spasmodic twitching of his lips. The murmur of men's voices was rising behind them, sure proof of their impatience, a certain sign of their desire for the action that had so far been denied them. Martínez heard it, too, and suddenly his jaws tightened and he stepped forward and threw up his head defiantly.

"I cannot answer for my men, but for myself, I choose to join you, if you will have me. I am skilled in navigation and I was for five years a gunner in the Spanish ships of the line. I can be of service to—"

MacMurran threw up his hand to cut off Martínez' frenzied flow of speech.

"We have many navigators, many gunners." He looked out across the harsh faces half seen in the flickering light of the torches. "Do you want this Martínez, you men? Do you want to sail with him and share your loot with him?"

The answer came rolling and thundering up out of the night.

"No! No!"

"Too many of us now!"

"Neither this whining dog nor any of his men."

Martínez' face had gained back a little of its color as he made his plea to the tall man at the top of the steps, but now it was as white as the sun-bleached shells that littered the beach. He flung up his arms as if to ward off a blow, and his voice cut through the torrent of sound in a rising wail.

"*Madre de Dios*! It was your own word that we should have our choice! Let us sail with you! Let us—"

But the wolf pack behind him howled him down and MacMurran threw out his hands in a careless gesture of resignation. It was obvious that the outcome was of little or no interest to him.

"I told you you could join us if the men approved. You can see, my friend, that they do not approve."

He motioned the captain of the guard. "Take them aside, now. You can deal with them after we have settled with these—" his voice grew acid with the sting of sarcasm—"these gentlemen and ladies who have come to visit us."

There was a brief scuffle, the sobbing pleas of Martínez, abruptly cut off as one of the guards slashed him in the face with a pistol butt. "Quiet, you dog!" He and his men were dragged away, already doomed to death and now left to agonies of terror and dismay, as their minds turned frantically upon the time and manner of its coming.

MacMurran was studying the little group before him now, weighing them as best he could in their tattered remnants.

"By the ship's papers, there was a Monsieur de Ternant. Which of you has that honor?"

There was a moment of creeping silence and then Etienne spoke in a voice that was hollow and as shaken as a broken reed. "He is dead, monsieur. They—they slashed his hands off at the wrists and left him bleeding on his bunk."

MacMurran nodded. "So it was Ternant they killed. A pity, for he was rich and could have brought a pretty ransom. Well, there is at least his wife. Yes, and his two children. They should do as well."

He shifted his glance to Julie and Manette, standing side by side. Manette was still and outwardly unmoved, but Julie was so racked by nervous sobs that she could scarcely speak. She caught her breath, her bare shoulders shaking and her whole figure a vivid picture of torn and tragic misery. "I am Julie de Ternant, monsieur," she whispered brokenly. "I beg you show us mercy! We will give you anything! Anything you ask."

He smiled a little, as scornfully as if no man, or woman either, should give way to such terror at being a captive on the isle of Bonneterre. "Why," he said, "you're very generous, Madame de Ternant. So generous that we must show you some generosity in return." He paused, stroking his chin thoughtfully as if he meditated the bargain he would offer. "Let us say forty thousand dollars for yourself and fifteen thousand for each of the children. Is that fair enough? As for the slave, perhaps another thousand dollars—although I'll grant you that's a trifle high, since we sell better ones straight from the barracoons at a flat rate of one dollar to the pound. How does that sound to you, madame? Will you accept that or will you have me be more generous still?"

Julie was staring up at him with her lips half open and her eyes fixed in an unbelieving stare. "Seventy thousand dollars, monsieur? Seventy thousand? *Mon Dieu,* monsieur, that is a fortune!"

"Seventy-one thousand, madame," he corrected. "Of course, if it is too high, the men are always waiting."

"But monsieur!" she pleaded. "You will strip us of everything. Our home, our land—"

"And would you rather be stripped of your clothes and thrown out there on the beach?" His voice crackled with sudden anger and he moved forward a threatening step. "Come, madame, I have no time to haggle with you. Take it or leave it, but do it now!"

She bit her lip, trembling with fear and almost too dazed to speak. Then from the darkness behind her, a great bull bass of a voice roared like a cannon firing.

"Give us the wench! Give us that woman."

In an instant she was on her knees with her arms held piteously out before her. "Oh, no! No!" she screamed. "I will send for the money. I will send for it tonight—but do not let them have me! In the name of God, monsieur—"

He hesitated an instant as if her delay had angered him so greatly that he was more than half inclined to give her to the mob, even in the face of her terrified capitulation. Then he shrugged his shoulders and lifted his hand in a command for silence.

"There are other women," he said half regretfully. "There are many other women you can use. But they do not all have access to so handsome a sum of money."

There was a mutinous murmur from the shifting, impatient mob and suddenly his eyes flashed fire and his voice was a harsh bellow of anger.

"Do you question me? By God, if you do—" He moved forward to the edge of the steps and his whole figure was tense with a scarcely withheld rage. The murmur died away and he stood there for a long breath of time, his eyes sweeping them all contemptuously, his hand tight upon the butt of the pistol in his belt. Then he relaxed and stepped back into the shadows again.

Etienne and Lessups and Gronier he dealt with briskly. A ransom of twenty thousand dollars each, to be delivered within ten days. They were almost pitiful in their eagerness to fall in with his demands, white and shaken when the guard led them aside to join Julie and Cécile and Désirée.

Then there was only Manette left upon the sand before him. Manette, with head held high and the brief shirt she wore only covering enough to add a touch of mystery to the slim erectness of her figure.

"And you." He half bowed to her and a smile seemed to flicker far back in the depths of his eyes. "You are Manette de Santiago, driven from Santo Domingo and lately a dancer at a Havana water-front café. I have seen you there, señorita, and you were most attractive, but I doubt that dancing girls and refugees have the money for ransom that we have discussed here tonight. My men will be glad of that, I think—especially since Madame de Ternant will not be able to entertain them."

Manette's eyes widened in surprise, but then, she told herself silently, there was no reason for surprise. Such men as these had been the favored patrons of La Sirena del Sur, the men who filled its coffers with stolen gold and cheered and screamed when she stood naked before them in the flare of torchlight. She shot a quick glance at Etienne, but he was staring stonily at the sand. Julie was a crumpled, half-unconscious heap of despairing misery. Well, so much for that! She walked slowly forward until she was at the foot of the steps and could look up into MacMurran's face.

"You are right, señor." Her voice was a carefully controlled whisper, so light that it barely reached his ears and could not carry to the guards and the massed men behind her. "I do not have money for my ransom, but I have something that can be of far more value to you."

He frowned in surprise. "More value? Why, there is nothing—" He broke off and half wheeled away, his face suddenly contemptuous. "A trick!" he said harshly. "A dancing girl's trick to try to win a little longer space of time. By God, I'll teach you—"

Her whisper cut into the rising roar of his voice.

"And has your life no value, señor? Your life and this establishment?" She leaned forward a little, staring up at him with eyes that were like hot coals. "Why do you think that I was on that ship? Do you think that dancing girls from La Sirena travel idly back and forth on trips of pleasure? Oh, no, señor! There was a reason I was there—and that reason can be of value to you."

His eyes narrowed and he studied her speculatively as he turned her words over in his mind.

"And this information?" he said questioningly.

"It is for your ears alone," she said decisively. "And then, only after we have made a bargain."

He stared at her and then exploded in a sudden burst of unexpected laughter. "By God," he swore, "you talk about a bargain when I could have you lashed until you begged me to listen to your lies!"

"And if I did not tell you then?"

"You'd tell me. But there's time enough for that." He motioned her forward with a quick jerk of his wrist. "Come up here. When you see how Martínez and his men are handled you may change your mind." He turned to face the men upon the beach and his voice was low and unexcited but so clear that it reached the outermost fringes of the crowd. "This wench has knowledge—so she says—that may be of value to us. We'll question her a little later and, if she lies, you'll have her yet tonight. Now you have your sailors. What are your plans for them?"

The crowd roared and two burly blackbeards stepped out from the crowd. There were cutlasses swinging at their sides and bright handkerchiefs bound around their heads.

"It's damned cold tonight." Ostensibly the speaker mopped the perspiration from his forehead, and the crowd behind him howled with cruel laughter. "It's damned cold tonight, and we thought we'd warm them up a little. Enough to take the chill out of their bones so they can exercise a little here on the beach."

MacMurran's lips curled but his voice was sober as he replied, "I knew the brotherhood would show them mercy. Get along with it, and we'll stand here and see how well they're treated."

There was a turmoil of confusion, but as Manette watched she saw that it was taking the form of two long lines of men stretched out across the beach. Standing some four feet apart, they formed two impenetrable and parallel walls, and at the end nearest the house a smaller group had stripped Martínez and his men of their clothes and were painting them with some dark substance that threw a bitter acrid smell into the air. Tar! It could be nothing else. The black, half-slimy tar that was an ever present necessity wherever ships sailed the sea. Tar that would burn like oil and cling to a man's body until the flesh fell away from the scorching bones.

As she watched, one of the guards thrust a flaming torch into Martínez' blackened side and, as he screamed in agony, the tar caught and trickles of fire spread like water across his body. Standing so, with a man holding each wrist, he threw back his head and his voice was a wild torrent of wordless sound, shattering the night and turning Manette sick with horror. For a long moment they held him so, while the flames seemed to cover him like a living robe and the stink of burning flesh mingled with the harsh odor of the tar. Then they thrust him forward toward the two lines of waiting men.

"Run! Run! Run for your life!"

Staggering, blinded by the thick smoke that billowed about him, tormented by the gnawing agony that devoured his flesh, Martínez plunged forward between the lines of men. As he ran, cutlasses flashed in the night, so that with every step his body was torn and ripped and blood spurted out to mingle with the tar and fill his footprints in the sand. His voice was like a madman's now, horrible, inhuman. He stumbled, fell, and then as the fire licked at his hair and face, he forced himself to his feet and stumbled on again, the cold steel of the knives still slashing at his body, the fire scorching and searing him. He dropped to his knees, his arms flailing wildly for support. There was a final sob, beastly and shuddering, from his flame-filled lungs. He fell forward on the sand and the flames blazed up triumphantly above him. The men howled in a yelping screech of delight, like demons let loose upon the earth. There was the smell of burning flesh in the air, the obscene blackness of fresh blood still oozing into the sand.

The guards dragged a sailor forward and he was bathed in sudden light as the torches were crushed against his body. His wail of agony was sheer, demoniac terror, and as it still echoed in the night MacMurran turned to Manette and dragged her roughly forward by the arm.

"Do you see?" he growled. "Do you see why I said you would beg to talk if I chose to use the lash or the fire upon you?"

She was dizzy with sickness and the horror that grew and flamed before her eyes, but she clenched her teeth together and stiffened her body until it might have been a statue carved from tawny marble.

"I see." Her voice was harsh with the tension she was trying so desperately to hide. "I see, but still I am not afraid, señor. When we have made our bargain, then you will know what I have to tell. But not till then! Not if you use the fire and the whip until I am as completely destroyed as that poor devil on the sand. I am not afraid of you, señor. I will never be afraid of you!"

CHAPTER EIGHT

GREAT white-winged moths swirled and fluttered around the flickering candles in Perpignier's council room. The air was heavy with the smell of rum, and outside the men still rioted and sang and fought around the charred bodies of Martínez and his ill-fated crew. Manette stood on one side of the dark refectory table that occupied the center of the room, and across from her, at ease in their wide-armed Jamaica chairs, MacMurran and Grenaldi and the still stupid-faced. Perpignier studied her with insolent eyes that still took pleasure from the almost naked body she exposed to them. MacMurran leaned forward a little, his eyes lingering on her breasts before his glance shifted to her face.

"We are ready to hear you." His voice was cold with doubt and disbelief. "What is this great secret you have brought from Havana that is so important to us?"

She shook her head, feeling the high-strung quivering of doubt and apprehension shake her body, acutely aware of the sudden dryness of her lips. "When we have made a bargain, señor. That was the agreement. My information in exchange for my freedom—regardless of the value you may set upon it."

Grenaldi stirred impatiently in his chair and there were sudden yellow flecks of anger in the small red eyes. "By God, we've wasted enough time on this wench! Call in a man with a whip and I'll guarantee to have the information out of her."

But MacMurran turned his head enough to stare at him, and Grenaldi's voice subsided in impotent frustration. "Would you like to handle this affair?" MacMurran's voice was low but there was an edge of ice and fire beneath it. "Have you persuaded yourself that I am no longer capable of dealing with a matter such as this?"

There was no mistaking his meaning. Grenaldi had overstepped his role of subordinate and the challenge to MacMurran's dominance had been instantly met and attacked. Grenaldi's lips tightened but he leaned back in his chair and picked up the glass of rum before him.

"Have it as you want it. It will all be the same in the end." He lifted his glass and drank with an air of casual disinterest, but his eyes were watchful and wary until MacMurran slowly turned away.

"You are a handsome wench." His hard eyes touched her breasts again. "And I do not think you are entirely a fool. So I will make a bargain with you. You shall have your freedom, but it will only be such freedom as this island offers. You will be protected against those howling animals on the beach, but I cannot deny that you may receive attention from the captains, or even from myself."

His hard lips twisted into a smile and his eyes were insolent upon her. "When I saw you dance at La Sirena it occurred to me that it might be pleasant to have you here on Bonneterre. Now you are here, and we would be fools to disdain the gifts the good God sends us." He leaned back in his chair and his mouth was suddenly tight and bleak again. "That is my bargain and the only bargain that will be made. Speak now, if you have anything to tell."

She searched his face and found it as coldly set and immovable as the dark stones in a fortress wall. This time there would be no appeal. She had won a little, and perhaps lost a great deal—but it was the best that she could do. Her breasts lifted as she drew a deep breath of air into her lungs. She moved forward so that her thighs touched the table and helped hide the treacherous trembling of her body.

"There is an agreement," she began, "with Don Francisco de Larra of Havana. An agreement that was concluded some two years ago but has since fallen into disuse."

"An agreement?" MacMurran's eyes stabbed her face. "What sort of agreement and what does it have to do with us?"

She faced him steadily, feeling a faint flicker of sudden hope at his obvious surprise. If she could create discord here …

"Why, an agreement between Don Francisco and Perpignier. An agreement that a certain portion of all the loot of Bonneterre was to be delivered to Larra at Havana. You did not know of it, señor?"

"Know of it! By God, if there was any such agreement—" He was leaning forward now, his eyes blazing and his whole body tense and rigid. "And what was to become of these spoils that you say were sent to Havana?"

She shrugged her shoulders, mocking him into a fiercer rage with the half-smile on her lips. "I can only guess, señor. But when a pirate, an outlaw, pays tribute to a governor who may be prepared to mount an attack against him, he surely expects some return. Protection, perhaps, señor? You would know more of this than I."

He stared at her as he revolved the matter in his mind.

"Why, yes," he said softly. "It could be—protection. A promise from Larra of immunity in case of capture or attack. An immunity bought with the loot we won—but an immunity that was not shared with us."

He swiveled around to face Perpignier, leaning forward across the table so that their faces were less than a foot apart.

"Is there any truth in this? Did you have some such arrangement with Larra?"

Perpignier lifted his head slowly, his eyes swimming from the rum he had consumed. "Larra?" he repeated thickly. "Larra? Why, yes, I paid him for protection. It was my right to do so as the master of Bonneterre." The slobber drooled from his loose lips as he spoke and his head nodded a little as if it were an effort to hold it erect. "What affair of yours is it if I—"

"What affair? By God, it's more than my affair. It's the affair of every man out on that beach! This protection that you say you bought—was it for every man upon this island or was it only for yourself?"

Perpignier's eyes narrowed and his mouth twisted in a sly grimace of drunken cunning. "Why, for every man, of course. For every man. Freedom of the seas, MacMurran. I bought you freedom from attack."

"The hell you did! If you did that—and I don't believe you could—why didn't I know of this? Why weren't Grenaldi, here, and the other captains told there was no danger of attack? If that was the truth, how is it we have lost six ships in the last twelve months? Are you going to tell me they were all sunk without a trace or that the men deserted and sailed away to nowhere? By God, Perpignier, you've sold us out! You've used the treasury of the brotherhood to buy protection for yourself and left the rest of us to shift for ourselves as best we could!"

He whirled back to Manette with the flame of rage still burning in his cheeks.

"How did you know of this?" he demanded. "Were you a party to this agreement when it was made?"

"No, señor, I was not." She was deadly serious now, intent on building up this flaming disagreement to its highest pitch.

"Don Francisco forced me to come here as his agent to find why there had been no payments for the past six months."

"Six months!" His forehead knitted in sudden thought and then he struck the table sharply with his open hand. "By God, that's it! It was just six months ago that this drunken fool become so dazed and worthless that I was forced to take over the command. Of course there have been no payments, for I knew nothing of them and he was afraid to speak!"

Suddenly he was on his feet and his fingers tight in the throat of Perpignier's embroidered coat. He shook him as a dog would shake a rat, the soft blubber of Perpignier's jowls quivering like jelly as his head was flung back and forth upon his shoulders.

"So you bought freedom of the seas," MacMurran snarled. "By God, what you bought was your own death warrant—and there are men outside who'll be glad to serve it on you."

"Lies! All lies!" Perpignier's head lolled back and his mouth hung slackly open. "Bought you—bought you—" His sodden mind lost the thread of his thought and he stared blankly up at MacMurran's livid face. Moving uncertainly, he tried to pull himself away, and MacMurran's hand lashed him twice across the face, so that the flesh broke open and blood oozed down across the swollen jaws.

"Yes!" MacMurran's voice was suddenly as cold as winter ice grating against a harbor wall. "Yes, the men are outside now—but this is not the time. When you are sober, when you can feel the pain and know every blow—that is the time to deal with you."

He lifted his voice in a shout of command and two guards came lunging through the door, swords gleaming in their hands and their eyes hot and red-rimmed at the prospect of whatever violence might be before them.

"Throw this mass of fat into the prison below," he commanded. "Chain him to the floor and set a guard over him. If he is allowed to escape, the men who are responsible will pay for it with a rope around their necks. Drag him out now and call me in the morning when the liquor has burned out of him and he is able to talk again."

The guards hesitated for an instant, their startled eyes darting back and forth from MacMurran's face to the shapeless figure half falling from the chair.

One of them stammered hesitantly, "Perpignier? It is Perpignier that you—"

MacMurran's eyes blazed with sudden fury and his voice boomed and echoed against the rafters of the room.

"Yes, Perpignier! Do you dare to question me, or shall I—" His own blade glinted suddenly in his hand and the men fell back in quick alarm.

"It was only to be sure, monsieur. Only that we might serve you best."

"Then serve me now by dragging this pile of filth away!"

The men leaned forward as if they had been lashed with a whip and in an instant they were dragging Perpignier through the door, his legs limber beneath him and his feet stumbling under the impact of the guards' urge to be out and gone.

MacMurran turned back to the table and poured a tumbler full of rum from the bottle that stood open before him. He drank it slowly, forcing down the tide of rage that had overpowered him, forcing himself to a degree of calmness that would allow him to consider the strange outcome of the information Manette had given him. He set the glass back on the table with an air of harshly bridled violence and looked across at her.

"So." His voice was still gritty with anger but there was a new interest in his smoldering eyes. "You did have news for me, and

I was right when I said that you were not a fool. Well, I will keep my bargain. As a beginning you will share my bed tonight."

Manette nodded slowly. There was no eagerness in her, but after the terror she had undergone, it seemed a small price to pay for her release. "I had expected that. You will not find me ungrateful, señor, or too unwilling to provide the pleasure you desire."

"Why, then—" He broke off as Grenaldi's fist smashed down upon the table and set the glasses rattling and the bottle swaying from the harsh violence of the blow.

"By God, you go too far!"

Grenaldi's voice was as harshly guttural as the snarl of a baited beast. His lips twisted beneath the flaming beard.

"You are the master here now, but it was my ship and my men that brought this bitch ashore! If she is to bed with anyone tonight, it will be with me." He shoved his chair back from the table with a gesture of sudden violence and sprang to his feet. "We have all signed articles together and I'll see that you abide by them. What I bring in is mine, to be divided among us as it has always been!"

MacMurran leaned back in his chair and scowled at the shouting Italian as if he were some trusted dog that had suddenly dared to snarl and slash at the hand of his master.

"So," he said slowly, "this is twice tonight that you have tried to deny my authority. By God, I've had enough of it! As for the articles we signed, you know, just as I do, that I share in every prize that is brought ashore at Bonneterre. Tonight it is my pleasure to take this woman as a part of my share from *El Audaz.* Do you question that, or have you come back to your senses?"

"Question it? By the living God, I deny it! You'll have your share, but this woman will not be a part of it."

There was the sudden gleam of a lean-bladed dirk glittering in his hand. He flung himself forward in a charge as furious as that of a wounded bull. Manette cried out in terror. Then there was the sharp bark of a gun and Grenaldi staggered in his tracks, his knees wavering and weak beneath him as he stumbled and collapsed face downward upon the floor. Across the table MacMurran was still at ease in his chair, but there was a pistol in his hand and a thin tendril of smoke drifted up from its muzzle and spread like a veil in the glow of the flickering candles.

Grenaldi was writhing on the floor, his hands clutching his waist and blood already spilling from his lips. He was groaning and trying to speak. Manette looked appealingly across the table to where MacMurran sat, a cruel smile barely touching his lips.

"My God, señor!" she pleaded. "Must he be left like that, to suffer and to cry out like an animal? This is horrible! It is like some den of beasts."

MacMurran turned his head slowly so that he could look up at her, the half-smile still on his lips. "I shot him in the belly so that he *would* die like this. It will be many hours before the pain will end and death will take him. Between now and then others will see, and they will know the reward that is ready if they think of challenging my discipline. It is a lesson, señorita—a lesson written plainly so that they will understand."

He turned a contemptuous and angry stare upon the miserable agony of the red-bearded man twisting and turning upon the floor. "He has been mutinous before," he said harshly. "It is no great loss to the brotherhood, or even to the men that he commanded."

He got to his feet, stretching himself and pausing to drain the last few drops of rum from the glass before him. "There is nothing more to do here." His voice and manner ignored Grenaldi and his pain. "I am ready for my bed, and for a woman like you."

He turned away and strode through the door that led into the center hallway, with Manette dutifully at his heels. She turned for an instant in the doorway, looking back at Grenaldi and seeing that now his whole face and the floor around him were wet with blood. His sobs followed her as she closed the door and slipped out into the hall.

MacMurran's room faced the open gallery and the sound of the booming surf. High-ceilinged, plaster-walled, it was as bare as a monastery cell except for the wide four-poster bed, a linen chest of polished cypress, and a stiff, high-backed Spanish chair ornamented with inlaid silver and the dull gleam of scarlet morocco leather. There was no glass in the windows but there were orange-colored jalousies hinged to the window frames, swung open now to admit the cool night wind from the Gulf. Thick candles flared above the six-pronged silver candelabra on the linen chest, and the purple silk *ciel* above the bed stirred lightly as the wind touched it and set its gold-embroidered border gleaming and fading in the candlelight.

MacMurran dropped down into the stiff-backed chair and groaned with weariness. His long legs sprawled straight out before him with his boot heels resting on the polished floor. "Bring me some wine." He indicated a straw-wrapped decanter on the floor beside the chest. "And then pull off these boots for me. They're most confoundedly tight and I'll be glad to be rid of them."

She brought the wine, watched him for an instant as he tilted the mouth of the decanter to his lips, and then dropped to her knees and began to tug at the wide-legged boots of soft Spanish leather that he wore. They were stubborn, tight as he had said, and she strained and pulled until it seemed that her back would break and her arms come free. He watched her with a gleam of derision in his eyes, quite evidently amused at having her at his feet, humiliated by her task. When the boots were off, he allowed her to help him out of his coat and shirt and trousers. She could see now that he was deep-chested, with a stomach ridged with bare bands of muscle. There were deep scars across his chest, faded now to a dead whiteness, but eloquent witnesses to a time of battle and injury that must have taken him close to the doors of death.

"You were slow tonight, as awkward as some Gullah from the barracoon." His voice mocked her, entertained by the quick flush of anger that surged up into her face. "But you will learn." He turned away and flung himself sprawling on the bed. "Strip off that rag you wear and then blow out the candles and come to bed."

He watched her pull off the ragged shirt and his eyes brightened as they followed her passage to the chest where the candelabra stood. There was a swift grace in her movements, a curving, soft-fleshed femininity that set the pulse beating faster in his throat. He turned toward her as she slipped into the bed and he felt her body curving against his, surrendering to the strength of his arms, suddenly alive and eager with an urgency that he had not expected.

His mouth was harsh against her lips but it was a strangely welcome savagery, a violence that roused some primitive response deep-hidden within her flesh and blotted out the ordered reason of her thoughts.

Like a violin string tuned higher and higher, her body vibrated as she clung to him, surrendering utterly to her sudden desperate need for him. Then she felt him relax against her, and she caressed his shoulder gently, feeling a peace and satisfaction she had never known before.

It had been a terrifying thing to see Grenaldi dying, but per-haps, since it had brought her this, it had not been too great a price to pay. She lay still and silent, staring up into the darkness. Even in this breathless aftermath of ecstasy she was planning, as she would always plan, how best to turn such incidents as death and passion and desire to her own account. Always and forever these things would stir her only briefly, for she was always and forever in love—in love with herself, Manette—concerned unendingly with her own precious security and advantage.

CHAPTER NINE

THE LANGUOROUS, sun-filled days ran into a week, and then the weeks slipped by and dissolved into a month, and Manette was still on Bonneterre. To all intents, she was the queen of this lawless island, for MacMurran had developed a strange, almost unwilling passion for her. He dressed her now in rich silks and brocades and draped her with the jewels ravished from a hundred treasure ships. Slaves attended her, and even the savage sea wolves in the huts and on the beaches touched their foreheads in respect when she passed by.

Julie and Etienne and Lessups and Gronier were long since gone, lighter in purse, but freed at last from the unending fear that had made their days upon the island a purgatory of misery and doubt. Perpignier was dead, and Grenaldi rotted in a shallow grave, forgotten almost before the last shovelfuls of sand were thrown upon him.

For the moment there remained only the problem of ensuring Margarita against Don Francisco's wrath. Manette had told MacMurran the story of that bloody night in Havana one evening as he lolled in a crimson hammock on the gallery that faced the sea. "She is safe so far," she had concluded. "Safe until word reaches Larra that Perpignier is dead and I am here with you. After that—"

"After that there will be nothing anyone can do for her." The hammock creaked a little as MacMurran shifted his position. "I know a great deal about Larra and none of it is good. He loves cruelty the way some men love wine and women. It inflames him and sets him afire. He has a hunger for it that is never satisfied."

Manette nodded, remembering the feverish wildness of Larra's eyes when the lash had bitten deep into Maria de Castellán's body and the fresh blood had dripped down on the stone floor of the palace dungeon. "And when he hears of this, his first thought will be to slake that hunger with the flesh of Margarita's body. We must do something, and do it now. I cannot let her suffer so. I cannot—I will not!"

She was sitting in a rattan chair beside him and he stretched out his hand to touch her shoulder. "I can't start paying Larra the way Perpignier did,' he reminded her. "If there was even a hint of that, there'd be mutiny on the island between now and morning. It seems to me that the only hope is to get her out of Francisco's hands—and all the men on Bonneterre couldn't storm Havana and fight their way into the palace. I don't know what to tell you, Manette. If you had friends there who could get her past the gates—"

"I have no friends in Havana." And then in a flash of sudden inspiration she remembered that bright evening when she had sailed and, remembering it, saw Ramón's frightened face before her. She leaned forward eagerly, the mingled threats and promises there on the quay flashing through her mind. "I have no friends, but one of Don Francisco's bravos has good reason to fear me, and he has access to the guards and men at arms inside the palace."

"He can be bribed? And you know how to reach him?"

"Oh, yes, he can be bribed, and I can send word to him through his brother's tavern in New Orleans—the House of the Two Parrots."

"The House of the Two Parrots!" MacMurran's voice was edged with amazement. "By God, you have connections in strange places. León Careaga, who owns that tavern, is one of my own men, placed in New Orleans to keep me advised of the affairs in the city when I am not there."

He sat up and swung his legs over the side of the hammock so that he sat facing her. There was no man on earth whose heritage and inclination led him more readily into intrigue than this Allan MacMurran. Of mingled Scotch and Spanish blood, he found intrigue an exciting game, a contest to try his wits and skill. He was all eagerness now, plotting a devious path that could, in the end, bring him nothing except the rich reward of snapping his fingers and roaring with laughter at the undoing of the forces of law and order that opposed him.

"Now, by God, we'll give Larra something to swear and rave about! I'll send a messenger tonight, and Careaga will be here in the morning. It will be his duty to send word to this Ramón that we're going to steal your Margarita out from between Don Francisco's fingers. He'll be supplied with gold—enough to bribe the palace guards—and Ramón must have her outside the palace gates at midnight on—" He paused an instant as his quick mind reckoned sailing times. "On a night exactly three weeks from tonight. We'll have men to meet her there and a fast schooner standing by." He threw back his head and roared with laughter. "And I'd give as much gold again, and more, to see Larra stamp and roar when he finds out she's gone."

He lifted his voice in a hail and a servant came running out of the house and across the moonlit gallery. In an instant he was gone again to rouse the three men that MacMurran required, and within the hour their pirogue was threading the twisted network of sloughs and bayous that would bring them to New Orleans.

In the days that followed Manette learned a deep respect for his genius of organization and the depth and rigidity of the discipline he maintained. A fast sloop sailed for Havana to contact Ramón and be sure that the arrangements could be made and Margarita delivered to them at the time MacMurran had appointed. Two schooners were equipped and manned, the first to slip into the harbor of Havana and other to stand off and on outside the harbor and cover their retreat if they were pursued. The fiercest of the captains, Domingo Sánchez, was deputized to rule in MacMurran's absence from the island, for he refused to delegate this adventure to any other, reserving for himself the amusement and prestige of robbing Don Francisco in the sanctity of his own fortress city. It was only at the last moment that there was any rebellion against his plans, and that came from Manette when she learned that he planned to sail without her.

"And leave me here!" Her eyes blazed and she stamped her foot on the uncarpeted floor of the room they shared. "When you sail, Allan, I'll sail with you. Margarita is mine, and when we pluck her out of Larra's hands, I too will be there! Try to leave without me, and I'll plant a dirk in your back that will put you in the sand beside Grenaldi!"

He laughed up at her in startled and hilarious amusement, as entertained as if a pet kitten had arched its back and spat at him. "By God, now!" His laughter choked him and the grim lines were startlingly erased from his face. "A dirk in my back! This island air has settled in your blood, *niñita.* You're as bad as one of my swashbucklers out there on the beach! Give you a knife between your teeth and a rag of silk around your head, and you'd scuttle a ship along with the best of them." He took a long draught from the wine bottle he held, but when he replaced it on the floor beside him, the laughter was gone and he was serious and intent again.

"When all's said and done, there's danger in this, Manette. Too damned much danger for me to risk you in it. God knows I've gone as weak and soft as any simpering popinjay as far as you're concerned—but there's far more risk for you in Havana than there is for me, and I want you waiting for me here when I come back."

He was not angry, she was sure of that, but there was a stiff determination in his voice that cut off even the possibility of further argument. She was too wise to rouse him into fury, but her own obduracy was as fixed and unchangeable as his own. She had used devious means before—and she could use them again if circumstances forced the need upon her.

When his ship sailed, she was concealed far forward in the hold, hidden in a cramped space behind a close-packed barricade of kegs of rum. He did not discover her until the evening of the second day, and by the time the morning came again the sweet fire of her body had burned away his anger so completely that they lay abed till late and he toasted her with brandy when the mess boy brought their breakfast to them on the afterdeck.

They found the advance sloop waiting for them in the green sea lane ten leagues out from the harbor of Havana, and the news it carried was good. Ramón, hesitant and dubious at the beginning, had been won over by the tide of gold poured into his pockets, and even more by the assurance that if he failed he would most surely be kidnapped and taken to Bonneterre to pay the penalty for his omissions and his weakness. Thus spurred by fear and led like a donkey by the carrot of avarice, he had ventured into the palace and found the guards singularly receptive to the click of the doubloons MacMurran had forwarded to him. Everything had been arranged, from the greedy fist of the matron who watched over Margarita to the ready hand of the guards upon the palace gate. At midnight those same gates would open so that Margarita would be free to pass. Before there was any alarm, they would be far at sea and lost beyond the horizon.

They slipped into the harbor just at dusk, with the flag of Spain fluttering bravely and falsely at the masthead. It was too late for the customs officers to bestir themselves and come abroad, and to the chance onlooker, the schooner was simply another of the countless trading craft that roamed back and forth across the Antilles, carrying hides and rum and sugar and tobacco, laboring in and out of any harbor that might offer a cargo to them. The moon came up and the water stirred and glittered beneath it like molten silver. Lights sprang up on the shore and the offshore breeze brought them the mingled odors of tar and rum and molasses from the crowded quay.

It was just before midnight when they went ashore, five of them: Manette and MacMurran, Diego Ramírez, Raúl Brizant, and Julio Tochadero. The four oarsmen in the longboat would wait beside the pier. Ramón came riding forward with the six saddled horses he had provided for them. His jaw sagged as he saw Manette, and almost instinctively his fingers moved again in the sign of the cross as if to protect himself from evil. But he was a diplomat, this Ramón, and instantly he was smiling and bowing in his saddle, sweeping off his wide-brimmed hat in salutation.

"It is good to see you again, señorita—and good that the little Margarita will be free to join you within the hour."

She surveyed him with some amusement, sardonically aware of the shallowness of his protestations, knowing all too well that his sword and his services were always at the command of the most generous patron. "Yes," she agreed, "it is good, if all goes as it should. You have left no knot untied, no palm unpaid that could bring us to grief?"

"I swear upon the name of my father that everything is complete, señorita! We have only to ride to the gate, assist the young señorita to her saddle, and it is done. I have served you faithfully tonight."

"*Está bien.* Lead on, Ramón, and remember that we will be close behind you."

The city was quiet except for the sound of the horses' hoofs and the creaking saddle leather. The few stragglers they encountered glanced at them with quick, surreptitious glances and then as quickly looked away. In the Havana of 1795, it was not healthy to be too curious about the activities of a band of armed riders in the night. The black mass of the palace loomed up before them, wrapped in darkness and silence except for a single torch burning fitfully inside the great barred gates. Ramón rode on ahead and there were muttered words with the guard, the click of coins changing hands, and then the gates swung open and Margarita, unrecognizable in a long black cape and cowl, came hurrying out into the street. In an instant Manette was out of her saddle and running to her.

"*Mi hermanita!* My little lost one! And now you are safe again!"

"*Ai, Dios!* Manette! Manette! It has been so long!"

Margarita was laughing and crying in almost hysterical relief as MacMurran swung down and lifted her into her saddle. He looked up at her, smiling, the moonlight carving deep furrows of shadow in his wind-burned face. "Laugh, little one." His voice was low but it was almost singing with the triumph of Don Francisco's humiliation. "Soon you will be at sea and then you will find a shelter with us at Bonneterre." He vaulted back into his saddle and lifted his arm in a gesture of command. "Let us be gone!"

Manette was riding beside Ramón, and at the second cross street he drew rein as if to turn aside. She whirled in her saddle and her voice was like a sentry's challenge. "Hold there, Ramón! This is not the quay!"

He pulled up reluctantly, his eyes troubled and his mouth sullen. "You have no further use for me," he protested. "If I leave you now, there is less chance of some passer-by seeing us together and carrying the news to Don Francisco. The quay is only a half-dozen squares away."

Her belt yielded the long pistol she was carrying, and its barrel gleamed dully in the starlight. "A half-dozen squares or a half-dozen miles, you'll ride on with us, *amigo*. I've had no reason to trust you in the past and there'll be no new beginning now. Ride on there ahead!"

He started to protest, and then, as the pistol barrel lifted a little, he pulled his horse around and fell in some ten paces in front of her. She was alert now, her eyes searching every shadowed alley and doorway, her ears tuned for the faintest sound that might mean danger. MacMurran and the men were too far ahead for her to call to them, and there was no certainty that anything was wrong. Her fingers tightened on the pistol butt and she spurred her horse a little to keep pace with the hurrying Ramón.

They rode past street after street and there was no alarm. Her nervous tension eased a little until there was no emotion except relief and exultation in her when they rode up to the quay. They slipped out of their saddles, seeing the bright waters of the harbor before them and their own schooner riding at anchor a few hundred yards offshore. MacMurran looked back at her and laughed like a boy.

"It is done, Manette! Don Francisco can—"

A burst of gunfire ripped through the night and his laughter turned into a scream as a bullet struck him and he went crashing to the ground. Ramón was squirming on the cobblestones with a flesh wound through the calf of his leg, and Margarita was swaying as a bloody stain grew and widened on the dark surface of her cloak.

Manette and the three corsairs who were still on their feet whirled to meet the attack. They could see the dark figures of men running toward them, climbing over hogsheads of rum and molasses with naked blades gleaming in their hands. Diego snapped a shot from his pistol and one of the running figures howled suddenly and collapsed in the shadows. Raúl's and Julio's pistols blazed and the charging men hesitated and sought shelter again. The crew from the longboat was swarming up over the edge of the pier and Manette snapped swift orders to them. "Get them into the boat—those three who are wounded." A volley of shots rang out and she saw Diego drop his pistol and clap his hand to a wounded arm. She fired at a head half seen in a shaft of moonlight and saw it jerk back as the bullet struck and a body sprawled, face downward, in the dirt.

Ramón and MacMurran and Margarita had vanished, safe in the longboat and hidden by the sharp-edged rim of the quay. She ran after them, seeing Diego and Raúl and Julio just ahead. At the edge she turned to snap another shot back at the moving figures on the wharf and then she was scrambling over the side and leaping across a foot-wide stretch of open water to gain the stern of the boat. She waved her hand in a fierce gesture of command. "Pull off! Pull off!" The long blades bit into the water and the boat seemed to lift its bow and become alive as it slid swiftly out into the harbor. Men were shouting on the pier now, their figures monstrous and grotesque as they ran forward. Rifle and pistol bullets spattered the water, and some few struck the boat itself. Tense and white-lipped in the stern, Manette leaned forward as if to urge the boat to a greater speed. Silently she thanked God for the mistiness of the light, the deceiving flicker of the reflections from the moving water that made it almost impossible for the raiders on shore to fire with accuracy. The boat sliced ahead as if it had wings, and gradually the bullets began to fall far behind them, and then the firing from the quay ended and there was silence again.

It was all plain enough, clear and tangible in the light of Ramón's attempt to leave them before they reached the quay. He had bribed the guards to let Margarita escape, true enough, but his itching fingers had not been content with the gold he had earned for that. No, he had made another bargain—a bargain to have them waylaid and captured or killed as they returned, so he might share the rich rewards the crown of Spain had so futilely offered for the heads of these buccaneers. They were about halfway to the schooner now and she leaned forward with a swift command for the oarsmen.

"*Paren!* We will stop here for a moment!"

Doubtfully, their eyes uneasy and uncertain, they let their oars rest. She leaned forward to the nearest one. "Give me your pistol." He pulled it from his belt and handed it across to her, shooting a swift glance of doubt at the man on the seat beside him. Ramón was huddled in the bow, his face white with terror and his hands clasped around the calf of his leg where the bullet had torn into the flesh.

She called his name and saw his head jerk up in a sudden spasm of fear.

"Ramón," she demanded, "could you swim from here to shore?"

"To shore?" There was startled amazement in his voice. "To shore? Why—why, yes, señorita. It is no great distance."

"And your wound is not too severe?"

"Oh, no, señorita!" His voice was tense now with hope. "It is a small wound, a matter of a little blood and that is all." He was leaning forward, his lips half open and his eyes bright with expectation.

"Very well, then." The pistol barrel gestured toward the open water. "In with you, and be quick about it."

"Señorita! Most gracious señorita!" He was on his feet now, still almost unable to believe that he was to be pardoned. "You give me leave to return?"

"I give you leave to go over the side." Her voice crackled like a wind-swept fire in dry grass. "Quickly, now."

He plunged headlong into the water and began to swim away with long, space-destroying strokes. She let him go until he was some twenty feet from the boat and then she called to him again. "Ramón, before you go farther—"

Treading water, he twisted around to face her, his head like a bit of dark driftwood above the surface. "Yes, señorita?"

"You are sure that you are able to swim to the quay."

"Oh, yes, without doubt, señorita."

"And once there, you are planning to take up your life again? To enjoy yourself as you have done before?"

"*Es verdad*—and how I will enjoy it! My life has never been more precious to me than it is at this moment!"

She shifted her body a little so that she could face him more squarely, and her fingers tightened on the butt of the pistol.

"And that, you traitorous dog, is what I have been waiting for you to say!" She lifted the pistol from her lap.

The bullet smashed through the thin ledge of bone between his eyes and for an instant there was a tumult and commotion in the water where he had been. Then the smooth sea flowed past again, unruffled and untroubled by the corpse that had found a grave beneath its silvershining breast. For a space that might have been measured by a score of heartbéats she stared at the spot where he had disappeared. Then she seemed to relax as she turned back to the staring boatmen who sat, slack-jawed, in the rigid stillness of amazement.

"Pull away!" The knife-edged tautness of her voice shocked them into a confused stir of activity. "He'll need no further care, but we've wounded here who will."

The oar blades cut the black water like knives and a white crest of foam lifted and curled about the bow as the boat raced through the starlight toward the black hulled schooner.

CHAPTER TEN

MANETTE lingered on the inner balcony in the December sunlight, looking down into the patio of the house on Bienville Street that MacMurran maintained for use as a headquarters on his frequent visits to New Orleans. It was in the heart of the Vieux Carré, presenting only a blank wall and iron-grilled balconies to the street outside. Originally it had been orange, or perhaps even a deep red, but the sun and rain had weathered it to a softly radiant umber, set off by its green shutters and the multicolored profusion of plants and flowers that grew in great pots along the edge of the balconies.

Outside and beyond those balconies she was continually aware of this strange half-French, half-Spanish city of New Orleans. It was like wild music or the sharp-sweet taste of brandied wine; an exciting fragrance in her nostrils that taunted and tantalized her without end. Flung down beside a great crescent of the dark-stained, brutally full-throated Mississippi, it was almost like an island lost and yet proudly self-sufficient in an unending wilderness of earth and water. It was a swift babble of voices speaking in many tongues; the excitement of bubbling laughter that never ceased; the red-eyed savagery of bestial brutality and sudden, flaring anger. Its streets were narrow, but they were sweet with the scent of potted flowers and filled with soft music from unseen courtyards. It was a town that never slept, a town with a strange, lighthearted pulse pounding in its veins so that its surging, constantly renewed vitality was a siren song whispering and calling to her.

Looking down, she could see MacMurran, correct and distinguished in black, broadcloth and ruffled linen, playing the graceful and urbane host to Vincent and Telesphore St. Amant, the two brothers who were said to own two thirds of New Orleans and control the rest. Her gaze shifted away from them to the pride-of-India trees along the back wall of the enclosed patio. Pleasant, she thought, as pleasant as the marble fountain casting a mist of spray over the bronze statue of Aphrodite, the curving flagstone walks, the wide-leaved banana trees, and the sweet olives and figs growing up among the rosebushes.

The sounds from the narrow banquettes outside the house were muffled here but she could hear the cries of the colored street vendors crying their wares of fish and coal and sweetmeats and fruits from the market. There was the babel of French and Spanish and English and Portuguese in the streets. Wooden-wheeled carts went screeching slowly by and a scarlet macaw she had brought from Bonneterre teetered back and forth in its willow cage and screamed in sudden anger before it fell to preening its feathers with its great hooked beak.

She considered it all thoughtfully, tracing back the days to that bloody night in Havana harbor when they had spirited Margarita away. Poor child, her wound had been painful and slow to heal, but she was safe enough now with the nuns of St. Theresa in their convent on Dumaine Street. There was protection for her there, protection and the schooling in the graces and charms a young lady would need when she went out into the world.

MacMurran had been another story. There had been almost a month when it had been touch and go as to whether he would live or die. She had commandeered the services of the finest surgeons in New Orleans and held them there on Bonneterre while the slow days of indecision waxed and waned. She smiled a little, remembering their frenzied protests when she refused to release them from their vigil; remembering, too, their bows and smiles and beaming faces when she finally sent them away with more money in their pockets than they could have earned in a year's uninterrupted practice in New Orleans.

MacMurran looked up and saw her standing on the balcony and his white teeth gleamed in one of the rare smiles he seemed always to have for her and never for any of the others with whom he came in contact.

"Manette! It is early for you to be out, *chiquita*. Come down and have your coffee with us this morning."

The St. Amant brothers were on their feet, bowing as courteously as if she had been some great lady instead of the mistress of an acknowledged outlaw. Not that mistresses presented any novelty in New Orleans. It was open knowledge that some of the lovely women who bore the most famous of Creole names had not hesitated to give themselves to lovers.

She lifted a hand and smiled acknowledgment of their greetings.

"Surely you do not want me to join you now, Allan. You have affairs of business to discuss."

He shook his head in denial. "The business is almost done—and it's business I think you'll find of interest, too." He got up and crossed the patio to stand with his hand on the railing of the stairway that led down from the balcony. "Come, *chiquita*, or our guests will think you are lacking in hospitality."

She laughed, surrendering. "Surely they know me too well for that." Her high heels clicked like tiny hammers as she came down the steps, quite well aware that her wide skirts were undoubtedly displaying an indiscreet amount of slim and silken-clad ankles, insolently unconcerned and a little amused at the St. Amants' heightened interest in her progress.

MacMurran led her to the table and she refilled their coffee cups, begging them to resume the slim black cigars they had been smoking when she appeared. "And this business?" she asked.

It was easy to see that MacMurran was pleased; pleased and so stimulated that his black eyes were bright and flashing as he tapped a sheaf of folded papers on the table before him.

"Manette, I have just bought the Constancia plantation from these gentlemen, and it is my purpose to make it our home!"

"Constancia!" Julie had told her the story of Constancia since she had come to New Orleans. One of the great show places on the upper river, stretching over uncounted arpents of land, manned by an army of slaves, without a master these past eight months since the Marquis de la Ronde had fallen in an *affaire d'honneur* at the Dueling Oaks and the mistress of Constancia had taken her own life in an access of grief and loneliness. "Constancia! But what of Bonneterre? Will you give up the wealth that it has brought you?"

He laughed a little, shaking his head, while his fingers still caressed the folded deed to the plantation.

"Domingo will be in charge as my deputy, and I will be here to market goods and slaves that Bonneterre provides."

She frowned, trying to grasp this new scheme that reversed so completely the previous violent tenor of MacMurran's ways. As a sea rover and a pirate chieftain, he was so well adapted to his role that he might almost have been born to fill it; but as a man of business and a sober planter of cane or cotton or indigo …

"I do not understand these things," she admitted, "but will you not lose your share of the prizes unless you are there to claim them?"

"I will retain a share, a smaller one, perhaps, but in return I will gain the profits of everything that comes from Bonneterre. Everything! The slaves, the rum, the linens, the silver, the oils, and the ivories—they will all pass through my hands before they find their way into the hands of the buyers in Louisiana."

"And Constancia?"

"Constancia will serve as my headquarters, a pleasant place to live and a place that should return more profit even than the trade with Bonneterre."

So—she was to be the mistress of Constancia. Already she could see the carriages of the great Creole families rolling up to the doorway for the galas she would give. It would provide a background that even the proudest of them could not ignore, a secure position that would force them to accept her in their homes. And then like a sickening shock came the realization that she was, after all, only MacMurran's mistress, and even Constancia could not clear the path for her unless she could attain the status of his wife. She bit her lip, shooting a quick glance at him, wondering as she had wondered a thousand times before if she had a hold on him strong enough to snare him into matrimony. As matters stood now, he represented her only chance to attain security, but he was a strangely unpredictable mixture of designs and emotions, infatuated with her beyond the shadow of a doubt but still giving no evidence of any desire to place the relationship upon a permanent and conventional basis.

She heard the murmur of Telesphore St. Amant's voice beside her and jerked her mind back to the present.

"The trade with Bonneterre has been profitable, yes," he was saying, "but in many ways it has been unsatisfactory and dangerous. It is fine enough to get these goods at a low price and escape the import duties upon them, but it has been hard to deal with those wild men and there have been stories of merchants who went into the swamps to barter with them and never came back. But now, with Monsieur MacMurran as the intermediary, all this can be changed, for he can control those wolves and he can also deal with our bankers and merchants and planters who are ready and eager to buy. For our own part, monsieur," he turned to face MacMurran again, "you can count on us for every possible assistance. I know you have large resources of your own, but if you should need accommodation at any time, we shall be happy to be of service to you."

The picture was beginning to take form now in Manette's mind. She had known almost from the beginning that Allan was a man driven onward by some secret lash that whipped him forward to constantly widening spheres of recognition and reward. He had fought and intrigued his way to absolute dominance at Bonneterre and now he was exploring the pathway to far vaster operations where the rewards, if he succeeded, would be no less than magnificent. Well enough—there was satisfaction in being allied to such a man; but the problem now was to make sure she would not be left behind or discarded along the way.

The brothers St. Amant were saying their good-bys and Allan was calling for his cloak, since he was to accompany them to the Cabildo, where the deed to Constancia must be recorded. Smiling, with courteously formal phrases on her lips, she expressed her pleasure at their visit and begged them to return again, but it was only the surface of her mind that dealt with them. Inwardly, she was entrapped in a swirling storm of plans and schemes and half-completed designs that this new development had thrust upon her.

When they were gone she had one of the servants kindle a small blaze in the fireplace of her dressing room, and she was sitting before it when he returned a little before noon. His cheeks were flushed with excitement and there was nervous energy in every move he made. He waved away her suggestion of a chair, standing broad-shouldered and alert, with his back to the fire and his hands clasped behind his back.

"I must go to Bonneterre today." There was the urgent cadence of eagerness in his voice. "The captains must be informed of this new arrangement, and there are goods to be started on their way to my warehouse here."

"Your warehouse?" There was a note of startled incredulity in her voice. "Have you become a merchant?"

He laughed as if he were already half intoxicated by the swift passage of events. "I must have a place to keep these goods till they are sold. I bought it from Jean Boudreaux after I left you this morning." He glanced around the room, seeming to scorn the polished rosewood and mahogany, the damask hangings, the crystal-glittering chandelier, and the warm pattern of the Oriental rug beneath his feet. "We will have something far better than this before the month is done. We will have Constancia, Manette! We'll live like kings. By God, I'll be a power in Louisiana before I'm through!"

He was flushed with enthusiasm, so afire with the tremendous scope of his plans that it was a moment or two before it dawned upon him that there was no answering enthusiasm in Manette. His torrent of speech broke off in midsentence and he stared at her with eyes that were suddenly serious and surprised.

"Manette—" He paused, his line of thought so abruptly diverted that he was almost at a loss for words. "Manette, you seem to be unhappy or disturbed. Is there something in all this that is displeasing to you?"

"Displeasing?" A slow fire of anger was beginning to smolder in her eyes. "Is it ever pleasing to a woman to have the man who shares her bed make plans in which she is not included? You will establish your warehouses and become the master of Constancia. You will be accepted on equal terms by the bankers and lawyers and merchants of the city. But what about me? Am I to continue to be nothing but your kept woman, your prisoner? Do you think your friends' wives will open their doors to me if I am no better than a quadroon *siréne* hidden away on Rampart Street?"

Her voice had risen as her furious indignation overwhelmed her, and at the end she was almost screaming at him, aware that she ran the very probable risk of rousing him into a sudden rage but unable to contain her anger at being ignored in these vast plans that so enchanted him.

He stared down at her as if he were seeing her for the first time, not as a beautifully fashioned nymph of soft flesh and flaming passion, but as an individual, a woman with a heritage of pride and blood that had not been erased by the degradation she had suffered at Havana and at Bonneterre.

"You mean—" Strangely enough there was no anger in his voice. Instead there was a paradoxical trace of resigned futility and even sympathy. "You mean marriage, of course."

"Of course," she flared out at him. "Did you think that I would be content to go on forever like some streetwalker you had taken into your house? Did you think—"

"But marriage—for me, Manette—is impossible."

The breath died in her throat and she stared at him with eyes that were wide and uncomprehending.

"Impossible? How can it be impossible?"

He lifted a decanter from the low mahogany table that stood before the fire and poured a glass half full of the fiery brandy it contained. He drank it slowly, avoiding her eyes as if he were trying to pull his thoughts together and find words that would suit the tenor of his thoughts. Then he turned back to her and she saw that his lips were tight and hard with some ancient bitterness and his eyes were flat and shiny, reflecting the light like polished planes of steel.

"I'm surprised that you haven't heard the story before this. It's an old one in New Orleans—although there may be some who've forgotten it by now."

It seemed to her that there was suddenly a cold wind blowing in the room; a wind that sent a chill of premonition coursing down her spine and carried within itself the certainty of failure for her hopes and needs. Her fingers gnawed at the yellow silk of her skirt and a murky skein of fear began to weave itself into her thoughts.

"When I first came to New Orleans, ten years ago, I was young and a fool. I had no money, no friends, no influence. Just another younger son sent out from Scotland with letters of introduction and my sword and passage money to Louisiana. My mother was from Granada and my letters were to relatives of hers who had come out here with Ulloa when he was appointed governor."

He lifted the decanter and poured more brandy into the glass, almost mechanically, as if the action were simply an expression of his inner turbulence and reluctance to drag out these old affairs long buried in the past.

"There was a girl here then, Dorothée d'Estrehan, who was supposed to be the handsomest woman in Louisiana. I married her, much against her family's wishes, and within a year she'd made me the laughingstock of the town. Her particular fancy was a fencing master with a salon in Exchange Alley. I challenged him and he cut me down the way a butcher would slice up a hog. I couldn't stay here then. That's when I first went to Bonneterre."

"Yes." Manette had to moisten her lips before she could form the words. "And after that—"

"I came back two years later and challenged him again. That time I left him under the oaks, but it was too late to make any difference as far as Dorothée was concerned. I wanted nothing on God's earth from her except my freedom, and I filed my petition for divorce the same day I killed her Spanish fencing master."

"It could not have been refused!"

"No." There was an infinite weariness in his voice now, an acknowledgment of defeat she had never known in him before. "No, it was not refused, it was simply laid aside. You see, Dorothée went stark, raving mad when she heard that her Spaniard was dead—and a divorce cannot be prosecuted against a person who has lost her mind!"

He turned and walked out of the room then, leaving Manette sobbing in her chair. The alliance with him had been her last and only hope of rescuing herself. She had even dared to dream of the day when they would share an empire of pride and power and position. But that was gone now and there was only the sickness of despair.

Her mind was dull and empty, frozen in the blurred pattern of a vague confusion that shrank away from the past and refused to contemplate the future. It was idle and unfair to blame MacMurran for the situation, and yet, illogically, the feeling grew in her that it was through him that she had been betrayed. Her lips twisted a little as she remembered how he had smiled at her that morning in the patio. He'd have little enough to smile about in the future. She looked up dully as a mulatto slave girl knocked and then came into the room.

"Get out!" Her frustration and anger found an outlet in the scalding fury of her voice. "Get out, I say! If you ever intrude on me like this again, I'll have you stripped and lashed in the Place des Armes!"

The Negro's eyes grew white with terror and she dropped the envelope she had been carrying on the table before the fire and scuttled away again. Without leaning forward, Manette could see that it was addressed to her, a soft, flamboyant handwriting that she had never seen before.

She leaned over to pick it up and ran her fingers beneath the red wax seal. The note inside was short enough:

Nuevo Orleans

17 de diciembre de 1795

Srta. Manette de Santiago
Calle de Bienville

Muy señorita mía:

I have not seen you now for almost a month and I would be most honored if you would receive me this evening. There is a matter of some importance to both of us that I would like to present to you.

Quedo de Vd. atto. y S.S.,

ETIENNE VINCENT CHRÉTIEN

So—Etienne again. She was unsure of her own feeling for Etienne; unsure and a little guilty, for since she had been in New Orleans he had called on her twice, and each time it had been when Allan was at Bonneterre. The meetings had been innocent enough—on the surface—but there was an attraction between them that was like the swift surge of a hidden river, concealed and yet ready to break forth in a torrent if it but found the proper channel. In a way, she despised Etienne, for he *was* weak. There was nothing about him of the steel-forged determination of MacMurran; nothing of his reckless courage and the flaming temper that welcomed and accepted every challenge. Perhaps, she thought ruefully, it was Etienne's very weakness that attracted her. She was a strong woman, emotionally and mentally, and it was possible that Etienne provided a distorted, half-romantic outlet for the maternalism that she supposed all women possessed to some degree.

She turned the letter over slowly in her fingers, considering the possibilities of allowing Etienne to call on her that evening. The frustrated irritation she had felt toward Allan still rankled in her, and in a sudden mood of vague vindictiveness she decided that she would entertain Etienne tonight, and perhaps entertain him in a way that would repay MacMurran for the position his earlier indiscretions had forced upon her.

She pulled the bell cord in the corner of thé room, and when the still frightened slave girl edged hesitantly through the door, she flung a question at her. "The messenger who brought this note—is he still here or has he gone?"

"He still here, madame. He say he told to wait for an answer."

"Wait, then." She crossed the room and scratched out a brief note, telling Etienne that she would be glad to see him at nine that night. She sprinkled fine sand over the paper to dry the ink and handed the folded paper to the waiting slave.

"Give him this."

She relaxed before the fire and a slow glow kindled in her eyes as she envisioned the night before her. Etienne was coming to her with no honorable proposal, she was sure of that. He had almost run through what heritage he had once had, and the money for his ransom from Bonneterre had completed the wreckage and driven him far into debt. He would not be there to talk of marriage banns, but then, for the matter, there were other things a man and woman could discuss, if they felt so inclined.

Smiling, she poured a little brandy into a glass and held it up. She could see the flames through it and they turned the pale liquor the color of blood and fire. Sloeeyed, she relaxed in the soft chair with the edge of the glass just touching her lower lip. After all, if Allan could not and would not offer her marriage, there was no reason for him to claim complete fidelity from her. The brandy was like velvet and fire upon her lips. Tonight, perhaps, they would burn from another fire ....

CHAPTER ELEVEN

N EW ORLEANS was a fantastic and incredible mosaic of lux-
ury and poverty, gaiety and violence, crime and loveliness,
shame and beauty. Its narrow streets were ankle-deep in mud
and edged by open ditches where the sewage and waste of the city
turned foul and stagnant and became a stench in the nostrils.
But in those same streets were great ladies in brocades and dia-
monds and gentlemen who imported their shirts from Paris and
their boots from the Triana craftsmen of Seville. They rubbed
shoulders with priests and pirates, nuns in snow-white coifs and
olive-skinned quadroons with chignons draped with emeralds.
There were planters and sailors and soldiers of fortune and gamblers; coffeehouses and slave marts and gambling houses and
cathedrals; a circus where fighting dogs were pitted against bulls
and bears; pillories facing the Cabildo for the accommodation of
debtors, thieves and runaway slaves.

It was through this olla-podrida of people and places and
restlessness and movement that Etienne came to MacMurran's
blank-walled mansion on Bienville Street. He was wretchedly
nervous, and even the brandy he had taken at Benedetti's had
done little or nothing to relieve his tension. His creditors were
dogging him like hounds behind a rabbit, and even a Chrétien
might find himself thrown into prison or locked into the pil-
lory for debt. If it ever came to that, it would be the end. After
such public disgrace there could be nothing left except a bullet through the temple or eternal exile to barbarous Mexico or

Texas. He felt the skin on his back crawl with revulsion and the corners of his lips were tight and pinched as he lifted the bronze knocker on MacMurran's door. It clanged and clattered like a fire gong in the night, and he checked himself in a sudden sweat of shame and embarrassment as he realized that he was pounding frantically upon the door, like some hard-hunted criminal demanding sanctuary at a monastery. He must pull himself together. He knew how quickly Manette could become arrogant and contemptuous, and tonight, of all nights, she must see him as brave and wise and altogether admirable.

The door swung open slowly, almost reluctantly, and he found himself facing the slave Kelcho. MacMurran's major-domo, he was a Kuafi Negro, captured somewhere in the Sudan, high-nosed, thin-lipped, with a bearing and appearance like an Arab prince. He was fanatically faithful to MacMurran, and he stared at Etienne now as if he was half inclined to refuse him entrance. But when he spoke there was nothing in his voice except the servility the barracoons and buffalo-hide whips had taught him.

"*Bon soir,* m'sieur. Madame is waiting for you."

He took Etienne's cloak and led the way down the hall to the great double doors that opened into the living room. His knuckles touched the panels respectfully, the knob turned and Manette turned away from the fireplace to greet her guest.

"Etienne!" She smiled at him, her shoulders white and glowing in the firelight, her whole body outlined in loveliness by the halo of the flames. "It is so good of you to come and comfort me when I am here alone—or did you know that I would be alone?"

His lips brushed her fingers and when he lifted his head his eyes were challenging and faintly insolent. "I knew," he admitted, "just as you did. I heard MacMurran's arrangements made at Gaspari's, and I sent a note to you at once. It was kind of you to accept me, Manette."

Amusement flickered in her eyes. Posture as they would, they were both rogues, adventurers. It was a secret knowledge shared between them. It provided a common ground, a hidden, carefully concealed area of unscrupulous chicanery where they could be at ease together, sharing an intimacy so close and immediate that they recognized each other's aims and purposes and stratagems without the need for words.

"I have looked forward to—accepting you."

She saw his eyes widen in surprise and then grow faintly smug and triumphant as he caught the secondary meaning of her words.

"Let me give you a little brandy, Etienne. It is cold outside and I can see that you are chilled and a little shaken by it."

There was a long sofa facing the fireplace, and she picked up a silver-chased decanter from the darkly gleaming taboret beside it. Her eyes mocked him now, and he damned her inwardly for having seen the agitation that possessed him, even in the moment that she offered herself to him. A woman like that—

"You are more than kind tonight."

He accepted the tall tumbler of brandy that she offered him, holding it between his palms to warm it a little, disturbed by this new turn affairs had taken. Manette was like a tawny fire, more passionately sensual in her appeal than any woman he had ever known, but he had not come here tonight to seek the sweetness of her flesh. Tonight his errand concerned his very life and there must be no diversion from it. And yet he was too practiced a cavalier not to know the rage and bitterness a woman could summon to assuage her wounded pride if her offered favors were taken lightly or refused. He sighed, lifting the brandy to his lips, all too well aware that she was laughing at him, almost as if she had guessed the entanglement in which he found himself.

"Tell me, Etienne, what have you been doing to amuse yourself?" She led the conversation away into shallow channels of news and gossip like a courteous hostess entertaining a stranger and finding it a little difficult to discover topics of common interest. The irritated frustration MacMurran had bred in her still stirred like fermenting yeast, and there was no doubt in her mind that she would give herself to Etienne before the night was done. But it was pleasant to delay it all, to postpone it a bit and prolong the savor of MacMurran's cuckoldry. Then to, there was a rare spice of amusement in it, for Etienne had plainly come with other matters on his mind, which he must now, in common gallantry, delay.

She guided the talk deftly, persuading him to tell of a dinner at De Neyrac's, the latest quadroon ball, a shooting party in the trembling sea marshes between the city and the Gulf. There was nothing to do but follow her lead, but his talk was only sudden spates of words, cut off as the memory of his difficulties poured back upon him. The hours drifted by and the fire burned lower and lower so that the shadows of the room crept in and pressed them together in a constantly narrowing circle of intimacy.

She took his arm and drew him down on the sofa beside her so that they faced the fire. She could smell the salt in the driftwood burning, catch the aroma of the brandy from his glass. It was quiet, except for the muted crackling of the fire.

"Etienne," she said softly, "do you remember the first night on *El Audaz,* and the second day when I told you there would not always be a Julie or a Monsieur de Ternant standing near us?"

She let her shoulder brush against him and her fingers sought his hand, then slid slowly up his arm inside the lace-fringed sleeve. The neckline of her gown had been cut so daringly low that she knew he could not glance down without seeing the curve of her breasts. Her fingers tightened on his arm.

"Do you remember, Etienne?" Her voice had dropped to a husky whisper. "Do you remember?"

She was a witch, a demon, an Ishtar or an Ashtoreth brought back to earth to steal away his senses and his resolution with the pale moon madness of her body. Her fingers were rings of fire upon his arm, and her breasts were like bright apples he could not refuse.

"I remember! My God, Manette, you know that I do!"

The prison and the pillories were vague and unsubstantial images, cut off by the curtain of rising passion she was weaving around him. They did not matter now, for they were lost along with the hordes of yelping creditors and the notes that were so far and so sadly overdue. Nothing mattered except this woman and the strange, sweet fragrance of her, the promise of delight bound up in the silken flesh that turned from rose to gold in the flickering light of the fire. He let his brandy glass fall to the floor as he flung himself upon her.

"Manette! Manette, my darling!"

Yet for a moment she withheld the softness of her body from him, lying still and almost rigid in his arms, savoring in the instant before surrender the bitter aloes of this sweet revenge upon MacMurran. He would never know, but she would know, and in that secret knowledge she would possess a walled tower of scorn and triumph. As for Etienne, he was weak and venal and self-seeking, but it was a weakness a woman could forgive and accept because it was so like her own.

She let the harshness seep out of her body like spring ice breaking and being swept away in the irresistible tide of a white-foamed torrent of water. His hands were eager upon her, so eager that they were hot and nervous and inept. She twisted her body a little, helping him, so that her bodice slipped down about her waist and left the glowing richness of her breasts uncovered. She drew his head closer, tighter, and her thighs set up a frantic quivering that she could not control. There was a broken, sobbing, endless instant of lying tense between the earth and sky, and then the bright star flame of ecstasy, growing and raging until it was a blaze that swept over her and soared into a tower of light and color and sound. Like a skyrocket at its highest arc it flamed into new magnificence, hung poised for an eternity, and then there were only the fading sparks falling slowly back to earth.

"Etienne." It was less than a whisper. "Etienne, I love you so! You are my heart, *querido*. Let me hold you always—always!"

He stirred a little, uneasily.

"You are very sweet, Manette." There was something forced, reluctant in his voice. For an instant it seemed as if she had not heard him, and then the passion died and the eyes that looked up at him were the familiarly appraising ones he knew so well.

"Bring me some brandy, Etienne."

She sat up and straightened her dress about her as he turned to the decanter on the taboret. When he swung around with the goblet in his hand, the passion-haunted nymph that he had known was gone and in her place was only a lovely woman, poised, entirely at ease, even, perhaps, a little amused.

She sipped the brandy slowly, not trying to escape the madness that had so unexpectedly possessed her, but rather holding it curiously in her mind, examining it and weighing it against the other facets of her life. Etienne, she knew, would never be one tenth the man MacMurran was. Even his love-making fell short of the passionate animal savagery she knew with Allan. And yet he had turned her into a babbling schoolgirl, whimpering of love and begging for his favors. Her mouth twisted bitterly. She was suddenly aware, with a withering sense of self-contempt, that she was in love with Etienne, would always be in love with him. With Etienne—as penniless and unscrupulous an opportunist as herself. She lifted the glass and held it to her lips until it was empty, as if she were trying to wash out and burn away the treacherous impulse that had overtaken her. She held the glass out to Etienne, smiling a little, her eyes dark and shadowed in the taut and withdrawn face.

"More, please, Etienne, if you will be so kind."

She cradled the refilled glass in her hand, her fingers moving slowly back and forth upon it as if it were some talisman to bind her to a world of reality again. Etienne watched her with puzzled eyes, eyes that even held a trace of fear in their farthest depths. He had clasped his hands behind him so she could not see the nervous twitching of his fingers, but his lips betrayed him.

She looked up at him and laughed and he could not tell whether she found amusement in him or mocked the memory of her own weakness and infatuation.

"Poor Etienne." Her voice was like soft velvet now, freed of its urgency, freed of the insane desire that had possessed her. "I did not mean to devour you or hold you forever, my darling. It is only that with a woman, sometimes, passion lingers for a little while and then she is a fool—as I was."

He roused himself to a protest. "You must not say that, Manette. You are very sweet. This gift that you have given me tonight I will never forget."

"No?" She surveyed him quizzically, seeing the all too apparent weakness in him, the egotism, the self-love so great and demanding that he could never truly give himself to anyone.

"Etienne, you did not come to make love to me tonight. What was it that brought you, *corazón*?"

His body shifted uneasily and his eyes sought hers and then flickered away again. His tongue touched his dry lips and he swallowed as though his throat were clogged with words that he found it hard to speak.

"I—I am in trouble, Manette. The most serious and dangerous trouble that could befall me."

He paused and his eyes implored her sympathy and understanding.

"Why, then, tell me, *corazón*. Who knows? There may be something I can do to help. What is this trouble that touches you so closely and so terribly?"

"Money!" He seemed almost to spit the word out upon the floor as if it were sour in his mouth. "Money! I owe money everywhere, Manette, and Jean Falaise told me only this afternoon that if he is not paid, he will land me in the prison or the pillories!"

"The pillories! Oh, no Etienne! He would not do that!"

She knew the pillories, as everyone in New Orleans knew them. Unpainted frames of heavy wood, rising not more than two feet above the ground, but pierced with four holes to contain a man's wrists and ankles so that when they were locked down upon him, he sat awkwardly upon the ground, his knees half bent and his face thrust forward like some drooling idiot's to the gaze of all who passed before the Cabildo or the Presbytery. You saw Negroes in the stocks, picked up and being punished as runaways. You saw drunken sailors there sometimes, and prostitutes, and petty thieves. They served their penances in indignity and terror and pain, for drunks and street urchins passing by pelted them with rotten fruit and dead animals and even, now and then, with rocks, so that many were finally released with dried blood caked upon them. Sometimes they lived, sometimes they died of their injuries, and no one seemed to know or care.

"Etienne, you are joking!" All the blindly senseless tide of love that she had choked back only a few moments before came flooding back again so that her eyes were wide with terror and her mind frantic and hysteric with schemes and plans to save him. "This Falaise—what is your debt to him? I have jewels that can be pawned or sold! We will raise the required money and pay this monster."

"It would not be enough, Manette."

Etienne's voice was like a dark sword of despair cutting off her flow of words. "Falaise is only one of many—one of the little ones. If we buy him off, there will be another and then another and another, until finally you will be stripped of all you have and there will still be a hundred others ready and eager to drag me down."

"But, *corazón,* there must be something!" She was pitiful, there in the firelight. Pitiful, because the damask and the satin and the jewels seemed like a grotesque mockery of her drawn face, the helpless quivering of her lips, the dark shadows of despair that were her eyes.

"There is only one thing, Manette." He paused, feeling the incongruity of their fresh-passed passion against his present need. "Only one thing. I must marry, Manette, and marry someone who has the money to free me from this filthy net of debt and disaster."

"Marry!" The sound died in her throat and she stared at him with stricken eyes. Tonight she had been in his arms, had discovered and beaten down a passion for him that was like the wild surge of a hurricane; and tonight, tonight he threw the brutal necessity for a venal marriage in her face as carelessly as if it were an empty glove. Her head dropped into her hands and the long sobs tore through her body. Until this moment, she had allowed herself to hope that someday, somehow ...

"Oh, Manette, my darling—"

She felt his arms about her, comforting her, stroking the smooth skin of her shoulder. "Do not cry so, Manette. Please, my sweet one."

She lifted her head and her breasts rose and fell as she drew long gasps of air into her lungs. The tears streamed down her face, but she was Manette again, calling upon the courage and the pride that she had always known, meeting the situation gallantly.

"Forgive me, *corazón*. I—I will be all right now."

She wiped the tears away and leaned forward to fill two brandy glasses from the tall decanter. She handed one to Etienne and even managed a parody of a smile as she lifted her glass and clicked its rim against his own.

"To your marriage, Etienne. May it be happy and——and profitable."

She drained the glass in a single draught and then, in a sudden flaring violence of anger and renunciation, sent it crashing against the brick back wall of the fireplace in a shower of splintered crystal and hissing flame.

She leaned back against the sofa, feeling her body grow slack and relaxed, the emotions that had ripped and torn at her fade and vanish like thin smoke. The smashing of the brandy glass had been a climax, a period set at the end of a long and painful paragraph. Now she was only tired, so tired that she could survey the whole affair with a certain sardonic cynicism, as if she had known that this must be the eventual outcome even while she struggled against it.

"And who," there was bitter amusement in her voice, "is to have the honor of becoming Madame Chrétien, my friend?"

Etienne stood up and moved forward to stand before the fireplace again. His own face was white with strain and fatigue, but he was like a man who had come at last to the end of a weary and toilsome road.

"Julie," he said flatly, and then, as if he were afraid she would not understand, "Julie de Ternant."

"So." Her eyes crinkled a little in sudden amusement. "Having been her lover, you will now become her husband. It seems fitting enough, Etienne, but from what Julie said on Bonneterre, I thought the ransom MacMurran got from her had left her almost without a picayune."

Etienne chuckled harshly. "Julie is French to the bone, Manette. She could no more avoid haggling over the amount of the ransom than she could avoid breathing. But Ternant had many properties, and he left them all to our little Julie. Today she is one of the wealthiest women in Louisiana."

"*Es verdad*? I did not know of this, Etienne. But if it is like that, why do you not marry her now and be done with it? She can pay your debts—yes, and provide the credit for you to acquire new ones. What are you waiting for, *amigo*?"

The light that had flamed briefly in Etienne's eyes faded away and his shoulders seemed to sag beneath the rich broadcloth of his coat.

"She will not," he admitted drearily. "Or, at least, she has not. Oh, she has never refused, but neither has she agreed. She waits and hesitates and turns this way and that way, and in the meantime, *mon Dieu*, my creditors drive me like a dog! I need your help, Manette. I need it now!"

"*My* help!" She roused herself to lean forward and stare at him in amazement. "You come to me for help in a matter like this?"

"But you can do it, Manette!" His voice was trembling with eagerness, with the sheer dark necessity of making her see his need and her place in it. "Julie has admired you, almost worshiped you since the night you saved us from her husband on *El Audaz*. If you urge her to do this, she will agree. She will—"

Manette fell back upon the sofa, her throat shaken with laughter that was perilously near a sob.

"So now," she gasped, "I am to be your marriage broker, your procuress, your—Oh, you are droll, Etienne! Tell me, what else can I do for you tonight?"

"You would let me go to the pillories, then?"

She sobered suddenly, aware that Etienne's eyes were like live coals, the macabre lines of complete despair slashed in his face.

"No," she admitted softly, "I could not do that. Even now, after all of this, I could not do that." Her eyes grew thoughtful as she stared reflectively into the heart of the leaping fire. "I will do what I can for you, Etienne. I will see Julie tomorrow and urge her to—to marry you."

It was like tearing her heart out and holding it in her hand. But there was no other way to save this man she loved except to throw him into another woman's arms. She caught her breath, closing her eyes to hide the shock and pain. Through the dark mists that swirled about her, she heard Etienne's voice babbling on almost hysterically in a spasm of long withheld release:

"—and for you too, Manette. When Julie and I are married there'll be money enough. I'll see that you're well paid."

It came to her with a sudden agony of surprise and humiliation that he was offering her a share of the spoils. She was to be paid—paid like some broker or banker or factor who had turned a successful piece of business! In the startling reaction from her own tragic mood of despair and self-sacrifice it was too much. She felt the mounting waves of hysteria rolling up inside her, felt her body shake and quiver from them. She fought against them, but the storm of her emotion swelled into a torrent of broken tears and laughter. She was on her feet, swaying a little, seeing Etienne's face suddenly shocked and terrified before her.

"Get out!" It was a stranger's voice, weird and high-pitched, and yet she knew it was her own. "Get out, I say!" She clawed at his shoulder and tried to push him toward the door while the crazy laughter wrenched and twisted her and echoed and re-echoed in the room.

" 'I'll see that you're well paid'! Oh, *por Dios,* Etienne! *Por Dios!*"

She struck at him savagely, feeling the flesh of his cheek tear beneath her fingernails, seeing him turn and twist as he tried to dodge away.

"Get out! Get out!"

Through the red mist that enveloped her, she was aware that he was crossing the room, that the door had been opened and closed and that she was alone. She collapsed on the sofa while the awful laughter still tore at her with maniac hands.

Still laughing, she fumbled for the decanter and lifted it to her lips. A log burned through in the fireplace and fell with a crash and a shower of sparks.

But all she could hear was the echo of Etienne's voice saying over and over and over again:

"I'll see that you're well paid—well paid—well paid!"

CHAPTER TWELVE

S HE WOKE in the morning to sunlight that forced its way in through the closed jalousies and lay in slanting lines of radiance between the windows and the floor.

There was the dull, dark taste of stale brandy in her mouth and the sunlight burned against her eyes. She shifted her position a little in the great four-poster bed, seeing the satin *ciel* quiver a little with the movement. There was a silken bell cord within reach of her hand and she jerked it three times as a signal that her maid was to bring her morning coffee to her.

As she waited, her mind ranged back to the night before. In the clear light of morning it seemed that she must have been insane and she closed her eyes as if to shut out the images that paraded before her in a mockingly licentious cavalcade. The interval of passion with Etienne was nothing. Since she had left Havana so many different men had possessed her that she had come to regard her body with something only a little above contempt. But the deeper matter, the emotion that had racked her and torn her and made her cling to him—that was sheer and utter madness. Seeing herself now as he must have seen her then, she recoiled from the image. A woman maddened almost into gibbering incoherence by her own desire. A woman calling upon a man for something he did not have to give. A woman trying to clutch and hold and transmute an hour of passion into a lifetime of devotion. Her fingernails bit into the palms of her hands as her mind writhed beneath this humiliation she had brought upon herself.

"You fool! You utter, hopeless, miserable fool!"

A sudden shocked awareness told her she had spoken the words aloud and they seemed to quiver in the air more vividly than the sunlight from the jalousies. She was strangely light-headed, but that would be from the brandy still in her veins. She turned to jerk the bell cord impatiently and even as her fingers touched it she heard the soft knock at the door.

"Come in! Come in!"

She was shocked at the harshness of her own voice. It was like the rasping cry of a sea gull. She shook her head vigorously to clear her thoughts, and watched the mulatto maid edge through the door with the wide silver tray that held coffee and brandy.

"Good morning, madame."

The maid sketched an awkward curtsy and then brought the tray across the room to the low table beside the bed. She glanced inquiringly at Manette.

"Madame will have brandy with her coffee this morning?"

Ordinarily, Allan drank brandy in the morning, but she did not. The maid's suggestion could only mean that the house servants were all too well aware of what had passed the night before. They had decided she would need a stimulant so they had provided one. And why not? she thought bitterly. Perhaps it could drive out the morbid ghosts that gibbered and chattered inside her brain.

"Brandy," she agreed. "Half brandy and half coffee." She reached for the extended cup eagerly and then was amazed to see that her hand was shaking too badly to hold it. She turned on one elbow, half raising herself from the bed, and took the cup in both hands as if it were a massive bowl rather than fragile china as light and delicate as an azalea bloom. It was hot, but the fire of the liquor was like a cleansing flame upon her lips and she gulped it greedily, feeling its glow spread through her and drive out the chill and the strangeness that had made her body and her mind not quite her own.

She relaxed against the softness of her pillow while the maid bathed her face and hands with warm water from a silver bowl, combed her hair gently into place, and touched her ears with a perfume that had in it something of the sharpness of spices and sandalwood. She was feeling better now. The images were not quite so clear and the sharp knives of remorse less keen.

"Fill the cup again," she ordered. "The same as before."

This time the single hand served admirably and she drank the mixture of brandy and coffee more slowly, feeling it widen and extend the area of well-being the first draught had established.

"Madame will bathe and dress now?"

"Not now. I will rest a little longer and call you when I am ready. Leave the coffee and the brandy."

There was the affair of Etienne and Julie to be considered. She had given Etienne her word that she would try to help—and, after all, there was no particular reason why she should not. At the worst, it could only end in failure, and at the best it would put Etienne deeply and inescapably in her debt. Last night, in the uproar of tangled emotions that had swirled about her, she had been outraged at his suggestion of a financial reward, but now, with the brandy lending a strange new clarity and objectivity to her brain, she was able to consider it in the light of the coolly calculating self-interest she had abandoned the night before.

MacMurran had been generous, even lavish with her; but he had made it plain that he could not offer her the security of marriage, so that always and forever she would be at the mercy of some sudden whim or infatuation or love affair of his that would force her out into the world again to seek a new protector. When that time came, and she knew that it was inevitable, a secret store of funds or a source of them could mean the difference between triumphal emergence and total degradation. Yes, for her own sake she must help Etienne to urge Julie into marriage. As for this infatuation for Etienne, which she still could not quite deny, why, that was something to put aside and thrust into the background until, being so neglected, it would most surely die.

The Ternant house on Esplanade was blood brother in shape and form and structure to the one on Bienville Street that sheltered MacMurran and Manette. But there was a difference in its atmosphere, a difference so elusive and intangible that Manette could feel it without being able to isolate or understand its source. She probed at the problem as she and Julie sipped their sherry before the crackling fire in Julie's living room.

"You are so safe here, so assured and protected—" She broke off, unable to explain or analyze the atmosphere of security that was so much a part of this gracious room where the firelight splashed like liquid silver against the satin-paneled walls.

Julie clucked sympathetically, sensing Manette's nervousness, disturbed because it was so unusual in this strange woman who could face ravishment and death and dishonor without fear or any plea for quarter.

"It is only that we have lived here so long, *petite.* There is no difference between this house and your own."

"No difference?" Manette's eyes were suddenly clouded with the weariness of a woman who has at last met and faced the truth as to her own situation. *"Corajo,* Julie! There is as much difference as there it between a banker and a bandit!"

Julie laughed, trying to distract her. "And is there so much difference always between them, Manette? Some bankers I have seen—"

Manette brushed the pleasantry aside. "Perhaps, but you and your house are secure, while Allan and I are nothing more than visitors and strangers under our own roof. We are here today and gone tomorrow. Why, Julie, if you only married again to make this house complete, you would have everything here that the world could ever offer you!"

"I have been married," Julie said. "It was not too—pleasant, shall I say?"

"Of course, but then you married for money and position, you married a man far older than yourself who was more like a father than a husband. Now you have the money and the position. This time you should marry for your own pleasure—some man you can love who is of your own age and background."

"And that would be—"

Manette shrugged her shoulders. "How can I tell? I am a stranger here and know less than a dozen people in the city. But you are young and beautiful, Julie. You cannot waste yourself by living here alone until you grow old and sour and wrinkled and some young cadet consents to sleep with you simply because you have gold that he can spend or jewels that he can wear."

Julie's lips twisted into a half-humorous *moue* of protest. "Oh, surely, Manette, it is not that bad. Etienne has been begging me to marry him for the past two months, and he is handsome and young and, as you say, of the same background as myself."

"Etienne!" Manette's voice was the perfect echo of startled amazement. "But I thought that Etienne—" She broke off in apparent confusion, and lifted the glass of sherry to her lips.

"You thought what?" It was a sharp-edged inquiry.

"Nothing, Julie. Nothing at all. Just some idle gossip that came to me."

Julie leaned forward and placed her glass carefully on the low table before them. Her mouth was suddenly thin-lipped and her eyes were keen and questioning.

"Manette, you are my friend. If you know something of Etienne that I do not, it is your duty to tell me." She laid her hand pleadingly upon Manette's. "Tell me, Manette."

Manette allowed her fingers to twist the stem of her own glass back and forth in apparent nervousness and indecision. Her eyes avoided Julie's face and the insistent questions so plainly written there.

"Why, Julie," she said at last, "it is simply that I have heard that Etienne has been most intimate with Renée de Neyrac of late and some seem to believe that he will approach her father before the week is out."

"Renée de Neyrac!" Julie's voice soared up in involuntary protest and disbelief. The Neyrac women carried with them a long tradition of being Louisiana's greatest beauties and the family fortune was fabulous, even in this land of tremendous wealth and uncounted arpents of plantation lands. "Oh, he could not turn to Renée de Neyrac! She has the temper of a wildcat and a list of lovers that would stretch from here to St. Ann's!"

"So? And yet she is very beautiful, Julie, and Louis de Neyrac could provide a dowry that would make Etienne independently wealthy for the rest of his life."

Julie sprang to her feet and began to pace up and down before the fire. Her heels clicked against the hardwood floor and the rustle of her silk petticoats was like a storm wind gathering in the trees. Her mouth twisted angrily as she walked and her eyes were brighter than the fire behind her.

"It is intolerable!" she burst out. "If it were anyone except Renée de Neyrac—She has beaten me and thwarted me and been my rival since we were children together in the convent. Every man I ever wanted she has taken! Every dress, every jewel I ever owned has been a little less fine than hers." She whirled and faced Manette, her whole body quivering with anger. "Did you know that my husband was her lover before he married me and turned to me only when she had made it publicly plain that she would not marry him? Did you know that? But it is true—as true as the fact that I am here and you are there! Oh, this I will not accept! Etienne has been my lover and my suitor—and now she would take him, too!"

She flung herself down upon the sofa and buried her face in her hands. She was not crying, Manette was certain of that, but her body quivered and shuddered with a passion so strong she did not even attempt to control it.

"Then why, Julie," there was a trace of acrid dryness in Manette's voice, "why do you not marry him yourself, since you say that he has been begging you to do this for the past two months?"

Julie's figure stiffened and she crouched there, still and unmoving as though Manette's question had opened up a new chain of thought that she must consider in complete isolation from the world outside. The silence grew until it was like a tangible presence in the room. The fire flickered silently, reflected in rosewood furniture and shining silver and gleaming mirrors. Rain spattered against the windows and the two women were still and quiet here in the seclusion of this shadowed room. At last Julie's taut body relaxed and she lifted her head and turned so that she faced the fire again. She picked up her half-empty glass of sherry and Manette saw that Julie's lips were set in a tight line of resolution and there was the glow of a fixed purpose in her eyes.

"I have waited," she said slowly, almost as if she were explaining something to herself rather than to Manette, "I have waited and held Etienne at arm's length because—oh, because I have known Etienne in the months that we were lovers! I know how his breath catches in his throat when he is proud and pointedly desirous! I know the songs he sings in the evenings and the way he grumbles and protests when he is first awakened in the early morning. All of these things about him were new and exciting to me in the beginning, but I know them now, and they are not new. I thought—I thought, perhaps, there would be someone strange and different and exciting."

"And if there were, and you were married to Etienne," Manette said in a silkily insinuating murmur, "would that prevent your sharing these new delights with this—this stranger that is yet to come?" Her mood changed abruptly to one of brutal reality. "You were not so punctilious when you were married to Ternant."

Julie lifted her eyes from the crystal wineglass to Manette's face and nodded in slow agreement.

"You are right, Manette. Etienne could not—perhaps would not—care to stop me if that happened."

"Then marry him!" Manette's voice drew a line of finality through Julie's doubts and questions. "Marry him, or else give him to Renée de Neyrac and forget him!"

Julie's lips twitched in sudden anger and her finger tips tapped the polished table top before her as if they were measuring the syllables of her words and the depths of her resolution.

"Renée de Neyrac shall never have him! She had my husband, and she has had the others, but she shall not have Etienne!" She leaned back and laughed suddenly, relaxed and pleased now that the decision had been made. "*Mon Dieu,* Manette, Etienne is coming here tonight, and if he is still in the mood for marriage, you may see our banns published on the cathedral doors before noon tomorrow!"

"And if he is not in the mood, you are wise enough to know how to deal with that situation, too?"

"I am wise enough." Julie was smiling now, a smile that was somehow reminiscent of a thousand long dead kisses that had touched her lips, the smile of a woman sure of her powers, sure of her ability to use it to gain her own desires.

Rain buffeted the carriage and the wind tore at it and shook it through all the empty squares that lay between Esplanade and Bienville Street. The people of the city had been driven indoors by the storm and night had begun to draw its veil across the houses and the trees so that it was like riding forever through a world of emptiness and wind and rain and small, flickering lights, half glimpsed through shuttered windows. At a stationer's shop on Bourbon Street, Manette sent the coachman inside for paper and a pen. Straining to see in the dim light of the coach, she scratched out a brief note to Etienne:

> When you call on J. tonight do not be surprised if she accuses you of courting the oldest daughter at the house where you had dinner two nights ago. Deny it—but deny it so that she will believe you are lying. Then press your own cause and I think you will find little difficulty in your way.
>
> M.

The stationer's colored errand boy was dispatched to carry the message to Etienne without delay and Manette leaned back in the carriage and tried to brace herself against the jounce and jolting of the potholed and uneven street. She and Julie had been through much together. Together they had seen men die, and now she had tricked Julie into a marriage from which other such men might be born. There was a vague, elusive sense of completeness there, a cycle she was too tired to think through to its beginnings. All she could think of now was a warm fire in her dressing room, a glass of brandy, and a hot dinner served her as she rested in the great four- poster bed.

Pray God, she thought, that Allan is still at Bonneterre.

She was too tired for Allan tonight; too tired for the lustiness he would bring back with him from the sandy isle of palms and barracoons and council fires and death.

CHAPTER THIRTEEN

THE NEW YEAR had come and gone in a riot of exploding anvils and bonfires and champagne before MacMurran and Manette left the house on Bienville Street to establish their headquarters at Constancia. There was a road, of sorts, along the twenty-mile stretch of river front between New Orleans and Constancia, but it was so rutted and mired that Allan ordered the plantation river sloop sent down to New Orleans for them. Now, after a slow, all-day trip upriver, the sloop was turning in for the plantation dock and Manette could see a stirring swarm of humanity moving and shifting back and forth at the edge of the levee.

The slaves were there, almost a hundred of them, the women in starched blue dresses and brightly colored turbans of calico, the field hands in clean gray cottonade with their wide straw hats in their hands and bright handkerchiefs around their necks. Wilson Grambling, the hard-mouthed white overseer that the Marquis de la Ronde had brought in from Georgia, was at the edge of the wharf, faintly ill at ease in unfamiliar broadcloth and white linen, prepared to welcome these new owners with the respect that was their due, and equally prepared to despise them silently and bitterly if they measured up to less than the masters of such an establishment as Constancia should be.

Clinging to MacMurran's arm as they came down the gang-plank, Manette looked over the heads of the assembled slaves to an avenue of oak trees a thousand yards long, an avenue that led as straight as an arrow to a great white house that was magnificent in its simplicity and dignity, breath-taking in its overpowering bulk and beauty. She saw the strange white man in the rumpled broadcloth walking swiftly forward to meet them, and wondered, for an instant, what sorry passage with life had left the dark look of insolence in his eyes and slashed his hard mouth into so thin a line. Then he was sweeping off his hat in an awkward bow.

"Mistah MacMurran an' madame, allow me to welcome you to Constancia. Ah'm Wilson Gramblin', overseah heah undah the Marquis, an' Ah've been kept in chahge heah since his lady passed away."

His Georgia accent was as wide as a muddy Southern river, and yet there was a touch of distinction in his voice that spoke of a gentleman's schooling somewhere far back in the past.

Allan stepped forward a little and held out his hand in greeting.

"I'm glad to see you, Mr. Grambling, and I appreciate the fact that you've been taking care of things. Vincent St. Amant has spoken very highly of you." He drew Manette forward so that she stood beside him. "My dear, this is Mr. Wilson Grambling. You have heard me speak of him. Mr. Grambling, the Señorita de Santiago."

"A pleasuah, señorita." Grambling sketched in the awkward bow again, but Manette was almost sure she saw a quick look of understanding and contempt in his eyes.

So, she thought furiously, you're already saying to yourself, And this is MacMurran's Spanish whore. You'll find I'm more than that, *cabrón*, before we're done!

Her eyes flashed fire for an instant and she could almost have sworn Grambling saw it and was amused, but she forced herself to smile at him, acknowledging the introduction, and then moved forward to the carriage that waited with wheels turned to one side and a colored coachman bowing and smiling beside it. Allan helped her in, followed her, and then without an instant's hesitation beckoned Grambling to them.

"Climb in, Grambling," he invited. "We'll want you to show us around and go over the operations with us."

The massed blacks had been standing in awed silence and MacMurran would have driven away without giving them a backward glance. As far as he was concerned, they were merchandise, to be taken from captured slavers and tamed in barracoons and sold at a dollar a pound from Bonneterre. Here, on Constancia, they were provided to till the fields and care for the house and run the errands and do all the other unending work this vast establishment demanded. But Manette had seen plantation life before and knew all too well how strong an influence for tranquillity or trouble these massed and silent slaves could exert. She touched his arm unobtrusively and drew MacMurran's attention to them.

"You should speak to them, Allan," she whispered. "These are not like the blacks you pen and sell at Bonneterre. These are your own. They belong to you—not just for a day or two, but month after month and year after year."

He stared at her in outright amazement.

"Speak to them! Why, good God, I haven't got anything to say to them! Let them do their work and—"

"They expect it, Allan," she insisted.

He gave her a glance of mingled disgust and exasperation and got to his feet in the open carriage, standing so that he faced the bunched rows of men and women and children who were as much his property as was the land beneath his carriage wheels. He stood silent for almost a minute, while his eyes ran over them slowly and appraisingly. Some of them shot him quick glances and then jerked their eyes away while others simply stared in blank-faced wonder at this new master and his mistress. He cleared his throat and lifted his hand as if to enjoin silence, though there was not even a breath of sound from the waiting Negroes.

"I am Allan MacMurran," he said slowly, "and this is the Señorita de Santiago. I am glad that you have come down to the levee to make us welcome." He paused, obviously at a loss for words, and then finished in a sudden burst of inspiration. "There will be no more work today, and there will be a ration of rum for all of you a little later in the afternoon." The dark mass stirred a little and there was a murmur of relief and a few shouts of jubilant exultation as he resumed his seat with an air of irritated impatience and motioned the coachman into action.

"Damned nonsense," he growled. "Didn't have anything to say to them, in the first place, and now I've wound up by losing a day's work and a couple of casks of rum. A damned fine way to start running a plantation, I must say!"

But Manette could see that he was secretly pleased. There was a little smile twitching at the corners of his lips and his dark eyes were bright and shining. He had commanded men in plenty, but this was the first time he had ever spoken to so large a group that was completely and entirely his own. For the first time, he had begun to catch the feudal atmosphere of Constancia and realize that he was its seigneur. It was no longer simply a convenient headquarters for his smuggling operations. No, it was more than that, for he had just been given his first glimpse of the intense paternalism that was the pride and power of the ruling planter caste.

The double line of oaks, planted a good half century before, formed a curving roof above their carriage, a roof hung with beards of gray Spanish moss and inhabited by shrill-voiced birds whose brilliant plumage shone and glittered in the thin mid-winter sunshine. The main house rose before them now, whitely gleaming, lovely and serene behind the rows of thick two-story columns that enclosed it on all four sides. The raised basement lifted the first floor and the lower gallery a dozen feet above the earth, and the second gallery, guarded by grilled ironwork that was like white lace, circled the house midway between the lower gallery and the steeply pitched roof. Fifty feet away on either side rose the octagonal columns of the *pigeonniers,* the dovecotes, perhaps twenty-five feet high and ten feet wide. The shingled roofs were topped with gleaming finials and the pigeons were a gray and white cloud about them, whirling and fluttering and cooing softly in the sunshine.

A little farther back was the *garçonnière,* almost an exact copy of the main house itself, but only a third as large. It was here that the cadets of the family had been lodged as they grew to manhood, and its wide fireplaces and great four-poster beds provided a ready welcome for any bachelors or unattended males who might honor the plantation with their presence.

The kitchen was housed in a squire brick building, some twenty feet back of the house, detached to spare the master and his mistress the heat and odors of the cooking and lessen the danger of the destructive fire that was the ever present fear of the isolated plantations. Reaching back almost to the fields was the good-sized village of slave cabins, stables, barns, carriage houses, cooling bins, storehouses, and all the other sheds and huts and buildings that went to make up Constancia.

The coachman pulled up with a flourish before the wide white steps that led up to the lower gallery. MacMurran leaped out, his eyes raking the magnificent façade. He offered his hand to Manette and she jumped from the carriage to the ground with a swirl of many colored petticoats and a flash of red silk stockings that matched the scarlet heels of her tiny slippers.

"My dear," MacMurran was smiling at her with something that was almost akin to tenderness, "welcome to Constancia. I hope you will be very happy here."

With a shock of surprise she realized that he had spoken to her as if she were a bride rather than a mistress taken by force and held only at his pleasure.

"Why, thank you, Allan. It is very kind of you to put it so."

She saw his eyes darken a little and knew she had unintentionally recalled the insane Dorothée to his mind, and spoiled a little of his sense of triumph in coming as a master to Constancia. She regretted it instantly, for Allan had been as kind and considerate as any man could be in the peculiar circumstances that bound them together. She still resented the fact of Dorothée, but that was neither here nor there. She was obliged to live in the present as it was, and not as it might have been. She forced a brilliant smile and let her eyes sparkle up at him so he would know she understood and shared his triumph.

"It *is* wonderful, Allan! Wonderful that you should have come from Scotland with nothing only ten years ago, and now you are the master of the greatest plantation in Louisiana."

She slipped her hand into the curve of his arm and let her body brush momentarily against him. "Show it to me, Allan."

He smiled down at her, his momentary depression gone, and his face relaxed and warm again.

"We'll see it together."

They climbed the wide steps slowly, their eyes busy with the ninety-foot sweep of the wide gallery and the row of tall double windows guarded by green jalousies that reached from floor to ceiling. The house servants were waiting to greet them just outside the door, the brown-skinned maids demure and curtsying in blue-and-white striped calico with snow-white aprons, the butler and the footmen in livery. A gray-polled patriarch with skin as smooth and black as ebony held the wide front door open for them and bowed with dignity as they paused before they went into the house. MacMurran cast an inquiring glance at Grambling, who was following a few steps behind, and the overseer hurried forward.

"This is yoah butlah, Mistah MacMurran—Cragon, they call him. He was with the Marquis foah almost thutty yeahs. If you want to, you can tu'n the entiah runnin' of this house ovah to him an' relieve yoahself of any worry in regahd to it."

"Well, I don't know …." Mac Murran's voice reflected his own doubts. "I rather imagine the Señorita de Santiago will want to take charge of that. But we'll see about all that later."

The door Cragon was holding open for them was of paneled cypress, polished until it was almost as brilliant as a mirror, hung on heavy silver hinges, and fitted with a silver doorknob and lock so massive they might have come from a medieval castle. The great central hallway stretched away before them, seventy feet long and a full twenty-five feet wide. They caught glimpses of gold-framed mirrors and a rose-carpeted spiral stairway that spun its way up from the hall to the floor above. There were oil paintings from France on the wide walls and three great chandeliers hanging from the ceiling with their copper and crystal gleaming like fire in the reflected light from the doorway.

Manette glanced up at MacMurran and saw that his dark face was fierce with pride. He was staring about him like a conqueror. His shoulders had stiffened and he was even more erect than usual. For the first time since she had known him, she felt a strange, illogical thrill of satisfaction at the idea of sharing even a part of such a man's life. He was wild and fierce and ruthless and almost completely amoral, but he was a man and she was the woman he had chosen to enter the doors of Constancia with him. They shared the common attributes of strength and courage, and as she stood there in the sunlight with the great house stretching away before them, she began to wonder again if between them they could not beat down the difficulties that opposed them and wrench some final safety and security from the greedy hands of destiny.

But those were thoughts to be considered in the empty hours of the night; now there was all of Constancia to see.

As they went through the house, the inventory of possessions they had acquired mounted until it became fantastic, incredible, almost a little frightening. Pleyel pianos, Aubusson carpets, spinets of rosewood, Sèvres vases, mahogany desks, cherry armoires, liquor cabinets, inlaid jewel cases, an ebony table mounted with mother-of-pearl, Dresden china, silver epergnes, cut-glass decanters, carved marble fireplaces and mantels—it went on and on until Manette was dazzled and confused and MacMurran collapsed in a vast chair in the master bedroom and shouted at Cragon to bring him brandy and plenty of it.

"My God, Manette!" He wiped the perspiration from his forehead. "What in the name of hell are we going to do with all this? I knew it was big, but good Lord! Why, I could quarter half the men from Bonneterre on the lower floor and hardly notice they were there!"

Manette laughed at him, pouring his brandy into one of the tall silver tumblers Cragon had provided.

"And that," she said decisively, "is something we won't do. Can you imagine those wild boars of yours testing their cutlass edges on the spinet? Oh, no, Allan—keep your men on Bonneterre, and we'll find other guests to stay with us at Constancia. We'll have—"

"Who?"

The flat monosyllable was like a pistol bullet smashing through her words.

"Who? What do you mean, Allan?"

"You say we'll find other guests to stay with us here. Who are we going to find, Manette? We're not accepted by society, either of us. And not just because of Dorothée, either. When all's said and done, I'm nothing but a pirate, and you—well, you're con- ·
nected with me. I can do business with these Creoles, but I'll do it in their offices and in the coffeehouses, and when it's done they'll pick up their papers and put on their hats and go home. What's the answer to that, Manette? Are we going to rattle around in this place by ourselves like a couple of pistol balls in an empty shot locker?"

Her eyes narrowed as she studied him in surprised conjecture. His earlier mood of exuberant triumph had given way to one of the rare periods of depression and melancholia that sometimes affected him. When he was like this, his past successes turned to ashes and he could see nothing ahead except loneliness and despair and a final, inevitable ruin. Usually he drank his way back to sanity in a wild, week-long debauch, but this time he had raised a question that even brandy could not answer.

"Why, Allan, I didn't know you were especially interested in being accepted by Creole society."

"Society? Hell, I don't care anything about society. But I don't want to be regarded as an outlaw, either." He filled his glass half full of brandy and leaned forward. "It's like this, Manette: We weren't nobility in Scotland—far from it, in fact—but we had the respect and liking of our friends and neighbors. Our hands were clean, even though there might not be any silver in them, and we were welcomed at the houses of our friends, just as they were welcomed at our own. It's different here. I've had to do things that roweled these people to the marrow of their bones, and they don't want to forget about them. But, by God, I don't want to be on the outside looking in, either! Before I'm done I want to be welcomed and honored in any house in Lousiana! I want to see men touch their hats and their ladies drop a curtsy when I ride by. That's what I want, Manette—and that's what I'm going to have!"

So it was this buried craving for honor and prestige and acceptance that had driven him out of Bonneterre and into New Orleans. It was the motive for the purchase of Constancia—but it was directly contrary to the fact that he still continued to outrage the Creoles' basic sense of conventional respectability by flaunting Manette boldly in their faces. A puzzled frown gathered between her eyes as she considered the paradox and then she jerked her mind back to his words and tried to find other words to answer him.

"You are not alone, Allan," she said slowly. "I had in Santo Domingo what you had in Scotland, and it has not been easy to give it up and take the crusts and curds instead. But Allan, gold washes many a memory clean. Most men, and women, too, find it easier to forgive wealth than poverty. There is something about wealth and success that fascinates them and draw's them like moths around a candle flame. They begin to make excuses for this so attractive sinner—to tell each other that undoubtedly half the evil reports are lies and the rest most grossly exaggerated. They move a little closer, accepting and allowing first a small intimacy and then a greater one, until one day the past is buried and forgotten and nothing remains but the fact of your fortune and your success. Believe me, Allan, these things do not come overnight, but they come as surely and inevitably as the morning follows the sunrise."

He stared at her reflectively, turning the brandy glass thoughtfully back and forth between his fingers. "By God, Manette, I believe you're right. Lord knows some of the most mealy-mouthed and sanctimonious men I deal with in the city got their money by tricks and trades so raw and slimy that they still stink to high heaven, but that's all forgotten now and it's 'M'sieur' this and 'M'sieur' that and 'M'sieur, how can I serve you best today!' "

He got up and took two quick strides forward so that he could put his arm about her waist and pull her to him.

"You're a wise young wench, and a damned cynical one, too."

His eyes were bright and eager again, all the despair and bitterness washed out of them by this new conception of his present position and its possibilities. "I'll tell you this, Manette: If it weren't for Dorothée—But there's no use talking about that now."

She felt her cheeks go warm in a sudden flush of triumph and exultation. If he would commit himself now …

"If it weren't for Dorothée—what then, Allan?"

But his mood had changed and he moved away to consider the brandy and the more immediate future that lay before them.

"There are the St. Amants," he mused. "God knows we're entangled together in so many enterprises now that they can scarcely refuse to come and bring their women with them. And Jacques Marnier and the Monteil brothers and Pierre Lucien—I think they'd all prefer to forget their scruples rather than their profits. If they once show the way, I've little doubt that there'll be others ready and willing to follow them."

He looked up and Manette saw that the fierce pride he had worn as he stood at the door of Constancia was his again.

"Manette!" His voice had the old bold ring of confidence. "Manette, we'll see the bastards bowing and scraping to us yet. It's going to be all right, Manette, it's going to be all right!"

"All right? Why, of course, *querido*. How else could it be?"

How else? And yet there was still Dorothée, as vague and intangible as thin smoke on a far horizon, as definite and forbidding a barrier as a high wall of fitted stone.

CHAPTER FOURTEEN

I T WAS an early spring that year; a fierce, pagan spring with the wild geese crying overhead and moons like yellow gold, and all the sweet intoxication and passion of the tropics in the warm winds that blew up from the south. The slim green lances of the sugar cane had pierced the warming earth and glittered like a vast sea of emerald from the river to the far horizon. The hearth fires were dead, for even the bright, stinging rain that swept down like a silver veil was warm and tender, ending as abruptly as it began and leaving a legacy of sky-dyed pools to reflect the fresh-leaved oak trees and the white columns of Constancia.

It was a time of almost enraptured relief to Manette, for now she could put the studied formality of the great house behind her and gallop headlong down the long plantation lanes or linger beside the river where there were green thickets of willow and poplar and sycamore and the flashing half-glimpsed brilliance of blue herons and green and orange parakeets. This was the life she had known as a girl in Santo Domingo, and sometimes the fantasy of a return to her carefree childhood was so strong that she could blot out all the harsh and violent years between and almost accept the future with the same grave confidence she had known then.

And then all the brightness and assurance would be lost, for she would hear the echo of Etienne's voice in the murmur of the river or see some stranger riding by with the same odd, square-set shoulders, and the destroying bitterness of his marriage to Julie would sweep over her and she would be forlorn and hopeless and alone. There was an added irony in the unmistakable fact that it had turned out to be an ideal arrangement, the very model of a marriage made in heaven. The new ménage was pleasant and lighthearted and appealingly attractive. When she had called to see them at the house on Esplanade there had been a curious warmth and gaiety and tolerance between Julie and Etienne that was as disarming as if they had been two children playing a game they found entertaining beyond all words. She had come back to the plantation with an almost murderous jealousy in her heart; but that had faded a little now, so that the black hours of hopeless envy and despair were more and more infrequent.

Sometimes Allan rode with her, but it was only now and then, for he had buried himself wholeheartedly in the management of the plantation and spent long hours conferring with Wilson Grambling or riding through the fields on tours of meticulous inspection. The concept of creating from the bosom of the earth itself had caught his imagination, and he was tireless in its execution, with the unwearying enthusiasm of a lover fascinated and enchained by some new and lovely mistress. He cursed the obligations that took him away to Bonneterre and to New Orleans, and would come galloping back through the mists of midnight to gain an extra day or hour with this land that was his new-found love.

Studying him as he succumbed to this new passion, Manette believed that she could discern in him a new strength he had never had before; a strong, unvarying integrity of purpose more sure and solid than the hotheaded recklessness he had displayed in the past. Even the fiasco of their social endeavors had not brought back his former mood of bitterness and resentment.

And it had been a fiasco; there was no way in which the fact could be softened or disguised. They had planned a plantation party and Allan had threatened or bludgeoned or coerced the St. Amant brothers and Jacques Marnier and Pierre Lucien into acceptance. There had been turmoil and commotion for two days before, but when Manette was done and stood ready to receive her guests, the house was bright and fragrant with great masses of flowers, the staircase was garlanded with roses, and an orchestra from New Orleans was ready to provide music for their dancing feet. For the midnight supper, the huge oak table in the dining room was covered with lace and shining silver, and there was a brave epergne of flowers with ribbons running from it to a gay bouquet that lay beside each lady's plate. The sideboards groaned with their burden of whole turkeys, roasts, cold ham, rich cheeses, salads, gelatines, cakes in richly iced pyramids, and nougat *pièce montée.* There were champagne, and wine in cut-glass decanters, and whisky and brandy and cigars for the pleasure of the gentlemen.

The guests were to come by carriage, since the river was wild with wind, and just before sunset Vincent and Telesphore St. Amant arrived with their ladies in a great coach with their escutcheon emblazoned upon the doors. Allan greeted them in the driveway and escorted them to the open door, where Cragon was all white smiles and bows and Manette awaited them with cold shivers of doubt and misgiving coursing up and down her spine.

The St. Amant women were awe-inspiring, there was no doubt of that. Vincent's wife, Céleste, was in her middle twenties, a slim, dark-haired beauty with a sensuous mouth and a devil of recklessness in her eyes. They were alert and almost brutally curious and probing as she acknowledged the introduction to Manette.

"So ravishing to meet you, señorita!" Her voice trilled up into a little laugh. "One has heard so much of the Señorita de Santiago." She leaned closer so that her lips were almost touching Manette's ear. "Sometimes I have envied you, my dear, when such a husband as Vincent is almost more than a woman should be asked to bear." She laughed again, half in mockery, half from the excitement and recklessness that possessed her, and Manette turned to greet Telesphore St. Amant and his wife, who stood waiting on the doorstep.

Where Vincent's wife was reckless, Telesphore's wife, Eulalie, was stolid and vinegary. She was a heavy woman dressed in black and her prim lips were pinched into a tight and disapproving knot. Her eyes snapped fire as Allan made the introductions, and when he was done, she snorted like a fly-stung horse and waddled contemptuously past Manette into the brilliance of the entrance hall. Telesphore shot Manette a swift apologetic glance and turned hurriedly away from the black mask of anger that had suddenly descended upon Allan's face.

In the drawing room, conversation flared up in brief spurts and then died away into unhappy deserts of silence. Manette pressed whisky upon the gentlemen and found, not to her very great surprise, that Céleste much preferred a tumbler of brandy to a glass of wine. She turned to Eulalie with a smile that she felt must be like a death's-head grin upon her face.

"And may I offer you a glass of sherry, Madame St. Amant?"

The beady eyes stared at her without blinking and the tight mouth unpursed itself just enough to release the words: "I do not care for sherry."

"Then perhaps some port, or a glass of brandy to warm you after the long chill of your drive?"

"I prefer to have neither."

The lips snapped shut again and Manette bowed to defeat and crossed the room to sit beside Céleste.

"We are so pleased that you could come to us tonight. You are the first guests who have honored us since we came to Constancia." She was almost rigid with the effort to keep her voice as warm and casual as it would have been under similar circumstances at Santo Domingo, but she was trembling, and her brain was still misty and envenomed with the brutality of Madame Eulalie's rebuffs.

"Honored you? Why, *mon Dieu,* señorita, it is, as I understand it, a matter of business." The brandy, and Manette guessed shrewdly that it was not the first she had taken since she left New Orleans, had kindled the fires of recklessness in Céleste's eyes and loosened her tongue so that now she was completely unrestrained and uninhibited. "It seems that your so handsome M'sieur MacMurran is going to make a great deal of money for my little Vincent. And since Vincent loves money above all things, we are here tonight because we were bidden to be here. La—honored indeed!" She threw back her head and the shrillness of her laughter echoed through the room. "Eulalie, the señorita says that we have 'honored' her by being here tonight. It that not droll, Eulalie? Are you not proud and glad that you have so honored the señorita and her—"

"Céleste!"

Vincent St. Amant's furious voice was like a blow across her face.

"You have taken far too much brandy and have no idea what you are saying. Be silent at once, I command you!"

He turned to Manette with a twisted smile and a gesture of abject apology. "I implore your pardon—and yours, M'sieur MacMurran. Céleste is overtired and the brandy has obviously gone to her head. If it would not be too great an imposition to have one of your maids show her to her room so she might sleep a little while—"

"Why, of course." Manette's hand was on the bell cord as she spoke. There was an uneasy silence until the maid appeared, and then Vincent helped Céleste up from her chair and steadied her uncertain steps as they started toward the door. She was still laughing and carried the half-empty brandy glass clutched against her breast. As the door closed behind them, her voice floated back into the room: " 'Honored'! *Ma foi,* Vincent, are you so hard pressed that you must make your money from buccaneers and their mistresses now?"

Tight-lipped, Manette looked up at Allan and saw that the veins in his temples were throbbing like voodoo drums and his eyes were black fires in his swarthy face. She managed to smile at him, lifting her shoulders in a shrug that was meant to dismiss the incident, and after a moment she saw that his hands were no longer clenched into fists and that he was beating down the fury of rage that had possessed him.

Cragon came in to announce that another carriage had just reached the entrance to the drive, and Allan excused himself and hurried away to welcome the belated guests. Telesphore bestirred himself to set up a screen of conversation with Manette, and they talked of the weather and the sugar cane and the beauty of the trees of Constancia, while Eulalie sat angry and withdrawn, a fat white toad before the fire, apparently bereft of speech for the time being.

They heard footsteps in the hall and the door opened to admit Pierre Lucien and a small, twittery woman whose birdlike voice and fluttery hesitation robbed her words of any meaning they might otherwise have had. She darted across the room to peck at Eulalie's cheek and was rewarded with another snort of contempt that sent her fluttering away again. When she was presented to

Manette, she seized Manette's hand in both her own and rubbed it briskly, as if she were trying to restore its circulation. The mass of tightly curled ringlets around her head bobbed and bounced as she accepted the introduction with a flurry of chattered speech and little nervous grimaces of her too red lips.

"Oh, it's just too wonderful—too wonderful to be here at Constancia again! We were here so often when the Marquis was alive, and even after that. His wife was such a sweet woman, so gentle and so dignified and so refined. She was a Tourtelot, such a charming family and so well bred. Did you know them, my dear? But of course you're new here, aren't you? And to find my dear, sweet friend Eulalie here! You're going to love her, my dear, simply love her! She is the most wonderful woman! And surely that darling Céleste is here." Her eyes darted around the room and returned to Manette. "Don't tell me Céleste isn't here tonight!"

"Céleste," Manette said dryly, "is a little indisposed. She has gone up to her room to rest, but I know she would be delighted to see you."

"Oh, yes, I must, simply must go to her at once! If you would have one of the maids show me the way to her room—"

She departed in a flurry of skirts and a babble of talk, and Manette glanced over at Allan with laughter bubbling up just below the surface of her throat. If this was the society of the Creoles ...

Dusk brought a messenger on a foam-mouthed horse, carrying a note from Jacques Marnier. Monsieur Marnier was prostrated with regret, but Madame Marnier had developed a most sudden and mysterious illness and they would be obliged to deprive themselves of the exquisite pleasure of a visit to Constancia at this time. With the most profound and abject apologies ...

Manette guessed shrewdly that Madame Marnier had flatly refused to come to Constancia, and Jacques had spent the time up until the last possible minute trying to persuade her to it. At the last, then, there had been nothing to do but dispatch the note—and small loss, if the Marniers were of the same caliber as the St. Amants and the Luciens.

The balance of the evening had been almost equally pleasant and successful. Eulalie had excused herself at nine o'clock and gone upstairs to bed. Lucien and his wife had quarreled violently when he danced too often with Manette, and Vincent St. Amant had proceeded to get himself quietly and completely intoxicated. By midnight the last efforts to make something of the affair had been abandoned and the musicians had been dismissed and the food left to Telesphore and Pierre and Allan to do with as they would. Céleste awoke sometime in the small hours of the morning and created a minor crisis by tumbling drunkenly down the stairs in her search for a further supply of brandy. She was duly bandaged and bathed with liniment and assuaged with the desired brandy. In the morning, Manette lay abed and listened to Allan bidding his guests Godspeed, as the last carriage wheels rolled away down the driveway.

When he came up to her room, still angry, ashamed, and a little confused, she cozened him into the bed with her and found means there to soothe his wounded pride. Since then, there had been no formal festivities under Constancia's roof.

Julie and Etienne came calling now and then, and neighboring planters passing by on horseback dropped in for a drink and an hour's talk. But the St. Amants and the Luciens and the Marniers had not come back to Constancia—nor would they, Manette vowed, ever again.

CHAPTER FIFTEEN

"BY GOD, ALLAN, I don't know what it is, but I know there's trouble building up as sure as I'm a foot high."

Captain Langley stretched his lean Virginia horseman's legs out before him and regarded Constancia's avenue of oaks with a troubled and accusing glare. He was out of the Old Dominion, a Royalist who had supported the King during the years of the American Revolution. With his cause defeated and his neighbors suspicious and unfriendly, he had shaken the dust of the colonies from his feet and come to Louisiana in the days of the French regime. By some hook or crook, and there was talk that it had been open and bare-faced bribery, he had managed to acquire the grant of land that joined Constancia on the north. He had dubbed it Britannia Plantation, with a stubborn clinging to the lost cause he had espoused, and settled down to raise a family of sons and daughters and oversee his fields and damn the American rebels acidly and contemptuously whenever the thought of them crossed his mind.

"The blacks have been sneaking off and drumming and making voodoo out in the swamp for two weeks now. I thought about locking them into their cabins at night, but hell, Allan, you can't close up the doors and windows on those kennels in weather like this. By morning, you wouldn't have a slave fit to go to the fields."

Allan nodded soberly, a tall glass of cold punch in his hand and his boots still gray with dust. "The overseer from Arlington, just the other side of you, was by here about two weeks ago looking for a couple of their boys that had run away. One of them was the hunter for the plantation. Now what in hell did that overseer call him? Martin? Meckling? Mingo? That's what it was—Mingo. Anyway, it seemed Russat had this Mingo whipped for some reason or other, and the next morning he was gone, along with his gun and his ammunition and some other buck that had had a touch of the whip a little while before. I wouldn't be a bit surprised to find that he's stirring up the rest of them and trying to get some sort of uprising started. They had one right along here, you know, back in '83, when Brentwood was burned to the ground and old Paul Curet got himself hung at his own gatepost."

"I helped cut him down—and then we started burning black men. I tell you, Allan, this river smelled like a fire in a slaughter-house for more than a fortnight!"

"So I've heard, and it might again. I'm just wondering if we ought to send the women down to New Orleans until this thing blows over."

"Russat's sending Madelaine and the daughters down on one of his sloops today. I hear he let the boys stay with him, those that are old enough to fire a gun, but I don't know, Allan—run from them now and the next time trouble comes up they'll be just that much harder to handle. I'm of a mind to face it out, come hell or high water. What's your situation here? Are your people quiet or have they caught the fever, too?"

Allan frowned, his mind ranging back over half-over- looked incidents, perhaps straws in the wind, perhaps nothing. "Hard to say, Captain. Grambling says they're restless and he caught a few of them wandering around at night, when they were supposed to be in the cabins, but they aren't insubordinate. They're doing their work and there hasn't been any more grumbling than usual. Why don't we organize some kind of committee and hunt this Mingo down and blow his damned head off? That ought to put an end to it."

Langley shook his head, his face and voice obviously regretful. "Almost impossible, I'm afraid, Allan. Mingo's a professional hunter. He knows the swamps the way we know the palms of our hands. You'd have to have an army to dig him out, and even then you'd probably lose some damned good men before it was done. No, Allah, the thing to do is watch your own cabins and your own people. He may try to slip in to stir them up, and if he does, there's a good chance to kill him before he can get away. Outside of that, there's damned little I know to do, except sit tight and see."

He got to his feet and slapped his wide-brimmed hat viciously against his dusty breeches. "Damn mutineers and rebels, anyway," he growled. "They ruined the colonies and now these black bastards are getting ready to ruin Louisiana." He adjusted the hat firmly on his head and held out his hand. "Let me know if anything comes up down here, and I'll do the same for you if there's any trouble at Britannia or Arlington."

He stomped down the steps into the saddle of the horse that one of the colored grooms had been holding for him. His hand lifted in a gesture of farewell, and Allan watched him ride away down the long avenue of oaks. When he had gone, Allan got to his feet and paced slowly down the gallery to a point where he could look out over the fields of cane, head-high now from the pounding rain and steaming heat of the spring that had come and gone, the tassels beginning to yellow in the sun. The crop was laid by and the slaves were scattered on a dozen different tasks. Some were cutting lumber and shingles at the edge of the timber, others sweated from dawn till dusk upon the unending task of raising and strengthening the levee. There were bricks to bake and supplies to unload and hogsheads to fashion. In spite of his exultant sense of satisfaction in the swiftly maturing crop, he was a little sorry that it was so far advanced. When the blacks were gathered in the fields, it was easy enough to keep track of them, but now that they were scattered like quail, it was a matter of luck and guesswork to maintain even the sketchiest form of "supervision. He and Grambling were the only white men on the plantation, and the direct management of the work gangs was delegated to colored foremen who had shown ability and intelligence above the average. Like minor tribal chiefs, they prided themselves upon exacting complete and absolute obedience; if they, too, were discontented ...

He swung back toward the gallery steps as he saw Manette, astride the gray gelding she had selected from the Constancia stables, flash around the corner of the house in a cloud of dust and a roar of hoofs and come to a sudden jolting stop at the foot of the steps. She slipped out of the saddle as a waiting groom ran forward and her heels clattered as she gained the gallery and ran toward him.

"Allan!" Her voice shook with her breathlessness and her face was streaked with sweat and dust. "They've killed Porter! Jock and Andio refused to work, and when he took the whip to them, they killed him with their axes! They've run for the swamp and he's down there with his head cut away and one arm chopped off!"

"Porter! Great God above!"

Porter had been the foreman in charge of the timber gang, an immense, coal-black man with a voice like a bull and a record of almost fanatical loyalty to Constancia.

"What about the others? Are they still there?" He was tense now, his lean body leaning forward as if he were about to spring, the fingers of both hands curling and straightening as if they were already clenched about Jock's and Andio's necks.

"They were when I left. They're muttering among themselves, but I think they're more scared than anything else." Her breath was coming more steadily now, but the slight trembling of the riding crop clutched in her white-knuckled fingers betrayed the agitation that still possessed her. "Where's Grambling? You'll have to send him—"

"Grambling's two miles away, clearing out the drainage ditches at the north end of the plantation. I'll send for him, but I can't wait." He lifted his voice in a shout that rang like a trumpet in the sultry heat of the sleepy July afternoon.

"Kelcho! Kelcho!"

He had brought the slave with him from New Orleans to act as his personal servant and bodyguard, and although he was sometimes out of sight, he was never beyond the sound of his master's voice. He came now, running through the open door, his fist clamped on the hilt of the cutlass that he alone, of all the slaves on the plantation, was allowed to wear.

"M'sieur." His eyes were as alert as a hunting dog's and there was a question in his voice.

"There's been a mutiny in the timber gang and Porter's been killed. We'll have to get out there right away. Get my pistols and fusil and the same for yourself." He wheeled around toward two Negro grooms who stared from the driveway in wide-eyed amazement. "Get two horses—mine and Kelcho's—and run, damn you! Run as you've never run before, or I'll have the black hide stripped off your backs!"

He turned back to find Manette's lips a tight line and her eyes dark with a premonition of approaching danger. "And this, I suppose, is some of Mingo's work?"

"Mingo?" His brows knotted into a scowl as he stared at her. "What do you know about Mingo and his work?"

"I was here when Russat's overseer came through two weeks ago. I knew then, Allan. This is the way it began in Santo Domingo. First a runaway, then recruits to join him, and then a mob killing and burning in the night." Her lips drew away from her teeth as she saw the horror of it all again. "My God, Allan, I can't go through that again!"

"You won't have to," he promised her. "I'll send you downriver as soon as I've settled this affair."

"And you'll go with me, won't you, Allan? *Por Dios,* I could not bear it unless I knew that you were safe!"

"With you? And leave all this?" The swift gesture of his arm took in the white walls of Constancia, the endless arpents of green fields, the *pigeonniers,* and the avenue of bearded oaks. He chuckled harshly, the sound of his laughter grotesque and terrible against the grim implacability of his face. "When I leave here they'll carry me away."

He broke off as Kelcho came running out on the gallery, his arms burdened with guns, his own two pistols already thrust into his belt. In the same instant, horses' hoofs drummed on the driveway and the two stable boys came running as if the devil pursued them, the saddled horses trotting at their heels.

"Allan! Allan!"

He stooped and kissed her quickly, his lips harsh and unyielding with the tenseness of his fury. "Send a messenger for Grambling and tell him to bring Matt with him. Matt can take Porter's place for the rest of the day."

He ran down the steps and vaulted into the saddle. His spurs gouged the stallion's flanks and he was gone in a roar of pounding hoofs, with Kelcho riding hard a half length behind. It was almost a mile and a half to the edge of the timber, and his mind turned bitter and hard as the arpents of tall cane swept by.

Never before had he given himself so completely and utterly to anything as he had to the fascination of Constancia. It had bred a love in him that was stronger than a passion for brandy or women or wealth, and he snarled deep in his throat at the thought that it was menaced by a pack of ragged savages from the depths of some African jungle. God only knew what he'd find at the timber. If the others had panicked and fled from the swamp, it would mean another thirty men for Mingo to lead against the plantations. But if they were still there, the thing was to get them back to work; to drive them so fiercely and unendingly that they would have no time to brood on the fact of Porter's death; no time to consider anything except the pain and weariness of their own bodies. They were almost at the edge of the cane fields now, and he slowed his mount a little and waved Kelcho up beside him.

"When we leave the cane, drop back about twenty feet behind so you can cover me. I'll ride in on them, but I can't watch them all while I'm on top of them. If they start trouble, shoot and shoot to kill."

He moved ahead again, seeing the tall crests of the timber rising against the sky, green and serene and almost tropically luxuriant, untroubled by the drama of savagery and death that had been played out on the ground below. In the space between two breaths, the stallion had shot out of the cane and was charging across the clearing where the blacks had been working. They were still there, white-eyed, bunched, their axes in their hands, balanced between fear and flight and the rigorous discipline that bound them to the land. The bloodied mass of flesh that had been their foreman sprawled in dust turned black and caked with blood. The head lay a half-dozen feet from the body, grinning up at emptiness. One arm had been chopped away and there was a deep gash across his waist.

The slaves seemed to shrink together as Allan rode in, and a few clutched their axes a little tighter as if they were prepared to defend themselves against him. He drew rein a scant three feet from the dark ranks, and he heard Kelcho check his horse so that the hoofbeats died a score of feet behind him. It seemed to him that the skin of his whole body had tightened so that he was encased in a binding shell that was alternately icy cold and then shot through with fire. He let his eyes range slowly over the dark faces that stared up at him, and picked out a tall man called Laton as the most likely to speak for the entire group.

He managed to keep the blind fury out of his voice, but there was in it the deep note of a distant sword clanging against a shield. "Laton, tell me, what happened here?"

Laton shifted his feet uneasily and his eyes shifted from side to side as if he sought support from his fellows. "I am not too sure, m'sieur. I working there." His arm indicated a patch of timber some fifty feet away. "Then I hear Porter yell. He say, 'You work and work now, by God!' He start for Andio with whip and Andio throw ax at him and cut his belly wide like a fish. Porter, he big man and he keep coming. Then Jock come running, swing ax like man cut tree. I see Porter go down and Jock chop at him till head, arm—all gone. Then they run, hide somewhere in timber. We wait here."

He was bathed in sweat when he finished and his eyes were wild and terrified, but Allan had the story. Jock and Andio had mutinied. God only knew why, but it was a thousand to one that Mingo had incited them. Now they were gone and the first seeds of rebellion had been sown.

"All right, let's get on with the work." His stomach had contracted into a frozen knot and his mouth was as dry as leather scorching in the sun, but he spoke as casually as if their obedience were a foregone conclusion. "Laton, you and one of the other boys rig up a stretcher out of a couple of poles and some branches and take Porter back. Don't take him to the cabins. Put him in the carriage house, in the shade, and then get back here as fast as God will let you. If I catch you spreading wild stories around the cabins I'll have you hung up and whipped until you can't walk. Go on, get started!"

The issue of obedience or rebellion hung in the balance for a long tense moment. Then Laton jerked his head at another slave who stood beside him and they moved off toward the timber to cut the poles and brush that would be needed for the stretcher. As if their acquiescence had been a signal, the other blacks seemed to relax and draw apart a little, holding their axes more easily, reassured now that it seemed certain they would not be held responsible or punished for Jock's and Andio's outburst of savagery. One by one,' they turned and went back to the work that had occupied them before Porter had been killed. When the last of them had gone, Allan let the breath escape from his lungs in a long gasp and felt the rigid stiffness begin to drain out of his shoulders and his loins.

He sat there, unmoving and inscrutable, while Laton and the other man loaded Porter's butchered body on the makeshift stretcher and trudged off through the cane with it. He was still sitting there when Grambling and Matt, a huge black man, came spurring in with foam dripping from the bridles and the horses heaving and sweating in the blazing heat.

"Put Matt in charge and stay with them until they're settled down, Wilson. Tell Matt I want them worked so hard today they won't have time to think about this now or talk about it tonight. Come up to the house in an hour or two. We've got to figure out a few plans, and the sooner we get started, the better off we'll be."

He wheeled the stallion and saw Kelcho remount and fall in behind him. The tall stalks of the sugar cane hid the bloody clearing and glistened with metallic greens and burning gold like an unending horde of treasure. There was a faint fragrance to it and now and then a vagrant breeze rustled the leaves with the sound of men talking in muted voices in the distance. The fierce lust of possession that only this land and these tapering stalks could rouse stirred in him again. He would hold this, some inner voice whispered fiercely, hold it and protect it against all comers. Even though the oak avenue of Constancia might grow sodden with blood and choked with battered bodies, he would never surrender it. This was his, created from the bosom of the earth itself.

While he lived, he would suffer no one to take it from him.

CHAPTER SIXTEEN

MANETTE was waiting for him on the upper gallery, her amber skin glowing against the snowy whiteness of the sheer lawn dress she wore, a frosted silver pitcher filled with Barbados rum punch on the rattan table beside her. She met him at the gallery doorway that led into the upper hall, cool and quiet and serene, a breath of loveliness and sanity after the heat and violence and sweat and blood of the clearing at the edge of the timber. He was hot and dirty and begrimed with dust. His shirt was plastered against his back and the two pistols he had taken with him still bulged from the white linen waistband that he wore. The soft-spoken, conservative planter who dined on silver plate and gravely considered the fluctuations of the sugar market was gone; this was the MacMurran of Bonneterre, hard-eyed, thin-lipped, terrible in bus fury, ruthless in reprisals. He glared at her before he strode across the gallery and tilted the silver pitcher to his lips, disdaining the empty tumblers on the table, intent only on the coolness of the punch that soothed his parched throat and relieved the painful tautness of nerves drawn tight as fiddle strings.

"Were—were the others still there, Allan?"

"They were," he said shortly, "and they're back at work again with Matt and Wilson driving them. But what I want to know," he flared out, "is what in hell you're doing in an outfit like that and why in the devil you haven't got your luggage packed and waiting to go."

She faced his anger steadily, although the blood rushed into her cheeks and some of the warmth of welcome died in her eyes.

"I'm not going to New Orleans, Allan. Not unless you go with me." She threw up her hand in a gesture of protest as he started to speak, and hurried on. "This is my home now, just as it's yours, and if you can stay, here, I can too. You told me once I couldn't go to Havana with you, but I went. Now you're trying to tell me that I can't stay here, but I will, Allan. *Válgame Dios,* I will not move from here until Constancia is safe or until we both are dead!"

He stared at her with hard eyes, his booted feet wide apart and the silver pitcher still in his hands.

"I could have you roped and carried on board that sloop and taken to New Orleans," he growled.

"Yes? And you would lose the men you sent to do the roping!" The white skirt swirled up about her thighs and the top of one red silk stocking yielded a silver-hilted poniard, its blade as narrow and keen as an adder's tongue, its razor-sharp edges glittering in the sunlight. "You will not send me away, Allan. If you stay, I stay. Is it understood?"

The hard lines around his mouth relaxed a little and there was the sudden flash of white teeth against the swarthy darkness of his face. "A tiger cat! By God, Manette, I'd almost forgotten that you carry the devil always inside you. Stay, then. And when they come howling up that line of oaks, I'll give you a cutlass and send you out to beat them off singlehanded." He lifted the pitcher and drank again, and when he lowered it only the dregs remained. He dropped into a chair beside the table and mopped the sweat and dirt from his face with a handkerchief that turned from white to gray as he progressed.

"Have Cragon bring me paper and a pen, Manette, and let him mix another pitcher full of that rum while he's about it. It's a damned fine drink for a day like this."

While they waited, he told her what had happened at the edge of the timber, and when the paper and the pen arrived, he wrote brief notes to Captain Langley at Britannia Plantation and Russat at Arlington, and dispatched a colored stable boy up the river with a good horse between his legs. It might or might not affect them, but at least they would be in touch with the progress of events and in a position to take whatever precautions might appear appropriate.

Grambling rode in to report that the timber gang was working steadily, and there had been no sign of Jock or Andio. Matt was driving the men hard and by night they would be so exhausted they would not spin too wild a tale in the dusty street before the cabins. They would bury Porter tonight with as little fanfare as possible to avoid exciting the other slaves. And what in hell were they going to do if the slaves up and down the river did decide to rise against them?

Allan considered the question silently, the smoke of his cigar rising in slow wreaths above his head. "Well," he admitted, "there's not much we can do until we begin to see what happens. We'll search the cabins for weapons this afternoon—not that it means a hell of a lot. You couldn't gather up all the cane knives and axes and scythes that are scattered around this place if you worked from now until hell froze over. But we can be sure they haven't any firearms, and the fact that we're searching may put the fear of the Lord into a few of them. Another thing we can do is get all our own guns out of the *garçonnière* and offices and bring them in here. We'll see that they're loaded and primed every minute from now on, and I want plenty of extra powder and lead on hand. Great God!" His fist slammed down on the table. "I wish I had those two little brass cannons I always kept on the gallery at the Maison Blanc in Bonneterre! They'd make short work of any damned uprising that came along!"

Manette leaned forward with sudden alertness in her eyes. "Send for them, then! Kelcho can go to Bonneterre and bring them back, and bring a score of your bloodiest cutthroats with him, too, while he's about it. I'll warrant there'll be no uprising here while they're at hand. You couldn't raise enough blacks on the river to attack a squad of those wolves from Bonneterre!"

Allan's eyes swiveled slowly around until they rested on her face. "It's not too damned impractical," he admitted slowly. "Kelcho could be in Bonneterre by noon tomorrow and be back here with the men and guns by a little after daylight of the second day. If the blacks hold off that long—"

He turned to stare at the impassive Kelcho squatting on the gallery floor some thirty feet away. "He knows his way through the bayous," he mused, "and he can lead the men back here without coming within a dozen miles of the Governor's men at New Orleans. Kelcho," he shouted abruptly, "get up and come over here. I want you to go to Bonneterre for me tonight."

The slow sun dropped out of sight behind the western rim of the world, its passing heralded by a funeral pyre of gold and orange flaming in the sky. The soft dusk came, and in its shadows Porter was buried in the plot set aside for slaves who died on the plantation. There would be no marker or tombstone above his head, but it would not be missed, for no one on Constancia would soon forget the time or manner of his passing. Allan and Grambling split the night into two watches and each in turn peered out into the darkness from the upper gallery like lookouts perched high on the crossarms of a pirate brig.

For Manette, it was an endless night of fitful and uneasy sleep. She rolled and tossed behind the sheltering mosquito netting that draped her bed, listening first to Grambling and then to Allan pacing back and forth across the gallery through the laggard, sullen hours. The strength of her own determination to remain at Constancia puzzled her a little, even now that it was fixed and immutable. Certainly, it was not for love of Allan. They had settled down comfortably together, still rich in the physical passion that they shared, but barren of the tenderness or sentiment that would have involved their emotions as deeply as their bodies. No, it was something else. A clinging to such security as she had, perhaps. As matters stood now, Allan was her only barrier against the world, and Allan and Constancia had grown so close together that in abandoning one she would have abandoned the other. While she was here, even subject to attack, there was always the possibility that she would escape unscathed; but let her run like some frightened child to New Orleans and it might be difficult or impossible to return again. She shifted restlessly on the silk sheet, watching the white bars of moonlight flow into the room. Illogically, the memory of the evening on Bienville Street with Etienne came unbidden to her mind. She could laugh about it now, a little ruefully, but still triumphantly. The imperious attraction that had driven her into his arms was still alive, still something to be beaten down and pushed aside from day to day, but her shrewdly calculating brain warned her that it was futile to pursue it further and that her single chance of survival was bound up with Allan and with him alone. She heard his tired footsteps passing by outside her window and on sudden impulse she squirmed out past the mosquito netting and drew a silken robe that was no more than mist about her. Fumbling in the darkness, she found her slippers beside the bed and slipped silently across the room to stand in the floor-deep window that opened on the gallery.

It was almost morning and the faint gray light in the east was beginning to be touched with the faintest hint of rose and purple. A dawn breeze had sprung up, rustling the scorched leaves of the trees and pressing the thin folds of her robe lightly against her. Allan was standing at the gallery rail staring out toward the river. His shoulders drooped in weariness and she knew that it was an exhaustion not only of the body but of the spirit. She called to him softly.

"Allan! Allan, is everything all right?"

He whirled to face her and she saw his shoulders straighten in an involuntary and instinctive refusal to betray the dragging weight of fatigue and nervous tension that he carried.

"I thought you were asleep." He came slowly across the moon-splashed gallery until he stood before her, his eyes warm and approving as he appraised the tawny figure so sensuously revealed through the fragile network of her gown. "You're a pretty thing to see at this time of the morning, *niñita*, but I'm damned if you wouldn't distract a sentry so badly that Mingo and all his men could climb up here and sit on the gallery rail without even being noticed."

She tilted her head and smiled at him from half-closed eyes, flirting and wooing him as flagrantly as any quadroon strolling up and down the levee. If she could make him forget his weariness and the strain of waiting …

"And you like that, *corazón*? You do not think I am too—indiscreet?"

He laughed then, pulling her to him so that her body was like fire and velvet in his arms, her lips half parted and turned up to his.

"You'd soon find that you're far too indiscreet if I could leave this gallery for half an hour." He kissed her, lightly at first, and then with a sudden violence that left her bruised and shaken. "But that will have to wait—a little while, at least. Ring for some coffee and brandy to help me get the sleep out of my eyes. And Manette." His voice halted her as she started to turn away. "You'd best put on a robe that covers you a little more completely. I've had Grambling leave his cottage and move in here so we'll all be together if we're attacked. He might come out at any time, and I prefer not to share your charms—or even the appearance of them."

He said it lightly enough, but there had been another note there, too; an almost indistinguishable tone of pride and owner-ship, more suited to some freshly bedded bridegroom still tingling with newly discovered ecstasies than to a hard-bitten sea rover who had begun their intimacy by mocking her as she knelt tugging at his boots. Her eyes were thoughtful as she slipped into a satin robe of gold and scarlet and straightened her hair with a jewel-encrusted comb of ivory. If there was such a thing as love between man and woman—a belief she had almost entirely abandoned—and if Allan was unconsciously yielding to it, her position here was far stronger than she had believed possible. There was always, of course, the gibbering Dorothée lurking in a murky shadowland of madness, but even that must pass in time, and if she could hold Allan until then …

She heard the dragging footsteps of the sleepy mulatto maid bringing the coffee and brandy down the hall and hurried out to wave her on toward the gallery, where Allan was pacing to and fro. The sun was out and the little breeze had died as silently as it had come. They could hear the stir of movement in the slave quarters at the rear, with cooking pots banging and women call-ing back and forth and field hands shouting at their mules as they harnessed them to plows and wagons for the work of the day that lay ahead. Grambling came clumping down the hall in riding boots, his eyes drugged with sleep and a two-day beard bristling upon his cheeks.

"Good mawnin', suh an' señorita." The dull eyes rested on her for an instant with the scarcely veiled insolence that seemed always to possess him when he addressed her. "Ah judge suh, theah's been no trouble since you came on guahd?"

"Not a sound anywhere." He gestured hospitably toward the coffee and brandy on the table beside him. "Fix yourself a coffee royal to help get awake, and then I think you'd better go to the back and get the gangs started for the day. They can work under their foremen, for a while at least, and you can come back here after you get them on their way. I'm damned if I can believe that we'd have an attack in broad daylight, but I've worked with these apes just long enough to know that you can't tell a damned thing about what they're likely to do next."

The day slowly dragged itself away. The heat mounted as the hours passed until the air danced and wavered above the burning fields. Even the birds fell silent; the river was like a stagnant lake; the oak leaves drooped and turned from green to gray under the coating of dust that settled upon them. On the gallery they played *écarté* until the figures on the cards blurred before their eyes. Grambling retired to his room to try to sleep and Allan paced restlessly up and down, tried to work on his accounts, and finally abandoned them when the sweat dripping from his forehead muddied the papers where he tried to write.

"By God!" His temper was strained to the breaking point, and his voice rasped like a file cutting against sheet steel. "I'll make that goddamned Mingo pay for this, if it's the last thing I ever do! When those buckos come in from Bonneterre, I'll take them into the swamp and we'll find that bastard if we have to run him into hell!"

Manette, lounging in a long wicker chair, stared out at the river and the oaks without attempting to answer him. The waiting had been hard for her that day, too, perhaps even more so than it had been for Allan, for she knew what a black mutiny could be. All day she had been trying to force the acid memories of Santo Domingo from her mind, but they kept crowding back with all their grisly cargo of violence and murder and rapine and unholy torture. It was like a nightmare that went on and on after the dream was done, a monster that gnawed upon her brain and tore her quivering nerves to shreds, over and over again.

Her eyes caught a flicker of movement on the river road far to the north, a cloud of dust above the unending flatness of the land. It enveloped the galloping horse and the rider spurring it forward through the choked stillness of the afternoon, but now she could hear the faint drum of hoofs against the earth, and she whirled to Allan with a startled ejaculation of dismay.

He had caught the sound and movement too, and he was leaning out over the gallery rail, his eyes narrowed as he tried to pierce the fog of dust, his knuckles white from the pressure of his fingers on the steel.

"Allan, can you see who it is?"

He shook his head, his eyes never leaving the billowing tower of dust. "From Arlington or Britannia, more than likely—and killing a horse to get here with whatever news he has."

The dust dropped a little as the rider slowed for the entrance gate, and they could see that it was a slight, bareheaded girl, still in the first flush of adolescence, mounted on a coal-black stallion that was flecked with foam. She sent the horse flying up the long oak avenue in a last desperate burst of speed, and Allan turned and ran into the house so he could gain the lower floor and meet her at the steps. Manette tucked up the skirt of her thin blue cottonade dress and went flying after him, her slim legs flashing and her black hair streaming behind her like a banner in the wind. She reached the driveway just as the child jerked the horse to a stop and flung herself out of the saddle. She was swaying with exhaustion, and the unbound mass of her tangled ash-blonde hair framed a face that seemed to be nothing but wide eyes almost screaming with terror and lips that trembled uncontrollably.

"My God!" The words seemed to be ripped out of Allan's throat. "It's Langley's youngest—Lucille, I think it is."

He strode forward and scooped the child up in his arms, just as she seemed about to collapse. "Get some brandy and some cold water and a cloth." He carried her up the steps and into the shade of the gallery, and Manette turned and raced toward the pantry at the back of the house. There was no time to wait for some confused and frightened servant now. She ladled water feverishly into an empty champagne cooler from the great earthern jar where it was left to cool and settle, jerked two snowy white dinner napkins from a cabinet beside the wall, and snatched up a half-empty bottle of brandy. Her heels rang like pistol shots as she ran down the hall and she burst out on the gallery into a shrill babble of words from the almost hysterical child.

" ...and then—and then after they burned Arlington, they came marching down the road to our house!" She was gasping so that she could hardly talk, and her young breasts rose and fell like birds fluttering in a fowler's net.

"And when was that, Lucille? How long ago?" Allan's voice was quiet and soothing. He had crumpled up one of the dinner napkins and plunged it into the water, and now he was wiping the sweat and dust and tears from her face.

"It was—oh, not over an hour ago. Papa put me on a horse when we saw them coming and he—he told me to ride here and warn you that they were at Britannia!" Her voice soared up into a wail of misery and panic and Manette brushed Allan aside and slipped an arm around the trembling child as she lifted a glass of brandy to the quivering lips.

"Don't cry, *muchachita*," she whispered comfortingly. "It will be all right now. Here, drink this and it will make you better."

The girl gulped the fiery liquor obediently, coughing and gagging as it burned her throat, and then relaxed a little as the alcohol was absorbed almost immediately into her blood. She fumbled at the pocket of her dress and brought a crumpled envelope addressed to Allan in a slashing, angular hand.

"Papa sent you this note." She held it out timidly and nestled a little closer to Manette as Allan ripped it open. When he turned back to them, his face had hardened into the furious mask Manette had seen in the instant that he shot Grenaldi in the house at Bonneterre. He held the note out to her and she read it swiftly, holding it so that whatever evil tidings it might bring would not be visible to Lucille's eyes.

It was brief enough, and quite evidently written in a moment of haste, snatched from the bloody claws of terrible and immediate danger:

Allan MacMurran, Esq.:

Arlington is burned and Russat dead. The blacks are within a mile of Britannia, and as they number near a hundred, I take it Russat's slaves have joined them. When this reaches you it will be too late to come to our aid, and I beg you not to attempt it. Keep Lucille with you and give her such protection as you can.

Sncrly,
DAVID LANGLEY

Manette turned back to Lucille and saw that the girl's eyes had grown heavy from the effects of the brandy and the reaction from the fear and nervous tension she had endured. Her pale face and ash-blonde hair had the quality of a cameo against the dark background of the Bombay blackwood chair, and the still immature curves of her young breasts and thighs suggested that someday this would be a beauty who would turn men's hearts to fire.

She turned to Manette, with the drowsiness drugging her so that her eyes were like deep blue pools. "I'm so tired," she whispered, "so terribly tired ….

"Of course you are, *muchachita*." Manette shot a quick glance of warning at Allan as he seemed about to speak. "Let us go upstairs, where you can lie down and rest a little while."

With her arm around the child's slender waist, she helped her up the stairs and into a jalousie-shadowed bedroom directly adjoining her own. She helped her strip away the sweaty, dust-caked garments she had worn and slipped a short silk chemise, such as she herself had worn in the islands, over Lucille's head. As she worked she heard the great plantation bell clanging in a peremptory summons to the slaves who were scattered from the river to the swamp. Lucille's eyes flew wide in sudden terror and her slim finger tips dug themselves into the flesh of Manette's arm.

"The bell! The bell! Papa rang our bell like that when he saw them coming! Are they here? Are they here now?"

Manette's hand smoothed the child's forehead reassuringly. "Oh, no, they are not here, Lucille. That is only the bell that calls the slaves in from the fields at the end of the day. Try to sleep a little while, *muchachita*." She eased the slim body down on the bed, feeling it relax a little under the comfort of her words. The brandy had been potent and she had given Lucille enough of it to befuddle a far more battered toper than this wisp of a girl. It was serving its purpose now, for as she watched the almost transparent lids closed over the wide blue eyes and Lucille's lips parted in a long sigh that was the prelude to almost instant slumber. Moving lightly, Manette tiptoed across the room and closed the door gently behind her. The night would almost certainly erupt in hell and horror. There seemed little enough doubt of that in the light of Langley's note, but for a few hours the blonde girl in the room behind her would be free from its terror and its mounting pressure.

She ran out to the upper gallery, where she could look out across the whole plantation, and found it empty and deserted. From every direction she could see the work gangs moving toward the house, hurrying down the narrow plantation lanes with a haste that reflected their own apprehension at this unprecedented signal to abandon their work while the sun was still high in the sky. She looked down in time to see Allan come down the steps and hand two envelopes to a waiting stable boy, who leaped into the saddle and raced away down the avenue of oaks that led to the river road.

"Allan," she called, and saw him turn and lift his head to look up at her. "Allan, where are you sending him now?"

"Downriver." His voice was tight. "I'm sending word to the plantations below us so they can prepare themselves. You'd best come down and be sure the house is well stocked with food and water. It may be we'll have to withstand a siege."

He turned and disappeared beneath the gallery and she picked up her skirts and ran for the stairway to the lower hall. The house servants were milling in an uneasy knot beside the pantry door, and she summoned Cragon to her with an impatient gesture of her hand. "The slaves at Arlington have risen and burned the house and murdered Russat and his sons." She saw him begin to tremble. "They are at Britannia now, and there's no doubt they'll be here soon. I want you to bring in a dozen hams, whatever bread there may be baked, such fruits as there are, and enough water to fill every jar and container we can find. See that every jalousie is closed and locked on the inside, and set two of the maids to gathering clean white cloths that may be used for bandages if they are needed."

She disregarded his stammering response and ran out into the patterned garden that lay behind the house. Allan and Grambling were standing at the end of the long row of cabins that housed the slaves. Negro women too old to work in the fields were scurrying back and forth and building crackling fires beneath the black iron cooking pots that stood on the narrow street.

"God only knows whether they'll stay neutral or join the others when the attack begins." It was Allan's voice, throbbing with a harsh note of urgency that underlined and emphasized his anxiety. "No way to lock them up, so there's nothing to do but feed them well and threaten them with sudden death if they do join in. I don't know how they'll take it."

Grambling nodded morosely, waving his arm to urge on the first file of workers who had just appeared at the far end of the lane. "They'll take it hahd, suh, but they'll take it." He patted the two pistols thrust into his belt and glared at the approaching line of slaves. "Theah's no chance that yoah men from Bonneteah might get heah befoah th' black bastahds come down on us?"

Allan shook his head wearily. "No more chance than a heretic in hell. They'll have to travel by night and drag the cannon behind them. We'll be damned lucky if they're here by midmorning tomorrow." He turned and saw Manette standing a little distance away. "Is the child asleep?"

"She's lost to the world. Allan, don't you think we should send that girl downriver while we can?"

A frown gathered between his eyes, and his left hand crept up to stroke his chin. "I'm afraid to now, Manette. God only knows whether this trouble is confined to the north of us or not. When it was like this in '83, they rose all up and down the river on the same afternoon. For all I know, there's as much danger below us as there is above, and I can't risk sending her into their arms. While she's here, she'll be as safe as any of us—and I'm more than half convinced that we'll be able to hold them off."

He took her arm and turned away toward the *garçonnière*. "You can help me gather up the guns and the powder and shot. Thank God you learned how to use a fowling piece when you were a girl in Santo Domingo."

She had to run to keep pace with his long-legged strides, and for the next hour it seemed to her that she did nothing but run frantically back and forth, supervising and managing and ordering and hurrying until her very bones ached with weariness and the sweat poured from her face and ran in an unending rivulet between her breasts.

Then it was done, all that could be done. The muttering, sullen-eyed field hands had made no move to leave their quarters, but they were restless and uneasy, a potential threat that could not be evaded or escaped. There was no way to confine or restrain them, except by the fragile bonds of fear and loyalty. The house servants, with a higher degree of intelligence and, presumably, of loyalty, were clustered like a flock of frightened birds in the serving pantry and the hall outside.

There were food and water on the upper gallery, and a startlingly complete array of pistols and fusils and muskets and fowling pieces and powder and lead. A section of the gallery that faced the river had been barricaded with heavy timbers to form a makeshift rampart. A half-dozen of the wickedly long-bladed cane knives leaned against the wall and softwood torches dipped in tar stood ready to be kindled and flung into the faces of the attackers.

Manette had changed into a boy's costume that she sometimes wore on these searing nights; an outfit of knee-length pantaloons of plum-colored cottonade and a yellow blouse with the neckline slashed so low it revealed the soft valley between her breasts.

The night came on and a full moon hung above the river until the land was bathed in yellow light, so that the grim group waiting on the gallery could trace the course of the river road and the levee a good two miles away. A dull, ominous glare reddened the sky far to the north just before midnight, and they knew Langley and his household had gone down to defeat and Britannia was ablaze.

Allan swung back from his post at the gallery rail to face Grambling and Manette. "It won't be too long now. As soon as they've run through Langley's brandy and rum, they'll start this way. Chances are they'll make it here just about daylight."

Manette's body quivered with an involuntary twitching of muscles she could not control, but Grambling's voice came up out of the shadows with the same drawl of insolent contemptuousness that it had always carried.

"That could be a damn sight wuss, suh. We'll be able to see weah we're shootin' an' it'll be hardah foah them to sneak past us an' catch us from the reah."

The conversation died again, and after a while Manette looked up to see Lucille standing in the doorway. The period of her drugged sleep had passed, and as she came but into the moonlight that bathed the gallery, Manette saw that she still wore the short chemise with one of Manette's filmiest and most transparent dressing gowns thrown over her shoulders. She caught Allan's look of startled amazement and saw Grambling's eyes light up with sudden interest. For an instant she considered sending the girl back into her room for a heavier robe and then she shrugged her shoulders and dismissed the matter from her mind. It was a night of stifling heat and, after all, Lucille was little more than a child. What difference did it make if the men did see the smoothly tapering legs and the smooth curve of ivory shoulders? They had both seen women and girls before. She held out her hand to Lucille and felt a quick flush of pleasure as the girl ran across the gallery to her.

"You are feeling better, *muchachita?* I believe the sleep has done you good."

"Oh, yes, thank you. I am rested now." She turned and her eyes searched the road to the north, but the glare in the sky was gone and there was only the soft arc of the night, splattered with stars and washed with the golden flood tide of the moon. "Has there been any word from Britannia?"

"Nothing at all, Lucille." There was nothing to be gained by telling her now of the glow that had throbbed and faded against the sky.

The empty hours ran on into infinity, the moon reached its zenith and disappeared behind the peaked rooftop, and Manette dozed a little in her chair. She wakened in startled alarm as she heard Allan's voice with a new note of urgency in it:

"I can hear them coming! Listen!"

She scarcely breathed and for an instant it seemed that there was only silence in the night. Then she heard them, far to the north on the river road. They were singing, some barbaric chant that she had never heard before. The empty air carried the deep, far-off murmur of their voices, rising and falling interminably, punctuated now and then by a wordless, quavering shout. Her breath caught in her throat and for a moment the impulse to turn and flee madly into the darkness was so strong that she clung to the arms of the chair in order to restrain herself. Grambling had leaped to his feet and run to the rail to stand beside MacMurran, and in an instant she was beside them, peering out through the fading moonlight in a vain attempt to catch a glimpse of the marching horde that was bearing down upon them.

"Where, Allan, where?"

Her voice was steady enough, but her heart was pounding as if it sought to tear itself free from her breast.

"Too far away to see. About two miles, more or less, I'd say. Just about where our land joins Britannia."

"Take 'em th' best paht of a half an houah to covah that much ground. Anything special you'd like to have done between now an' then, suh?"

"Check all the guns. Be sure they're primed and ready to fire. Then bring them over here against the rail where we can get them as we need them. Manette, go downstairs and have Cragon bring up a pot of red-hot coals from the kitchen. We may need them to fire those torches, if they get in close enough for us to use them."

As Manette hurried across the gallery, she saw that Lucille had collapsed in one of the tall Jamaica chairs and buried her face in her hands, as if she could not bear to see the horde of howling blacks a second time. Her robe had fallen away so that she seemed to be almost naked, the slim figure of ivory and rose tender and undefended in the last wash of the moonlight.

They had come into view by the time she had sent Cragon stumbling on his errand and regained the vantage point of the upper gallery; a shifting, shouting mass of shadowy, half-seen figures, distinguished for a moment in sharp-edged silhouettes, as the torches they carried flared above them, sinking back into black and shapeless anonymity as the night wind died and the torches guttered and sparked. There were three in the lead who rode on horseback, transformed by the cruel alchemy of the moonlight into giants towering above the earth. They drew rein at the gate where the oak avenue entered the river road, and Manette could hear them shouting, ordering their straggling followers to close in behind them in preparation for the imminent attack.

Manette felt Allan's hand on her arm, and looked up to see his lips twisted into a half-rueful, half-reckless smile.

"We'll know the answer in a little while, and I think that we'll make out all right. But in case anything should go wrong, I just want you to know—you've been damned lovely, Manette."

"Oh, Allan—Allan!" She flung herself against him, pressing her face against his chest and pulling him to her as if she would never let him go. But then his hands were on her wrists and he was forcing her away. A jerk of his head indicated the shelter behind the heavy timber barricade, where Lucille was already crouched.

"Your post's back there, *niñita*—and keep your head down." The reckless smile flickered on his lips again, and she stared up at him with a new respect for this man who could laugh in the face of death and find time and courage to pay her a compliment while his enemies were almost at his very doorstep.

"Get along now." His voice was as warm and pleasant as it had been before, but there was no mistaking the fact that this time it was a command. She turned and hurried away to drop down behind the barricade, peering over its top at the dark mass of men on the river road.

As she watched, one of the riders lifted his arm and they began to pour in through the gate.

CHAPTER SEVENTEEN

THEY DID NOT come on the run, as Manette had half expected. Indeed there was a certain air of leisurely and unhurried arrogance about their advance, as if they were so confident of their power that victory was a foregone conclusion. As they drew closer, she could see that the rider who had motioned them on was a short, squarely built Negro, with shoulders so wide and arms so long that he was grotesque and monstrous. The narrow forehead slanted back, sharply from above his eyes and his lips were thick and pendulous below a wide, flat nose that seemed scarcely to emerge from the puffed heaviness of his cheeks. He rode with Jock on one side of him and Andio on the other, promoted to be his lieutenants because of their familiarity with the terrain and buildings of Constancia.

Allan swore softly as he identified them and half lifted the musket in his hands. But the distance was still too great, and he relapsed into his former frozen immobility with only his hard eyes moving as they ranged up and down the column of the approaching slaves. The blacks moved unhurriedly, but they were loud and boisterous, flushed with their successes at Arlington and Britannia, half drunk from the brandy and rum they had pillaged and swigged as the plantations burned. Their trampling feet raised a cloud of dust about them, and now and then a high, wavering shout shrilled out somewhere in the column and traveled up and down its length.

Peering over the barricade, Manette could see that the three riders carried muskets across their saddle bows, and each of them had a brace of pistols thrust into his belt. Behind them the first thin light of the morning gleamed dully on muskets and fusils and fowling pieces that the blacks handled with the reckless carelessness of total ignorance of their danger. Those who had not been fortunate enough to obtain a gun from the pillaged plantations carried long, razor-tipped cane knives, and many of them had completed their armament with heavy oak or cypress clubs, hacked out of the stretches of timber through which they had passed.

The leading rider, who was almost certainly Mingo, drew rein and threw up his arm in a gesture of command when they were about three hundred feet short of the house. The undisciplined horde crowded up around him, pushing and shoving each other in a babel of sound. Mingo stood up in his stirrups and they could hear him roaring like a caged lion as he tried to beat down the voices that bubbled and eddied about him.

Grambling lifted a musket and steadied it against one of the pillars as he drew a careful bead on the wide-shouldered figure towering above the milling swarm of blacks. His finger tightened on the trigger, but before he could fire Allan's voice cracked in his ears like a bull whip snapping above his head.

"Hold it, Wilson. It's too long a shot to be sure, and there's no use wasting powder and lead. Let them come in closer, and as soon as you fire, grab another gun and throw your empty one back behind the barricade so Lucille can reload. Manette, I want you to stay behind that barricade as much as you can, but I want your gun in action, too, when they charge. Keep shooting unless you see that Lucille is falling behind on her reloading. If that happens, give her a hand. We can't afford to be caught up here with all the guns empty at the same time." His eyes shifted to

Lucille's crouched and gleaming figure. "I wish to God you had more clothes on, but it's too late to do anything about it now. You stay down behind that barricade, no matter what happens. By God, if I see your head sticking up, I'll take a shot at you myself! You do know how to reload these guns, don't you?"

She nodded dumbly, her eyes wide with terror and excitement, and then as his gaze continued to bore into her, she seemed to find her voice again. "I—I've reloaded lots of times for Papa and my brothers when they were shooting on the river."

He nodded in satisfaction, and his voice lost some of its harshness. "You'll make it, all right. Just stay down behind those timbers and you'll be safe."

He whirled back to the railing as a shout sprang up from the attackers and grew into a monstrous, bestial roar. They had spread out to a full forty-foot front between the double lines of oaks, and even as he turned they broke into a shambling charge that gained speed as they advanced. Mingo and his two lieutenants cantered a little ahead, their reins loose, muskets in one hand and a raised pistol ready in the other. Manette had been trembling like a leaf from the moment they left the river road and turned into the avenue, but now, as she lifted herself to her knees and felt the unyielding metal of the brass fowling piece beneath her fingers, the quivering died and she experienced a sense of almost icy calmness. Her eyes measured the gun sights against the blackness of Jock's sweating chest, and when she heard Allan's husky whisper, "Let them have it!" her fingers tightened on the trigger as smoothly and evenly as though she were firing at a flight of ducks wheeling down upon some still lagoon. The roar of the heavy charge deafened her and the walnut stock kicked back against her shoulder like a hard-swung sledge, but through the smoke and the acrid smell of powder that eddied about her, she saw Jock reel in the saddle and then slump limply to the ground.

Andio was down, too, but it seemed that Mingo was wrapped in some invisible mantle of protection, for his horse had swerved at the last moment and Allan's bullet had sent a shower of splinters flying from his cantle and then crashed on to bury itself in the plunging horse's hip.

She flung the empty fowling piece aside and snatched up a loaded musket that stood ready to her hand. Allan was cursing savagely in a bitter monotone that cut its way through the noise and turmoil like a cutlass slashing away a field of cane. Grambling was firing as calmly and steadily as some inanimate machine, sliding the empty weapons across the floor to Lucille's feet and aiming slowly and carefully before he sent a ball smashing down into the black bodies that came nearer and nearer. Manette jerked aside as a pistol bullet rang on the railing, not three inches from her head, and then, with a motion so swiftly unthinking that it could only have been instinctive, she snapped a shot at the half-naked black who had run a little ahead of the line and stood staring up at the gallery with his pistol still smoking in his hand. He threw his hands up to his throat as the heavy musket ball tore through his flesh and stumbled backward a half-dozen faltering steps before he turned and fell with blood gushing out between his fingers.

A half dozen of the blacks sent the blazing torches they had carried hurtling through the air to sputter and flame on the gallery floor, and Manette dropped her gun and scuttled forward on hands and knees to dispose of them before they set fire to the wood. It was easier and faster to fling them back over the rail than to try to put them out, and she sent them flying through the air, turning and gleaming like gigantic pinwheels, trailing long comets of black smoke behind them.

The blacks' charge had carried them to within a scant thirty feet of the gallery steps, but they had begun to waver under the pitiless and unceasing fire of Grambling's and Allan's guns. Mingo raged up and down before them, shaking his musket above his head as he tried to urge them forward. Manette snatched up a musket and fired at him, with the half-formed thought in mind that if she could destroy their leadership, the mob would break and run, but the ball kicked up a puff of dust at his feet, and as he turned and fired furiously she heard first a musket and then a pistol ball crash into the heavy timbers that protected her.

Lucille was working like a demon, her lips half open as she gasped for breath and her fingers flying from muskets to powder to ball and back to the guns again. Thanks to her, Allan and Grambling had been able to maintain a continuous stream of fire, while the running blacks below had been given no chance to halt and recharge their weapons, so that now they had only the cane knives and the clubs to help them press home the climax of their attack.

The acrid gray smoke of battle settled like a fog upon the gallery, but flashing through it there was the split-second lightning of the guns as they dealt out death and destruction and defiance. Manette had regained her old vantage point behind the barricade, and now the shattering roar of her own guns joined those of Allan and Grambling.

Slowly at first, and then in increasing numbers, the blacks in the lead began to dodge aside to shelter behind the oaks, and then fall back to the rear. The contagion of their desertion spread, and almost as quickly as it had come, the charge degenerated into a rout with the black figures running frantically for the road, and Mingo howling and screaming in rage behind them.

The strip of land that had been directly within the defenders' range of fire was rough with new-made mounds of crumpled flesh and astir with the slow movement of crippled wretches who tried to crawl and drag themselves away from this field of agony and blood. The main body of blacks had bunched into a knot at the end of the avenue, well out of range of the gallery's guns. Mingo was exhorting them, throwing both arms up into the air in spasmodic gestures of excitation. Still gasping for breath and shaken by the storm of death that had been unloosed upon them, the blacks stared at him with sullen faces, unwilling to brave again the terror from which they had just escaped.

Manette got to her feet with a moan of weariness and wiped the back of her arm across her forehead. Allan had stepped back from the railing and Grambling was still watching the blacks with a sneer of contempt tugging at his lips. Lucille, her hurrying fingers stilled, was staring up at them with questioning eyes, and Manette held out her hand and helped the girl to her feet so she could see out over the field of battle.

"We've beaten them off!" The girl's voice quivered in spite of her attempts to steady it. Her face was grimed with smoke and dirt and she had thrown aside the clinging folds of Manette's robe so that she was like some young Diana staring out into the dawn, with only the short chemise to cover her. "We've beaten them off and now we are safe again!"

Manette felt a wry grimace tugging at the corners of her lips. It was sheer cruelty to smash this youngster's mounting hope and confidence, but it would be far worse to let her delude herself and then be shocked and destroyed by the impact of harsh reality. "We have beaten them off, that's true enough, but I don't think there's any doubt that they'll be back. And if our own slaves decide to join them then—" She looked across at Allan, standing a half-dozen feet away with the grim tension of battle still carving his face into a bitter mask. "That's right, isn't it, Allan? They won't give up just because we've turned them back?"

He tore his eyes away from the confusion at the gate, silent for a moment as if his thoughts had been so far away that he was obliged to stop and analyze the meaning of her words. "Give up? Hell's fire, they can't give up! They're outlaws now, and the first time they're whipped it means a rope around the neck for every one of them. They'll be back, but I don't think they'll try a straight charge from the front again."

Grambling turned away from the railing and came walking slowly across to join them. His eyes swept up and down Lucille's body and then lingered insolently on the half-exposed curves of Manette's breasts, molded plainly beneath the sweat-soaked shirt.

"Ah wouldn't wondah but what they'll come at us from all foah sides this next time," he drawled. "That way they'd split up ouah fiah an' stand a bettah chance of at least one or two of theah pahties gettin' inside the house. If they do that, it's goin' to be right mean around heah—especially if they take a notion to set that lowah floah afiah an' smoke us out."

"They'll be fools if they don't. If they'd tried that at the beginning, they'd be on top of us by now. Say they do get inside, all we can do is try to hold the stairway, and if we can't do that—hell, if we can't do that, I don't know what happens next."

Allan strode across the gallery and picked up a decanter that was still three-fourths full of brandy. "We might as well drink a little of this." His lips twisted into a hard smile that had no laughter or amusement in it. "If they ever get past that stairway, they'll do the drinking, and I'd rather have it than turn it over to them." He filled three glasses halfway to the brim and splashed a little into the bottom of a fourth glass for Lucille. Still smiling, while the dark fires blazed in his eyes, he held the glasses out to them. "Drink up, *compañeros,* you've nothing to lose and everything to gain by it. God knows it's early yet, but for all we know, the men from Bonneterre may be at the edge of the timber now."

Feeling the fire of the liquor flow through her and replace the weariness with a new warmth of confidence and courage, Manette allowed herself to wonder just where the squad from Bonneterre might be. Her mind jerked back to their present danger as she heard Lucille's voice lifted in a wordless shivering cry. She spun around to look out toward the river and saw that the rabble of mutineers had re-formed and started toward them up the avenue again.

Mingo was on foot this time, swaggering a half-dozen paces ahead of his men, with his long arms swinging threateningly and his face evil and bestial in the glare of the mounting sunlight. There was no singing or shouting now; the blacks moved with the terrifying silence of wild beasts closing in upon some wounded but still dangerous animal. While they were still far out of range, they split up into four separate bands, with some fifteen to twenty men making up each group. Two of the groups straggled through the line of oaks and swung far out to the right, while another took a similar course to the left, as if to make it unmistakably plain that they planned to flank the house. While the third group advanced, the fourth lingered beneath the green archway of the oaks, giving the others time to arrive at their positions.

Allan looked across at Grambling and shook his head. "It's going to be bad. They're going to hit us from all four sides, just as you said they would."

"Couldn't rightly expect 'em to do anything else, suh." His eyes swung around the little group, lingering a little longer than they should upon Lucille and pausing again as he surveyed Manette. "Theah's foah of us heah, so Ah reckon that means one on each side an' th' devil take th' hindmost."

Allan's teeth gnawed at his lip as his eyes followed the two lines of advancing blacks. "I suppose that's it," he agreed reluctantly, "but great crying God!" His eyes measured Lucille's slim figure and the clear innocence of her eyes. "I hate like hell to put that child off somewhere by herself with a gun in her hand and tell her to fight off a pack of drunken rebels!"

He splashed more brandy into his glass and gulped it down as if it were water. "Do you know anything at all about using a gun, Lucille?" he demanded.

Unexpectedly, she smiled confidently up at him. "Why, of course I do, Mr. MacMurran. Papa taught me to shoot at the same time he taught me how to ride. If I can hit a duck, I ought to be able to hit a man."

Her complete naiveté and the utter absence of any reluctance to kill another human being was disarming, a brief but all-encompassing commentary upon the relationship between the planters and their slaves. Allan stared down at her tn blank amazement for an instant and then threw back his head and roared with laughter.

"By God, Lucille, you're as right as rain in the springtime. I'm damned glad I m not going to be out there in front of your gun." He jerked his head peremptorily at Grambling and started for the hallway that led to the back of the house. "We'll drag out some furniture and rig up the best barricades we can on the other three sides. You take one side and I'll take the other and we'll put Lucille at the front and Manette at the back. Some of those oak chests of drawers ought to serve pretty well if we can get them out." His voice faded as he passed on down the hall with Grambling swaggering carelessly along behind him.

Manette slipped her arm around Lucille's waist, remembering that Margarita had been just this girl's age when they fled from the fire and carnage of Santo Domingo. "We must recharge all the guns and carry a supply of powder and shot to the new barricades that they are building." Like sisters, they knelt side by side in the midst of the confusion of weapons and ammunition and in an instant they were engulfed in the feverish turmoil of preparation.

From her post at the rear of the house Manette could overlook the slave quarters, and she caught her breath as she saw that almost a score of the men had left their cabins and were milling uncertainly back and forth in the open space at the center of the slave quarters. Mingo's four groups had reached their assigned positions, so that there was a band of them on each of the four sides of the house. The disaster of their earlier charge had made them wary and they kept well out of range of gunfire as they waited for their leader's signal that would send them forward.

She heard a hoarse shout go up from the band that Mingo led on the avenue, and as it still echoed in her ears she saw that the knot of Constancia blacks was moving slowly forward to join the column of rebels massed beside the quarters. For an instant she knew the blinding despair of utter hopelessness, and then the anger grew in her like a white flame and she lifted the musket beside her and drilled the leader of the Constancia slaves cleanly between the eyes. She heard the others cry out in alarm as they fell back, and she sent another shot crashing into their midst, almost without taking time to aim. The mass of Mingo's rebels was rushing forward, shouting for the Constancia Negroes to join them, but the two dead bodies on the ground cried out too loudly for the waverers to misunderstand their meaning. They hesitated, eyes white-rimmed and suddenly afraid, and then they scattered like quail and vanished into the safety of their cabins. Howling, the renegades of Mingo's men were coming in at a stumbling run, and she turned back to them, damning the insubordination that had forced her to waste two precious shots on the rebellious Constancia blacks. She had marked the magnolia tree some eighty feet away as the point she would let them reach before she began to fire, and as the leaders surged past it, she lifted a musket to her shoulder and let its sights fall into line with the belly of the Negro who ran farthest to the front. The gun roared in her ears, and without waiting to see the effects of her shot, she dropped it and scooped up another that stood ready to her hand.

The blacks were howling and screaming as they advanced, guns flashing in explosions of brilliant light and waving cane knives glittering in the sun as their owners flourished them above their heads. She could hear bullets crashing into the wall behind her and tearing at the wood of the chest that was her barricade, but there was no time to think of that now. She was firing as rapidly as she could throw aside one gun and seize another, and between the puffs of smoke she could see black bodies twisting on the ground beside others that lay still and motionless.

Then the last fowling piece and musket had been fired and there remained only two slim-barreled dueling pistols. The attacking force had been almost cut in half, but there were still seven or eight of them on their feet, charging forward with a desperation that turned her cold with fear. If the pistols did not stop them …

She fired twice and saw each bullet find its mark, but the charge rolled on almost to the edge of the gallery now, black arms stretching out toward the rose-covered trellises that would serve as ladders between the ground and the lower gallery floor. She fumbled frantically for powder and shot, jolting the ball down into the barrel as she ran to the railing and peered down over the edge. But it was too late. There was a fleeting glimpse of dark bodies hurling themselves over the rail and into the shelter of the gallery and then they were out of sight and she could hear them ripping and pounding on the locked jalousies that guarded the tall windows.

Still clutching the musket in her hand, she turned and raced toward the north side of the house, where there was still the intermittent crackle of gunfire echoing beneath the eaves. Allan was standing up behind the barricade, his arm outstretched and a pointed pistol in his hand. As site ran toward him the gun flashed fire, and then she saw him hurl it furiously into the face of the attackers who surged below. So that had been his last shot.

She called to him as she ran down the long gallery and saw him turn in quick alarm. "Allan," she gasped, "I couldn't stop them and they're tearing the jalousies off the windows now."

"Yes," he growled, "there'll be plenty of them there by now. Mingo and four of his men just got through here." He ran over to the wall and his hand closed around the hilt of one of the cane knives leaning there. "I'll try to hold them at the stairway. Tell Wilson to join me there and see what you can do about loading up some of these guns again." He whirled and charged into the long center hall and Manette raced after him.

As she passed the wide landing of the stair, she caught a glimpse of white eyes gleaming from dark faces as the slaves charged up the winding steps. Allan had run down to meet them, the cane knife slashing and jabbing so viciously before him that the foremost blacks had stumbled back a little. She ran on, just in time to meet Grambling coming through the doorway, a naked knife thrust into his belt and a musket reversed in his hands so that he held it by the barrel and its stock became a murderous club.

"On the stairs! Allan's on the stairway!" She wheeled and pointed frantically and saw Grambling's face harden as he ran past her and went charging down the stairs to wedge himself in at Allan's side.

Lucille—But there was no time to think of Lucille. Breath sobbing in her throat, she ran out on the gallery where Grambling had made his stand and where his empty guns lay scattered about the floor. There were two pistols there, and she loaded them with fingers that trembled so terribly that the stream of powder washed back and forth like a pendulum on a clock, and it was only by holding it hard against the muzzle that she was able to pour in a charge and cram the lead ball in behind it. She had been crouching on her knees and now she twisted erect and turned to run back into the hall. Allan and Grambling had been forced back to the top of the stairs, and blood was pouring from Allan's shoulder. His left arm hung limp and helpless at his side while his other sent the blade flickering back and forth in the faces of the surging mob that almost engulfed him. Grambling had lost his musket in the melee and now he was lunging and stabbing with the knife he had carried in his belt. She ran up beside them and fired point-blank into the faces of two brawny Negroes who had almost gained the level of the upper hall. She saw their faces suddenly transformed into torn masks of blood-stained meat; saw them waver in their tracks and then go crashing like logs into the howling mob behind them. For an instant Allan and Grambling pressed forward into this new opening, but they were borne back by sheer weight of numbers. Screaming, snarling like animals, the blacks surged up and over them, crushing them to the floor beneath a storm of flashing blades and swinging clubs. She heard Allan cry out in helpless rage and then threw up her arm as a cypress club in the hands of a fierce-eyed black poised for an instant above her and then came whistling down to crush out sight and sound and consciousness.

The world came back to her slowly. At first in a nauseating sensation of wheeling, whirling dizziness and then with a sudden realization of blinding pain that ate its way through her body like white fire feeding upon her flesh. She tried to open her eyes and found that she could not, and when her exploring fingers touched them she found a coating of dried blood that had sealed them shut far more effectively than any mask. Only half aware of what she was doing, she picked at the clotted scab until it loosened enough to let her lift her eyelids and stare up into a shaft of sunlight that was beating mercilessly upon her face.

She was on the upper gallery, entirely alone except for a sprawled and indistinct figure some thirty feet away. She tried to focus her eyes upon it but the sunlight had blinded her and it was only gradually that she was able to recognize it as Lucille. The brief chemise had been torn away and the girl's thighs and breasts were black with blood. A thin stream of crimson still trickled from the corner of her torn lips and gathered in a pool upon the floor, and as Manette watched the child's face was contorted in sudden agony and a quavering moan forced itself out between the battered lips. Manette pulled herself up on one elbow with the confused idea of crawling to her. She realized that her own blouse had vanished and that her cottonade pantaloons were ripped open from waist to knee. So the blacks had ravished them both, the blonde child and the dark woman who had lain unconscious through it all. But why had it ended, and why were they here alone? At Santo Domingo the slaves had not spared the planters' women as long as breath remained in their bodies, or, for that matter, while the warmth and softness of life still lingered in them after they were dead. Something had drawn the blacks away. She became aware of a rising babel of voices in the driveway and managed to pull herself to the edge of the gallery, where she could look down on the scene below.

The blacks were swarming like bees, their voices loud and strident under the double intoxication of victory and of the bottles they passed so freely from hand to hand. The mass parted a little and she gasped in terror as she saw that the object of their attention was a naked figure, prone on the dust before them. It was Allan, his ankles bound and his wrists crossed and lashed together behind his back. The blood was still dripping from his shoulder and his whole left side was caked and coated with it, darkened by the dust of the driveway, clinging to his body like some evil and malignant growth that had fastened itself upon him. He was so still that it seemed to her he must be dead, and with the thought the blinding nausea possessed her again so that she turned her head aside and gagged wretchedly, the shivering convulsions sending new waves of pain slashing through her body.

The movement had pulled her eyes away, and as she turned back she caught a glimpse of Grambling, stripped, sagging against the ropes that held him upright against the wide bole of an elm tree. His head drooped on his chest and there were two great gashes across his belly that oozed blood.

Her gaze turned back to Allan, and as she watched she saw Mingo step forward and throw a rope over the low limb of one of the nearby oaks. There was no noose at its end, but she was suddenly certain that Allan was to be hanged, here in the clear brilliance of the sunshine, under her very eyes and in spite of anything that she might do. Mingo's arm shot out as his fingers fastened themselves around the end of the dangling rope and pulled it to him. His voice rumbled in a command Manette could not understand, and two Negroes stepped forward and jerked Allan to his feet. He was still alive, for he tried to stand erect and she saw his eyes sweep up in a flashing glance that scoured the upper gallery so swiftly she could not be sure that he had seen her face. The two bucks half dragged and half carried him to where Mingo stood. They swung him around so that Mingo was at his back, and then he was hidden from her as Mingo dragged at the rope and bent above him.

She had expected to see the rope knotted around his throat, but when Mingo stepped back she saw that it was lashed to his bound wrists. The two guards steadied him, holding him on his feet as a half-dozen chattering blacks laid hands on the other end of the rope that swung suspended from the limb above. She saw the rope suddenly grow tight and Allan's arms swing up between his shoulders so that he was thrown off balance and teetered perilously forward with the rope holding him upright and his feet slipping out from beneath him as they clawed for purchase in the shallow dust. Mingo's voice rumbled again and the Negroes threw the weight of their bodies against the rope as if they were engaged in some fantastic tug of war. Allan screamed as his arched arms were pulled back and then high above his head. The shoulder joints had been jerked out of their sockets and now he was hanging with his feet a good two feet above the ground, his weight suspended by the tortured arms that were attached to his body only by the broken fibers of torn muscles and the thin sheath of skin. The pain was almost unbearable and he moaned like an animal tortured beyond the limits of endurance.

They jerked the rope twice again. His arms seemed to be elongated now, and as Manette stared in horror she saw the skin tear open beneath his armpit until the bloody gash had run halfway across his back. His head had fallen forward upon his chest and a froth of blood oozed and bubbled between the twisted lips. Only, the choked sobbing of his groans told her that he was still alive.

She had no wish for anything except the blessed surcease of a merciful death; oblivion for herself and for those who had shared the defense and terror of Constancia with her. It came to her that if she could lay hands upon the guns again, she could release them all from the torture that lay ahead. She lifted her head and saw that the guns Allan had used were still scattered across the floor and the powder and shot were still intact, just as she had placed them there in an hour that seemed a million years ago.

Her body pressed tightly against the floor, she managed to work her way back from the edge of the gallery so that she was shielded from the eyes of the blacks below. She moved stiffly, consciously willing herself to perform each movement that made up her slow progression. Twice the walls and the sky dipped and wheeled in eccentric circles and she clenched her teeth and clung to the fading shreds of consciousness like a shipwrecked sailor clutching a floating spar. When her head cleared a little she moved on again, and finally her fingers touched the sun-warmed metal of a musket barrel and she drew it stealthily to her. She could reach the powder and shot from where she lay, and she measured out a charge of powder in the palm of her trembling hand.

It seemed to her that the thread of time spun itself out into an endless eternity as she fumbled at her self-appointed task, but eventually it was done; two muskets to bring release to Allan and to Grambling, a dueling pistol for Lucille, and another for herself. She put the pistols a yard away from Lucille's torn and ravished body and began to crawl back toward the railing, dragging the muskets behind her, shivering with fear when one of them scraped loudly across a roughened plank in the floor.

She pressed her face against the iron tracery of the railing and whimpered in sudden pain as her eyes reached the spot where Allan's body swung and twisted beneath the tree. The blacks had raked up a pile of straw and timber directly beneath his feet and the fresh-lit fire was just beginning to crackle through" it. His legs contracted in sudden agony as the tongues of flame licked at his naked feet, and he gasped and coughed, throwing his head back in search of air as the smoke billowed up and wound its choking tendrils into his nose and throat. The movements threw a fresh strain on his shattered shoulders and his voice rose in a wordless shriek.

With a sudden desperate access of strength, Manette pulled one of the muskets to her and slipped its barrel silently through the open grillework of the iron rail. An inner voice of doubt nagged in her brain, warning that she must move swiftly and surely if she was to carry out her purpose. Once the first shot was fired, there would be a storm of bullets from the blacks below, while others charged upstairs to wrest her weapons from her. And there were four shots to fire, and each one must travel unerringly to its mark.

She rested her cheek against the musket stock and let her eyes follow the long line of the barrel that was aimed straight at Allan's heart, and her lips formed the words "God forgive me." Her finger tightened on the trigger and a phrase from an almost forgotten prayer of her convent days seemed to echo in her brain:

"O holy Mother of God, despise not our prayers in our necessities."

There was the sudden roar of an explosion somewhere to the south, and as her head jerked up in swift alarm she saw the mass of blacks pitched and scattered like leaves flying in the wind. The sound of the belching cannon came again, and in its wake she heard the same rising storm of harsh voices that had split the sky when Grenaldi's men came swarming over the rail of the bark-entine *El Audaz.*

"*Muerte! Muerte!*"

The wolves of Bonneterre stormed into view from behind a fringe of trees, cutlasses flashing in the sun, their blazing pistols throwing a solid curtain of fire before them. The terrified blacks broke and ran like frightened deer, but the buccaneers pulled them down, screaming like fiends freshly released from hell. From her vantage point Manette saw Kelcho kick the fire away and slash at the rope before he lowered Allan gently to the ground. She tried to drag herself to her feet and call to them, but the weakness she had fought off for so long enveloped her like a cloud. The earth began to spin slowly around her and she crumpled to the floor, the shouts and pistol shots as soothing as a lullaby so that she smiled a little, lying there, unconscious, where a shaft of sunlight struck the floor.

CHAPTER EIGHTEEN

KELCHO took them to New Orleans in the plantation sloop that afternoon. It was a sun-scorched, windless day, but the current of the Mississippi carried them along at a steady six miles an hour, and even without the sails they would reach the river wharf at the foot of Bienville Street while the sun was still in the sky.

Allan's upper arms and shoulders were swollen into grotesque monstrosities beneath skin stretched so tightly that it had turned to a deep purple and threatened to split like the rind of a rotten melon at any movement. Strips of scorched flesh dangled from his feet and ankles and great blisters blossomed in crimson and black above them. There was little that could be done for him at the plantation except to drug him with brandy until the pain receded and only an occasional moan reflected the torture that he endured.

Grambling had been cut free and the gashes across his stomach bathed and bandaged. He was conscious, but the pain was not completely unendurable, and he was able to relax beneath the canvas awning Kelcho had stretched above them with a thin cigar clutched in his teeth and a palm-leaf fan moving slowly back and forth in his hand.

Lucille had gone from unconsciousness to a state of semi-delirious shock. The blood had been washed away and she had been wrapped in heavy blankets and almost drowned in brandy, but it was not enough to bring an end to the trembling that racked her torn and violated body.

Of them all, Manette had suffered the least physical injury from their ordeal. There was a tremendous throbbing knot of swollen flesh running back from her temple where the cypress club had smashed her into unconsciousness, but she had been able to direct the treatment of the others and even confer briefly with Trinidad Morales, the leathery, one-eyed Spaniard who commanded the troop from Bonneterre. He had sought her out as the trembling plantation slaves carried the wounded down to the river wharf, his hands still red with blood.

"It is over, señorita. Not even one of these black dogs has been left alive."

"Nor should they be. You have done a good day's work, Trinidad. And your own men?"

He laughed, with lips curled back like a snarling wolf. "You do not think those pig-born dogs could stand against my men, señorita? I have not lost a man—nor has a man of mine lost as much as a single drop of his own blood." He spat contemptuously upon the ground as his fingers caressed the butts of the pistols in his belt. "Ai! This is child's play. But I believe we reached you just in time, *verdad?*"

"Another second and you would have been too late." She felt the skin crawling on her back as she remembered that awful instant when the musket had been trained on Allan's heart and her finger quivering on the trigger. Merciful Mary! She would burn many candles in the cathedral to give thanks for this intervention.

"You are taking Don Allan and the others to New Orleans, señorita?"

"Immediately! They must have the services of the most skilled *médicos* Louisiana can provide if they are to live. Even then there is a doubt."

He nodded gravely. "For the little one, perhaps, but I think Don Allan will survive. I have seen him wounded and hurt before; there is some devil inside of him that forces him back to life. And what of this place, señorita? Will you abandon it to your own slaves?"

Abandon it? She had to wrench her mind away from its preoccupation with Allan and Lucille before she could grasp the implication of his words. Abandon Constancia? After they had fought and suffered so to save it? That would be like abandoning a part of themselves, and yet it was essential that she go with Allan to New Orleans and supervise at least the beginning of his care. Her eyes strayed past Trinidad's lean figure to where three of the half-naked corsairs were cheerfully ripping a rosewood table apart to provide fuel for a fire that they had kindled. As God was her witness, she knew they would not treat Constancia with gentle hands, but at least they would keep it safe and control the slaves.

"Trinidad." There was decision in her voice now, an acceptance of the obligation of authority that circumstances had thrown upon her. "I want you and your men to stay here until you hear from me. It may be a week, or it may be a fortnight. Until I return or send someone to take my place, you are in charge. The slaves have their own foremen who can direct their work, and you need not concern yourself with it. I want you to protect this house and its furnishings and see that it is not looted or ravaged or destroyed."

He stared at her doubtfully, uncertain whether she spoke as MacMurran's deputy or simply as a willful woman who had no right or reason to command. She could guess the thoughts that were passing through his mind and she threw back her head and stared him into submission with a glare as truculent and intolerant as MacMurran's own. His eyes slipped away from hers, uneasily, and then his shoulders rose and fell in a gesture of resignation and acceptance.

"As you say, señorita. We will stay until other arrangements can be made." He turned away to pass the word on to his men, and Manette felt a new tide of strength flowing through her. From this moment on she would be indeed the mistress of Constancia. Until Allan could return, she, and she alone, would control the life and destiny of this estate.

The sun was like a fading torch burning on the river to the west when Kelcho warped the sloop in beside the almost deserted Bienville dock. She snapped out an order that sent Kelcho running up Bienville Street to send the coach and coachman to them; once that was done, he was to summon the doctors Lammierre and Portebain and Fortozar, accepting no excuses for delay and making it his business to assure their presence at the house at Bienville Street by the time the injured were delivered there.

Her own head was pounding with unending pain and sometimes the cobbles of the street danced and blurred before her eyes, but she directed the loading of the others into the carriage and then urged the coachman on with the grim warning that any avoidable jars and jolts would be repaid with a bull whip stripping the flesh from his naked back. She found the doctors waiting for them in the inner courtyard, and under the crackling lash of her commands the house servants carried the other three inside and laid them in wide beds. After the physicians had finished attending to them, she asked Portebain to apply a dressing to her head and listened with chill attention as he interpreted the facts of the patients' condition to her and outlined the attention they would require through the night.

Allan, he felt sure, would recover, although the convalescence would be slow and he would be obliged to remain in New Orleans for several months in order to enjoy the benefits of daily medical attention. As to Grambling, his wounds were neither deep nor severe and he should be on his feet and ready to return to Constancia within a fortnight. Lucille, he hinted, was another affair entirely. She had undergone a terrible experience and there was a question as to whether or not she would be able to rise above it and survive. Time alone would tell, and in the meantime the señorita herself should seek her bed, for it was obvious that she had reached the final limit of her strength. He lifted his tall hat in a courteous salute, promised to return with his colleagues early in the morning, and took himself away into the darkness of the hot, star-spangled night.

A week went by and Allan was sufficiently recovered to talk to her for a few minutes every day, although his arms were still strapped tightly to his sides and he had a disconcerting way of dropping off into slumber in the middle of a conversation. Grambling was up, moving stiffly about the house with the color back in his cheeks and the slow insolence restored to his eyes as they followed Manette's movements. Lucille's fever was gone and she was quieter now, but there was a strange lethargy in her face and an incoherence in her speech that led Manette to wonder if the shock had burned some foul scar in the child's mind that would never heal again.

She did not mention it to Allan, for she knew that he had been disturbed by the fact of Lucille's presence at Constancia during the attack and she had no wish to hinder his recovery with doubts and fears that she could bear alone. As it was, he fretted endlessly about conditions at Constancia. The crop of cane, the slaves, the mules and cattle—all left without even a trace of adequate supervision. When he talked of them the feverish flush mounted into his cheeks again and his body twisted restlessly on the soft surface of the bed. Watching him, Manette realized that this situation must not continue, for it had checked the progress of his recovery and was tearing down the gains Portebain had so far been able to achieve. Grambling was still too stiff and weak to go back to the plantation, but her own strength had returned and was fortified with a new vitality born of her determination to assume the active management of Constancia.

As soon as the idea entered her mind, she set about making her plans, and two days later she and Kelcho were stepping from a sloop onto the river landing at Constancia.

The management of Constancia was no child's play, nor was it made easier by the task of repairing the damage that had been done by the mutinous blacks and by the buccaneers who had been quartered there. It turned her heartsick to come up the long avenue of oaks and find the wide lawn trampled into dust and defaced with burned out fires, rotting bits of food, and empty rum and brandy bottles. Two drunken corsairs quarreled beside the open door and stopped to leer at her as she swept past. The delicate railing that had guarded the graceful staircase was smashed and splintered on the floor, and the mirrors had gone down to destruction under the pirates' pistol practice. She ran up the stairs and flung open the door that led into her bedroom. There was a shriek of alarm and a mulatto girl tumbled out of the great bed and fled through the open window to the gallery. Trinidad, his one eye glazed with drunkenness and his tongue thick and unruly, raised himself to stare up at her.

"Hola, señorita!" He started to grin at her and then his face twisted into a sudden frown. "You have driven my little brown bird away." He threw his legs over the side of the bed and came

unsteadily to his feet. He staggered across to the window and stared uncertainly up and down the gallery, his body swaying back and forth as he balanced himself with a hand outstretched against the wall. He managed to turn and face her and his thin lips twisted in a lewd smile of invitation. "Now you can take her place, señorita. Damn fine-looking wench." He stumbled toward her across the room and her fingers closed on the base of a heavy brass candlestick that stood on the table beside her. "Nobody here but you and me." She lunged at him like a tigress and the candlestick crashed down upon his head. His mouth gaped open as f he were about to shout out a protest and then his knees gave way and he fell face forward on the floor.

She bound him with the tie-back cords from the brocade curtains and gagged him with a wad and a strip of cloth ripped from the sheet that had been upon the bed. Gasping for breath, she dragged him into the alcove that served as her dressing room and slammed and locked the door upon him. His pistols, loaded and primed, were on the floor beside the bed, and she tucked one of them into the bodice of her dress and carried the other in her hand as she ventured out into the hall again. She found two more men sprawled in drunken slumber in the bedroom Lucille had occupied and left them trussed, gagged, and bound to opposite posts of the bed, after she had prudently ensured their lack of resistance by cracking them smartly on the heads with the barrel of her pistol.

Back on the lower floor again, she caught the muffled sound of riotous voices from the cellar below and tiptoed out of the house and down the outside stairway to peer into the gloom and catch a glimpse of light from the doorway of the vast cooling room where butter and milk and fruits and vegetables were stored to protect them against the ravages of the heat. She kicked off her slipper so there would be no sound as she made her way stealthily across the wide tiled floor to a point from which she could see into the room. Two wide-pronged candelabra flared like torches, and in a close-packed circle around the hub of light the sea wolves swore and shoved and shouted as the dice rolled and coins of gold and silver rang against the floor. The room was strewn with bottles and thick with smoke and the odor of the unwashed bodies and the liquor was like the miasma from some stagnant and fetid swamp, sour and sickening in her nostrils. The heavy oak door stood halfway open and the padlock that was used to secure it hung open on the hasp. Shrinking back out of the light, she counted the men who crouched and gambled there, and her eyes narrowed in satisfaction as she totaled fifteen of them, the entire strength of the band outside of those who were bound and gagged upstairs and the two who lounged on the gallery at the front.

With a movement as swift and silent as a striking snake, she slipped across the open space of the lighted doorway and dodged into the security of the shadows behind the door. She waited breathlessly for some challenge from the depths of the room, but they had been too intent upon the whirling dice to see her pass. Working with silent fingers, she pulled the padlock free of its hasp and held it ready in her hand. Her breasts rose and fell as she gathered her strength together, and then she hurled herself against the open door, feeling it resist at first and then swing free and echo like a cannon's blast as it slammed shut against its casing. A roaring tumult of startled voices swelled inside the room, but her fingers had jammed the padlock into place and she felt it snap shut as the first charging tide of bodies crashed against the oak. Still-faced and rigid, she listened to the tide of noise swell into a crescendo of baffled shouts and curses and finally fade into a muffled monotone of angry argument and discussion. She smiled a little then. There was no other entrance into the cooling room and no liquor except the bottles they had carried inside with them. By midnight that would be gone, and by morning they would be sick and chastened, sober and ready to return to Bonneterre. There were still the two men she had met on the lower gallery to be secured, but her success thus far had built up a heady confidence in her own ability to cope with them and she turned back toward the cellar steps with a faint trace of a swagger that was new to her.

She found them much as she had left them, and before they realized that she was there they were gaping into the muzzles of the two pistols she had taken from Trinidad and staring up at her with amazement in their bloodshot eyes. She saw Kelcho hurrying up the avenue from the river and held them under the threat of her guns until he was at her side. Her voice crackled like heat lightning as she ordered them to their feet.

"Face the wall, you dogs, and keep your hands high above your heads unless you want a bullet in your backs." They stared at her dumbly, and the pistol muzzles lifted a little to give weight to her commands. "Move! *Por Dios,* will you force me to shoot you down in cold blood?"

Her eyes snapped fire and they turned hurriedly around so that their backs were presented to her. She jerked her head at the wide-eyed Kelcho. "Move over there and take their guns and knives and put them in a pile at the edge of the gallery." He acted quickly, stripping the corsairs of their weapons and then hurrying back to stand beside her with his lean face as impassive as before. "Shall I bind them, señorita?"

She nodded grimly, her eyes never leaving the figures of the men before her. "Tie their hands behind them and halter their ankles with a short rope so they cannot run." She watched the orders carried out and then herded them through the lower hall and down the cellar steps. She dared not open the door of the cooling room to thrust them in with their fellows, but there was another, smaller cell nearby, and she drove them inside and secured the door so that there was no chance of their escape. It was, she thought ruefully, a sorry return for the rescue they had effected, but she had watched Allan deal with them on Bonneterre enough to know that when they were inflamed with liquor they were like wild beasts and the only course that would remove them from Constancia was to let the brandy die out in their veins and then force Trinidad to muster them and lead them back along the road that they had come.

By sundown she had flushed Cragon and the maids from the sanctuary at the edge of the timber where they had taken shelter and flung them into the task of restoring order to the chaos of the house. She had left word at the quarters that the black foremen were to report to her without delay, and as the work gangs straggled in she interviewed their leaders on the gallery at the back of the house with a pistol, a dog whip, and a tall bottle of brandy conveniently at hand on the table beside her. As she had expected, the work had lagged. Unnerved by the task of burying their fellow slaves who had fallen before the pirates' guns and unaccustomed to working without direct and constant supervision, they had muddled through in a confusion of uncertainty and fear that was as ineffective as it was inept. She dealt out praise and blame impartially, issued crisp directions for the tasks that were to be undertaken on the following day, and sent them back to their quarters with new vigor in their steps and an obvious sense of relief at being freed from the responsibilities of authority and decision.

When they were gone she had Cragon bring her dinner to her on the gallery and washed it down with a liberal glass of brandy as the dusk began to settle about her. Sitting there alone, as the slow rising moon began to paint the earth with splashes of soft

silver, she had to fight down a brooding sense of doubt and hopelessness as her mind measured the magnitude of the task she had
undertaken. Even under the best of conditions the plantation's
thousand and one problems required untiring attention and
supervision. Now, in its state of almost total disorganization, the
difficulties were multiplied a hundredfold. And there was Allan
to be considered and cared for in New Orleans, and Grambling,
who would be coming back to Constancia before a fortnight
was done. She frowned a little, considering this hard-mouthed
stranger with the slow drawl that was like molasses in his mouth.
His attitude had been insolent and contemptuous from the beginning, and she had not failed to catch the insult of the half-closed
eyes that had stripped her bare while they shared the defense of
the gallery a week before. Well, he was not the first man who had
looked at her with desire in his eyes, and the slim poniard was
still sheathed against the smooth flesh of her thigh. There would
be time enough to deal with Grambling after his return. For the
present, another glass of brandy and then the rest and sleep her
exhausted body demanded.

CHAPTER NINETEEN

S HE HAD BEEN at Constancia almost two weeks when Grambling came riding in from New Orleans just at sunset. He pulled himself stiffly out of the saddle at the foot of the steps and whistled shrilly for a stable boy. Manette, waist-deep in the tub of hot water that had been ready for her when she came in from a long day in the fields, caught the slow drawl of his voice as he talked to the groom and felt the sharp stab of resentment at his intrusion. Since she had been in charge here at Constancia, a new sense of power and responsibility had begun to grow in her. She had not felt isolated or alone. Margarita, by special dispensation from the mother superior, had spent a week with her, a new Margarita, sweet and charming and unafraid, full of excited gossip and enamored of a schoolmate's Creole brother she had seen but once. It had been sheer delight to display Constancia to her, dwelling on its excellencies and even finding an odd inverted pride in its difficulties. Margarita had gone back downriver the day before, but even then Manette had not been alone, for she had turned back to Constancia as eagerly as a passionate woman losing herself in the arms of an adored lover.

The plantation was no longer an inanimate composition of land and trees and buildings; by the very fact that she had poured herself into it, Constancia had come alive so that it was like a lover and a child and an enemy, all blended into one. There were days when she fought it doggedly, beating down its perversity through hours that turned grim and sullen as they slipped away.

There were other times when she cherished it, and now and then a moment when its beauty and spendthrift luxuriance stirred her like a triumphant symphony or a lover's bittersweet caress. But in all its moods she had made it hers, and hers alone—and now Grambling had come riding in.

Her eyes narrowed a little as she considered a plan that was slowly taking form in her mind. She selected an ivory and crimson gown she had brought with her from New Orleans. Her bare shoulders and arms gleamed above the revealing calyx of its bodice and the skirt spread and swelled about her. She added a scarlet mantilla of lace that was lighter than a dream, a Chinese fan of yellow silk and burnished jade. There would be a sadistic amusement in watching Grambling's eyes burn with a brightening flame, and then seeing that flame flicker and die as she laughed at his desire and humiliated him with the withering scorn of her rejection.

He was waiting for her in the lower hallway, pacing arrogantly back and forth as if he were the master of Constancia. At the click of her footsteps on the stairs, he whirled around and then stood rooted in his tracks as if he had been turned to stone.

"Gawd almighty!" He stared up at her and the tip of his tongue moistened the sun-chapped skin of his lips. "Ah'm mighty glad Ah didn't wait any longah to come back to this plantation. You look a sight diffunt from what you did that mawnin' up on th' gallery."

She smiled at him, letting the fan swing open with the soft whisper of silk so that it was like a bright butterfly wing to set off the tawny brilliance of her skin and the dusky richness of her hair.

"Yes? But you did not seem to dislike my appearance then."

"Ah liked it well enough." His bold eyes lingered on her bare shoulders and on the soft curve of her breasts, which were only half covered by the swooping bodice. "But you'ah moah like a woman this evenin'. That mawnin' you were a hellcat, pure and simple."

"And are you sure that I am not, Mr. Grambling?" She came slowly down the stairs; slowly so that he could fill his eyes with the smooth curve of her hips, the sculptured pride of her breasts, the lips that were a scarlet challenge, softened now into a smile that was half invitation and half mockery. She knew he had despised her since first she came to Constancia, but now that the lust she had surprised in his eyes provided her with a weapon, she would use it to humble him and bring him crawling to her feet.

She slipped her hand confidingly into the crook of his arm and let her body sway dangerously close to his, secretly amused by the look of startled and triumphant surprise that betrayed him for an instant and then vanished as quickly as it had come. "Dinner will be ready soon. Would you like to go out on the gallery and have a drink while we are waiting?"

Her eyes clung to his, waiting for his answer as if her only desire was to please him and adapt her own wishes to his pleasure. He stared at her suspiciously, as if some inner voice was warning him against this new and unexpected deference.

"Why not—if you don't object to such presumption from yoah hiahed ovahseah." There was a thread of resentment in his voice.

She let her fingers tighten on his arm and laughed up at him as if she believed he had been joking. "Oh, Wilson!" She had used his first name deliberately and had her reward as she felt the muscles twitch sharply in his arm. "I don't know why you talk like that." Her eyes flashed up at him and fell away in the very image of demure confusion. "You know, you're far more than an overseer—now!"

On the gallery she prepared his drink against a background of little deferential questions as to how much brandy he preferred and whether or not she should mix it for him. He had little enough to say, but his eyes were shrewdly calculating as he followed the lithe movement of her body and puzzled over this new and unexplained attitude

She touched her glass to his, leaning forward in her chair so his eyes could not escape the warm sweep of her breasts. "To our better—knowledge of each other, Wilson." The word assumed an undisguised meaning on her lips, the ancient scriptural meaning of carnal knowledge between a man and a woman bound together by passion.

His lips tightened a little in satisfaction at this proof of his long held belief that this woman of bronze and ebony was as completely amoral as some impulsive, untamed savage. He had hated her from the moment she first set foot on Constancia six months before. For him she represented all women who openly flaunted their utter disregard for convention and morality. He had hated them a long time now, so long that it had become a fixed obsession with him; ever since that bitter night ten years ago in Georgia when he had come home to find that his child-wife, Suzanne, had decamped with a cotton buyer from Virginia and made him the laughingstock of the county. He tore his mind away from the gnawing humiliation of that ancient memory. Before he was done he would exact some repayment here.

"Ah'll enjoy acquirin' that knowledge—with yoah assistance, of coahse." His eyes challenged her while she smiled up at him and then he lifted the glass and drained it without removing it from his lips. He held the empty glass out to her with a brusque request that was nothing but open arrogance.

"Ah'd like to have anothah—mixed just like th' one Ah had."

She accepted the glass humbly and turned her back on him as she mixed the drink to hide the deadly smile of triumph that flickered at the corners of her lips. He was beginning to be sure of her now, and she wanted him to be sure; so confident and certain of her surrender that when she turned upon him the blow would be all the more startling and devastating. She let her fingers touch his and linger there a moment as he took the glass. She knew the magic of even the slightest touch, and as she saw him stiffen in his chair she turned away and strolled languidly across the gallery to lean against the rail, where the early starlight could bathe her in new mystery. After all, this was only the beginning of the game.

"And how was Allan when you left New Orleans?"

"Why, to tell you th' truth, he seemed to be fah bettah. He's had some visitahs—" He checked himself as if he had almost said too much. "He's brought one of th' bookkeepahs up from th' office to look aftah his business an' write his lettahs foah him." He fumbled in the pocket of his linen coat and produced a sealed envelope, which he tossed carelessly on the table. "He asked me to delivah this lettah to you, but Ah'd fo'gotten it until this minute."

"I'll read it when we go inside, where there's more light. And Lucille—is she improving, too?"

"That's mighty hahd to say. Some days she's just as bright an' chippah as a mockin'bi'd, an' th' next mawnin' you can't hahdly get a wo'd out of her. Ah don' know about that girl. Sometimes Ah thinks she won't nevah get ovah it."

They moved into the rosewood dining hall for dinner, with Manette's hand clinging again to Grambling's arm. She knew that he had the scent of her body and her perfume in his nostrils now. The brandy had reinforced and heightened the desire that had been growing in him for weeks and months, and even though he could despise her with the old hate that was as much a part of him as the flesh upon his bones, he could not renounce or even hide the lascivious hunger she had aroused. He stared at her across the table as he ate, his eyes probing her so fiercely that after a while the feeling crept upon her that his gaze had stripped her clothing away and left her naked and undefended before him.

After dinner she let him lead her to the upper gallery. There was only the reflection of the moonlight there beneath the shelter of the eaves, and until her eyes became accustomed to the darkness she could see him only as a dark blur lounging in a chair a half-dozen feet away. Slowly the outline of his face and figure began to emerge more clearly, and the tenor of his desires became open and unmistakable as he began to present and press his case.

"Ah've looked foahwahd to bein' heah alone with you, without anyone else around. Ah thought about it all th' time aftah you left New O'leans, an' Ah thought about it every step of th' way comin' up heah today."

She let a hint of breathlessness creep into her voice. "And now that you are here?"

"Why, now that Ah'm heah, an' you'ah so pleasant an' amiable, Ah'd like to carry ouah relationship a little fuhthah." He stood up, and two quick strides brought him to the side of her chair. She felt his hand touch her hair and then move down to linger on the soft curve of her shoulder. "Ah'm a man an' you'ah a woman. We both know what we want, an' it seems to me like we'ah both wantin' th' same thing."

She could almost feel her skin crawl beneath his touch and there was an instant of madness when the steel of the poniard seemed to burn against her thigh with a heat that could be cooled only in Grambling's blood. She closed her eyes and forced the insane desire away.

"But Wilson!" She seemed to be pleading with him now. "We couldn't! You know we couldn't! There's Allan."

"Allan's not heah now." His voice had deepened with the growling intensity of his desire and his fingers had slipped inside her bodice so that her breast lay cradled in his hand. "Theah's nobody heah but you an' me, an' what we do is ouah business an' nobody else's."

He pulled her to her feet and his arms were suddenly hard and cruelly possessive. His lips were harsh and defiling upon her mouth, and even as he kissed her he lifted one hand to rip the front of her bodice away. For a moment she felt a twinge of fear at this ruthless bestiality her deliberate seduction had awakened, and then she pressed herself so tightly against him that the clawing hand was trapped between them and she felt him grow tense and rigid as she allowed her body to move tantalizingly against him. His arms relaxed a little in the assurance of her subjugation, and in the same instant she tore herself free and ran across the gallery to pause in the lighted doorway.

"We can't do this! We can't!" Her voice broke a little as if she were forcing the words out against her will. "You must give me time, Wilson, and even then—"

He lunged across the gallery toward her, but she was down the hall and safe behind the closed door of her bedroom before his pounding footsteps could overtake her. She twisted the key in the lock as his hard fist hammered on the door.

"Manette! Manette! Open this doah befoah Ah break it down!"

She laughed silently, her fingers feeling the outline of the poniard through her gown. "Please, Wilson—not tonight! Perhaps tomorrow or another day. But not tonight! Not tonight ...."

There was a silence outside the door as her final half-promising phrase sank into his mind. It was bitter to be balked tonight, but there would be many nights before Allan came back to Constancia. Only a fool would rouse her to an enduring antagonism now.

"Ah'll still be heah tomorrow." There was a warning in his voice, a warning and the shadow of a threat.

"I know, I know! I'll think of nothing else till then. Good night, *mi corazón*. Good night!"

She could hear the thump of his boots as he turned back toward the gallery and threw up her hands to muffle the wild torrent of her triumphant laughter. He would sit late and drink tonight, cursing his own weakness in letting her escape, spinning erotic dreams of the nights that lay ahead. It would not be a peaceful or a happy night for him, nor would it be the last that he would spend like this. She knew that her twisted rope of mingled allure and retreat would weave a noose around his throat that would bring him to the brink of madness. Then, when the pent-up heat of his desire was at its highest pitch, she would turn on him and rip the last shreds of pride and self-complacence from him. Never again would he dare look at a woman with the contemptuous insolence with which he had stared at her.

She turned away from the door and settled herself beside the dressing table to read the note that he had brought from Allan.

CHAPTER TWENTY

FOR GRAMBLING the three days that followed his arrival at Constancia were beset with a nightmare confusion. Always, in the brief coolness of the mornings and in the languid warmth of the tropic nights, she was almost within his grasp, and always she managed to elude him. She had taken to wearing her brief boy's costume during the day, so that when he saw her then every curve and contour of her body was so brazenly and unmistakably revealed that she might almost as well have been naked before his eyes. In the evenings she tempted him with an even more cruel subtlety, for then the deliberate seduction of her gowns and the intoxication of her perfume affirmed the magic of her womanhood and swelled the tide of his breathless impatience to an almost unbearable crest of urgency and desperate desire.

There were new lines of tension carved beside his lips and he had slept so little that his eyes burned deep in his skull above sagging crescents of flushed and wrinkled flesh. As the long days and empty nights went by, his smoldering hate grew like a wind-whipped flame until it was so much a part of his blind determination to possess her that he was like a ravenous dog, ready to snap and tear at the very hand that held food out before him. It was on the upper gallery, on the evening of the third night, that the dammed-back tide of overwhelming frustration boiled up in a maelstrom of rage and final recklessness. He had been pleading with her and she had demurred and hesitated, advancing the argument of her obligation to MacMurran.

"*Damn MacMurran!*" The roar of his voice jerked her erect in her chair. "By the time he's able to travel he'll be back with his wife again an' you'll be out on th' streets beggin' some drunken sailah to take you foah a picayune! An' yet you sit heah an' bait me like some schoolboy because you think you have to play faiah with MacMurran!"

"His wife! Dorothée?" Her fingers dug into the arms of her chair and her eyes widened unbelievably. "You're out of your mind! Dorothée has been mad for years, a lunatic, caged in her room with an attendant always beside her!"

He laughed mockingly. "An' so that's what he told you? An' what would you say if Ah told you his wife an' her mothah spent the entiah aftahnoon with him in his room only two days aftah you left New O'leans? What would you say if Ah told you th' house on Bienville Street had been swa'min' with lawyahs and priests an' it's plain that she's sane again an' he's plannin' to take her back?"

She leaped to her feet and faced him with clenched fists trembling at her sides and her face drawn and tortured.

"It's a lie!" Her voice was shrill and panic-stricken. "Dorothée could never recover. You're telling me this to drive me away from him so that you can take his place!"

"An' so it's a lie, is it?" His hand slipped inside his coat and reappeared holding a folded sheet of letter paper. "Then maybe you'd like to see this. It's th' note he got from her th' very day you went away." He waved it carelessly back and forth, and with a choking cry she dashed forward and snatched it from him. Her eyes burned as she tried to decipher the spidery handwriting, but there was no light here except the flickering mist of the

moonlight; she whirled and ran into her own room, where a candelabra flickered beside her bed.

> Mon cher Allan,
>
> We have been dismayed at the report of your inju-
> ries at Constancia and beg that Dorothée and I may call
> upon you Thursday to offer our felicitations upon your
> escape and best wishes for your speedy recovery. There
> is also another matter of mutual interest that I feel we
> should discuss with you at this time. You will be over-
> joyed, I know, to learn that Dorothée is at last freed from
> the illness that has possessed her for so long.
>
> With all wishes for your good health,
>
> MARIE TÉRÈSE D'ESTREHAN

She stared at the paper with a sick disbelief that slowly gave
way to a blinding sense of despair. She glanced at the date of
the note and saw that it was, in truth, the very day upon which
she came back to Constancia, just forty-eight hours before the
afternoon Madame d'Estrehan had suggested for their visit. She
looked up to see Grambling leaning against one of the thick posts
of her bed, his mouth twisted into a sneer of sardonic triumph,
his eyes derisive and insolent again.

"How did this note come into your hands?"

He laughed at her, mocking her panic-stricken struggle to
escape this brutal reality that he had forced upon her. "Ah stole
it—an' Ah planned to use it just this way. Would you rathah
have waited to find out until MacMurran ordahed you out of
Constancia an' brought her heah to take yoah place?"

She shook her head, her mind still whirling. It was grotesque,
fantastic, a monumental tragedy of errors that must dissolve

before some still undisclosed explanation. And yet—there had been no word of this in the note from Allan that Grambling had delivered to her. Surely, if it had been barren of significance, he would have told her of the incident. This shroud of secrecy and silence could only mean that plans were under way that she was not to share; plans that would thrust her out of Allan's life and cut her adrift in a hostile and savage world.

Grambling's voice cut across her thoughts, domineering and openly complacent, the voice of a beggar on horseback.

"Theah's no need for us to hold off any longah as fah as Ah can see. It doesn't make any diff'runce what MacMurran thinks about it now."

The words pounded in her head like muffled hammers striking a leaden gong. It would be like this forever now; a woman to be possessed by casual strangers who would not try to disguise their contempt even in the passionate hour they shared with her. It seemed to her that she was sinking into some murky slough that fastened slimy tentacles upon her as she was dragged down into the pitiless limbo of despair and darkness. Out of the well of wretchedness that consumed her, she heard her own voice, as alien and disembodied as if there were some stranger in the room.

"No, it doesn't make any difference now."

Like a woman in a dream her hands crept up to her throat and her fingers began to loosen the ribbon that supported the bodice of her gown.

CHAPTER TWENTY-ONE

"MADRE DE DIOS! Must I do this work myself, or would a touch of the whip brighten your wits today?"

The irritation that seemed always to be smoldering in her crackled in her voice, and the blacks who were piling the newly made molasses hogsheads against the brick wall of the sugar factory measured her anger in panic-stricken glances from the corners of their eyes, and then swarmed like bees about the mule-drawn carts that had hauled the casks down from the shaving- and sawdust-cluttered carpentry. They lived in constant terror of her now, this strange, foreign woman who had lately turned as cruel and ruthless as the devil himself.

She was cruel. She knew that she had changed, turned bitter and vindictive under the prodding of her own insecurity and the problem Grambling's contemptuous possessiveness had created for her. After she had surrendered to him, he had dropped even the pretense of courtesy. Three nights before on the upper gallery he had said, "In th' mawnin' Ah want you to go down to th' quahtahs an stay theah until those Nigrahs have scrubbed out every damn one of 'em with hot watah an' lye. They smell wuss than any pigsty Ah evah saw."

"You want me to—" Her rage almost choked her so that she had to stop for an instant to catch her breath. "Why, damn you, I'll see you stretched in hell with a stake in your guts before I'll take orders from you! I'm in charge here!"

His insolent drawl smothered her storming revolt. "You'ah not in chahge heah. MacMurran's just keepin' you out of sight up heah till he gets straightened out with his wife again. Soon as that happens he'll send you trottin' down th' road with th' hounds yappin' at yoah heels. Ah said foah you to get out to th' quahtahs in th' mawnin' an' that's what I meant." He leaned forward, reaching for the bottle that waited on the table. "When Ah tell you Ah want somethin' done—Goddamn!"

He threw himself back, in the chair, his arms thrown up to protect his face, and as he struggled to rise Manette lashed out at him again with the heavy riding crop she had snatched up from the floor beside her chair. His cheek was torn open where the first blow had struck him, and now she lashed him like a dog, the flail of the whip cutting at his eyes so that he fell back from the assault, his voice rising in a roar of fear and anger.

"Stop! Goddamn it, stop! Ah'll kill you foah this, Ah sweah to God Ah will!"

She threw the whip aside and in the same instant there was the swirl of her skirt and then the poniard was naked and deadly in her hand. He had lunged toward her when she dropped the whip, but when the light flickered on the cold steel, he checked himself in mid-stride and stood staring at her, his head thrust forward on his shoulders and his half-clenched hands clawing at empty air.

"*Cabrón*! Fifth from a stinking gutter! Son of a pig and brother of a rat!"

She moved forward threateningly and he stumbled backward.

"Now wait! Wait a minute theah." He raised one hand in a cautious gesture of appeal. "You don't want to do nothin' you'ah goin' to be sorry foah latah on. Ah reckon Ah did go too fah, but Ah shoah didn't aim to set you off like this. Aftah all, we been pretty good friends heah lately."

"Friends? I've hated you from the day I first set foot on this plantation! I've let you share my bed, yes, but it wasn't because I wanted you. I used you to wipe Allan out of my mind, just as I'd use a dirty rag to wipe the mud off of my shoes—and when I was done, I'd value the filthy cloth more highly than I value you!"

She could see the rage deepening in his face as he absorbed the jeering insult. His lips twisted in and out and his hands began to tremble with the force of his impotent fury.

"No woman evah talked to me like that."

She moved the point of the poniard a little, watching his eyes flicker down to it and then come slowly back to her face.

"You're lucky that it's only talk—so far." Still facing him, she moved enough to put the gallery railing at her back. "Now get out! Get off this gallery and get out of this house and get away from this plantation. If you ever come near me again, I'll kill you!"

That had been three days before, and now, sitting astride the gray gelding here in the sunlight while the casks rolled and rumbled into place, she tried to decide what action she could take in regard to Grambling's continuing defiance of her order. He had taken himself out of the house that night, but he had gone only as far as the overseer's cottage some fifty yards away. He had barricaded himself there, and she knew from the house servants that he had been drinking steadily for the past three days and nights. He had found other consolations, too. She was sure of that, for from her vantage point on the gallery in the evenings she had seen stealthy mulatto girls stealing in and out of the cottage and heard their high-pitched, giggling laughter in the night. It was little enough to her if he chose to turn himself into a drunken animal, but it was a situation that was swollen with danger. As long as he was on the plantation, driven half mad with anger and brandy, she could have not even the semblance of peace or dignity or safety. And yet there was no one to help her drive him away, and she shrank from the thought of attempting it alone.

It was hot that night in Grambling's cottage; so hot that, even though he wore only a pair of thin gray cottonade pantaloons, the greasy sweat stood beaded on his face and soaked the mat of hair that covered his chest. His hair was rumpled and uncombed, and a three-day stubble of beard darkened his face. But he had been drinking too long to care or even to know these things. When the sluggish torment the debauch was building up in him came to the surface of his consciousness he numbed it with more brandy, until the tortured flesh and nerves grew dazed again. Numberless times in the last three days and nights he had spurred his body on to exhaust itself with some mulatto wench from the quarters, but that had been a nostrum for the mind rather than the flesh, a confused defiance to blot out the humiliation of Manette's rejection.

He cursed her now, sullenly, resentfully, watching the growing apprehension of the mulatto girl who crouched on the floor before him.

"A damn whoah, that's all she is! Layin' up theah with MacMurran so she can have th' fine clothes an' th' purty fixin's he can give her. She slept with me—an', by God, she liked it, too! She found out what it was to have a real man in bed with her foah a change. But Ah couldn't buy her no fancy doodads from New O'leans, so she says, 'Wilson, you get out. You ain't got nothin' Ah want except one thing an' th' world's full of men waitin' to give me that.' Goddamn her dirty soul. Come heah, girl! She ain't got anything you ain't got an' you'ah a damn sight easiah to get along with."

The girl cut her eyes uneasily toward the door, her face sullen and unresponsive with the fear that was building up in her. This was white folks' talk, and bad talk, at that. It was sure death for a colored girl to even think such things about a white woman, and worse to sit and listen to a white man say them. She gathered her legs beneath her and stretched out a tentative hand toward the flimsy dress that lay discarded on the floor.

"I force' to go now, honey. I be back when you—"

"Go, hell!" The blind resentment that was like a poison inside him boiled over in a searing rage, welcoming this opportunity to release itself without regard to reason or direction. "Ah'll teach you to talk about goin' when Ah tell you to come to me!" A perverse demon inside his brain was jeering at him as he lunged up from his chair: You can't even hold a colored wench, can you? You're willing to bring them in here and talk to them and sleep with them and give them liquor out of your own bottle, and even then they don't want to be around you. Nobody wants to be around you, Grambling.

His slashing blow was born of his sudden desperate need to silence this mocking enemy that was the only accuser he truly feared, the traitorous heretic that exposed his secret weaknesses, dragging his hard-hidden doubts and fears out into the light, threatening the very foundations of the image of himself he had so painstakingly constructed and displayed.

The girl had gained her knees when he struck her, and the hard sledge of his fist sent her lurching to the floor with sprawled legs and her body twisted. She buried her head in her arms in a futile gesture of self-protection, but he tore even that poor defense away as he jerked her to her feet and held her erect with one hand twisted in her hair.

She opened her mouth to scream and he struck her again, feeling the lips tear beneath his knuckles, the teeth shatter like broken glass.

"You sit theah an' tell me that you'ah foahced to go now! You'll go, goddamn you!" His breath came in sobbing gasps so that the words were almost unintelligible. "You'll go a damn sight fahthah than you planned to. You'ah goin' clean to hell befoah Ah get done with you tonight!"

Her knees buckled beneath her and her arms jerked wildly and ineffectually, but he held her erect with the torturing hand upon her hair, while his other fist beat her face into a pulpy mass that finally lost all human shape. He let her fall then, and when she was on the floor he kicked at her breasts with his bare feet until the swelling mounds were puffed and distorted. She stopped struggling. Standing over her, legs wide astraddle and his chest rising and falling with the hurricane of his anger, he realized vaguely that he was smeared with her blood—on his hands and his arms, across the puffed and bearded jowls, dark splotches on the wrinkled gray of the sweat-soaked cottonade.

"Ah reckon you leahned yoah lesson tonight, didn't you? " He had spoken aloud, in a drunken mumble of loose lips and a thickened tongue. He swayed back and forth, staring down at her, and the demon inside him chose that moment to strike again:

But the one you really hate—the woman up at the big house—you haven't taught her any lessons, have you, Grambling?

"By God," he said aloud, "Ah will teach her—an' Ah'll teach her now!"

He stumbled toward the door and halfway there his rolling eyes fell on the coiled blacksnake whip it had been his custom to carry with him to the fields. It was a good eight feet long, with a lash that tapered from the thickness of a man's wrist to a slim tip braided over a dozen strands of wire, so that the stiff ends of the wire protruded like nails and ripped and gashed whatever flesh they touched.

He coiled the whip and tucked it beneath his arm before he opened the cottage door and stepped out into the darkness of the night. It was well past midnight and Constancia was asleep. The lights were out in the quarters and in the big house. There would be no one there at this hour except Manette. The house servants slept in their own cabins in the quarters and MacMurran was far away in a rose-walled house on Bienville Street. Grambling's tongue shuttled greedily back and forth across his lips as he slipped through the open door and into the wide hallway. He was silent now, moving through the darkness on bare feet that did not waken even a whisper of a sound. He crept up the curving stairway, his breath whispering lightly in and out, the knuckles of his fingers white around the butt of the coiled whip. At the top of the stairs he stopped to listen, but there was no sound or movement. The night was hushed, without even the murmur of a breeze or the sleepy twittering of a bird. One arm outstretched so that his fingertips just brushed the surface of the wall, he stole forward through the darkness; forward toward the room where Manette was sleeping as he had so often seen her sleep, her body a darker blur of gold against the silver of the silken bed, her hair like a dark halo to frame the loveliness of her face. He caught his breath as he remembered, giving himself up to a shudder of sadistic desire that racked him from head to foot.

His fingers touched the edge of her unlatched door and he felt it give and swing slowly open before him.

CHAPTER TWENTY-TWO

S HE HAD BEEN SO exhausted that night that after dinner she
had dropped off to sleep as she relaxed in her chair on the
upper gallery. There had been the faintest whisper of a breeze
coming in from the river and the quiet coolness there had been
a blessed sanctuary after the heat and tumult of the day. She had
tried to think about Allan and Dorothée and Grambling, but her
mind had been too drained by weariness to concentrate upon the
problems that they posed. Little by little, she had yielded herself
to the serenity of the night, until at last she fell asleep with the
moonlight in a bright pool about her feet.

It was past midnight when she stirred and wakened, still
drugged with drowsiness, half-consciously aware that she should
seek her bed. Thrusting herself reluctantly through the waves of
sleep that still swirled about her, she found the doorway to her
room and shrugged off the three light garments that she wore.
The bed was a soft sea that beckoned to her and she collapsed
across it. The mosquito netting fell into place behind her and in
an instant she was asleep again, her head pillowed on her arm,
her dreams pursuing the problems her conscious mind had long
since thrust aside.

But the dream would not be denied. It led her through a
strange, unending land of bleak and awful desolation. Dark thun-
derheads of turgid clouds rolled and muttered like angry waves
above her. There was a cold wind, a cruel wind that stripped her
bare so that she ran naked and whimpering before it, seeking

some shelter in this sheer and terrifying emptiness. But there was nothing. Nothing but the vast void of tainted and reeking earth that stretched on and on to some murky and unclean horizon. And then she heard them howling behind her, running with feet that never touched the ground. Black, hideous, yellow-fanged. Suddenly there was a high wall before her with a great door that stood half open, and Allan, with a sword in his hand, beckoning her on. The black horrors snarled and howled at her heels, but she had almost gained the refuge of the wall when Allan's face twisted into a distorted mask of hate and he thrust the sword at her quivering breast. The door clanged shut against her and she was alone in the terrible desert of this empty land, with the rabid hounds of darkness leaping up so that their foul breath sickened her and she was smothering beneath their weight.

Her shriek of terror echoed through the room. In the same instant the barbed tip of Grambling's whip cut through the mosquito netting and stripped the soft flesh from her throat.

She screamed again, entrapped between the dream and the reality, flung headlong into a nightmare labyrinth of fear and delirium. The beasts had pulled her down, and now there was blood upon her throat. Her mind whirled as she tried to fight her way back to sanity, and with the panic instinct of desperation, she tore the mosquito netting aside and fled toward the safety of the open window and the gallery.

When she was halfway across the room, the whip licked out again and brought her to her knees with slashing waves of pain. She tried to stagger to her feet, and it was then that she saw Grambling, just inside the door, his face distorted, the whip writhing like a live snake in his hands. He threw back his head and laughed when he saw her eyes upon him, a wild, insane cackling. It ended as abruptly as it had begun and in the same instant the lash flashed out and the tip snapped so closely before her eyes that she could feel its threat in the sudden movement of air against her face and hear its sharp explosion in her ears, like the echo of a pistol shot.

"Ah could of ripped them purty eyes right out of yoah head then." His voice was flat, expressionless, the dull monotone of a madman so fully committed to a course of action that there was no need for consideration or discussion. "Reckon prob'ly Ah'll do that yet—just befoah Ah kill you, maybe."

She began to tremble, her control swept away in a deluge of nervous frenzy she could not control.

"Grambling!" This was some stranger's voice, this pitiful, quavering sound that seemed scarcely strong enough to pierce the shadows. *"Por Dios,* Grambling, what are you trying to do to me?"

"Goin' to teach you a lesson you won't nevah fo'get." He moved toward her, and now she could see the drying blood upon his face and body. She tried to shrink away.

"You figuahed you weah puttin' me back in my place when you pulled that knife on me an' drove me out of yoah house." He leaned forward, close enough now for her to see the glaze of madness in his eyes. "Goddamn you, Ah'm goin' to rip th' hide off of yoah body foah that! Ah've already killed one wench tonight an' they can't hang me no highah foah two than they can foah one."

His hard fingers bit into her wrist and he jerked her to her feet and sent her spinning across the room to crash into the wide rosewood dressing table. She heard the glass shatter and felt the sharp pain as the jagged edges of the broken mirror ripped into her shoulder. The fragile bottles of perfume and the cloisonné vials that held her creams and the rouge for her lips came crashing down about her in a wild confusion that seemed, somehow, a fitting part of this maniac ordeal that had fastened itself upon her. The lash followed her, searing her like smoking iron as the barbed tip slashed and tore.

She was lost in a mist of horror now. A tempest of sobs tore at her throat and choked back the shrieking terror that exploded in her brain. There was a strange languor in her body, a languor than sank beneath the surface of the flayed and tortured flesh and seemed almost to invite the lash again. She heard it singing in the air and then her body jerked and quivered as the braided rawhide wound itself about her thighs. Helplessly she surrendered herself to its dark caress. She could hear Grambling cursing her, but the voice was far away and the words were only a meaningless blur of sound. He was going to kill her, she knew that now. It would be slow, with the whip draining the life out of her little by little as it flayed the skin from her body. A long death. A hard death.

She tried to twist her head aside to escape the insistent odor of ammonia that was dragging her back to an unwilling consciousness, but the thick rug was saturated with it, soaked with the contents of a bottle of her smelling salts that had been shattered when Grambling sent her reeling into the dressing table. She moaned a little, seeking to hold this warm fog of stupor that had overpowered her, but the ammoniac fumes were all about her, driving the vague shadows out of her brain and forcing her back into a monstrous world besieged by bloody violence and unending agony.

Her eyes had cleared a little and she saw that Grambling, inexplicably, had thrown open the doors of the armoire and was jerking her dresses down and piling them in a clumsy heap against the wall. As she watched, he crossed the room to Allan's desk and began to jerk out the piles of papers and correspondence that it contained and add them to the pile. Her still numbed brain struggled sluggishly with the problem, confused by his abandonment of the beating to plunge into this new activity. Her dresses and Allan's papers ...

With a sudden flash of sanity, she realized that he was planning to burn Constancia!

Her drugged resignation fell away as swiftly as it had come and she was no longer a beaten animal, but a woman of fire and murderous violence, intent on her own need to save herself and the allied obligation to destroy this bestial renegade who had dared to attack her. A pistol that had been on the dressing table lay at her fingertips, but the priming had been spilled when it fell and now it was only so much wood and steel. Her eyes darted about the room in search of a weapon and paused at the slight pile of garments she had thrown down beside the door when she came into the bedroom from the gallery some two hours before. Somewhere beneath those crumpled garments was the poniard that she always carried. It was hidden now, but when Grambling swept up the blouse and skirt and undershift to add them to his pile, the knife would come clattering out upon the floor. If she could reach it first ...

His back was turned to her as he rummaged among the papers in the desk, and she lifted herself to her elbows and began to crawl silently toward the little mound of crumpled cloth. A shard of glass tinkled as she touched it and she froze into instant immobility with her eyes riveted on Grambling's back. It seemed to her his hurrying fingers were still for an instant and her heart stopped while she waited for him to turn and see her there. But he plunged his hands back into the open drawer and she inched forward again.

Her fingers touched the edge of the blouse and she began to pull it to her. Gently, softly, slowly, so that there would be no betraying click of metal against wood, if the poniard was entangled with it. The blouse came free and her trembling fingers explored it feverishly—but the knife was not there. The skirt, then. Her fingers stirred again, probing, searching, sifting the soft folds for the cold reassurance of the steel. But there was no steel, no razor-pointed blade, no deep-carved hilt to nestle snugly in the hot palm of her hand.

Her brain whirled with the hopelessness of defeat. She had been more than half asleep when she had come into the room and thrown her clothes aside. Perhaps she had left the blade beside her bed or on some nearby chair. Her nails bit into the palms of her hands as she tried to force the recollection of that sleep-jaded moment back into her mind, but it was gone.

With a sudden start she realized that the sound of crinkling papers from the desk had ceased. She jerked her head around and saw that Grambling had turned and was watching her, his fingers already closing again around the butt of the whip. Paralyzed with despair, she saw the quick flip of his wrist that brought the lash to his feet in a black coil of latent torment. In an instant his hand would move again and the barbed thongs would beat her back into the unconsciousness that she had just escaped.

In a final frenzy of desperation, she snatched at the crumpled undershift and sobbed in an ecstasy of relief as the lean poniard clattered out upon the floor. There was no time to charge him with it in her hand; the ready whip would cut her down before she could even gain her feet. But there was another way, a better way. For a fraction of an instant the naked knife seemed to gather strength in her open palm. Then her arm swept up and forward in a silver arc and the poniard flashed through the air like a hawk swooping upon its prey. Grambling tried to cry out and raise his arm, but the cry gurgled away into a blood-choked bubble-of sound as the blade pierced his throat and the arm fell limp and nerveless at his side. He clutched feebly at his throat, stumbling back against the disordered clutter of the desk. His eyes had widened into great moons of terror and his jaw jerked feebly as the blood spurted out in a darkly spasmodic flood that poured down across his chest and dripped and overflowed upon the floor below. He crashed down on his knees and for an instant he stared across the room at her, wildly questioning this inconceivable thing. Then his head fell forward so that his chin seemed to rest on the poniard hilt and he collapsed in the shambles that his own lifeblood had made.

In the silence that settled upon the room the first whisper of the dawn wind stirred the curtains of the windows as if to herald an end to the fearful night and the coming of another day.

Drained of emotion, spent to the final limit of exhaustion, Manette lifted her head and felt its coolness on her face. Then, like a tired child, she dropped her head upon her arms and slept.

CHAPTER TWENTY-THREE

GRAMBLING and the mulatto girl he had killed had been buried for a week. The bedroom where he had died, with the hot blood bubbling from his throat, had been cleaned and put in order, but Manette had found that too many gibbering memories still lingered there in the long hours of the night and had transferred her belongings and herself to another room on the opposite side of the hall. Restless and uneasy during the slow days of her convalescence, she cursed her whip wounds and the bandages that sheathed them, fretting against the perilous inactivity they imposed upon her.

Her position was dangerous, and the danger grew with every hour that slipped away. It was too much to expect the slaves not to chatter of the drama of the two deaths to other blacks from the adjoining plantations. Then the neighboring overseers would pick it up and carry it to their masters, and in a fortnight the gaudy scandal would be the gossip of New Orleans. She knew only too well what would happen then—a military guard dispatched from the Cabildo to bring her before the Governor for questioning. A hurried message to Don Francisco de Larra of Havana that the woman who had made a fool of him had fallen into the clutches of the law and could be punished as he desired. The long weeks of waiting in a dark cell for his reply, and then the trial that would not be a trial but only a farce and a mockery to serve his ends. After that there would be His Gracious Majesty's plantations on the southern islands, where she would be put to work in the fields and lashed into obedience and docility.

She closed her eyes and shuddered, unable even for a moment to conceive the possibility of resignation to such a fate. And yet, what was to save her from it? It was possible that Allan might have saved her, but now that he was reconciled with Dorothée he could scarcely afford to espouse the cause of a murdering wanton whose name was already linked too closely with his own. No, she must disappear before the hue and cry was raised, and there was only one person in all the world who could be forced to aid her. Etienne! Etienne, who owed her a secret and an unpaid debt for her assistance in the matter of his marriage to Julie de Ternant. Etienne, whose house of cards would come crashing down about him if she even hinted at the conspiracy they had shared. Yes, she could demand protection from him, and it must be done at once, before the grim Cabildo walls enclosed her and she was denied even this narrow avenue of escape.

The deep-cut slashes that scarred her body had begun to heal, but they were still so raw and inflamed that the slightest movement was a torment. The thought of the long trip down-river turned her sick with weakness, but there was no alternative. Better a long day of agony than a lifetime surrendered to misery and despair. She tugged at the bell cord suspended beside her bed and waited, husbanding her strength, for one of the mulatto maids to appear.

"I am going to New Orleans in the morning," she told the sloe-eyed girl who came at last. "Everything that is mine must be packed and placed aboard the sloop by sunrise. You'd best begin now, for there are many things to be collected and much to do."

"But—everything? Surely, when the señorita returns—"

Her lips twisted in a wry smile. "There will be time enough to replace them—when the señorita returns. Get one of the other girls to help you now, and begin at once. *Vamos!*"

Propped up in bed with her pillows behind her back, she watched the two girls scuttle back and forth. Dresses of satin and gowns of silk, rich robes of embroidered brocade and lingerie as filmy as a dream; hats and slippers and the heavy golden bracelets from Peru; an ivory jewel box that had come from Vienna by way of Paris, emeralds and rouge and Chinese fans, and a long strand of limpid pearls Allan had given her the day they left Bonneterre. One by one, her treasures vanished into the depths of two brass-bound trunks until there was nothing left except the simple dress of Irish linen that she would wear on the weary journey from Constancia to New Orleans. She saw the trunks carried to the hall below and then dismissed the maids and resigned herself to the long hours that must be endured until the dawn. The room seemed strangely empty, as empty as her heart, and she was possessed by a sudden illogical impression that the great house was desolate and sad because of her decision to abandon it. But that was utter imbecility, a reflection of her own unhappiness at leaving this spot that she had loved so well. In a few more weeks the house would welcome Dorothée as graciously as it had welcomed her, and after a while not even a memory of her life there would remain; not even the fragrance of her perfumes or the echo of her footsteps on the stairs. Uncomforted and alone, she watched the moonlight creep across the floor until the first gray wisps of morning gathered like pale smoke in the dawn.

It was sundown when she came at last to New Orleans, parched by the blazing sun that had poured down upon the muddy river, her body a solid mass of pain from the exertion of guiding the sloop and handling the sails. She had come unattended, for it was far too dangerous to bring one of the Constancia slaves to New Orleans with the story of Grambling's death trembling on his lips. Almost moaning with fatigue, she warped the sloop in to the pier. She sent a colored lounger scurrying to bring one of the shabby public carriages to the wharf, and when she had seen the trunks loaded on it and collapsed against the cracked leather of its worn upholstery, she gave the driver Etienne's address and gave herself up to weariness and exhaustion. She managed to rouse herself when they reached the house on Esplanade, and a part of her weariness gave way to a profound sensation of relief at having gained this sanctuary.

The major-domo summoned Etienne to greet her and he came into the living room with hands outstretched and the brightness of undisguised pleasure burning in his eyes. "Manette, it is wonderful to see you here, *ma chère,* and you are more beautiful than ever—" His voice died as he saw the dark circles etched beneath her eyes and the tight lines at the corners of her mouth that betrayed her nervousness and pain. "But have you been ill, *petite?* Or did the journey from Constancia tire you?"

"I have been beaten, Etienne. Beaten with a blacksnake whip until I could not crawl across the floor."

She saw his eyes widen in amazement and his quick glance took in the bandages on her arm and the mottled bruises that were still livid upon her cheeks.

"Beaten! *Ma foi,* Manette, that is impossible! Who would have dared?"

She told him then, as she sat on the sofa and sipped sherry, just as she had that long-ago afternoon when she had persuaded Julie into marriage. She told him of Grambling first and then, at the last, of the news Grambling had brought of Allan's return to Dorothée.

"What have you heard of this, Etienne?" she demanded. "Is it true that Dorothée has regained her mind and Allan plans to return to her?"

His eyes flickered away and he caught his lower lip between his teeth, but when he replied it was to nod in sympathetic agreement.

"It's true enough, Manette." He let his fingers cover hers as if to comfort her. "It is a miracle that she should be sane again, and yet who knows what the *Dieu Seigneur* plans or proposes? I have not seen her myself, but it is common talk that her madness has vanished, and she is to take her place as Allan's wife again."

"But she was unfaithful to him! She drove him away to Bonneterre in the beginning and he had already sued her for a divorce when she—"

"I know, I know, Manette. But Allan was younger then and he cared nothing for the opinion of the city or the people in it. Now—why, now he is bent on laying the foundations for a dynasty. He has Constancia and his affairs here in New Orleans. He lacks nothing except the acceptance of society, and his return to Dorothée will ensure that."

She nodded slowly, remembering that first afternoon in an upper bedroom at Constancia, remembering the bitterness that had been in his voice, the defiance and the desire in his words: "I don't want to be on the outside looking in! Before I'm done, I want to be welcomed and honored in any house in Louisiana! That's what I want, Manette—and that's what I'm going to have!" Yes, it was true enough. He had chafed beneath the irregularity of their relationship, loyal to it because of the physical bonds that held them together but all too well aware that it was a handicap he would eventually be forced to surmount or discard.

She forced her mind back to the present, realizing that Julie had not come forward to welcome her. That was strange.

"And where is Julie tonight, Etienne?"

He laughed a little, his dark eyes brightening with an anticipation she could not understand. "Julie is not here," he said slowly. "She went upriver to visit her cousins at Philomene plantation almost a week ago. It will be a fortnight or more before she will come back to New Orleans again." His fingers tightened on her hand and she knew that for him her presence and Julie's absence could only mean a providential opportunity to renew the relationship that had been abandoned with his marriage. And that was well enough—for even as small a thing as the touch of his hand aroused the old tempestuous turbulence that she could never deny—but first they must solve the problem of her escape from the dangers that pressed so closely and relentlessly about her.

"Perhaps that is for the best," she admitted. "Julie might or might not be inclined to help me in this matter. But you will help me, Etienne"—her eyes challenged him—"for you remember an agreement that we made, and now I need your help, just as you once needed mine."

He stirred uneasily, making a great business of refilling their glasses and restoring the decanter to the taboret. "But what is this help that you require, Manette? I have no power or influence with the Governor."

"I know that, Etienne." She was a little impatient now, a swift resentment mounting in her at his obvious reluctance to become entangled in the skein of her affairs. "I need nothing from you except a spot where I can be concealed from the Governor's anger until this matter is forgotten or until I can get away. Some place where I can be safe. Surely I am not the first refugee who has ever been hidden in New Orleans. There must be some establishment—"

"Yes," he said slowly, "there is a place. Pierre Le Marche lay there all one winter when he was accused of a treasonable plot against the crown. It was well enough for him, but as for you—"

"If it served his purpose, there is no reason it should not serve mine. What is this place, Etienne?" She leaned forward so that she could stare into his eyes. "What is this secret establishment that even the Governor cannot reach?"

"You have money?"

"A reasonable amount. If it is not enough, you will give me more."

He stared at her in amazement and then his lips parted in a flashing smile as he slapped his hand down on the taboret. "Yes, by God, I will," he agreed. "Well, then, this refuge that I mentioned is a house of assignation. Oh, most discreet, known only to a very limited number of the gentlemen of the city. It is managed by a Señora Carlota Calderón, who came here from Navarre and is the mistress of Don Pedro Antonio de Valera!"

She caught her breath, for Valera was the most feared and hated man in all the colonies of Spain. Judge advocate of His Majesty's private and extraordinary tribunal, he held such power that governors and viceroys shuddered at the mention of his name. Responsible only to the King, he commanded the same fear in the field of secular political affairs that was tendered to the Inquisition in matters of churchly and clerical import. If the Señora Calderón was under his protection …

"But a house of assignation," she protested. "It would not be expected to—"

Etienne laughed again and waved her objections away with a careless hand. "You would be an honored guest. The matter of the assignations is a blind, a screen thrown up so that men may come and go without exciting comment as to their political activities or the information they may possess. It is a great convenience for Valera, and as for your part in it, it is common talk that he has no love for Larra. You will be safe enough there—and it will be easy for me to see you while you are in seclusion."

"Seclusion. Yes, I suppose that is as good a word as any other." There were harsh lines of bitterness around her mouth and her eyes were dark and brooding. Now as if to cap everything that had gone before, she was to exchange the sweeping graciousness of Constancia for the sordid shelter of a bordello; the sound of the wind whispering through the tasseled cane for the shallow tinkling of a bawdyhouse piano; the strength she had found in Allan for the weakness in Etienne. And yet she had hungered and grieved for Etienne while she was separated from him. It was a fruitless relationship, rooted in the wind, with an inevitable finale of stinging emptiness and ignominious frustration, but she could not escape it. She shrugged her shoulders in a gesture of fatalistic resignation.

"Take me there now, Etienne." She forced herself to her feet, feeling the intolerable weariness like a great stone upon her shoulders. She caught the startled disappointment in his face and laughed ruefully, knowing that they were both remembering the passion they had shared on a certain night in Bienville Street. "If you could see my body, you would not even want me now." She jerked open the bodice of her dress so he could see the purple bruises above the bandages that bound her breasts and saw the torches of desire burn out in his eyes as they were replaced by a stare of mounting horror. His mouth fell slack with revulsion; he tried desperately to speak words of sympathy, but he was rendered speechless at the sight of her mutilated body.

"There will be time enough for that when I am whole and clean again. Will you take me to the Señora Calderón now?"

He nodded silently.

CHAPTER TWENTY-FOUR

ARLOTA CALDERÓN was a petite, honey-colored blonde, as debonair as a swordsman and as cold and calculating as a Gascon money-changer. Her fair skin and clear blue eyes bespoke the heritage bequeathed to the provinces of Navarra and Huesca and Zaragoza in those long dead days when the hordes of the invading Vandals swept into Spain across the Pyrenees. With the brilliance of the chandeliers blazing down upon her in this shuttered house that overlooked the Place d'Armes, she was a woman of silver and steel, alert, reckless; she was gracious enough, but perpetually *en garde* against the world.

Her eyes had brightened with a sudden interest when Etienne had presented her to Manette, and as she listened to his explanation, she measured the other woman almost as warily as a duellist would have measured the capacities of his opponent. When he was done, her fingers drummed thoughtfully on the arm of her chair as she considered the possibilities of the situation.

"You have not tried to call on the Señor MacMurran for assistance?"

"And be humiliated by his refusal?" Manette's slim arm sketched a quick gesture of impatience and disdain. "I have had no word from him since the single note that Grambling brought, and Etienne tells me it is common knowledge he will resume his life with Dorothée. No, señora, whatever is to be done, I must do alone. If you can help me, I shall be grateful to you, and if you cannot—why, then I must seek assistance elsewhere.'"

Señora Calderón nodded in agreement, as if it were no more than the answer she had expected. "Yes, that matches with the reports that I have heard of you. You are not entirely without a reputation in New Orleans, señorita, and many who deplore your—ruthlessness—have still found occasion to praise your spirit and your courage." Her white teeth flashed in an unexpected smile of scarlet lips and approving eyes. "We have no place here for cowards, señorita, but there is always a welcome for those who have retained their gallantry and boldness. Sometimes it is even possible for us to work together and gain a mutual benefit. But there will be time enough to talk of that. You are tired now and I will take you to your room, if M'sieur Chrétien will excuse us." As slim and supple as a rapier, she was on her feet in a single fluid movement, smiling again as if she found some secret and unexpected satisfaction in this dark stranger whose reputation for impetuous audacity was so like her own. "My house is yours, señorita," she said gravely. "It is an honor to have you here."

The city began to stir in the first flush of the dawn, and it was a pleasant thing to enjoy the day's first cup of fragrant coffee in a jasmine- and oleander-scented courtyard while the jade-green laves of the banana leaves were still shining with dew and the coolness of the night lingered in the air. The pigeons resumed their soft-voiced murmurings and mocking-birds and swallows that would be silent in the blaze of noon loosed the splintered silver of their songs here in the glowing rose light of the morning. Swathed in a scarlet dressing gown, Manette sipped coffee and surveyed the vast square of the Place d'Armes from the balcony outside her room. To the north, the great gray masses of the Cabildo, the Cathedral, and the Presbytère loomed up against the cloudless turquoise of the sky; the Church and the State, one and indivisible in this tropic outpost that flourished beneath the gold and scarlet banners of ancient Spain.

A night's rest and the shining brightness of the morning had combined to cleanse Manette of the nerve-racking dejection that had burdened her since Grambling's death. Constancia was gone, and Allan with it, but its corollary was a new freedom she could share with Etienne and the half-glimpsed prospect of some new adventure in Carlota's oblique suggestion of the night before. If she could win Carlota's confidence and, through her, the favor of the all-powerful Valera, the danger of her arrest and punishment would be at an end. The slightest hint of his displeasure might effectively scuttle any punitive action the Governor might undertake and release her from the necessity of hiding and dodging like some runaway slave. She turned back to the room as she heard someone rapping on her door and threw it open to find Carlota just outside.

"Hola, señorita! Will you share my breakfast with me today?" Her gesture indicated two demurely smiling colored girls who waited respectfully behind her, their arms extended to support immense silver trays. "The others in this cursed house sleep like the dead." Her voice rippled up into mocking laughter. "Their exertions of the night exhaust them and yet they consider it a pleasure and a profit." She wrinkled her nose in a grimace of contemptuous disgust. May we come in, señorita?"

"But of course! It is more than kind of you to join me. On the balcony, perhaps?"

"Most certainly the balcony. I know of nothing more enjoyable than to watch others scurry back and forth about their work while I am relaxed and at my ease." She tossed a careless word of instruction to the colored maids and paused for an instant to preen herself before the full-length mirrors that were the doors of the armoire. "I am not sure … this green …" Her fingers caressed the surface of her transparent taffeta dressing gown. "Is it too dark, Manette? Does it turn me sallow?"

"It becomes you marvelously." There was the warmth of sincerity in Manette's voice, for Carlota was as sleek and shining as some Chinese figurine, straight-backed, head held high, proud with an arrogance that could come only from an inner assurance as certain and unquavering as finely tempered steel.

The maids withdrew and Manette, assuming the role of hostess, poured *café con leche* and put aside the heavy silver covers that had guarded the warmth of the toasted brown brioches. "Your household serves you well, señora."

"The two who were here? They are not bad. Tell me," her eyes looked up to probe Manette's face with sudden intensity, "are you ill at ease here because it is a rendezvous for certain men and women of the town?"

Manette considered the question thoughtfully, her eyes straying out across the square and finally coming to rest on the grim gray walls of the Cabildo. "There was a time, when I was a girl in Santo Domingo, that I might have been distressed by it," she admitted. "On the other hand—who knows—I might have found it fascinating and romantic." She turned back to Carlota, recognizing the basic similarity between them that made it possible for her to answer honestly and without pretense. "Now it is a matter of indifference to me. Actually, there's little enough difference between these women and myself. They give their bodies to strangers in return for a handful of silver. I lived with Allan in an effort to gain my own security." She smiled ruefully. "Perhaps they are the wiser, after all. At least, they have the silver, while I have nothing!"

Carlota shook her head. "No," she said slowly, "I do not think it is the same. You played for high stakes—just as I play now—and the cards ran against you. But these addlepated *putas* want nothing more than a few coins in their hands that they can throw away on fripperies or on some gaudy popinjay who has chanced to catch their fancy. A good half of them have husbands they cozen and deceive, with the result that every now and then the *garde* finds one of these pretty birds floating face downward in the river—and small blame, as far as I'm concerned, for the men who put them there."

"And yet—" Manette hesitated and Carlota's laughter filled the balcony again.

"And yet I am the mistress, the procuress of this house! Is that what you were about to say?" The laughter ebbed away and she was suddenly grave and intent. "It is a role that I must play a little while, Manette. Don Pedro Valera has need of such a place as this, where he can confer in secret with certain other men, and if they are seen going or coming, it is put down as an affair of passion rather than of power or politics."

"And that was what you meant last night when you said we might work together?"

"I believe it could be arranged. But only Don Pedro could discuss these matters with you." She hesitated, her eyes withdrawn and thoughtful. "He should be here later today. If there is an opportunity, I will try to have him talk to you."

He was a man of captious temper and a sarcastic tongue, this Don Pedro Antonio de Valera. One of the great caballeros of Spain, a noble of Aragon, he had followed a tortuous road from the ancient castle of Sietamo in the red hills of Huesca to the fever-ridden swamps of Louisiana. He had begun conventionally enough. After his graduation from the royal military school, he had, quite as a matter of course, assumed his acknowledged position as the proprietary colonel of the famed Castilla regiment, a troop that had been the private possession of the Valeras for uncounted generations. He took as his bride the still adolescent Doña Ana, third daughter of the Duke of Hijar, promptly got her with child, and as promptly lost her in the throes of her first accouchement. He turned away from the regiment then, to travel in Italy and Germany, to become the ambassador to Portugal, to be made a knight of the Golden Fleece, a governor of Valencia, and, finally, the captain general of New Castile.

But there was a sourness in him that turned men's hearts against him, a skepticism that offset the advantages of his intelligence, his ability, and his almost fantastic capacity for intense, unending work. He quarreled with his king and with the queen, María Luisa. He was no friend of the powerful courtier Godoy, and his contempt for the *golillas,* the stiff-collared lawyers and public servants Godoy was prone to name as colonial governors, was bitter and unrestrained. Arrogant, intemperate, tremendously ambitious, he fitted nowhere at the court of Spain, and yet his blood and his achievements demanded recognition. So, then, he was exiled to Louisiana. Exiled with an exalted title and a position of almost unlimited power. Exiled with great honors and protestations of affection from his sovereign—but exiled nonetheless. He used his power savagely, seeking an outlet for his furious resentment, but even as he used it, the seeds of rebellion sprouted and flowered within him and he began to dream of greater power, a power that would not be subject to the crown of Spain.

Manette was summoned into his presence just at the hour of sundown.

He was bent over a long table piled high with papers and he glanced up briefly and then returned to his work as Carlota ushered Manette into the room. A lean, tense, hard-faced man somewhere in his middle years. A tightlipped, angry mouth, and eternally suspicious eyes. Pale, long-fingered hands and a hacking cough that rasped and rattled in his throat. Don Pedro Antonio de Valera.

The two women crossed the room until only the wide table separated them from Valera. He worked on, engrossed in his task and seemingly oblivious of their presence. As she watched him, Manette felt an irrepressible tingling in her body that was almost a shiver of revulsion. With only a fleeting glance he had managed to convey the impression of an icy and unbending isolation, a dedication to some unknown purpose that was almost inhuman in its stark austerity. She shot a quick glance at Carlota and was reassured with a fleeting grimace of quickly lifted eyebrows and the faintest possible *moue* of disrespect. More plainly than words, Carlota had told her that this attitude must be accepted but was, in its essence, unimportant and even insignificant. Manette breathed more easily, relaxing a little, and in the same instant he slammed the papers down on the desk with a scalding curse and shoved back his chair so he could stare up at her.

"Manette de Santiago." His voice suggested almost unbounded impatience and contempt. "Is there any reason I should not deliver you to the Governor and have you hanged?"

"Hanged?" She laughed at him then, piercing the brittle armor of his self-assumed truculence. "Have you no better use for me than that, Your Excellency?"

"Any man could find a use for you for an hour—or for a night—but whether you are good for anything aside from that—I have my doubts."

"But you could put the matter to the test."

He nodded sourly. "Yes, and end with a knife in my throat, like the one you killed only a week ago." He saw the surprised alarm aflame in her eyes and chuckled derisively. "Oh, yes,

I know the story. I knew it within an hour after you entered this house last night."

She whirled to rake Carlota with accusing eyes, but the blonde woman only smiled and lifted her hand in a brief gesture of resignation. "Don Pedro is the master here, Manette. This is his house. I think your secret is safe enough with him." She turned back to Valera and her blue eyes searched his face with the impudence of a long and intimate relationship. *"No es verdad?* There is no need to frighten this girl. It is my thought that she can serve you well."

"Your thought!" The sneering deprecation of his voice was unmistakable, insulting, but the eyes were attentive, even a little commendatory as he put his question. "What could this pirate's woman do for me?"

Carlota let the question hang unanswered in the air until Manette felt her whole body grow tense and rigid with the strain of waiting. Then she said softly, "There is the affair of Manuel García and *intendencia* of Valladolid."

"García! And what connection has she with García?"

"None, at the moment. But he will be here soon, and as you said yourself, any man can find a use for her. Perhaps, before they were done, she would be able to discover the truth of his intentions."

He scowled at her, his fingers restless and uneasy as they pawed at the papers on his desk. "And another mouth to babble the secrets she would have to know," he growled. "And what assurance would we have that she would not carry the whole matter to the Governor in exchange for a pardon for herself?"

"And place her head in a noose so that she could be sent to Don Francisco's torture chambers in Havana? There is no fear of betrayal here, Don Pedro. Her own salvation would depend on the success of the things you plan."

"Perhaps. Perhaps." The basilisk eyes glared up at Manette. "Let me hear your story in your own—" He broke off as a torrent of coughing racked him until his face was flushed and the breath choked in his throat. "And if you lie to me, I'll strip you naked and have you flogged through the streets from here to the blackest cell in the Cabildo."

She told him, and then withstood the hour-long ordeal of his searching cross-examination. Over and over again he questioned her as to her relations with Larra, probing and exploring for some weakness or discrepancy. But there was no need for her to disguise the facts or hide the truth, and she faced and answered him steadfastly, even at the last when wave after wave of weariness washed her strength away and his face grew blurred and indistinct before her eyes. In the end, he threw himself back in his chair and turned a questioning glare upon Carlota. "You are a woman and should be able to judge another. Do you think she speaks the truth?"

"I am sure of it. I was convinced of it last night and again when I talked to her this morning. She can do this for you, Don Pedro, and the good God only knows where you would find another that would serve as well."

His fingers drummed thoughtfully on the table and then he thrust the matter aside with a petulant gesture of resignation. "As you desire it, then. Your neck will crack as quickly as my own if you are wrong." He turned back to his papers and issued a final order without bothering to look up at them. "You can instruct her and give her such information as she must have. I can waste no further time on this affair. Take her away, and let me know when M'sieur Rodale arrives."

Manette felt Carlota touch her arm and followed her to the door, so drained of strength by her weakness and fatigue that she stumbled a little as she crossed the threshold. She caught herself and looked up to find Carlota smiling at her, the brightness of an undisputed triumph shining in her eyes.

"You are under the protection of Don Pedro now," she said softly, "and you are safe—as safe as any of us here can be."

"And this commission I am to undertake for him?"

"We'll talk of that tomorrow. For tonight, go to your room and I will have your dinner and some wine brought up to you. After that, you can sleep and dream—dream that someday soon you will be one of the *damas ricas* of an empire!"

"An empire!"

But Carlota had turned away, her tiny heels clicking like castanets as she hurried down the hall.

An empire! But she was only a fugitive with the danger of torture and death still as closely allied to her as her shadow. She tried to find some meaning in Carlota's words but her brain was too spent to grapple with the problem. She felt the railing of the staircase beneath her fingers and began the slow ascent that would take her to her room. Tomorrow would be time enough.

CHAPTER TWENTY-FIVE

"AND SO that is the plan." Carlota had been pacing up and down the room as she talked, and now she stopped and turned to face Manette, silhouetted against the open window that overlooked the balcony and the square. "You are surprised? And yet there is a natural destiny in it—a confusion of anger and resentment and discontent here that cries out for such a man as Valera to set it straight again."

Manette nodded slowly, her imagination aflame with the possibilities of this coup Don Pedro planned, but still only half persuaded that it was practicable or even possible.

"Only a man of tremendous vision would have dared to dream of it," she admitted. "To weld Louisiana and Texas and all of Mexico into a single empire, and then throw off the rule of Spain!"

"But these colonies are ready for it! They demand it! Look, Manette." Carlota's eyes kindled as she pressed home her point. "Louisiana is a French province, even though we rule it now, and the French Creoles would rise in a moment to free themselves from the Spanish crown. Mexico is a hotbed of discontent. It has been seething since the Jesuits were expelled in 1767. It has been throttled by the taxes and the restrictions the King has put upon it. The Creoles hate the governors sent out from Spain and they know the endless confiscations and exactions will strip them bare if they continue. The Viceroy of Mexico has already pledged allegiance to Don Pedro, and with him the governors of the *intendencias* have also pledged their support."

"But not Manuel García, who rules in Valladolid."

"That is the question." The blue eyes darkened like a stormy sky. "We are not sure of him. He blows hot and cold. *Por Dios,* if this were my affair, I'd have him stabbed in the back and let the Viceroy appoint a governor who'd fall in with our plans!"

"It has been done before."

"I know, I know, and I have told Don Pedro so a thousand times, but García has a tremendous following among the *ricos* of Valladolid, and Valera hopes to draw them to him through this wavering García. That is your task, Manette. To dazzle and enchant him so while he is in New Orleans that there will be no question of his loyalty to us. To wind him so tightly around your fingers that even though he cares nothing for the empire, he will support it because you ask it of him as a favor."

"And if that fails?"

"Then you must lead him on until he tells you exactly what he plans to do. We can take measures then to be sure his opposition comes to nothing."

Somber-eyed, oppressed by the coupled shadows of doubt and distaste for this role that she must play, Manette forced her mind to range ahead to the day, less than a fortnight away now, when García would arrive in New Orleans and she would be presented to him. It would be a hiatus, a parenthesis in time cutting off any association with Etienne; and now that she had seen him again, she was as breathless and starry-eyed as any schoolgirl sighing from a convent window. Cover and coat it though she would, the fact remained that she proposed to lend herself to a deliberate entrapment, a fraudulent illusion of tenderness and passion, as false as the farcical burlesque of ecstasy that any of the women in Carlota's house enacted for every stranger who came to her door. The bitterness of self-contempt was like gall upon her lips, but even as her conscious mind shuddered away from the shabby image, the deeper, unappeasable compulsion of her own self-preservation urged her on, stabbing her with the immutable fact of Grambling's death, the black pits of the *palacio* in Havana, the single slim chance of survival that hung on the tenuous thread of Valera's favor.

She looked up and met the question in Carlota's eyes, aware that her own hesitation had already frayed the unsubstantial fabric of unanimity and confidence that she had tried to weave so carefully. With a flash of sudden anger, she damned García silently into the foulest depths of hell. What in the name of God was this unknown Spaniard to her? If it was his pleasure to twist and turn and conspire and intrigue, that was his affair; there was no reason why she should risk her life to keep him free from harm.

"I'll lead him to you with a ring in his ugly nose," she promised grimly. "But there is one thing." The movement of her hand encompassed the smooth contours of her body. "If these cuts and bruises are not healed by then, the affair is hopeless. Men are such sentimental fools that they demand perfection."

"Don't worry about that. I'll send Ajona to you this afternoon. She's as black as coal and as wild as if she were still in Africa, but she has a gift of healing. Put yourself in her hands and I can promise you your body will be smooth enough by the time you're ready to display it to García."

Manette laughed, reckless and impatient now that the die had been cast and she was committed to this new adventure. "The poor, unhappy Manuel! If he accepts me, he becomes a traitorous rebel, and if he does not—"

"If he does not, there will be no Manuel."

Their eyes met and clung in silence for a lengthening moment, as if they had both suddenly realized that there was grim reality behind the glittering network of intrigue that they had woven. Before this affair was done, many men would die and there would be the smoke of burning cities black against the sky. But in the end there would be an empire born, and they would be a part of it.

Manette swept up the half-filled decanter of brandy and tilted it invitingly above a glass. "Brandy, Carlota? Brandy to drink a toast to the seduction of Manuel?"

Carlota's lips softened into a smile and her eyes were gay and arrogant again. "To his seduction—and to your success."

Their glasses touched in a shaft of sunlight—an omen of good fortune, an assurance of a complete and perfect consummation. Yes, beyond any shadow of a doubt, these women would be important in the new empire.

Ajona was of the Bantu blood, a statuesque, coalblack woman who had come to maturity in the shrouded rain forests of the Congo. The ridged triangular scars that stood out on her cheeks and forehead marked her as a *menlekale,* a witch woman learned in the dark sorceries of fetishism and the voodoo rites. No one knew her age, herself least of all, but she was young enough for her breasts to be firm and erect under the cottonade she wore and her thighs round and smooth. She came to Manette's room in the early afternoon, her secret salves and charms wrapped in a square of purple cloth, her face as still and inscrutable as a Mebali ceremonial mask.

"*Yo soy Ajona.*" She had picked up a trace of Spanish from Carlota, a little of the gumbo patois from the other servants in the house. "You take off—" She groped vainly for the strange word that eluded her and then touched the edge of Manette's dress as a sign that it was to be removed so she could see the wounds she was to heal.

Manette's eyes swept over her in a searching glance of swift appraisal. She was a little reluctant to entrust her body to the care of this half-tamed savage, but her memory brought back the image of a woman her father had owned on Santo Domingo; a woman with those same sharp scars upon her face. She had nursed and cured the blacks, and on one desperate, fear-ridden afternoon she had snatched Margarita back from the jaws of death after a poisonous snake had buried its fangs in her flesh. It had been done with charms and incantations and some strange poultice pressed against the wound, but it had been successful. She stood up and let the thin dress that was her only garment fall in a crumpled circle about her feet.

Silent and impassive, the woman began to unwind the bandages that covered Manette's breasts and back and thighs. Her fingertips touched the half-healed slashes and there was a tingling in them, a static electricity as unmistakable and positive as the magnetism that lifts a cat's fur high and stiff upon its back at the touch of its mistress' hand on a frosty morning. Manette's eyes narrowed in speculative surprise. There was something here she did not understand; some secret, primitive power in this black barbarian.

Ajona turned away and Manette saw her fumbling in the depths of the purple bundle. The hand emerged with a stoppered vial of colorless liquid. When the woman opened it, there was the odor of musk and coriander in the air. In the first fractional instant of application, it was like a searing fire eating its way into the depths of the torn flesh; then, suddenly, the scorching flame was gone and there was the buoyant sensation of a complete escape from pain, a blessed coolness that was as refreshing as the foam of sea spray against her naked body. She looked down and it seemed to her that already the welted flesh seemed a little less inflamed and angry.

"That was good, Ajona—*muy bueno.*" She probed the Woman's face to see if she had been understood and was rewarded with a solemn nod of the head and the quick gestures of some incantation that she could not follow. "I must be well and whole again within two weeks, a fortnight. Do you understand?"

Ajona nodded again and her lips twisted silently in an effort to find the words that would express her thoughts. "All gone." She spread her hands a foot apart to indicate a space of days. "If not here," her eyes swept the room and then flashed back to Manette's face, "we use *voudou* one night when sun is dead."

"Voodoo! To heal these cuts upon me?" Instinctively she shrank back from even the suggestion of this mystery. The thin-lipped Jesuit friars had outlawed it with all the exorcisms of book and bell and candle, denouncing it as a bloody and savage superstition, but there were many, even among the whites, who could not escape the conviction that it was real and terrible. They had heard the drums throbbing in the night, seen the feared grigri snatched up in panic terror from a shabby doorstep, watched men sicken and fade until they were no more than ghosts or zombies, the living dead walking the earth with empty eyes.

"Voodoo! Oh, no, Ajona!" The color had drained out of her face and her hands quivered uncontrollably. "I could not! I—"

Unmoved, Ajona stared at her with a gaze that was almost hypnotic in the dark depths of its fixed intensity. "No danger." She threw back her head, her eyes still blazing like live coals, and Manette knew with a certainty that went far beyond knowledge or experience that this dark stranger was a priestess of that strange and savage cult.

She shook her head wearily, confused by the implications of this twisted labyrinth that gaped before her. "I don't know, Ajona—I don't know. We'll wait and see." She turned away to pick up her dress, and when she looked back again Ajona was gone. Gone, but she had left behind her a suggestion of darkness and secret evil.

It was a relief to have Etienne call for her that evening. As his shining barouche rolled through the narrow streets her eyes grew bright and she found that she could even laugh easily and carelessly again. She had been careful to wear a veil, drawn taut from her bonnet to a gay bow beneath her chin, so that even anyone who knew her well would have found it hard to recognize her in the dimness of the poorly lighted streets.

A narrow road had been hacked out of the wilderness between the town and Lake Pontchartrain, and at Etienne's direction the Negro coachman turned the horses into it and sent them jogging briskly toward the north. There was no danger of discovery here, and Manette let herself relax in the warm and passionate circle of Etienne's arms. "It is so good to be with you again, *mon cher*," she said softly. "I have dreamed of you in the nights and wanted you near me in the emptiness of the afternoons. I tried not to think of you, but you kept coming back to me over and over again."

"And yet you had Allan."

She nodded, remembering MacMurran's strength and gentleness. "Just as you had Julie—and have her still. There was no other course open to either of us. And yet that has not kept me from missing you and wanting you and needing you."

He bent his head to kiss her and suddenly the heat of her desire was a throbbing turbulence in her blood. Breathless, she knew a devouring hunger for the feeling of his hands upon her flesh; a demanding, insatiable need that turned her weak with eagerness, intolerant of the restraints imposed by her torn body and the sheaths of bandages that encased her.

"Etienne! My darling! My dear one! *Mi Corazón!*" she murmured, clinging to him.

They had come to the shore of Pontchartrain and Manette looked up to see an inland sea girdled in jade, lustrous and bespangled in the quivering sheen of moonlight. The narrow beach ended in a cloudy mist of palmettos and flowering shrubs so that there was a lush fragrance in the air. Without a word she slipped out of the carriage, feeling the soft shifting of the sand beneath her slippers as she waited for Etienne to issue his instructions to the coachman. The barouche turned sluggishly on the yielding surface of the beach and then clattered away into the darkness so that they were left alone beside the shining water.

She slipped off her dress and stepped out of the two satin and taffeta petticoats that she wore, suddenly ashamed to have him see the bandages upon her body. Always before, at Bonneterre and on Bienville Street, she had revealed herself to him without a hint of any flaw or imperfection. With a sudden shyness of uncertainty and doubt, she wondered if he would turn away, seeing her so marred and broken. But there was only a shocked pity in his eyes, a compassion that checked the force of his eagerness.

"*Mon Dieu,* Manette! I had no idea you had suffered so." His hand touched the coil of bandages that bound her thighs. "You must not try to—"

Her eyes flamed in quick protest, for now the need to give herself to this man had become imperative.

"Oh, it is nothing, *corazón*—nothing!" She could sense his hesitation, his reluctance to violate the ravaged body that cried out for tenderness and a passive season in which to mend itself.

The storm of her emotion swelled into a tumult that foamed and pounded in her brain.

"See, *querido,* it is only a scratch and nothing more!" Her fingers turned clumsy and awkward by their frantic eagerness, she stripped the gauze away and stood trembling before him.

"You see, *corazón?*" Her empty arms and her eyes implored him, and then she knew the ecstasy of his body against hers and in the sudden access of relief her head fell back so that her face was like a golden flower bathed in the flood of moonlight. The white sand received them and there was even a fierce exultation in the pain that leaped again in the gashes covering her body. The mingled pain and passion was a scarlet mist that blinded her so that, at the end, it was like a voluptuous dream that had come out of nowhere and vanished into emptiness.

"I love you so, my darling! I love you so!"

Her voice was no more than a whisper, transient and evanescent in the soft sweetness of the night, protesting the disparity between the dream and the reality, seeking the elusive core of substance and finding only shadows there.

CHAPTER TWENTY-SIX

L IKE FIRE thrown off by a whirling St. Catherine's wheel, the days went plummeting away until a week was gone. A week of plotting and planning with Carlota; a week that included two searing inquisitions at the hands of the still suspicious Valera; a week when the nights were enchanted tides of time, because they were shared with Etienne. And through it all, every morning and every evening, Ajona came to bathe her body with the liquid fire that had the fragrance of musk and coriander and to talk, in her broken, half-intelligible patois, of the mysteries of the voodoo cult.

It was as old as the legend of man, as old as the world itself. A part of the ancient, earth-wide worship of the serpent, it was akin to the Biblical legend of the great snake that opened the eyes of mortals to the tree of life; the scaly monster that guarded the golden apples of the Hesperides; and the Aztec serpent-deity Quetzalcoatl, who gave his people an abundance of maize and wisdom and freedom from disease. Men had worshiped it as the Naga of Kashmir, which ruled the countries beneath the seas, and as the dragon of Lesbos, which was a beneficent god only so long as it was propitiated twice each day with a human sacrifice. But most important to Manette was its powers as a healer of the wounds of men. Even as the Greek god of healing, Aesculapius, had adopted as his symbol a serpent coiled around a staff, so had the untamed blacks of the Congo ascribed to the great snakes of the earth the occult powers of exorcising pain and sorrow, of palliating wounds, and even turning aside the grisly hand of death.

With the Negroes, the worship of the snake was an affair of drums and dancing, of sacrifice and smoky fires and orgiastic frenzy. Manette shrank away from it as an impiety that was unclean, debasing. But her wounds were slow to heal and Ajona shook her head as she bathed them now, muttering that human hands alone could never mend the broken flesh in the few days that remained before the coming of García. She grew desperate then, so desperate that in the hush of midnight she stole out of the house with Ajona at her side, to be borne silently away in a black carriage.

They left the civilization and the safety of the town behind them and followed a narrow road, dark under its shroud of lowering trees that paralleled the misty path of the river. Spasmodic bursts of rain spattered against the carriage windows and a hungry wind rattled the doors and set the treetops tossing under the murky sky. Thunder, roaring and growling like a savage beast, pursued them, and their outriders were the lashes of the lightning that crackled and glared in intermittent frenzy.

Her nerves as taut as tight-drawn bowstrings, Manette fought down the mounting whirlwind of hysteria that threatened to engulf her. In her overwrought condition, the storm outside became the tangible measure of celestial wrath that sought to turn her back and block the culmination of this satanic folly. Her eyes flickered to the still figure of Ajona, silent and withdrawn, oblivious of her surroundings. With the abruptness of a falling star it came to her that this dark, scar-faced woman was no better than a savage, and yet she had trusted herself to her and even concealed her own absence from Carlota's house, so that now no living human would know where she had gone or where to search for her, if she did not return. There had been whispers in

Santo Domingo of human sacrifices to the bloody voodoo gods, and other tales of men—and women, too—who had vanished from their plantation houses between dusk and dawn and never returned to them again. She had an almost overpowering desire to throw open the carriage door and leap out into the sheltering darkness, but even as she leaned forward, she felt the restraining touch of Ajona's hand upon her arm.

"Soon now." Even in the obscurity of the carriage there was a luminous quality in Ajona's eyes, a mesmeric power that drained her will away and left her docile and submissive. They passed the fire-gutted ruins of a burned plantation house, the shattered columns of its façade like dead men's fingers clutching at the empty air. Then the carriage wheels slowed to a stop and through the mist and rain she could make out the outlines of a long, two-story building standing almost at the edge of the river. There was no light or sound to indicate that it was occupied, and the panic fear that she had been lured to this isolated spot for some murderous, obscene purpose surged up in her again. Reluctantly, with her hand close to the poniard concealed beneath her skirt, she followed Ajona through the rain and darkness to the half-seen outline of a door. It swung open before them, as if some sentry had been watching their approach, and she edged forward into a smoke-filled vault that might well have served as one of the anterooms of hell.

In the days of the plantation's glory, she decided swiftly, it must have been a warehouse, for it was strongly built of native brick and the roof was so high above her that she could barely see it through the twisting smoke. Some sixty feet long and perhaps forty feet across, it was dimly lighted by fat pine torches thrust into rude sconces on the walls. Midway of the room, a crude stone altar had been erected in the center of the floor, and the fire that blazed upon it cast a shifting patchwork of light and shadow on the massed rows of dark faces that stared at her from across the room. A grotesque idol hacked out of some strange black wood towered above the altar, fat-bellied, gross, immense, its eyes formed by jewels that reflected the light. As she stared at it, the idol seemed to stir and move, and she suddenly realized with a shivering chill of. horror that live snakes clung to it, twisting and winding their sinuous bodies back and forth as their tongues flickered between the open jaws of their scaly, sharp-pointed heads.

Hesitating beside the door, she watched Ajona discard her dress, emerging with only an abbreviated skirt, not much larger than a man's pocket handkerchief, that fluttered from her waist. She was a magnificent woman, strong-thighed, narrow-waisted, erect, with full, pointed breasts that were like cones of polished ebony. She knotted a bandeau around her head, and when she turned to face the altar, Manette saw that it had been embroidered with garnets and sequins and bits of crystal so that it picked up and reflected the light of the fire.

A brooding silence had gripped the room from the moment that Ajona entered it, but now she threw back her head and the rafters rang with the shrill resonance of her summons.

"Voudou magnian! Voudou magnian!"

Like a cresting wave, the dark mass of half-seen worshippers threw back the sound.

"Voudou magnian! Voudou magnian!"

In the instant that the roar still lingered in the air, Ajona dashed across the room and leaped to the top of the altar, halfway between the crackling flames and the mass of snakes that writhed upon the idol. She threw her arms high above her head and two drums began to throb somewhere in the shadows; a rhythm of deep-toned, staccato notes so swiftly piled one upon the other that Manette felt as if some rigid band were being tightened around her lungs to leave her weak and breathless. The drummers were beside the altar now, two brawny Negro men, naked except for the merest twist of scarlet cloth wound around their hips. Ajona cried out again, her voice rising high above the steady pounding of the drums, and the communicants surged forward to form a crescent before her, their eyes staring up at her and their bodies swaying in an uneven cadence that matched the harsh syncopation of the drums.

Ajona's voice was rising and falling in a chant that Manette could not understand, but a half dozen of the women stepped forward, holding up great earthen jugs as if they waited for a benediction. With a movement that was almost too swift to follow, Ajona whirled toward the idol, and when she turned back again each hand held a green-scaled, jet-eyed reptile as thick as her own wrist and a good foot longer than a tall man's height. The ugly triangles of their heads swayed slowly back and forth as if they searched the faces of the men and women before them; beady-eyed, they coiled and convoluted into the very symbols of labyrinthine evil. Bending forward, Ajona passed their bodies over the extended jugs, consecrating them with some devil's sacrament. The roar of the worshipers surged up again, and with the sound Ajona turned and flung the two snakes straight into the heart of the flames.

Manette gasped in horror as the fire leaped up about them. In spite of the oppressive heat of the room, there was an icy coldness in her veins, and her thoughts wheeled in a pattern of confusion that refused to accept the scene before her eyes. The drums had pounded on, unfaltering, so that now it seemed to her that there had never been an hour or a moment when they had not been raging in her brain. She shrank back against the wall as she saw one of the women coming toward her with a wide bowl filled with some liquid that had been poured from the earthen jugs.

She shook her head in blind refusal, her arms stiff and rigid at her sides, as the woman held the bowl out to her. Instinctively, she knew that its acceptance would mark her own transition from the hard-held sanctuary of sanity to an acceptance of this Black Mass that was being celebrated with fires and serpents and voodoo drums. As irresistibly as if she were being coerced by physical force, her eyes turned to Ajona, and she saw that the black priestess was staring at her with a hooded glare that seemed to gather up all of Manette's will and consciousness and strip the last thread of her self-determination from her.

"Drink!" It was a command that she was helpless to disobey.

"Drink!" Ajona's arm stiffened, poised like a spear that she was powerless to deflect.

White-faced, so entrapped in this dream that her body was like a stranger to her, Manette held out her hands and felt her fingers tighten on the edges of the bowl extended to her.

"Drink!"

Mechanically, her empty eyes never wavering from Ajona's face, she lifted the bowl and held it to her lips until the last bitter drop was gone. Ajona turned away, and as her fingers relaxed and the bowl shattered on the floor, the sound of the drums grew louder and louder in her ears.

It was an inferno now; an inferno of blinding light and utter darkness; an inferno of billowing smoke and moving bodies that revealed themselves in gold and brown and ebony skins, as the dancers stripped their cloths away and shouted and postured in the glare of the altar fire. The drink had numbed her brain, sweeping away the restraints that she had always known, and in the same instant it had roused in her a primitive, deep-buried need to give herself to this orgiastic rite. She felt fingers fumbling at her dress and, looking down, she discovered that they were her own. Completely aloof, her mind registered a strange sensation of freedom as the clothing dropped away. Even the bandages were gone. It seemed only natural and right that she should stand before them so. Her lips half parted and her eyes burning like live coals, she moved steadily forward until she stood facing the dancers, with her back pressed tightly against the rough stone of the altar.

A hard-muscled Negro stomped and whirled before her, his body twisting and jerking. She felt his hard hands on her wrist, and her body stirred until it made itself one with the tempo of the drums. Her eyes were glazed and staring and the room had receded into a vague blur of sound and tumult when he swept her up in his arms and laid her quivering body on the altar. Against the raging background of the drums, she vaguely saw Ajona with a glittering knife in her hands, slashing at the body of a snake, and she shivered under its chill as the black priestess pressed the raw fragments of the butchered reptile against the cuts and wounds upon her body. She tried to thrust her aside and saw Ajona's hands moving in cabalistic conjurations before her eyes. The fire leaped up like a great torch and the tumult of the drums raged about her. She screamed, feeling the smoke sear the inner flesh of her throat and nostrils; and then there was only silence and emptiness and, at the last, a torrent of blackness that enveloped her like a shroud.

CHAPTER TWENTY-SEVEN

S HE WAS the prisoner of her own tremendous weariness. The sunlight battered against the closed portals of her eyes but she refused to open them, for that would let the world and its demands and memories come rushing in upon her, and she was not ready to admit them now. This was a time for resting, a time to forget the past and repudiate the future. She heard a door close softly and then the sound of footsteps that crossed the floor and stopped beside her bed. Perhaps, if she was very still and did not open her eyes …

"*Caramba,* Manette, 1 had no idea Etienne was such a man that he could make you sleep the day away!" It was Carlota, her voice tinged with half-derisive amusement. And she had said—Etienne! But she had not been with Etienne. Manette tried to sort out the memories of the night before, but there was only confusion and a vague impression of something foul and horrible. Involuntarily her eyes flew open and she saw Carlota standing beside the bed and laughing at her.

"So you are still alive. You have slept so long that I almost believed you were dead. See, I have brought you coffee to help you open your eyes." She motioned to a colored maid who waited in the doorway and pulled a small table over beside the bed to hold the silver tray. She measured the depths of Manette's exhaustion with experienced eyes and then nodded decisively as if to confirm some unspoken thought. "The first cup laced with brandy, I believe, and perhaps the second, too, if one is not enough." She poured the coffee and the brandy deftly and held the steaming cup out to Manette. "Drink this, *hermanita*. It will bring you back to life again."

Reluctantly, Manette accepted the cup, lifting herself on one elbow so she could bring the fragrant liquid to her lips. It was strong and bitter on her tongue, but it was a familiar and matter-of-fact reality. The gnawing fantasies that had plagued her began to fade away, replaced by the clear constancy of sunlight, the conventional pattern of street sounds drifting in through the open window, the smiling urbanity of the blonde girl smiling at her across the coffee cup.

"I am as tired as if I had dragged a loaded dray through every street of the town!" She stretched her arms lazily above her head, twisting her body like a cat, and realized with a sudden shock of surprise that she was free from the pain that had been her constant companion since that nightmare hour in the bedroom at Constancia. She jerked herself into a sitting position and her eyes searched her body for the livid wounds that had defaced it only the day before. But they were almost indistinguishable now. Where there had been crimson welts of swollen flesh, there was only a thin line that might have been no more than the stroke of a pen. Unbelievingly, almost fearfully, her fingers touched her breasts and the smooth skin of her thighs. Her head jerked up as she stared at Carlota in startled amazement.

"Look, Carlota, look! They are gone!" She threw her legs over the side of the bed and stood erect, revolving slowly so that the other could see. "You can hardly see them now, and by tomorrow no one will ever know that they were there!"

"*Es increíble!*" Carlota leaned forward to touch the thin lines that still showed faintly on Manette's skin and then lifted her head with a puzzled frown gathering between her eyes. "But only yesterday they were as red as cinnabar," she protested. "I have never seen such a healing in the space of a night and a day." Her fingers drummed meditatively on the table and her quick glance surprised the look of mingled confusion and secrecy that Manette could not hide. "And you slept all day today."

Manette's lips tightened into a rigid line of stubborn reticence. Regardless of what had happened the night before—and even now she was none too sure where the reality ended and the dream began—she was determined not to betray herself to any man or woman who walked the earth. It was enough to suspect that the bestial memories would confront her again and again in the emptiness of sleepless nights. It would be unbearable to know that someone else was privy to this buried ugliness.

"It has been better than a fortnight." She forced her voice to a tone that was casual and unconcerned. "After all, these things cannot go on forever."

"No." The doubt still lingered in Carlota's voice. "And yet to have them disappear so quickly—" She shook her head as if to throw off the questions that perplexed her. "At least, you will be ready for Manuel when he appears, and Don Pedro had word this morning that he will be here within the next two days."

"So soon?" The excitement faded from her eyes and her spirits sagged under the oppression the prospect of García always bred in her. "How long will he stay, do you you think, Carlota?"

"*Quién sabe*? No longer than he requires to conclude his business with Don Pedro, I can assure you. It would be fatal for the King's men to even know that he was in New Orleans, and worse if they discovered that he was nibbling at the edges of a plot against the crown. No, he will be in and out as swiftly as he can manage. You will have no time to waste, once he arrives."

Manette's breasts rose and fell in the suggestion of a sigh. "Like one of your *putas*," she suggested bitterly. "A matter of business to be dispatched as soon as possible, without letting the poor fool know that there is any need for haste."

She turned away and stood looking out across the balcony at the bustling activity of the dusty Place d'Armes. If I could only get away from all this, she thought. If I could go back to Constancia ... For a moment it seemed as if she could see the tall cane rippling in the wind and smell the flowers that ran riot beside the river. Then the image faded and she was staring down at the bustling square again. Constancia had vanished into the mists of yesterday, but the obligation of García was real and tangible and very, very near at hand.

The music of the guitars and violins filled the air like the swirl of swallows, flying silver-winged. Candlelight brightened the colors of the dancers' costumes and laid a patina of gold on bared shoulders and the half-revealed curves of the women's breasts. Crimson wine lent its vividness to long-stemmed crystal glasses and there was an unending tide of bubbling laughter. For it was Valera's pleasure to honor his guest, Don Manuel Armando García y Valdés, *el gobernador* of the *intendencia* of Valladolid—and, just at this time, a tremendously significant pawn on the board of Don Pedro's hopes and plans.

Don Manuel was dancing with Manette, flushed a little with the wine he had consumed. He was a tall, broad-shouldered man with the coldest eyes Manette had ever seen, his mouth a hard, suspicious line that betrayed his ruthless consecration to the cause of his own ambition and egotism. Here was a man, she decided, who would be contemptuously unmoved by any motives of loyalty or generosity or tolerance. In his pragmatic world the good or evil of any action could be judged only by its practical consequences and the effect it might have upon his own comfort or happiness or fortune. She had a secret abhorrence for such men as this, men who had no bright-hued core of recklessness or generosity to temper the pitiless inflexibility that drove them on. But in this affair her personal feelings were of no importance. She smiled up at him, feeling his arm demanding about her waist as he swung her through a measure of the dance, allowing her body to linger and soften against his own in an unmistakable suggestion of surrender.

The song reached its triumphant ending with a bright plume of cadenzas, and she turned away toward the shadowed balcony that overlooked the patio, with García eager and attentive at her side. "A most attractive establishment, this home of Don Pedro's." It was an empty compliment, designed only to disturb the silence that had fallen upon them as they looked down at the bubbling fountain ringed with flowers.

"*Es muy hermosa,*" she agreed, "but undoubtedly your own *palacio* is far more magnificent than this. We know so little here of Valladolid." Her fingers lingered on his arm and she looked up at him with the wide-eyed admiration of a child. "Tell me about it, señor."

Let this fool boast a little, she thought contemptuously. All men love to talk at length about themselves, and in the end he will have a higher regard for me, since I provided him with an audience.

"Valladolid?" He was obviously pleased by her question. "Why it is an old city some fifty *leguas* west of the Ciudad de México. They say Mendoza founded it some two hundred and fifty years ago and made it the capital of the state of Michoacán. In some ways, for a colonial town, it is handsome enough. We overlook the valley of Guayangareo, although the town itself hangs on the very edge of the plateau."

"And are there wide plazas and great buildings there, such as those that I have seen in Havana?"

"There are some, although at best it is only a mountain town. But we have a cathedral with an onyx font and wood carving in the choir and silver doors to the shrine in its chapel. There is the *palacio* and a Capuchin convent—yes, and a third establishment." His voice dropped into a sudden growl of anger. "The cursed College of San Nicolás de Hidalgo! The core and center of the clericalism and conservatism that holds Michoacán in dry rot and strangles every progressive measure of mine!"

His fingers tightened on the iron railing of the balcony and his face was harsh and bitter with the remembered fury of his rebuffs.

"But perhaps," her voice was a soft whisper of insinuation, "all that will change if Don Pedro is successful."

He whirled around to stare at her with eyes that were suddenly cold and suspicious. "Don Pedro! Do you mean that you are in Don Pedro's confidence?"

"And why not, Don Manuel? Everyone who is here tonight is in Don Pedro's confidence to some degree. It was my understanding that while you were here you were to be incognito, so obviously the only guests Don Pedro could invite to meet you are those who are in some way associated with the matter that brings you here."

"Yes—yes, I suppose that is all true enough. But I had not realized there were so many concerned with it here." His fingers stroked his chin thoughtfully and she saw that her words had opened up a new avenue of conjecture in his mind. "But what part is it that you play here, señorita? Surely you are neither a politician nor a filibustering bravo."

She laughed deprecatingly, throwing her head back so he could not escape the beauty of the smooth column of her throat and the tantalizing softness of the curved breasts so generously revealed by her deep-slashed bodice. "Oh, I am nothing. An old friend of Carlota's, a refugee from Santo Domingo. I interest myself in this because it offers entertainment, and perhaps before I am done, a little romance." She let her eyes meet his with an unveiled boldness that carried an unmistakable invitation. "Do you think that I will be so fortunate, señor?"

His hard eyes appraised her proud breasts, the smooth curve of her hips, the skin that was like amber silk. "Perhaps that is a need that can be supplied while I am here."

She turned to face him, her lips half parted and her face an image of eagerness and unqualified assent. "At your pleasure, señor," she said softly. *"Pues estoy lista y a las órdenes de usted*—I am quite ready and at your service."

She saw his face relax into an expression of arrogant self-satisfaction. As plainly as words, it said that this was no more than Don Manuel García should rightfully expect. In that instant she hated him, and an irrevocable resolution was born in her that before the affair was done, he would pay dearly for this cavalier acceptance of her favors. Don Manuel Armando García y Valdés though he was, she was still—and would always be—Manette de Santiago, a free woman and a woman of pride.

He sought her out at Carlota's house that night, long after the dance had ended and the music was dead, for it would have been inconceivable to soil Don Pedro's home with the shabbiness of such a rendezvous. She was expecting him, and the room was soft with candlelight, cool with the freshness of the night wind that came creeping in across the balcony. A sleepy colored maid had dressed her hair and touched her breasts and the lobes of her ears with perfume. There were bottles of wine and brandy and bowls of small sugared cakes and tartly spiced shrimp for his pleasure. She wore a Chinese dressing gown of scarlet silk that she had never worn before, flowers in her hair, jeweled bracelets tinkling on her wrists. He strode into the room with the high handed arrogance of some dragoon shouldering his way into a filthy barrel house on the water front, ripping off his coat before he was inside the door and dropping into a chair to tug and pull impatiently at his boots.

Her cheeks flamed with humiliation but she tried to mend the matter as best she could. "You will have a little brandy, Don Manuel, and perhaps sit on the balcony a little while until you are cooled and rested?"

"The balcony?" His eyes raked her contemptuously from head to foot. *"Por Dios,* we have a surplus of balconies at Valladolid! Here, help me with these boots—and throw that gown aside so I can look at you!"

For a moment the room seemed to swim and whirl around her, and her hands clenched into fists as she fought down the tide of insane fury that almost blinded her. She turned away as she slipped off her robe, so that he would not see the teeth gnawing at her lip, and when she knelt before him to help him with the boots, her face was docile and worshiping again.

"I am quite ready and at your service." She repeated the phrase she had used on Valera's balcony and heard him grunt in satisfaction. Tugging at his boots, she remembered the night she had performed the same service for Allan on Bonneterre; but there was as much difference here as there was between night and day. With Allan, it had been a jest, a matter for merriment and laughter so that she had been able to save her pride, but with this overbearing stranger, it was only a mark, of cringing servility that he forced from her, a symbol of her subjugation to him.

He was a lusty lover, once they had gained the bed; but there was a rough cruelty about him that denied her any pleasure in their union. He used her with the same impersonal indifference he would have bestowed upon a slave who blacked his boots or a glass of wine that contributed to his purely physical gratification.

When he had spent himself, he rolled away from her without a word and was almost instantly asleep, snoring with a raucous harshness that was like the sound of alligators roaring in a swamp.

She slipped out of bed and made her way to the peace and isolation of the balcony. She had known many men, but none of them had ever left her with this feeling of having been soiled and cheapened. Her fingers writhed in her lap as she raged against the circumstances that had brought her to a pass where he could treat her as if she were no better than some trash or rubbish.

"I am quite ready and at your service." Yes, she had told him that, but now the words took on a new meaning in her mind. She was ready enough and there would be no lack of service, but in the end it was to be a service that would strip his pride from him and send him whimpering down to hell. Hard-eyed, her fingers caressing a tall glass of the brandy he had spurned, she began to plot his ruin. In spite of Don Pedro and Carlota and all the rest, Don Manuel García would never live to see the red roofs of Valladolid again.

CHAPTER TWENTY-EIGHT

THE CITY sweltered and groaned and panted under a pall of heat that burned the spirit out of men's souls and seemed to melt the very flesh upon their bones. The stagnant sewage in the open gutters turned foul and stinking under a green scab of slime. Swarms of flies and mosquitoes and gnats bred on it and winged away to spread its filthiness through the taverns and coffeehouses and homes and restaurants. An uneasy miasma of fear began to settle over the city, for there were strange stories of a mysterious death that had been loosed in the streets, a plague that was minimized and concealed behind an official veil of silence, even while the hearses rolled somberly through the streets and the death knell of the cathedral bells tolled unendingly.

"They say now it is the cholera." The worried frown deepened between Carlota's eyes as she moved restlessly back and forth across the room. "Don Pedro tells me it began with a trading schooner from Brazil that dropped anchor here three weeks ago. There were half a dozen sick on board, and before it was known the rest of the crew had jumped their ship and gone into hiding."

Manette felt an icy shudder of fear ripple across her shoulders. There had been cholera in Santo Domingo in the summer of '85, and she could still remember her brother dying in an agony of retching nausea and distorted limbs, his body bloated into a grotesque horror and the green bile dribbling from the corners of his mouth. She could remember the stinking piles of the unburied dead, the choking smoke from the burning tar that was believed to clear the air.

"If that is true, our only hope is to run as if the devil were at our heels—to get out of New Orleans before this damnable pestilence strikes us down!"

"I know." Carlotta lifted her hands in a gesture of exhausted resignation. "But how can we leave now? García is here, and Don Pedro swears that if he himself leaves the city, everything we have already done will fall into waste and ruin. There is nothing we can do but wait and, perhaps, pray a little." Her lips twisted into an ironic grimace of self-contempt. "Although I've little faith that *el Señor* would look with favor on any prayers you or I might send up to Him. How goes it with García, *hermanita?* Has the stiff-necked fool given you any hint of his intentions or is he still stubborn and secretive?"

"That stinking *cabrón!*" Manette's scorn was as scathing as the bite of a lash. "I tell you there is nothing to that *borrachón!* He can think only of brandy and himself and a night spent in my bed. He is eaten up with jealous ambitions that he is not man enough to carry out."

"And yet they say he has many followers in Valladolid."

"*Absurdo!* If they know him there as I have come to know him, he can have no influence at all. For my part, a knife in his back and a stone around his neck before he is kicked into the river would suit me best!"

"You may be right. Don Pedro makes no progress with him at all. *Es una lástima*—but let us try it for a few days more." She started to leave the room and then paused for a moment with her hand on the edge of the open door. "If he is too obstinate, it 'must be as we said in the beginning—'There will be no more Manuel.'"

The door closed silently behind her and the words pounded and roared through Manette's brain in a rising crescendo of vindictive resolution.

"There will be no more Manuel!"

She whispered the words over and over to herself. Not today, and perhaps not tomorrow—but soon, soon he would be repaid for all that she had suffered from him.

They had decided to go horseback riding that afternoon. She and García went up the river to a spot they had found a few days before where there was a carpet of grass at the edge of the water and an almost impenetrable growth of shrubs and underbrush to hide them from the road. It was an effective way to escape the searing heat, for they could swim in the cool water of the wide Mississippi and then rest and refresh themselves with wine in the shadows of the trees that rimmed the grassy beach.

Today Manuel had been drinking heavily before he joined her, so that his face was flushed to a deep brick red and his boasting and blustering reached new heights she had never been forced to endure before. She had expected the fresh air and the swimming to enforce some measure of sobriety upon him, but he had continued to drink so steadily all through the afternoon that by the time the first hush of the evening began to descend, he could only flounder awkwardly in the water, splashing and puffing as she swam smoothly and effortlessly beside him. Water was as natural an element as air to her, for the plantation house at Santo Domingo had turned its back upon the fields of cane and looked out across the blue-bosomed Caribbean, and she had learned to swim there almost as soon as she was able to walk. The fact that he was uncouth and inept in this, as in 'so many things that he attempted, only deepened the scornful loathing that festered and grew in her with every added moment she was forced to spend beside him.

Pot-gutted and thick-jowled, as hairless and bare as a lump of yellow clay, he sprawled on the grass beside her now, one hand gross and almost insufferable upon her leg, the other maintaining a precarious grip on a halfempty brandy bottle that he waved like a baton.

"Damn their souls!" His tongue was thick and the words stumbled awkwardly on his lips. "Pedro de Valera and that yellow-headed bitch of his that calls herself Carlota! They've split their guts to try to get me in because they know I can do more for them than any other man they've got, and then they offer me a governorship if they're successful! A governorship!" His loose lips gaped open in a sagging sneer of truculence and he glared at Manette with bloodshot eyes. "Why, damn their miserly souls, I've got a governship now!"

Manette leaned forward eagerly. At last, after the long days of waiting, the veil that had shrouded García's intentions was being thrust aside. "But surely," she protested, "you would rule a far greater state than Michoacán. Perhaps you would even be one of the councilors of the Viceroy himself."

"Councilor?" His body shook with drunken laughter. "A councilor to the Viceroy? By God, before this thing is done, I'll be the viceroy to Mexico myself, and Don Pedro and that fool who is the viceroy now and all the rest of the squalling pack will be kicking their heels in the sunshine with a rope around their necks!" He broke off as a new idea found lodging in the confusion of his mind. "All but you. You're a high-headed wench, but I can beat that out of you when I get you to Mexico." The brandy splattered on the grass as he waved the bottle in a sweeping gesture. "I'll leave you out of it when I see the Governor tonight, and—"

"The Governor!" Her nails bit into the palms of her hands as she groped frantically for his meaning. "What business have you with the Governor here?"

"Why, the business of uncovering Don Pedro's plot for him, and for the King of Spain. And then," he shook a rigid finger in her face as if to emphasize his words, "do you know what my reward will be? I'll be the next viceroy of Mexico, for there'll be a need for one when His Excellency's been burned and hanged in his own courtyard. Oh, you'll do well enough with me. Far better than you deserve."

She pressed her hands against her eyes, trying to grasp the fact of this betrayal, forcing herself to realize that before the night was done this sodden fool would be babbling to the Governor, and Don Pedro and Carlota would be shackled to the floor in the death cells of the Cabildo. At the best, there was only an hour or two of grace, for once they left the river there would be no escape. If she could stop him, or even turn him aside …

With her mind a seething caldron of desperate schemes and stratagems, she stared out at the brown flood of the rolling river, and suddenly she seemed to see García there again, his awkward arms flailing the water, his mouth half open as he gasped and struggled.

"*Aie, corazón!* It is no wonder you are a governor and will soon be a viceroy." Eyes bright with admiration, she turned to smile down at him, her whole figure straining forward in a graceful arc as if she could hardly restrain the impulse to throw herself into his arms. "You are so wise not to become entangled with them, Manuel, for you are destined for greater things than they can offer you."

His loose lips twisted in a sneer of sottish contempt. "They can offer me nothing—but I can assure them a slow and miserable death." He pulled and pushed himself to his feet, staggering a little and clutching at a tree to regain his balance. "Help me dress and then get into your clothes. I'll see the Governor tonight and—*Por Dios,* what's the matter with you now?"

She had picked up his shirt as if to help him into it and then cast it aside with a little exclamation of annoyance. Her hands brushed at the skin between his shoulders as he tried to twist his head around to see what she was doing.

"Now, by San Patricio—" he began, but her voice, apologetic and distressed, cut across the rising tide of his impatience.

"Your back is covered with mud, *corazón*. It must have been here beneath the tree." He felt her fingers scraping at his back again and then she stepped aside and threw up her hands in a gesture of futility. "You will have to go back into the water and wash it off." She saw the scowl of protest gathering on his face and hurried on. "Certainly you do not want to present yourself to the Governor with mud above your collar and matted in your hair."

Scarcely able to stand alone, he staggered toward the bank of the river with Manette supporting him and urging him on. He would have stopped when the water reached his waist, but Manette was an arm's length ahead, pulling him forward so vigorously that he was in momentary danger of toppling forward and could not release her hand.

"*Estoy cansado!*" he bellowed. "I am tired and this is far enough. In the name of the sacred saints! Must I swim the river before I can have a flake of dirt washed from my back?"

"Only a little more, *querido*," she coaxed him. "Only a little more so that the water will reach the mud and I can remove it more quickly for you."

She led him on until the muddy ripples slapped his chin and she was treading water to keep her own head above the surface. Suddenly she whirled like a striking snake and her cupped hands deluged his face with a cataract of water. Choking and gasping, he tried to cry out and she splashed his open mouth so full that the cry died in a strangled gurgle of sound. She could feel his hands beating and clutching at her, and for an instant one of them closed about her wrist. He tried to drag her to him, but she plunged her head into the water and buried her teeth in his wrist until his fingers grew limp again and she was able to escape.

She ducked under his flailing arms and emerged behind him, gasping for breath as her heart pounded like a great drum. She allowed herself to sink to the soft bottom of the stream for an instant and then threw herself straight up into the air with every ounce of strength she could command. For a moment her head and shoulders gleamed high above the water, and in that fraction of a second she clamped her right arm around his throat and let her weight drag him backward in an awkward, stumbling retreat that brought him crashing down.

He was like a wild beast then, throwing himself from side to side and clawing frantically at her arm beneath the roiled surface of the river. She could feel her strength slipping away and her tortured lungs cried out for air. Flaring pinwheels of light spun and shattered before her eyes, but the liquor García had consumed and the halfchoked condition to which she had reduced him at the beginning fought for her. His hands dropped away from her arm and his body was sluggish and inert. Almost insensible with exhaustion and the need for air, she threw herself blindly toward the surface, gasping in quick, tearing sobs as her head emerged above the water. At first she was too weak to stroke her way to shore, and she floated on her back, eyes closed, stripped of every emotion. Slowly her strength returned and she opened her eyes to see that she had drifted almost a hundred yards downstream from the spot where she had entered the water. The current had washed her in toward shore and she clung to the bent knees of a riverside cypress tree until she was able to pull herself out of the water. Stumbling like a woman half asleep, she made her way up the bank and located the brandy bottle that García had propped carefully against a tree.

"*Válgame Dios!*" she whispered. "That was good."

She lifted the bottle again, welcoming the fire of the liquor, the new courage and strength it lent her. She dressed slowly, as painstakingly as if she were preparing for a ball, and when she was done, she knotted García's clothing around a heavy stone and threw it far out into the stream.

Back in the saddle, with the reins of García's horse looped about her arm, she looked out at the dull tide of water that was already washing Manuel's body downriver to the sea.

"There will be no more Manuel," she said softly, and with the sound of the words, she realized fully for the first time that she was free of him forever.

"There will be no more Manuel."

Like a chant, the words fell into the rhythm of the horses' hoofs, and she lifted her head and smiled as she jogged down the dusty highway toward New Orleans.

CHAPTER TWENTY-NINE

ON PEDRO had raged like a maniac at the first news of García's death, but as the days went by it faded into insignificance and seemed almost to be forgotten, submerged beneath the more immediate question of survival as the plague swept through the streets. The pestilence was like a creeping fire that had flickered obscurely in the beginning, spreading so slowly that the change was almost imperceptible. Then, almost overnight, it was transformed into a raging horror, a holocaust that bred a wild, unreasoning panic and choked the river roads with refugees who fought like animals to escape their doomed and desolate city.

Stores and taverns and business houses of every kind closed their doors, either because the clerks and proprietors were dead or because their accustomed patrons were afraid to venture forth. The streets were empty, abandoned to the mobs of thieves and cutthroats who roamed the city bent on loot and murder and rapine. Carts and drays and wagons had been pressed into service to carry the dead to the cemeteries, where sweating gravediggers toiled all through the night beneath the fitful flare of torches, and found more bodies waiting in the morning than there had been at dusk the day before. Barrels of pitch and tar burned at every corner, ruddy and infernal in the night, hiding the sky with the black pall of their choking smoke so that even at the crest of noon the city lay in a murky, unclean twilight. Sometimes the wind carried the sparks to a tinder-dry roof or through an open window and then whole blocks of homes and business houses burned away because there was no one left to fight the towering sheets of flame. There was an incessant roar of cannonading on Royal and Bourbon and Chartres Streets, for some believed, or tried to believe, that the discharge of these heavy guns cleared the air and helped to drive away the dread effluvia of the cholera. And through it all, in the ravaged mornings and in the reeking havoc of the dusk, the mournful wail of the death-cart drivers was like the litany of the city's sorrow.

"Any dead today? Any dead today? Bring out your dead so we can carry them away!"

Manette watched a dray piled high with uncoffined corpses jolt past the Cabildo and disappear into St. Peter's Street. The smoke and the heat and the unending crashing of the guns had set her head throbbing like a beaten gong, and the thought flashed through her mind, with a strange impersonality, that this might be the first symptom of the cholera breeding in her flesh. She turned away from the balcony, smiling a little at Carlota's efforts to clear a space of unsullied air about her with the dustdry fronds of a palmetto fan.

"You exhaust yourself for nothing, *niña*. As soon as the fan is quiet the smoke comes back again. Look, I can show you a better way." Manette poured two glasses half full of brandy and added a little *bière douce* to chill its fire. "Now, you see—this is cool and it will wash the dryness from your throat. Then, if you drink enough of it, you will be able to laugh at the plague. That is better than fighting it I promise you."

Carlota laughed and dropped the useless fan on the floor, still gallant and unafraid, as if some steady flame of courage burned forever inside her slender body.

"Dr. Manette—and from what I can see this treatment is as effective as any other doctor has been able to prescribe, and far more pleasant." Her sharp eyes studied Manette speculatively as she took the glass. "Tell me, *hermanita*, what holds you here? Is it Etienne—and has his Julie come back to him again?"

"His Julie is fifty miles upriver, and will stay there. We'll see no more of Julie until the heat is over and the plague is gone. And as for Etienne, I think he stays here because I am here, and I stay because I have nowhere else to go."

"There is Constancia."

"Constancia! And beg a sanctuary from Dorothée if I found them there?" She laughed bitterly. "I may die here on St. Ann's Street, Carlota, but that's far better than living, if that means crawling on my hands and knees before Allan and Dorothée!"

She turned her head at the sound of a soft tapping on the door. "Come in," she called, and one of the maids slipped into the room with a white envelope in her hand and gave it to Manette.

"For me?" She ripped it open and Carlota cried out in sympathy as she saw the color drain out of Manette's cheeks to leave her face a stark mask of misery and fear.

"Manette! What is it? What is the matter?"

Wordlessly, her eyes fixed in an empty stare, Manette held the fluttering paper out to her. The lines wavered unsteadily across the page, as if to reflect their author's weakness:

> Manette—
> I pray you come to me. I am sick and the servants have run away and I am here alone. I need you, Manette.
> ETIENNE

"But you can't go! You can't expose yourself when he has already been stricken with the plague! You will die, too, and then—"

"And then it will be over."

She lifted her head and Carlota saw that the shocked emptiness of her eyes was gone, driven out by a look of weariness and resignation she had never seen on Manette's face before. "He never really needed me before, Carlota, but he needs me now." She stood up and began to unfasten the buttons of the sheer silk dressing gown she wore. "If I may borrow your carriage to go to him—"

The street was almost empty as she stood at the doorway waiting for the carriage. Empty except for a tall Negro with an odd look of familiarity about him who was hurrying along the banquette toward the river. She stared at him, her mind so absorbed in Etienne that she was only half conscious of a fleeting effort to remember where she had seen the man before. Then, between two houses, a shaft of sunlight struck his face and she realized with a sharp shock of recognition that it was Kelcho, the Kuafi slave they had sent to Bonneterre when they were besieged at Constancia, as close to Allan and as much a part of him as his own right arm. She turned with the thought of concealing herself inside the house till he had passed, but the movement caught his eye and for an instant he stood stock-still, staring at her.

"Ma'mselle! Ma'mselle! I must talk to you!"

He began to run toward her, the cutlass he always wore swinging at his side and his usually impassive face alight with excitement. He jerked off his hat and his fingers touched his heart, his lips, and his forehead in the swift salute of the followers of Mohammed. "For three days I have searched everywhere for you, mam'selle. You must come with me to Constancia!"

"Constancia! I have no business at Constancia." Her voice trembled with bitterness. "Nor with the Señor MacMurran, although I suppose he is safe enough there on the plantation now."

Kelcho's eyes narrowed in perplexity. "But of course he is there, señorita. When he had no word from you, he insisted that we take him back to Constancia, even though the doctors swore that the trip would mean his death. And then when we arrived you were gone, and he sent me back to New Orleans that same night to find you and bring you to him."

Her mouth twisted contemptuously. "I suppose he was afraid to come himself. Once he was safe on the plantation he'd run no risk of exposing himself to the plague again."

"Oh, no, señorita!" Kelcho threw up his hands as if he were pleading with her to believe him. "But his weakness and the long trip in the heat was too much. He collapsed as we helped him across the gallery, and when I left he could not raise himself upon the bed."

"And what of his wife?" It seemed to her that she was tearing the words savagely out of her breast. "Does she care for him as a good wife should?"

But Kelcho's face was suddenly impassive and with-drawn again, as blank and expressionless as if he had donned a mask. "It is not for me to talk of Madame MacMurran, señorita. He will have to tell you of that him-self."

"Tell me?" The fury she had repressed was raging in her now, turning her voice hot and ugly. "There is nothing that he can tell me—but I have something that you can go back to Constancia and say to him!" Her lips quivered with her anger and her eyes were burning brands that seemed almost to sear the slave before her. "Tell him that I have no need for him now or ever! Tell him that I will see him burned in hell before I will come back to Constancia! Tell him to take his idiot Dorothée and keep her there, and I pray God she'll bring him as much unhappiness now as she has done before!"

Carlota's carriage had swung in beside the banquette and Manette turned blindly away, stumbling across the wooden side-walk and slamming the carriage door behind her viciously.

"Go! Go! Go on!" she cried, and felt the carriage lurch into motion. Kelcho was calling to her from the banquette, but she shrank back against the cushions as the carriage bounced and rattled on the untended roughness of the street. She was crying almost hysterically in a violent reaction from the emotional tempest of her anger. It was bad enough to know that Allan and Dorothée were together at Constancia, but to have him send a Negro to bring her back, as if she were some runaway slave ...

The carriage spun around a corner to the left and she felt its motion slacken and then die away as the driver reined in at Etienne's door. It was unlocked and she thrust her way inside, finding the house as silent and deserted as a tomb, strangely sepulchral, without the white-aproned maids and the snowy-haired major-domo who had always been in evidence before.

"Etienne!" she called. "Where are you, Etienne?"

There was the faint croaking of a fever-ridden voice from the floor above and she gathered up her skirts and raced up the curving stairs. She threw open the door of the bedroom he had shared with Julie and almost staggered at the sickening stench that suddenly engulfed her.

The jalousies had been closed to shut out the smothering heat of the sunlight, so that the room was dim and shadowy, as if had already become a vault of death. She could make out Etienne's figure, thin and wasted, in the wide expanse of the bed. His cheeks were as hollow and yellow as old parchment drawn tight above the bones of his face, his eyes so glazed and blood-red with fever that she was not sure he even saw or recognized her.

"Oh, Etienne, my darling! What has this horror done to you?"

She ran to him, feeling her stomach twist in choking revolt at the filth that stained the wrinkled surface of the bed. He had been nauseated, as all men were when the cholera descended upon them, and there had been dysentery, too, so that he lay in an unclean welter that spoke all too plainly of desertion and unsuccored nights and days. He stared up at her and it seemed as if some measure of relief replaced the stark hopelessness in his tortured eyes.

"Manette ..." His voice was a quavering whimper. "I am dying, Manette, and everyone ran away."

She dropped on her knees beside the bed, her hands stroking the cracked, fever-parched skin of his forehead. "You will be safe now, my darling." It was almost impossible to hide her terror and despair under a tone of comforting assurance and conviction. "I will be here with you."

He tried to lift himself on his elbow and one clawlike hand clamped itself around her wrist.

"Don't leave me, Manette!" he pleaded. "Don't go away and leave me here alone!"

She touched his eyelids gently, hiding the evidence of the stark fear that had drained away the last shreds of his courage. For an instant she felt a faint tremor of revulsion that was perilously hear contempt. No man escaped forever the finality of death, and she had seen many meet it bravely.

But he is sick and delirious, she admonished herself guiltily. He has suffered so that he is like a man upon the rack.

She found clean linens for the bed and heated bowls of water and washed and cleaned him until a part of the stench and filthiness was gone. A dressing table yielded a tall flask of eau de cologne, and she scattered the liquid in the room and opened the jalousies so that the air was no longer foul and sickening. Awkwardly, burning her hands and shrinking back from the heat, she kindled a fire in the detached kitchen behind the house and prepared a bowl of soup for him, lacing it with a generous cupful of sherry to give him strength. When it was done, she pulled up a chair beside his bed and held his wasted hand in hers until he dropped off into a fitful and uneasy sleep.

Alone, besieged by death in this empty house in a ravaged city, she tried to fight away the hopelessness that was like a dark cloud around her. She knew so little of the plague or what to do for it. She studied Etienne's face, watching the yellow pigment of the skin give way to a murky leaden cast, and she knew, with the hollow emptiness of despair, that his life was slipping away through the inept and untrained futility of her helplessness. With a sudden urgent desperation, she snatched up her hat and gloves and raced down the stairway and out into the street. If she could find a physician and persuade him to come back with her ...

Vaguely she remembered hearing Julie talk of a doctor on St. Philip's Street, not far from the Rue Dauphine, and she turned and ran down Esplanade in the panting heat of the late afternoon, gasping for breath and feeling her clothing plaster itself against her as the perspiration sprang out on her body. In Barracks Street, a pile of the dead had been heaped up and set afire, but the flames had guttered out, untended, so that now the funeral pyre was a noisome abomination of half-consumed bodies with fire-bared bones projecting from the scorched formlessness of distorted limbs.

She turned her head aside, her perfumed handkerchief clamped against her mouth and nostrils, and ran on as if her feet could carry her away from this malignity that was without a beginning and without an end. Her frantically darting eyes found the small brass plate that indicated Dr. Prudhomme's door, and she pounded frantically upon it until the sound of the brass knocker echoed like gunfire in the street. At first there was no response, and she was almost ready to turn away when she heard the sound of footsteps and the door swung open against its chain, only far enough for her to make out the angry, pinch-mouthed face of a whey-skinned slattern who stared out at her resentfully.

"Get on away!" the voice croaked like an angry raven. "The Doctor's not here, and when he does come in he'll have to eat and sleep. He can't take any new patients, anyway. He's already got more than any three men should be asked to see."

"But this is Etienne Chrétien!" Manette pleaded frantically. "On Esplanade. The husband of Julie de Ternant. Prudhomme has always been their family physician, for Julie told me so. He can't refuse them now! He must try to help M'sieur Chrétien!"

"He can't do any more than he's doing." But there was the faintest flicker of doubt in the woman's refusal. "I know he's looked after the Ternants, but they're no better than any of the others now."

She started to close the door, but Manette flung herself against it, holding it ajar with the sheer desperation of her trembling body. "Please tell him I was here," she begged. "Tell him that it is the husband of Julie de Ternant and ask him to come to him. In the name of God, I implore you, tell him this for me!"

"I'll tell him when he comes in." There was a grudging resentment in the woman's voice. "I'll tell him, but it won't do any good. He's doing all he can and he can't do any more."

The door slammed shut and Manette heard the rasp of the key turning in the massive lock. For a moment she was too exhausted to move and she let her body sag against the casing, closing her eyes and feeling her head throb with the boom of the cannonading that rocked the town. And as she relaxed there, her grief and dejection were like an anesthetic that dulled the temper of her resolution and her courage. It would be so easy to run away, to follow those others who were streaming out of the city with no thought of anything but their own self-preservation.

No one would ever know, and she would be free forever from this horror. She pushed herself away from the door and stumbled down the steps to the banquette. Only a few miles outside the town there would be safety—and then she seemed to feel the beseeching pressure of Etienne's bony fingers on her wrist and hear the entreaty of his voice: "Don't leave me, Manette! Don't go away and leave me here alone!"

She turned back toward the Rue Dauphine, her hope and courage as drooping and lifeless as broken plumes. She found herself repeating a paternoster, so long forgotten that the words were dry and meaningless upon her lips. The cannons shook the air and the black smoke was a clinging pall about her. Past the dead and dying, past the reeking pile of the unburned, unburied, and unshriven, she hurried through the streets of the stricken city to rejoin Etienne.

There was a desperate hunger for life in him, so that he clung to it while younger and stronger men went down to unmarked graves. Dr. Prudhomme had come at last, shaking his head when he saw the emaciated body and the dark skin. He had left opium and a jar filled with leeches, but in the end there was nothing he could do. The cholera was an affair of God, and no man could truly say that he knew whence it came or how to drive it away again.

On the fourth day, Carlota came to say farewell, all of the brightness burned out of her so that she was like some gray ghost. Don Pedro was dead, dead between a dawning and a dusk, and with him the dream of empire that no other could retrieve and quicken into life again.

"And what will you do now?" Manette's eyes searched Carlota's wasted face, wondering if she, too, presented the same despoiled image of corrosion and fatigue.

"I am going back to Spain, back to the little village of Estadilla where I was born."

"But there is nothing for you there!"

"Nothing," she agreed, "nor is there here, now that Don Pedro's gone." She rested her chin on the palm of her hand and her eyes seemed to be looking far away, into the blue depths of the Pyrenees that looked down upon the ancient province of Huesca. "There is a convent there, a quiet place. I would like to live and die in the peace and shelter of those walls, if they will have me."

When she was gone, the vast house seemed to be even more lonely than before. Etienne had fallen into a coma, broken only now and then by brief flashes of lucidity that were almost instantly submerged beneath the swirling tides of his delirium. His face was an evil purple, scarred by swollen lines of black that marked the throbbing and distended veins. It seemed to her that afternoon that his very breath was choking him and the black bile bubbled up between his cracked lips almost more swiftly than she could wipe it away.

It was no longer a labor of love that she performed, but a grim task that she discharged resentfully. For sometime during the bitter and unending siege—and even now she hardly knew when the change had come—she had awakened to the blinding realization that she despised this whimpering weakling. She knew now that there was no courage in him, no pride or gallantry to serve as a buckler and a staff in the face of this calamity. He was like a frightened child, crying and gnawing at its knuckles, frantically promising great gifts to the Church if he was spared, begging her for some reassurance that would lift his awful cloud of fear. She could remember now how he had skulked in the shadows when her own life hung in the balance that night on Bonneterre. She could remember how he had come trembling and pleading to the rendezvous on Bienville Street, caring nothing for her own pain and disappointment, intent only on saving himself. He was not even half a man, and as she looked back along the twisted road of her infatuation for him, she cursed herself for a blind fool.

She leaned forward as she saw that his eyes had cleared in a moment of consciousness and he was trying to speak.

"What is it, Etienne?" She touched his lips with the moistened cloth and saw them twist and tremble. "Don't try to talk unless you must. It is so hard for you."

"Dorothée … Dorothée … still mad. That day … she and her mother at Allan's … she … tried to stab Allan. Kelcho stopped her … got her away."

"Still mad! But then Allan could not take her back. She isn't at Constancia! And you knew this, Etienne! You knew, and yet you would not tell me!"

"Wanted you … myself … Manette. Didn't contradict Grambling's story when you told me … because I wanted you." The broken lips twisted into an awful parody of a smile. "Grambling knew, too. We both … knew … both wanted you. Too late … now …"

His head jerked back as if some unseen demon had struck him in the face. Something bubbled in his throat, clacking like tiny hammers falling on wet wood. For an instant his eyes were wild, imploring, and then his lips writhed in a final agony and the eyes were flat and empty, staring up at the face of this unclean death that had overtaken him.

CHAPTER THIRTY

S PONGE AWAY the dark stain of the bile that is like a scab of
blood upon the lips. Close the death-dazed eyes that still
stare fearfully into a dreadful eternity. Comb out the matted hair
and wind the body in a pale white sheet so that its twisted impo-
tence will be spared the indignity of strangers' eyes. These are
the things that must be done at the last. And then go and sit in
the open doorway of his house, with a loaded pistol at your feet
and your mind a sick, slow-bubbling slough of wretchedness and
despair, while you wait for the clumsy death cart to come jolting
down the street and bear your dead away.

Even then, Manette could hardly grasp the extent of the
cataclysmic outrage Grambling and Etienne had visited upon
her. Because they had desired her they had destroyed her, casting the pattern of her life in a grotesque and futile design that
had brought her to emptiness and desolation. There had been no
reconciliation between Allan and Dorothée and there could be
none now, with her mind still lost in its shadow world of haggard aberrations and gibbering lunacy. And by the same token
there would be no divorce, even if Allan had wanted one after
all that she had done. She buried her face in her hands as her
tortured mind called up the images of Grambling, the dalliance
with Etienne, García's strangled scream as the dark waters closed
above his head. No, Allan would not want her now. Then, too,
there was the virulent brutality of the defiance she had flung
at Kelcho only four days before. It had all grown into a coil of

ugliness and evil that was unforgivable, a barrier that barred her forever from Constancia and from Allan.

The day was almost gone and the dusk was blotting up the last lingering pools of light when she heard the wailing dirge of the scavenger, as callous and uncompassionate as the choking gobble of some carrion-fed vulture.

"Bring out your dead! They're piled high and we'll pile them higher before we're done. Bring out your dead, you sniveling rats! Drag them into the street so I can haul them away and there'll be room here for you tomorrow!"

The unpainted cart was piled high with the stiff bodies; young and old, clothed and naked, contorted in a grisly mass that slid and shifted as the cart lurched from one pothole to another in the rutted street. The driver was singing now, a raucous tavern song that broke off in midnote as Manette ran out to stop him.

"*Hola,* my handsome one!" His grin was a drunken leer as he stared down at her. "Will you ride with me, or shall I come into the house with you and leave this stinking pork to rot a little more?"

"There is a dead man inside the house, on the second floor. You must go in and bring him here, for I cannot carry him out alone."

"Bring him here! *Por Dios,* he'll turn to whey and bones if you wait for me to fetch him! Drag him out if you want him hauled away, but I'll have no part of it."

"You pig-faced *carbón*! You drunken son of an alley cat!" Her voice was as harsh and menacing as the pistol that had materialized in her hand. "Get that man now before I supply the devil with another passenger for that stinking cart of yours! Move, you scab-faced heap of gutter filth!"

His jaw dropped open and his eyes widened in amazement. Without a word, he lashed the reins around the rough plank that served as a seat and stumbled clumsily to the ground. Her pistol indicated the open door. "Inside and up the stairs."

She followed him into Etienne's room, standing well out of reach as he heaved the stiffening body up on his shoulder and turned back toward the street. Silently she watched him add the white-shrouded body to the pile of dead, and when he climbed back into his seat, she followed a half-dozen paces behind the creaking cart.

She was alone now, alone without a friend or lover or a roof to give her shelter. In all the length and breadth of Louisiana there was no one who cared a picayune whether she lived or died. Only half conscious of their destination, she stumbled along behind the dead, not to mourn and weep for Etienne, but to free herself from the burden of the past by watching the clods of earth conceal him and, in their falling, hear the epilogue of the drama that had ended on an empty stage.

The tide of traffic thickened at the cemetery gates. From Esplanade to Iberville, and from the river to the Rue Rampart, the city was giving up its dead. In carts and wagons and even in wheelbarrows they came, these lifeless ones that sought a refuge in the hallowed ground. The torches flared like evil beacons, and the workmen, moving wearily back and forth between the lights and shadows, seemed like fiends toiling in the depths of hell. Long, shallow trenches scarred the earth, and as soon as they were done, the waiting dead were tossed in helterskelter, so that finally no man knew the spot of earth that sheltered those of his own flesh and blood. Carts overturned as they smashed together, and the unprotesting dead littered the earth like jackstraws scattered by a giant hand.

Trembling, gasping, she saw Etienne's body thrown into an open ditch to find its place among a score of others who shared with him the anonymity of death. A cascade of the parched earth veiled his face and she turned and ran blindly into the darkness, seeking only an escape from the confusion and tumult of this devilish Saturnalia. Sharp-pointed branches scratched her face and she stumbled and almost fell, but somehow she gained the road and turned back toward the town.

Her hair had fallen down around her shoulders and her head drooped so that she saw only the square of ground before her hurrying feet. Vaguely she was aware of the sound of hoofbeats coming toward her, but she did not look up until she realized that they had spurred on past her, stopped, and then turned back. She lifted her head, and suddenly she was staring into Allan's face, peering down at her through the dusk and smoke, incredulous as he tried to recognize her as the woman he had known and loved.

"Manette! Manette!" He was out of the saddle now, sweeping her up in his arms in a storm of such passionate relief that she swayed and trembled like a willow tree caught in a blinding tempest. "I've looked everywhere for you—the house where Kelcho saw you, at Etienne's, in the streets and on the wharves, and finally here! I had to find you, Manette! I had to find you and take you to Constancia!"

"Constancia!" The word rang emptily in her ears and then her eyes flamed with sudden rage and she tore herself out of his arms with the fury of a snarling cat. *"Por Dios,* you'll have no more of me at Constancia! I've slept with you there! I've fought for you there! I've held it together while you lolled on your bed in New Orleans and entertained your slobbering idiot of a Dorothée!"

"Manette! Manette!"

He moved forward to take her in his arms again, but her hand shot out with fingers curved into claws and he fell back as the sharp nails tore across his cheek.

"Yes, I've done all that for you and for Constancia, but when your drunken overseer tries to horsewhip me and I have to run and hide like some runaway slave, you don't even lift a hand to help me. No, you run away from the plague to the Constancia I've helped you save!" Her voice soared up into a scream of bitter rage. "I'll sleep in the streets and sell myself to the sailors before I'll have any more of you and your cursed Constancia!"

It was true enough, she told herself savagely, true enough, and yet renouncing Constancia was like tearing the very heart out of her body. A sob choked her and she turned away and began to run blindly into the darkness. There were heavy footsteps behind her and then she felt Allan's fingers biting into her shoulder and felt herself whirled and held so securely she was powerless to lift her arms or attack him.

"By God, Manette, you're a fool!" His voice was harsh with anger and even in the darkness she could see the lips drawn hard and tight across his teeth. "I've hunted for you through this hellhole for a week. I've moved heaven and earth to find you. Listen, damn you!" He shook her so roughly that her head rolled back and forth on her shoulders. "Dorothée is dead! Dead of the plague. And there's a priest waiting for us at the plantation, if you want to go there as my wife. Now, by God, you'll make up your mind and make it up damned fast or I'll haul you down and turn you over to the sailors myself!"

"Dead!" She shook her head and found her mind an empty vacuum, unable to understand or accept what he had said. "Dorothée is dead?"

"She's been dead for a week, and I want to marry you. Marry you! Can't you understand that?"

He was glaring down at her, so shaken with exasperation that the angry breath whistled between his teeth. "If you don't want that—"

He started to turn away but now she clung to him, struggling to force out the words that would save this final chance for happiness.

"Want it! *Por Dios,* Allan, I've never wanted anything so much! It will be pure heaven to be—"

They had sent Kelcho to the wharf on foot so Manette could have his horse, and now as she rode beside MacMurran through the narrow streets she looked up in sudden surprise to see the white walls of the Convent of St. Theresa looming above her. She checked her mount and turned to Allan imploringly.

"Margarita! We must not leave her here, *corazón! Por favor,* may we take her to Constancia with us?

"Take her?" He threw back his head and roared with laughter. "I took both Margarita and Lucille with me when I went to the plantation ten days ago. They're waiting there now to be your maids of honor."

"My maids of honor!" For the first time it was real; something magnificent and glorious that she had only half believed before. For a moment she surrendered herself to this new warm tide of honor and security and success. Then she lifted her head proudly and urged her horse forward with her heel.

Tomorrow, and through all the tomorrows that lay ahead, she would be the mistress of Constancia!

THE END